Singing Spears

E. V. Thompson was born in London. He spent nine years in the Navy before joining the Bristol police force where he was a founder member of the 'Vice Squad'. Since then he has been an investigator with BOAC, worked with the Hong Kong Police Narcotics Bureau and was Chief Security Officer of Rhodesia's Department of Civil Aviation, before returning to England to become a full-time writer. This is his sixth novel.

Singing Spears

E. V. Thompson

PAN BOOKS
in association with
Macmillan London

First published 1982 by Macmillan London Ltd
This edition published 1984 by Pan Books Ltd,
Cavaye Place, London sw10 9pg
© E. V. Thompson 1982
ISBN 0 330 28180 1
Printed in Great Britain by
Richard Clay (The Chaucer Press) Ltd, Bungay, Suffolk

BOOK ONE

Southern Africa

in the 1880s

ANGOLA

S.W. AFRICA

Otjimkandje

Whalefish Bay

Zambezi R.

KALAHARI DESERT

MATABELELAND

Tati

Khami

Limpopo R.

See separate map

MOZAMBIQUE

Tete

Sena

Quelimane

Shupanga

Sofala

TRANSVAAL

WITWATERS RAND

Pretoria

Delagoa Bay

Kimberley

Orange R.

DRAKENSBURG MTS.

NATAL

Durban

Cape Town

N

MILES

0   100   200   300   400   500

CHAPTER ONE

An air of intense excitement enveloped the thatched mud huts of the King's kraal in the valley of Khami. Hearts beat faster and the mouth dried involuntarily. It was as though the village itself lay beneath the huge dust cloud that hung high above the red, dry-parched Matopos Hills like a giant umbrella.

The dust was being kicked up by the hooves of more than six thousand cattle. Pouring down the rounded slopes of a hill, they streamed towards the village, a wide, living ribbon extending for half-a-mile to the east.

The beasts were by no means prime cattle. They stumbled along with heads hanging low, red-rimmed eyes bulging from fear and exhaustion. A man could hide two fingers between their bony ribs. The cattle caught in the centre of the herd coughed and choked, swinging horned heads against the flanks of their neighbours as they breathed in more dust than air.

Yet, until a few weeks before, these scrawny animals had represented the proud wealth of a village of Manica tribesmen in their homeland around the foothills of the Inyanga mountains. Men had died for them.

Herding the cattle along their way were five hundred trotting Matabele warriors. Bedecked with ostrich feathers, they jogged along, hammering on taut hide war shields to keep the sea of cattle moving. Sunlight glinted on the gleaming, broad blades of their assegais.

The excitement in Khami was for the return of these warriors. The Matabele regiment — an 'impi' — had been away from its home kraal for three anxious months. Now it was almost home and the success of the foray was plain for all to see. The dust cloud of the captured cattle had been visible for hours before they came into view.

There would be a great celebration in the kraal tonight, in which all but a handful of mourning families would join. These warriors were part of the finest army in Africa and they had encountered little resistance during their campaigning. Those few tribes foolish enough to make a stand against them had been overwhelmed and slaughtered by the ruthless Matabele fighting-men.

Working in a back room of his stone-built store at the edge of the kraal, Daniel Retallick was aware of both the excitement and its cause. Twenty-six years of age now, he had been living in the royal kraal for almost five years. He had seen many victorious impis return. He knew that in addition to the cattle they would be bringing back prisoners. Captured children to be assimilated into the Matabele tribe, the girls as servants and chattels, the boys as warriors. There would be women prisoners too, to provide savage entertainment for the evening festivities.

Gritting his teeth against the images conjured up by the memories of previous 'entertainments', Daniel swung a wooden keg filled with gunpowder from the hard-packed dirt floor to the top of the three-tiered stack of barrels already against the stone wall.

Daniel loved the country of the Matabele, with its ancient hills and deep fertile valleys. Parched brown by the dry winter, it would erupt in a riot of flowering trees and shrubs in the rains of summer. He loved its people too and worked hard to protect them from the greed and exploitation of the English and the Boers who crowded Matabeleland's southern borders. But Daniel recognised the shortcomings of the tribe and its despotic ruler.

In his own quiet way, Daniel had tried to wean Mzilikazi, the Matabele King, away from many of the barbaric practices that more civilised nations found unacceptable. He was succeeding – but very slowly. He feared his efforts would be overtaken by the pressing needs of those men seeking entry to the riches they believed Matabeleland to hold.

Suddenly, the sound outside the store became a great roar that echoed from the surrounding hills. Leaping on the barrels of gunpowder, Daniel peered through a high, barred window. The returning warriors and the cattle were still more than a mile away. The object of the crowd's approbation was much closer.

Another roar, and the word 'BAYETE!' thundered to the sky from a thousand throats, setting a stack of tin plates rattling on a shelf in the store. 'Bayete' was a greeting by the people to their Paramount Chief – their King.

Daniel eased the keg of gunpowder further on to the stack before jumping to the ground. Wiping perspiration from his face with the crumpled kerchief he wore about his neck, he made his way to the front door of the store.

To cries of 'He comes! The mountain walks among his people', Mzilikazi was going out to meet the returning warriors, accompanied by many of his three hundred wives. Daniel realised this raid must have been something out of the ordinary.

Absolute ruler of the Matabele nation and the suzerain of a dozen lesser tribes, forty-six years had passed since Mzilikazi's break from Shaka, the Zulu Chief. Heading northwards from Natal, Mzilikazi had taken his own people first to the Transvaal, then, later, across the Limpopo River. Here, in the hills and plains that would one day be known as Rhodesia, and later as Zimbabwe, he had welded them together as the powerful and much-feared Matabele nation.

In those days Mzilikazi had been a great chief and a warrior in the prime of life. Now, in 1868, he was almost eighty years of age and rarely left the royal enclosure. Monarch of a greatly expanded nation, heavy drinking and the cares of his warrior people had dulled his mind and taken a toll of his once-fine physique. Mzilikazi now weighed more than three hundred pounds and his gross body needed to be supported wherever he went by two of his strongest bodyguards.

But the eyes of Mzilikazi were still as keen as ever. He missed nothing. Surrounded though he was by hundreds of shouting and applauding subjects, Mzilikazi saw Daniel. Shaking himself free from his helpers, he held up a massive hand for silence. Immediately, all sound was cut off, leaving behind a stillness so unexpected that a startled flock of red-billed quelea birds took to the air in a whirring cloud from the trees in the King's royal enclosure.

'The day is too warm for work, trader,' called Mzilikazi to Daniel. 'Come! I go to meet my son, Kanje. He returns from his first raid against the Manicas.'

He waved an overweight arm in the direction of the hills, where the tail end of the cattle herd had just come into sight,

'See? The cattle he has brought to me move across the land like locusts. He has done well.'

At Mzilikazi's side one of his favourite younger wives beamed her pleasure at his words. She was the mother of Kanje and had worked hard for this moment. At night, in the sweaty darkness of Mzilikazi's hut, with no one near to remind the King of her lowly status as a junior wife, she had used every wile known to woman to further the career of her only son. Sired by Mzilikazi when she was hardly thirteen years old, Kanje was but one of many hundred such royal 'princes'. Less respectful subjects declared they were as numerous as ticks on the great royal herds. Few would even rise high enough to command one of the King's impis. Kanje's mother was determined that *her* son should profit from his royal heritage – and one day take the throne from his father.

'Are you coming with me, trader? Would you look upon the faces of the Manica women and their spawn? My runner tells me there are many.'

Over the King's head, Daniel could see the blood-red leaves of the royal msasa trees. He shuddered, then shook his head. 'This is a day for your warriors and their families, Mzilikazi. I have much work to do in my store.'

The mother of Kanje glared malevolently at Daniel, incensed by what she considered to be a slight to her son.

'You are not pleased that my warriors have won a great victory . . . ?' Mzilikazi's narrowed angrily and Daniel's heart sank. He was probably one of the King's most trusted friends and, in return, had a great affection for the despotic old ruler, but in recent months drink and senility had combined to make Mzilikazi dangerously unpredictable.

'I'm happy at the success of your army, Mzilikazi,' Daniel chose his words carefully. 'I congratulate you on having such a brave warrior for a son – but I am a white man. Looking upon the faces of those who are soon to die gives me no pleasure.'

To Daniel's relief, the frown lifted from Mzilikazi's face. Daniel's dislike of the Matabele's more violent ways was no secret to anyone. With an expression of amusement on his face, Mzilikazi looked at Daniel speculatively.

'Very well, trader. Stay and continue your work – but I insist that you attend the celebrations tonight. You understand me?'

The King's eyes held Daniel's and, sick to his stomach, Daniel could only nod his head in agreement. He knew he should have swallowed his pride and accompanied Mzilikazi to meet his son and the victorious Matabele warriors. True, there would have been isolated acts of cruelty perpetrated against the unfortunate Manica prisoners by the jeering villagers but it would be nothing compared to what he would be forced to witness at the evening's victory celebrations. After consuming gallons of thick, kraal-brewed beer, the Matabele had no inhibitions. They would lay the dust about the celebration fires with the blood of their prisoners.

Daniel looked wearily along the valley. The first cattle of the stolen herd were now passing the low wooden shacks of the mission station that occupied an isolated position beside the main track to the kraal. There was no sign of the missionaries, but Daniel knew they would not be missing a single incident happening outside. The quill pens would be scratching the pages of their journals in a fury tonight.

There were two missionaries resident at the mission station. One was a single man, the other accompanied by his wife. Theirs was a lonely and frustrated existence. The station had been established as the result of an unguarded promise made by Mzilikazi to the veteran missionary, Robert Moffat, some years before. But giving his word to allow a mission station to be built was one thing – permitting it to function successfully was something quite different. Mzilikazi was adamant that the missionaries must not preach to his people. Summary execution was speedily imposed on any subject who appeared ready for conversion to the white man's faith.

Daniel did not like the missionaries. Both were quarrelsome and bigotted men. Their ambition of converting the Matabele to Christianity involved sweeping away all tribal traditions and pride. Covering the people's nakedness with western-style clothing and modelling the Matabele along the lines of Sunday-school children. In pursuit of this aim the missionaries schemed and connived to bring Europeans to the country, ignoring the dangers of such a policy. They argued that there was nothing wrong in using powder and shot to blast the benefits of The Word into the lives of Mzilikazi's reluctant savages.

Nevertheless, in spite of his dislike for them, Daniel sympathised with the missionaries in their well-nigh impossible task. He felt a grudging admiration for their tenacity in remaining in this land, where they were so patently unwanted. Mzilikazi would not go back on the promise he had made to Moffat, but he made no secret of the fact that he would be happy if the two men abandoned the mission station and left the Matabele to the Devil – and Mzilikazi. In an attempt to achieve this aim, he insisted they perform various menial tasks for him that were beneath the dignity of his own warriors. In addition, he demanded that they grow produce for the royal household and gather wood for his fires.

The missionaries took up these additional burdens without complaint, but both men kept carefully detailed diaries of their humiliations. They hoped that future publication, together with information of the happenings in Matabeleland might arouse the passions of the British public and force the government to send an army against the Matabele and their despotic ruler. At the very least, the diaries should ensure appropriate recognition for their devotion to the Christian cause.

Thinking of the ordeal he would have to undergo that evening, Daniel wished the missionaries were men he could talk to. It would be even better if Sam Speke were in Khami . . . Sam and his daughter Victoria.

Sam Speke had come to Khami many years before, with Daniel. Married to a girl of the Herero tribe from South West Africa, Sam was currently on a visit with his family to his wife's village, almost a thousand miles away.

A solid, reliable man, Sam Speke had been with Daniel's parents when they were shipwrecked on the treacherous Skeleton Coast of South West Africa. Only three years old at the time, Daniel, with his family, had been given sanctuary by the Hereros and lived in their village for many years. Daniel's parents had returned to England when he moved to Matabeleland, but Sam Speke came with him. He helped run the Matabele end of a remarkable trade route extending more than half the breadth of the African continent. From Mzilikazi's capital to Whalefish Bay, on the Atlantic coast. The South West African end of the operation was looked after by Aaron Copping, Daniel's partner. Aaron had been trading in

Africa for most of his life and knew more about South West Africa than any other man alive.

Theirs was a unique trading venture. Initially, it had begun as a trading link between Whalefish Bay and the Herero heartland. Daniel had extended the route first to the Bechuanas at Lake Ngami, in the Kalahari Desert, and then to the land of the Matabele. It was a hazardous life, at best – but Daniel was the envy of a great many white adventurers. These were the men who were gradually edging the frontiers of exploration and commerce closer to Matabeleland. Only Mzilikazi's impis, jealously guarding the rich lands over which their King claimed jurisdiction, kept them at bay.

Mzilikazi did not trust white men. He occasionally befriended certain individuals, but their numbers could be counted on the fingers of one hand and their friendship did not change his opinion of their fellows. What he learned from these select few convinced Mzilikazi beyond all doubt that if ever his country were thrown open to them the way of life of the Matabele would end forever. Mzilikazi was determined it would not come to pass in his lifetime.

As the sun sank below the summit of the range of hills to the west of Khami, the taut monkey-skin drums began to beat out from the great square in the centre of the capital. Others took up the rhythm eagerly. Soon the sound of a hundred drums echoed back and forth between the rocky crags about the town. In the centre of the square many fires sprang up and impromptu dancing began. As the dancers shuffled and swayed together in the flickering light the rapidly growing crowds about them sang and clapped in time to the music.

Daniel had hoped to arrive late at the festivities and slip away at the earliest moment without being noticed. His plans were dashed when Jandu, another of Mzilikazi's many sons, arrived at the store with orders to escort him to the square.

'You are to be honoured tonight, trader,' Jandu called from the store-room as he weighed a new percussion rifle in his hands while Daniel dressed.

Daniel entered the store fastening the long sleeves of his shirt at the wrists. The mosquitoes were always worse at night and it paid to leave as little skin exposed as possible.

13

'Honoured . . . ?' he frowned at Jandu. 'I'm damned if I see it that way. There's no honour in watching unarmed women being hacked to death by young boys!'

Jandu looked very much like his father when he was amused, 'Those young boys will one day be men – and men must be warriors. They need to know the feel of a spear entering the body of an enemy . . . to know which thrusts kill and which only maim. Such knowledge can make the difference between life and death to a warrior in his first battle . . .'

Jandu held the gun in his hands close to the spluttering animal-oil lamp and peered down the barrel. 'Why should you care what happens to Manica women? Are they more to you than Matabele women?'

Mzilikazi's son voiced the curiosity felt by many of the Matabele at Daniel's apparent celibacy while living among them. It was in marked contrast to the behaviour of the few other white men who had visited Khami, seeking permission to hunt, or search for precious metals – or simply explore the land of the Matabele. Their eagerness to have a 'slave girl' was the subject of many ribald tribal jokes. It was rumoured that this was the real reason why so many white men wished to enter Mzilikazi's kingdom. Indeed, before the arrival of the mission-ary's wife it was believed by the Matabele that there could be no white women in Africa.

'They are no more, and no less, than any other women,' Daniel retorted, but Jandu had already dismissed the matter of Daniel's taste in women from his mind. He held the rifle out towards him.

'This is a good gun?'

'The best. A man's family would never go hungry if he hunted for food with one of those – but it will cost you more elephant tusks than you could collect in a full year.'

Jandu lowered the gun. With a snort of derision he tossed it carelessly aside on a pile of colourful blankets. 'My family has never been hungry – and I hunt only with a spear. Such guns are for white men – and my father's son, Kanje.'

Daniel looked at Jandu sharply. 'Kanje has one of these? I've traded only one since they arrived – to Mzilikazi.'

'Are such guns made only for you, trader? Kanje's raid took

him far from our home. He met with the bearded men who come on horses from the south.'

Daniel knew Jandu was talking about the Boers. Their mounted commandos often rode to the borders of Matabeleland in the hope of surprising a small group of tribesmen and stealing their cattle.

'Kanje captured rifles from the Boers? I don't believe it!'

Jandu allowed himself a quick smile. 'Had Kanje *captured* guns from the bearded ones the Matabele would have a future King who even I would follow without question. No, trader. Kanje and twenty of his men were *given* the guns when the bearded ones learned he was a son of Mzilikazi.'

'If Kanje's accepted gifts from the Boers he's a fool!'

Jandu nodded. 'I see you understand the situation. Kanje does not. As you say, he is a fool — a young fool. He would rule our people, yet does not realise he has already put himself in debt to the bearded ones. If ever he becomes King they will be here, demanding the right to trade.'

Daniel remembered the look Kanje's mother had given him earlier in the day. She was a strong-willed woman who would always influence her son. If Kanje ever ruled in his father's place Daniel's trading days with the Matabele would be over. The Boers would move in to take his place. Daniel knew this. So did Jandu.

'You and I should be of one mind, trader. We both have much to lose should my brother be chosen to lead our people. You, your trade. I . . . my life. While I and my other brothers live we would always pose a threat to him. Unfortunately, there is little I can do to prevent Kanje having his way. I am just one of Mzilikazi's many troublesome sons. But you have my father's ear. You are a trusted friend. He will listen to you.'

Daniel looked at Jandu suspiciously. About thirty years of age, the Matabele was tall, even when judged by the standards of his own tribe, and he had the massive chest of his father. He also had remarkably large eyes that at first glance appeared docile, but when given a direct glance, a man felt they were burning into his very soul. Jandu had only recently returned to Khami, after serving as an Induna, or commander, of one of the King's impis in a far-off border district.

A man of exceptional intelligence and presence, Jandu

would pose a threat to the ambitions of any of Mzilikazi's sons. Daniel hoped, for Jandu's sake, that he had not yet attracted too much attention. But, although he was impressed by what he had seen of the other man, Daniel was reluctant to be drawn into their accession feuds.

'You would like me to put in a good word for you, of course?'

To Daniel's surprise, Jandu shrugged his shoulders nonchalantly, 'There are many of my brothers who would rule better than I – but Kanje is not one of them. Under his leadership Matabeleland would become a skeleton, picked clean by the jackals who squat about our borders. I have no wish to see this happen.'

Daniel stared thoughtfully at Jandu, wondering whether all this was no more than a devious ploy by Mzilikazi himself to draw him into the intrigues of the King's court, and so declare himself. He dismissed the idea immediately. Mzilikazi knew him better. He had always been very careful to remain aloof from the constant scheming of those who surrounded the King.

'You need make no reply now, but do not take too long to think about what has been said here today. Mzilikazi is an old man.'

'True – but he is still King of the Matabele, and tonight I've been ordered to witness Kanje's triumph. Let's go and get it over with.'

CHAPTER TWO

When Daniel arrived in the great square the victory celebrations were well under way, huge wood fires blazing furiously.
The area surrounding the kraal had long since been denuded of
trees and the wood had been brought from the river valley,
more than two miles distant from Khami. No effort was being
spared to make this a night the King's subjects would long
remember.

Around the fires beer gourds were passing from hand to
hand, and mouth to mouth, the drinking accompanied by
shouted bawdy jokes and loud, uninhibited laughter. Many of
the men, particularly those with sons in the returning impi, had
been celebrating from the moment the first warrior had been
sighted on the hills beyond the capital.

In the cleared space between the fires the women danced
in long, linked lines, stamping their feet, bodies newly anoin-
ted with animal fat, swaying in time to the music of the drum-
mers.

The women of the royal harem, dressed in their finest beads
and feathers were performing their own exclusive dance in the
very centre of the square, watched by their happy and relaxed
husband. Mzilikazi sat on a pile of cattle hides, drinking vast
quantities of beer. He was far too close to the nearest fire for
comfort, but seemed not to mind the glistening rivulets of
perspiration that formed salt pools in the deep creases of his
body.

Seeing Daniel, Mzilikazi roared for him to come and sit at
his side. Daniel would have preferred to sit further away from
the heat of the fire, but he dared not refuse. A gesture from the
King dismissed Jandu, and Daniel chose a place on the heaped
cow hides, accepting the gourd of beer that was quickly passed
to him by one of Mzilikazi's wives.

The beer, brewed and drunk by the Matabele, had the
consistency of a well-watered porridge. It smelled sour but the

taste was not unpleasant. Under the watchful eyes of Mzilikazi, Daniel took a deep draught before setting the gourd down on the ground beside him.

Resting a heavy hand briefly on Daniel's shoulder, the Matabele King beamed at him benignly. 'I am pleased to see you are still one of us, trader,' he boomed. 'Now you will hear of my son's first raid.'

Clapping his hands, Mzilikazi ordered the dancers from the square.

As the women hurried to find space on the ground behind their menfolk, the crowd's excitement increased in volume, drowning the complaining lowing of the captured cattle, penned within the royal cattle kraal, just beyond the village.

Another signal from Mzilikazi, then he sprawled back on his hide throne to enjoy a re-enactment of the raid on the Manicas.

First to take the stage was the King's 'Inganga' – his 'witch-doctor'. Accompanied by two assistants, he wore a hideous mask and a tall headdress of fur and feathers and made a frightening giant figure in the capricious light from the fire. After performing a series of incredible leaps and contortions that had the appreciative crowd gasping in awe, the Inganga stood in front of Mzilikazi and scattered a variety of powdered potions to the four winds. Then he began extolling the virtues of the King, reminding his subjects of past victories. As each one was mentioned the great crowd let out a sigh of appreciation.

When he felt enough had been said to satisfy the King's vanity, the Inganga began telling his listeners of the success of Kanje's raid in the unknown lands of the Manica tribes. He reminded King and the subjects that it was he, the Inganga, who had sent the raiding-party on its way protected by some of his most powerful 'medicine'.

'Powerful it may have been,' interrupted the King. 'But some faces were missing from the returning impi. How many of my warriors died?'

The Inganga turned to the Induna of the impi, who fell to his knees in front of his King.

'Seven, Kumalo.' Kumalo meant literally 'Majesty'.

'Name them.'

The Induna called out seven names. As each rolled off his tongue there was a groan from the listening crowd, and a wail from the women of the dead warrior's family.

'How did they die?' asked the King, when the names were known.

'They died bravely, Kumalo. They were truly Matabele warriors.'

Mzilikazi nodded his satisfaction, 'Each elder son, or father of the dead men is to be given ten captured cattle.'

There was a sigh of approval from the crowd. It was a generous gesture.

Next, the Inganga gave details of the number of their enemies killed, cattle gained for the Matabele, and the number of prisoners secured.

As the Inganga spoke, evidence of his statistics were produced for the benefit of his audience. A dozen cattle, terrified by the din about them, were dragged into the square and Mzilikazi immediately ordered them to be killed and roasted over the fires for his people. Next came the unfortunate prisoners, women and boys, herded into the firelight to the derisive jeers of the spectators. Many of the captured women fell to their knees in front of Mzilikazi, begging him to spare their lives. The children who were to be assimilated into the tribe clung to their mothers, too bewildered to understand what was about to happen. After no more than a brief glance in their direction, Mzilikazi dismissed them from his presence.

Next, the Inganga's assistants ran towards Mzilikazi carrying two bulging hide bags. As the bags were upturned before the King a dozen dust-smeared heads thudded to the ground and a great roar of approval went up from the crowd.

Daniel had been prepared for this display of barbarism. He had witnessed such incidents before – but he was not expecting Mzilikazi's next move.

The Inganga peered at each head in turn, finally selecting one topped with short, curly grey hair. Carrying it to the King, he handed over the gruesome object, declaring it to be the head of the Chief of the Manica tribe.

Mzilikazi took the head and held it up before him, studying the features. Suddenly, he tossed the head through the air towards Daniel who caught it in an involuntary action.

'There, trader. Does he look as noble as a Matabele?'

Aware of the laughter of the watching Matabele, Daniel shrugged, carefully concealing the revulsion he felt. 'He looks like any other man. No doubt he was proud of his tribe, and honoured his ancestors.'

Daniel placed the gruesome trophy next to the King. Mzilikazi hurriedly pushed it to the ground and ordered the main event of the evening to begin.

Daniel had played upon the King's own superstitious beliefs. The Matabele were taught that if a man honoured his ancestors throughout his own life, his own spirit would be welcomed by them after death. These ancestral spirits would not be pleased with any mortal who made their task more difficult by separating head from body.

The Inganga's two assistants removed the heads of the dead Manica warriors and now the victorious Matabele impi marched proudly to the firelit square, applauded loudly by relatives and friends. Dressed in their warrior feathers and carrying tall, hide shields and broad-bladed assegais, they spread across the square, assuming the extended-horn battle formation of an attacking Matabele impi. This was the Zulu manoeuvre that had struck terror in the hearts of enemies from Natal to the Zambezi River.

Chanting slogans and thudding their feet heavily to the ground with each step, the impi advanced across the square until it was within a few paces of Mzilikazi. Then, with a great shout of 'Bayete!' it broke ranks and the warriors moved off to one side.

Their Induna stepped forward and began giving Mzilikazi a lurid account of the raid. He was a good narrator and the crowd remained absolutely silent, straining to hear the Induna's every word. As each man was mentioned, he stepped forward and re-enacted the incident that had provoked such an honour, each stroke of his assegai signifying the death of an enemy at his hands.

Finally it was the turn of Kanje to step forward and impress the King with a display of his prowess. Glistening muscles rippling, the junior son sprang from the ranks of his fellow warriors, scornfully discarding his shield. Brandishing an assegai in his right hand and a rifle in his left, he performed well. To the accompaniment of the Induna's recital, he vividly relived the highlights of his great adventure. The watching subjects held their breath as Kanje crept from the broken rocks of a Manica hillside towards an unsuspecting sentry. They gasped as he fought with three enemy warriors in desperate hand-to-hand combat and shouted an urgent warning when, hard-pressed by the Manica warriors, he was attacked from behind.

When the last of the Manicas had been overwhelmed by the ferocity of his lone attack, Kanje stood facing the King, his father. Head thrown back proudly, he awaited the praise that was his due. Behind him, the crowd exploded in a frenzy of applause. Kanje was the hero of the moment. This was assuredly the greatest day of his young life.

Kanje's moment of glory might have lasted longer had not the Induna been so carried away by the enthusiasm of the crowd that he forgot the suspicious and jealous nature of the Matabele King. Enthusiastically, he concluded his contribution to Kanje's realistic performance by declaring to Mzilikazi, 'Truly, Great One, all who saw Kanje in battle said that he fought as bravely as his father once did. You can be proud of him, Great King.'

'Proud? Proud of a warrior who has hardly left boyhood behind, yet returns from his first raid convinced he is as brave as Mzilikazi?'

The King struggled to his feet, throwing off the bodyguard who rushed to his aid. Standing unsteadily, glaring from the Induna to Kanje, he boomed, 'I have defeated warriors who were said to be unbeatable. Yes . . . and the bearded white men from the south too. You would liken a first-blooded boy to me? Induna – I spit upon you!'

Mzilikazi matched words with the deed as the terrified Induna stood before him, not daring to move a muscle.

'Guards! Bring the prisoners to me.' Mzilikazi roared the words and there was hurried movement from his bodyguard.

The spectators had maintained a frightened silence during the King's angry outburst, fearful lest the slightest sound be interpreted as criticism and so attract the ever-vigilant court executioners. Now they relaxed, eager for what they believed was to follow.

The Manica women and children were herded forward, but now they had been divided into two wailing groups, women in one, children in the other. The paths of their lives would divide sharply now. Life for the young boys would take an upward surge. Given to families among the Matabele people, they would be set to work as herd-boys until they were of an age to join one of Mzilikazi's impis.

There was no such future for the women. They would take only a few steps more along their particular path. It was Matabele tradition that they should be turned loose in the square and there hunted down and slaughtered by the older herd-boys, many themselves sons of earlier victims. Those boys who showed a particular aptitude for killing would be drafted to an impi to begin their training as Matabele warriors.

This was the moment Daniel had been dreading. He had witnessed a similar 'spear washing' ceremony in his first year with the tribe. The memory of the savagery had haunted him for many months.

The prisoners were brought before Mzilikazi and the herd-boys raised their assegais and waited in quivering anticipation. The moments of waiting grew longer, but still the order to release the Manica women did not come. Daniel had dropped his gaze when the women were pushed forward, now he looked up, to see the King studying him.

'You do not wish to see the women killed, trader? If you were King of the Matabele what would you do with them?'

'Let them join their sons and brothers and become useful members of the tribe,' declared Daniel, unhesitantly.

Mzilikazi shifted his gaze to the face of Kanje, still standing proudly before him. But when he spoke it was to Daniel once more. 'You have never given me bad advice – and your honesty is greater than that of my son. So be it.' To the Induna of his personal bodyguard, he called, 'Release the Manica women. They will become servants to the Matabele. Take them away now.'

As a howl of disappointment rose from the throats of those villagers close enough to hear Mzilikazi's words, one of the Manica women who had been following the conversation closely, broke away from the others and flung herself at Daniel's feet.

A guard seized her arm to drag her away, but Mzilikazi waved him off.

'Leave her!' Grinning broadly, he said to Daniel. 'You have saved their lives, the least you can do is contribute in some way to their keep. This girl shall be yours.' To the guard he said, 'Have her taken to the trader's store.'

Mzilikazi's good humour was short-lived. Before Daniel could reply, Kanje took an angry pace forward. 'The prisoners are mine. It has always been the custom for the herd-boys to kill captive women. Since when have the Matabele looked to a white man for orders?'

Mzilikazi was a huge man, yet at Kanje's words it seemed to his awestruck people that he swelled to twice his normal size, so great was his wrath. Lunging forward, he snatched the rifle from the hands of his recalcitrant younger son.

'The Matabele put themselves in the power of the white man from the day warriors accept gifts such as this from his hands. Do you think it was given to you because a white man wants you for a brother? Fool! Black men and white can never be brothers. He gives you guns because he knows it will make you put aside your spears and rely upon this alone.'

Mzilikazi shook the rifle above his head for everyone to see. 'One day you will find you have an enemy to fight – but no bullets for your gun. Then you will need to turn to the white man and plead with him for more. In exchange he will demand that you allow traders, hunters and gold-diggers in the lands of the Matabele. Once they are here they will multiply like weeds in a field tended by a lazy woman. Where one white man places his foot you will soon find a hundred. For every hundred there will one day be a thousand. When that happens it will be the white man and not the Matabele who rules this land and we will be as the Mashona – men of no account.'

Mzilikazi waved the rifle in Kanje's face and gave him a look of withering scorn. 'I taught the Matabele to fight like men. To look in the face of an enemy and be close enough to smell the fear ooze from him. A brave warrior draws strength from the terror he sees in the eyes of an enemy. A gun is for a coward, a man who knows he is less than his enemy.'

Gripping the rifle as though it were a throwing spear, Mzilikazi hurled it from him, into the fire. It landed at the heart of the blaze, scattering sparks high into the night air.

Turning his back on Kanje and ignoring the wife whose earlier pride had given way to tearful dismay, Mzilikazi tottered from the square on the arms of his two attendants.

Just as he was about to enter the royal enclosure, there was a sudden sharp explosion from the fire. Fragments of burning wood were hurled over the assembled impi and the nearby spectators. They fled in momentary panic.

One man was left behind, lying face downwards in the dirt. It was the Induna who had led Kanje's raid.

Daniel leaped from his seat of skins and kneeled beside the still form. Turning the Induna over he saw an ugly blue-edged wound, just beneath the man's ribs. He was dead, killed by the single bullet in Kanje's gun.

The bullet had merely saved the Induna from a far more unpleasant fate. After praising the younger son in such glowing terms, Mzilikazi could not have allowed him to live. Only Induna's who were unswervingly loyal to Mzilikazi led his regiments. Indunas who favoured younger sons were particularly dangerous to an aged king. After all, Mzilikazi had himself broken away from the Zulu nation and founded the Matabele empire with only a single impi.

But the incident with the rifle meant that Mzilikazi would not need to worry about a challenge to his authority for a very long time. His subjects regarded the Induna's death as an awesome example of their King's power. He had used his son's gun to kill one who had offended him, without any man's finger being on the trigger.

But if the King had consolidated his own position, Daniel had made a dangerous enemy. He saw the look that Kanje cast in his direction before hurrying off to choke on his humiliation. Not only had Daniel deprived the Matabele of their anticipated 'spear washing' spectacle, he had robbed Kanje of the adulation of the herd-boys who might have proved themselves tonight. They would have made the name 'Kanje' ring around the square, committing it to the memories of those elders who one day soon would meet to appoint Mzilikazi's successor.

Back in his store, Daniel found that Jandu was the warrior who had brought the Manica girl to his living quarters and he was waiting with her.

The girl told Daniel her name was Suliyana. She was younger than she had appeared during the brief glimpse he had of her in the square. Looking at her slim body, naked from the waist up, Daniel thought she was probably an undernourished sixteen-year-old.

It seemed that Jandu's thoughts were moving along similar lines. 'You will need to feed her before you send her out to till your fields. She would be blown away by the first breeze that came along.'

'I can work as hard as any Matabele woman,' retorted Suliyana, scornfully. She had a soft, pleasant voice together with a disconcerting and challenging way of looking directly at the person to whom she was talking. 'And I will eat less than the women I saw in Mzilikazi's household.'

Jandu frowned and Daniel said hurriedly, 'I doubt if you'll be here long enough to impress me with your work – or lack of appetite. There's little enough room for one to live in this store.'

Jandu's frown became a smile. 'She'll have to stay here tonight. Mzilikazi will be very angry if you turn her out – and one night should be long enough to cause you much trouble, as Mzilikazi knows well. Just before you saved the lives of the Manica women a runner arrived with a message. Your friend Speke has returned to Matabeleland with his Herero wife and their daughter. They should reach Khami in the morning.'

CHAPTER THREE

Victoria Speke galloped her horse up to the door of the store a bare two hours after dawn. The manner of her arrival raised a cloud of choking dust in her wake and scattered bleary-eyed Matabele women, dogs and chickens.

She rode like a man and, with her short black hair and boy's clothing, an onlooker might have been excused for thinking she was an excited and boisterous youth, and not a lively young woman of twenty.

Sawing her horse to a slithering, foam-blowing halt, Victoria swung a leg across the pommel of the saddle. Kicking her other foot free of the stirrup, she slid to the ground with an agile, easy movement.

Running inside the store, she collided heavily with Daniel. Before he was able to recover his balance, her arms went about him and, while he pressed back against an uncomfortable stack of iron kettles and small cauldrons, Victoria kissed him with an ardour that would have raised eyebrows in even the most advanced-thinking European community.

'Daniel! It's good to be back. I've missed you . . . I feel I've been away from you for years! Have you missed me too? What's been happening?'

At that moment, Victoria caught sight of Suliyana.

The Manica girl was wearing no more, and no less, than she had on the day she was first captured. A string of beads about her waist, from which hung a brief leather apron, no more than eight inches square, at front and rear. She was standing by the store-blanket bed Daniel had provided for her in a corner of the store.

Victoria's hands dropped away from Daniel and went up to her thick, black hair in an automatic gesture. Stepping back from him, she looked from the girl to Daniel, her face registering incredulous disbelief, 'Who . . . who is this?'

Daniel had hoped to have Suliyana out of the store by the time Victoria and the others reached Khami. Victoria's early arrival had taken him by surprise. His embarrassed explanation was garbled and disjointed and did nothing to lessen Victoria's growing dismay.

'. . . at least she and the others are alive,' he ended, lamely.

'Others? You have more of them here?' Victoria cast a hurried glance about the store.

'No, of course not. Mzilikazi ordered Suliyana to be brought here. The others will be put to work in Khami.'

'And she's only been here since last night?'

'Of course. I was hoping to be rid of her by the time you arrived. You took me by surprise.'

'I can see *that*,' Victoria smiled again and Daniel relaxed. Fortunately, Victoria would never learn how difficult it had been to convince the Manica girl that she would not be sharing his bed.

Victoria took Daniel's hand and squeezed it so tightly she hurt his fingers. 'All right, I'll forgive you – but she can't stay here. She can come and work for us. We'll need some help in the house after all these months away.'

Sam Speke had built a large wooden cabin for his family. It was about fifty yards away from the store.

'Get your horse and I'll take you back along the trail to meet Dad and Aaron. On the way you can bring me up to date on all that's happened while I've been away.'

'Aaron is with you? Why? What's happening to our stores in South West Africa?'

'The fighting is bad, Daniel. While we were at home in Otjimkandje the village was raided three times, and most of the while the warriors are out raiding someone else. On the way we've passed through villages that have been razed to the ground. The stench of death is everywhere. Nobody is trading. Whatever one tribe needs it takes from another. It's dangerous for a man to have anything worth stealing. Even so, it took Dad a long time to persuade Aaron to leave with us . . . but there'll be time enough to talk about things like that when we meet up with the others. Let's just talk about you and me for a while.'

Since arriving in Khami, five years before, theirs had been a warm and easy relationship. Even then the fifteen-year-old Victoria had adored the twenty-one-year-old Daniel, already experienced in trading and the harsh ways of nineteenth-century Africa. Nothing had ever been said, but it was assumed by those about them that one day they would marry and set up home together among the Matabele.

Suliyana watched as they walked away, hand-in-hand, Victoria leaning her slight body against Daniel. The Manica girl was filled with an emotion she had never before experienced. She did not recognise it as the pangs of jealousy.

Daniel was not the first European Suliyana had met. She came from a village which was frequently visited by Portuguese traders. Occasionally she would also see a Portuguese official who had reluctantly forsaken the comforts of coastal life in order to undertake a tour of inspection through the interior of Manicaland. It was an area to which Portugal laid a vague and somewhat indifferent claim.

But none of the Portuguese men Suliyana had met were like Daniel. The Portuguese would sit with the village elders, sipping the brandy they had brought with them, their bloodshot eyes following the swaying bodies of village girls as they passed by. As soon as night fell the officials disappeared into their huts. Giggling children would creep to the low doorways and listen to the Portuguese grunting like wart hogs as they made sweaty love to the women the village headman was obliged to provide.

Daniel was different. He was an altogether gentler man. Suliyana would have given herself to him willingly, but he had not taken her. She had been both hurt and confused at the time. Now she thought she knew the reason. He had been saving himself for the girl who touched his hand now.

Suliyana had also met those with skins the colour of Victoria – but never before a woman. There were many half-caste renegades roaming the hills and forests of the land that lay between her country and the sea. The Manica's called them 'Pombeiros'. They were bastards and descendants of bastards. The result of four centuries of haphazard colonisation by the men who had introduced God and the sword to the tribes of Mozambique.

The Pombeiros were the scourge of the land. They resented the fathers who had sired them so carelessly and scorned the tribes to which they did not – and would not – belong.

Outcasts from both societies, their numbers grew rapidly and they joined together to form formidable rebel forces. They traded in ivory and slaves and sold their military skill to warring chiefs. Between wars they terrorised the countryside far and wide.

Yes, Suliyana had met Pombeiros before. It was only because her own tribe was strong that she did not remember such meetings with shame. Suliyana believed that Daniel was worthy of more than a Pombeiro girl.

Daniel and Victoria met up with Sam Speke, Mary and Aaron with their half-dozen ox-wagons in a narrow, dust-dry valley, five miles west of Khami. About the valley towered rounded granite hills, worn smooth by the wind and rain of twenty-five million African years. Here and there, giant rocks balanced one upon the other in defiance of the elements, recording the incredible depth of the aeons of erosion.

The men exchanged boisterous greetings before Daniel asked Aaron about the South West African end of their trade route.

Much of the humour left the aged Jew's lined face and he spread his arms wide in a characteristic gesture. 'How can you set a few shillings profit against a man's life, Daniel? The country is in turmoil. Not only is tribe fighting against tribe, but village against village. I've spent days negotiating a safe passage through the territory of a chief, only to be attacked by one of his own kraal heads who has changed sides. I stayed as long as I could – longer than any other trader, but I had to make the decision to get out while we still had some trade goods left. There will be no more business in South West until the wars are over.'

The finality of Aaron's statement left Daniel stunned. The whole of the Matabele trading operation depended upon being able to carry ivory, ostrich feathers and animal skins to the South West African port of Whalefish Bay.

'Don't let it worry you, Daniel,' the bearded Jewish trader tried to make light of their problems. 'I hear the Boers are trekking all the way from the Cape to the borders of Matabeleland. If they can do it, so can we. We'll carry our goods to Natal, use Durban . . . or Delagoa Bay.'

Daniel shook his head. 'We'd be crossing the country of both the Boers and the Zulus. Neither would think twice about killing us. If we escaped them our oxen would be eaten alive by Tsetse fly.'

'So, what do we do? Are you suggesting we throw away all our years of hard work? Become shopkeepers in Cape Town, maybe?'

Daniel said nothing for a few minutes. He had ruled out Aaron's proposed route to the Indian Ocean, but there *was* an alternative. . . .

Thoughtfully, he said, 'A few months ago Mzilikazi sent me to warn off an expedition trying to enter Matabeleland from the Kalahari. With the party was an artist. During a conversation I had with him he told me he'd travelled up the Zambezi River from the Indian Ocean in company with a missionary. On that occasion they only got as far as some rapids at Cabora Bassa, three hundred miles upriver. Later, the missionary followed the river on his own and reached the Makololo tribe. Their country is well to the north east, so a trading route along the Zambeze River is feasible. Not only that, the artist had heard of a route inland from Sofala, well to the south of the Zambezi. That would suit us even better.'

'There! Didn't I say you'd think of something? But how do we find this route?'

'I suppose I'll have to go and search for it. The main problem will be the tribes along the way. The first will be the Mashona. I don't anticipate any trouble with them. I've traded with them before and they owe allegiance to Mzilikazi – but I'm more worried about the Manicas. Their lands are beyond the Mashona and one of Mzilikazi's impis has just returned from a raid against them. They're hardly likely to welcome us with open arms.'

'Oh, I don't know,' interjected Victoria, mischievously. 'I saw the look your little Manica girl gave you before we left. I wouldn't say they seem *un*friendly people.'

Victoria had made the remark sarcastically, peeved because she had been back for no more than an hour and Daniel was already talking of going away. But, much to her dismay, Daniel seized upon her words, the sarcasm ignored.

'I think you've come up with the answer.' Seeing the puzzled expressions on the faces of the others, Daniel explained quickly about Kanje's raid and its consequence. 'It means that not only have we someone who knows Manicaland, but her family should be grateful enough to have her back to be ready to help us.'

'Wasn't I right to leave South West?' Aaron lifted his hands to the sky in gratitude. 'Lord, I should have known you wouldn't slam a door in my face without opening another.'

Daniel grinned ruefully. 'Save your thanks until we reach the Indian Ocean, Aaron. A lot can happen between here and there.'

Victoria also had misgivings, but for very different reasons. Daniel would be taking a Manica girl – a *grateful* Manica girl, on a long journey through unknown country. Together they would share dangers and new, exciting experiences. Victoria had no doubt the Manica girl would use her big, expressive brown eyes to good purpose along the way. Tears of frustration stung her eyes like grains of fine sand. Angrily she blinked them back. Pulling the reins of her startled horse towards her, she leaped upon its back and rode away along the track.

Sam Speke watched her go, a troubled frown on his face. He understood what was upsetting her. If only Daniel would say something to her about their future together . . . . Victoria was of an age for marriage – and Daniel was the man she had chosen. Sam Speke had always given his daughter everything she wanted. He would not allow the one thing she desired more than any other to escape from her now.

With a sigh, he cracked the long, rawhide whip over the flanks of his oxen. As the patient beasts leaned into their yokes, Sam Speke spoke to his wife, Mary, who clung to the seat beside him. 'I reckon I'll need to go with young Daniel on this trip of his to the coast. Our Victoria would never recover if he got lost somewhere along the way.'

Riding ahead of the others, Daniel caught up with Victoria where the rough path from the west joined the main track into the valley from the south. The mission station was only a few hundred yards distant and Victoria was talking to the two missionaries.

This was not the moment to ask Victoria why she had ridden

off so hastily, and one of the missionaries was beckoning to him. 'I've been waiting to have a word with you, Retallick. You know, of course, that Mzilikazi's impis have been on the rampage again? One returned only yesterday with thousands of stolen cattle and at least a hundred women prisoners. It sickened me to see them. The good Lord alone knows how many more were slaughtered. Can't you put a stop to such ghastly happenings? I know you live in the kraal with these savages, but you're a white man, after all. You *must* do something.'

The Reverend Farewell Loveday had been born in the Cape Colony thirty years before. At the age of seven he had accompanied his missionary parents on a recklessly misguided evangelistic voyage to the Natal coast, almost a thousand miles beyond the protection of the nearest British garrison. Only two days after they landed, the infant Farewell Loveday saw his parents hacked to pieces by the broad-bladed assegais of Shaka's Zulus. The experience rendered him totally unsuited for missionary work but, brought up by missionary colleagues of his late father, Farewell Loveday's future role in life was never in doubt. Now he was labouring amidst the Matabele, an off-shoot of the Zulu tribe he both hated and feared.

Leaning forward in his saddle, Daniel said cryptically, 'Plead with the Lord, Farewell. He's the only one who can influence Mzilikazi. I certainly can't – and I didn't see you outside registering a protest when the impi passed by the mission station.'

'You know as well as I do, they'd have overrun me with their stolen cattle.'

Swinging his horse's head away from the Reverend Farewell Loveday, Daniel spoke to the second missionary who stood nervously dabbing his unnaturally pale face with a damp handkerchief. 'How about you, Reverend Pugh-Williams? Didn't you think of pointing out the error of their ways to the warriors of the impi?'

'I . . . I was sick. Too sick to leave my bed. I should be there now . . . I'm not a well man.' The Reverend Pugh-Williams stammered the words unhappily in his sing-song Welsh voice.

Daniel's scornful look was tinged with pity. Arnold Pugh-Williams was a weak man. His failings would have been apparent in whatever calling he chose, in any country. Here, in the heart of Africa where a man needed to be strong to survive, he was an object of derision. His only defence against the harsh world about him lay in his illnesses, some real, but most imagined. When things became too much for him he took to his bed, tended in a somewhat desultory manner by his wife. He would have left Khami within weeks of his arrival had it not been for her. Helena Pugh-Williams insisted that The Lord's will had brought them to Khami – so here they must stay. The daughter of an English Anglican Bishop, Helena Pugh-Williams was an attractive and strong-willed young woman. Malicious Cape Town gossip had it that *she* had persuaded her timid husband to go to Khami – in order to be near the more ebullient Farewell Loveday.

'This heathen country is in sore need of red-blooded white men,' Farewell Loveday complained bitterly. 'I have a great many Boer friends who wouldn't stand by and stick their heads in the sand while Mzilikazi's warriors hacked innocent women to death. I trust their screams didn't keep *you* awake last night, Retallick?'

'They didn't,' replied Daniel, truthfully. 'And I hope you didn't report their deaths in your diary because they are still alive! Oh, and so that you might keep your journal accurate, there were only forty prisoners brought in, not a hundred.'

Jerking the reins of his horse, Daniel rode on to the store, Victoria falling silently in place behind him.

A basic difference of opinion separated Daniel and the two missionaries. Farewell Loveday, in particular, was working to have Matabeleland thrown open to white settlers, many of whom had already tried to obtain land grants from Mzilikazi. By far the most persistent were the Boers. Chafing at the petty restrictions imposed upon them by the rapidly expanding authority of the British administration in the Cape Colony, the Boers had set up their own Republic of Transvaal, extending to the southernmost limits of Mzilikazi's lands.

Only the ferocity and weight of numbers of Mzilikazi's warriors kept the Boers to the south of the Limpopo River. Missionaries of all denominations constantly fired their hopes of a northward trek, believing the Boers to be the only hope of forcing Christian standards on the Matabele and their vassals.

Daniel's experiences in South West Africa made him rather more sceptical of the outcome of such a white invasion. In that unfortunate territory traders had set one tribe against another, selling arms to each of the combatants in turn and making huge profits. In Matabeleland a confrontation between Boer and native would be bound to result in bitter and bloody fighting. The Boers wanted to carve out farms and homesteads to pass on to their sons and grandchildren. Those of them who had seen Matabeleland enthused about its lush, rolling hills and bountiful rivers and streams. Here a man could raise two crops every year.

Mzilikazi knew the worth of his lands. In order to keep them he and his warriors would fight to the death. However, his policy of maintaining a huge, well-trained army, coupled with the firm exclusion of whites from Matabeleland had succeeded in giving his people peace – so far. Many years before, a Boer adventurer *had* brought a large party to Matabeleland. Mounted and well-armed, they were confident of their superiority. They had stolen a great many Matabele cattle – but never got them back to Transvaal. Mzilikazi ambushed the raiders among the hills of the Matopos. Wounding many Boers, he slew all their retainers and recovered his cattle.

Since that day no European had entered Matabeleland without first obtaining Mzilikazi's permission. If relations between Matabele and white man were cool, at least they were not spilling each other's blood.

Daniel tackled Suliyana later that evening in Sam Speke's house, to which she had reluctantly moved. Victoria brought her to the room where Daniel, Aaron and Sam Speke were enjoying the brandy carried from the coast of South West Africa. Suliyana stood before them without any show of self-consciousness, and her eyes went instinctively to Daniel.

He smiled at her with more friendliness than he had dared display the previous evening. 'Suliyana, we've been talking here about setting up a new route to the coast for our trade goods. If it went through the country of your people do you think they would welcome us?'

Suliyana was an intelligent girl and she realised immediately how important she might be to the white man who had saved her life, but she contained her excitement as she answered.

'My people have never fought the white man. You will be welcome in our villages.'

Daniel's interest quickened at her words and he removed the pipe from his mouth. 'Other white men have been to your land?'

'Many come there, but they do not speak your language. They are the Mapunga – the rice eaters.'

'The Portuguese! Do these men bring trade goods from the sea?'

'Some do. I too have seen the sea upon which the white man floats his great wooden houses.'

'You've been to the sea and seen ships?' Daniel's excitement was shared by the others. 'What was the name of this place – and how far is it from your village?'

'The Mapunga call it "Sofala". It is ten days walk through the hills from my village.'

'Suliyana, if I return you to your people will you guide me to Sofala?'

'You are going to take me back to my village?' Now Suliyana's delight could not be hidden.

'Yes . . . that's if there's anyone left alive after Kanje's raid.'

Suliyana looked disdainful. 'The Matabele killed only old men and boys. They raided the working kraal of one of the headmen responsible for the chief's cattle. The headman was my uncle. I was visiting him from my own kraal, two days walk away. The Matabele would not dare attack such a place.'

She smiled happily at Daniel. 'Yes, I will guide you to the coast. I, or some of my people. But do not tell them you are Mzilikazi's friend, only that you trade with his tribe. My people have heard much of Mzilikazi from our neighbours, the tribes you call the Mashona. They have suffered much from the Matabele.'

The Mashonas occupied the high plateau to the north west of Matabeleland, forming an uncomfortable buffer between the Matabele and the Manica.

'Will you travel alone to Manicaland, Daniel?' Victoria asked the question very quietly.

'I haven't given it any thought yet. I'll probably take a few Mashonas with me to look after the pack animals.'

The Mashonas and their allied tribes did most of the work about the Matabele capital. Their situation was scarcely better than that of slaves, but for most of them it was enough that they lived. The means used by Mzilikazi to subjugate them came very close to genocide and the whole tribe lived in constant fear of Matabele raids.

Daniel looked to where Aaron sat back in an armchair, contentedly puffing at his pipe. 'Would you like to come with me to Sofala, Aaron?'

'Me . . . . ? Go gallivanting about the country searching for the Indian Ocean? No, my boy, to me one stretch of water is the same as another. You go off and find your ocean, you are the young pioneer. I have spent many months journeying from the Atlantic and have had enough of travelling. I'm just a poor old man who should have retired many years ago.'

Daniel smiled. Aaron had spent all his adult life travelling through the trackless wastes of southern Africa, trading as he went. He could not change his way of life now, even if he were so inclined. But he *had* just completed a very exhausting journey. He had earned a rest.

'You know, I've got a hankering to see the Indian Ocean, Daniel.'

Sam Speke's words came as a complete surprise to everyone except his wife. No adventurous traveller, Sam was usually quite content to remain at the kraal, manufacturing furniture for the store and the mission church, and building wagons for Mzilikazi. They were wagons that would never be used because Mzilikazi refused to allow any of his oxen to haul them. The oxen, in common with his cattle, were as children to him. To set them to work would be 'cruel'.

Before Daniel could reply to Sam Speke, Victoria spoke to her father. 'If you go, then I can come too.'

Anticipating Daniel's objections, she said quickly to Suliyana, 'Would *I* be safe in your country too?'

It was a difficult question for the Manica girl to answer. Suliyana had her own plans for the journey. After struggling without success for the right reply, she shrugged and said noncommittally, 'My people do not attack women.'

Victoria turned triumphantly to Daniel. 'There! Now there's no reason at all why I shouldn't come with you. I'll be safe in Manicaland and we'll be under Mzilikazi's protection until we get there.'

Victoria knew she would eventually get her own way with her father, she always did. But she expected Daniel to object. To her surprise, he did no more than raise a nominal protest. Then he too accepted that she would go with him to the east coast.

Daniel knew full well that Victoria had over-simplified the difficulties they would encounter, but he would be happy to have her along. Not only was she an attractive girl, but she could outshoot and outride most men. All were welcome qualities in a companion for a long journey in Africa.

Before leaving Matabeleland it was necessary for all would-be travellers to be 'given the road' – permission to leave the country – from Mzilikazi. The Matabele King was far from enthusiastic about Daniel's proposed new trade route to the sea.

'You will find many Tsetse flies that way, trader. You will lose your horses and oxen.'

'Tsetse flies shouldn't bother me at this time of the year and I'll be back before the rains begin.'

The rainy season would begin in November or December and last no longer than three months. It was now June, the coolest month of the year. Daniel felt he had allowed himself ample time to reach the coast and return safely to Khami.

'You will meet with tribes who are enemies of the Matabele. I cannot spare warriors to protect you from them.'

'I have no wish to take any of your warriors, Mzilikazi. I'm setting out to establish a trade route to the coast. In order to do that I need to make friends. I'd find that difficult if I were travelling with one of your impis. Your warriors would attack anything that moved.'

Mzilikazi was suspicious of Daniel's motives, but he accepted that a new trade route had to be found. The Matabele king received half the profit on all the ivory Daniel shipped out and he needed the money to keep his wives supplied with the beads and baubles Daniel brought in for them. Mzilikazi's motive in not wanting Daniel to leave was not entirely mercenary. He was genuinely fond of the young trader who had made his home among the Matabele. Daniel was honest and forthright, and cared for Mzilikazi's people. The King had come to rely on his advice. Mzilikazi feared that Daniel might find another tribe that suited him better and not return to the Matabele.

'Oh, very well, go if you must. But you will take my son Jandu with you. One Matabele warrior will not provoke a war, but his presence will mean that an attack upon you is an attack upon Mzilikazi. Go, trader, but return quickly. I am an old man and will not live forever.'

Daniel smiled, Mzilikazi had been saying the same thing to him for years.

CHAPTER FOUR

Daniel set off for Manicaland at the end of June 1868. He planned to return to Khami by the end of October. It gave him four months to make a round trip of a thousand miles through unknown country. After giving the matter some consideration he had ruled out ox-wagons. Ponderous and slow, oxen could only make fifteen miles a day given the best of conditions. Across country it would have been necessary to select longer routes for them, or cut a track for them. Instead, Daniel took riding horses for himself, Victoria and Sam Speke and a dozen pack mules.

Jandu scorned the horses. He and Suliyana chose to travel on foot with the fifty Mashona tribesmen Daniel was taking along to look after the mules and the trekkers. The Mashonas would also act as an escort without exciting the animosity of those tribes who feared and hated the Matabele.

Most of Khami turned out to see the party off. Mzilikazi himself braved the chill morning air to bid a safe journey to his trader, and to his junior son. Only the two missionaries remained in their cabins, behind closed doors, but Daniel placed no significance on their churlishness.

Daniel felt he had remained in Khami for far too long. There had been many times when he wanted to make expeditions about the country, or travel to the unknown lands of the Mashona. Mzilikazi had always found a reason to refuse permission for Daniel to leave the royal kraal for more than a day or two.

Now Mzilikazi seemed to have run out of reasonable excuses to prevent Daniel from leaving. It was a sign of the King's advancing years. There had been a time when he would not have needed to find an excuse. A curt refusal would have been sufficient. Taking a last look back at Khami before he passed out of sight, Daniel wondered how many years Mzilikazi had left to him, and what changes his death would bring about. It was certain there would be a fierce dispute among his many sons before the leadership issue was decided.

Daniel looked to where Jandu strode along behind the riders and speculated on his chances of becoming the King of the Matabele. Daniel wished he knew more of the enigmatic younger son, but was satisfied he would get to know him better on the long journey that lay ahead.

For five days the party toiled through high veldt country that presented them with a wide variety of landscapes. There were thickly wooded valleys, wide rolling plains where the dry, coarse brown grass was higher than a man's head, and endless folds of broken-granite hills.

Up to this point the country had been familiar to Jandu, but on the sixth day they began to descend a rock-strewn slope to where a river could be seen winding its way through well-treed country below them. This was the furthest Jandu had ever been from his home village in this direction. Suliyana would be guilding them from here.

Although the river was no more than fifty yards wide, the muddy brown water was deeper than Daniel had expected. It was also well-stocked with crocodiles. Looking for a place to cross, Daniel walked his horse carefully along the bank of the river and stopped opposite a series of low mud-flats, lying cracked and summer dry in mid-stream.

On the mud-flats a great number of crocodiles lay belly down, like so many harmless, rough-barked logs. Then, no more than six feet from the bank where Daniel stood, the eyes and nostrils of a crocodile rose above the surface of the sluggish river without making a ripple. The eyes, black slits in an orange marble setting stared malevolently in Daniel's direction.

Beside him, Victoria reined in her horse and shuddered. 'I hate crocodiles. There's something evil about them.'

'I agree, but we have to get across the river and this looks the likeliest spot.'

Daniel slid his heavy double-barrelled elephant gun from the scabbard hanging in front of his saddle. Raising it to his shoulder and lining it on the almost submerged crocodile, he eased back the pin-firing hammers with his thumb. He fired both barrels in quick succession and the result was immediate and spectacular. The crocodile turned a cartwheel in the water before dropping back to thrash about in a dying frenzy that churned the water to blood tinged froth. Then the great reptile rolled over to expose a bright yellow stomach and disappeared beneath the surface of the river.

As the sound of the shots rolled away, the crocodiles on the mud flats raised themselves on short, stocky legs and flung themselves at the river with surprising speed, sliding beneath the surface with a protest of expelled breath.

Reloading his rifle, Daniel snapped off two more shots at crocodiles not sufficiently startled to swim well clear of the area of the proposed river crossing.

Calling for Victoria to cover him against any unexpected attack, Daniel coaxed his horse into the river. Snorting with fear, the animal eased forward gingerly and twice slipped out of its depth before emerging safely on the far side of the river.

Sam Speke took over the task of guarding the other bank of the river and Victoria crossed with the first of the pack-horses. Some horses were more reluctant to enter the river than others, yet all went well until the last animal was almost across. Then a piece of dead wood drifted slowly between the animal and the bank. Mistaking it for a crocodile, the horse reared and fought against the Mashona who struggled desperately to hold it.

Sliding his rifle into its scabbard, Daniel kneed his own horse into the water to go to the rescue of the hard-pressed African. Reaching from the saddle, he grasped the bridle and was turning to lead the terrified animal to safety when it reared up again, catching Daniel off-balance. Pulled from his saddle, he was unceremoniously dumped in the river.

Victoria sat on the muddy bank, rifle across her knees, and surveyed the scene with great amusement. As Daniel floundered ashore, followed by the belatedly subdued pack-horse, she leaned back on her elbows and laughed at his bedraggled appearance.

Suddenly, something moved beneath Victoria's right arm and her expression changed to one of horror. She leaped to her feet, a snake, fangs sunk deep into the flesh just above her elbow, dangling from the bare arm.

The snake dropped to the ground and Jandu darted forward and cut off its head with a single stroke of his razor-sharp assegai. But the damage had been done. Victoria stood clutching her arm, grimacing at the pain.

Daniel splashed through the last few feet of water and scrambled up the river bank to Victoria's side. Glancing at the decapitated snake, still squirming on the ground, his mouth set in a grim line. Putting an arm about Victoria, he led her to a nearby grass-covered hillock and lowered her gently to the ground.

'Lie back and stay as still as you possibly can.'

Calling the Mashona tribesman in charge of the pack-horses to him, Daniel took his whip and cut off a few feet of its length. Making it into a loose loop, he put it about Victoria's upper arm and drew it tight, making an effective tourniquet.

Victoria was in great pain now and Sam Speke, last man to cross the river, leaped from his horse and dropped to his knees beside his daughter. He had not seen the incident and looked to Daniel for an explanation.

Daniel nodded to where two of the Mashonas were examining the snake. 'Boomslang. We need to work fast. Hold her, Sam. Get Jandu to help you.'

A boomslang was one of Africa's deadliest snakes. A member of the cobra family, its bite was invariably fatal.

'You won't need to hold me, Daniel. You're going to cut?'

'Yes.' Daniel avoided her eyes, nodding his readiness to Sam Speke.

Daniel looked down at the back of Victoria's arm. It was no more than a couple of minutes since the snake had bitten her, but already the area about the twin punctures were ugly and puffy. He would have liked time to sterilise his skinning knife over a flame, but every second was precious now. Sam Speke held his daughter to him and Jandu took her arm in his strong hands, holding the elbow joint immobile.

Daniel sucked in a great gulp of air, steadied his hand, then made a deep slash diagonally across the puncture marks left by the hollow, poison-filled fangs of the boomslang.

Victoria twitched as blood welled out, but Daniel was not satisfied. He made another cut, half-an-inch above the first. This time Victoria cried out in pain, but Daniel already had his mouth to the incisions he had made. He sucked at the wound in a bid to draw out the poison, spitting blood on the ground. He repeated the treatment eight or nine times, then removed the tourniquet. He allowed the blood to flow freely from the knife-inflicted wounds for some minutes before applying ammonia from his medical bag and binding up the wound.

Standing up, Daniel discovered he was perspiring heavily, despite his recent ducking, and his knees felt weak and shaky. Smiling down at Victoria, he said, 'That should fix it. You'll be as fit as a grasshopper by morning.'

Daniel spoke with a cheerfulness he did not feel. Victoria made no reply and as Sam Speke turned her over in his arms, her head fell back loosely.

'She's fainted.' Sam Speke turned a worried face up to Daniel. 'Do you really believe she's going to be all right?'

'Of course.' Daniel did his best to sound convincing. He did not want Sam Speke to share his misgivings. The burly ex-sailor adored his daughter and Daniel was reluctant to add to his concern. 'We'll stop here for a while and let her rest. You make her comfortable, Sam. I'll get a camp organised.'

Daniel gave the orders to the Mashonas, but Suliyana already had a fire going. She had pushed a pot to the crackling heart of the fire and was carefully 'milking' the remains of the venom from the boomslang's fangs.

'What are you doing?'

Suliyana raised her head briefly. 'I'm making a soup from the poison of the snake. It will help Victoria – if we are in time.' Adding water to the pot from a gourd, she asked, 'Victoria means much much to you?'

'Yes.'

Suliyana looked at Daniel sympathetically. 'You need not worry about her. She will live. I know . . . .'

Suliyana's confident prediction was no more reassuring than her snake-poison soup had been when morning came. Victoria was still unconscious and her breathing had become shallow and laboured.

Sam Speke was beside himself with worry. He had remained at his daughter's side all night, keeping her warm with blankets, applying more ammonia to the snake bite when he could endure his own helplessness no longer.

When Daniel examined Victoria's arm he shared Sam Speke's concern. The arm was swollen to more than twice its normal size, the skin dark and mottled. The arm was hot to his touch and a trickle of yellow oozed from the wound.

'We've got to get help. She needs more treatment than we can give her here.'

Sam Speke looked at Daniel in desperation. 'But where can we take her? There isn't a doctor within five hundred miles . . . and not a missionary closer than Khami.'

While the two men were talking, Suliyana stood beside the still form of Victoria. When she turned to them it was evident that she had arrived at an important decision.

'We must take her to the White Mondoro.'

'The . . . who?'

'The Mondoro is the voice of Chiminuka – the great spirit worshipped by the Mashona and Manica people.'

The explanation came from Jandu, but for once he did not use the scornful tone that was usual when he spoke of the despised Mashonas. 'Chiminuka speaks only through the White Mondoro. He is said to be a great man.'

Daniel and Sam Speke exchanged glances. Both had lived in Africa far too long to scoff at the thought of a medium speaking with the voice of a god, and able to heal sickness. Besides, where there was an important medium there would also be a native doctor, skilled in the use of herbs and with some experience in treating snake bites.

'Where is this Mondoro?' Daniel asked Suliyana.

She indicated a direction about forty-five degrees south of the course they were on. 'That way. He lives in the Great House of the Chiefs. It is no more than half a day's walk.'

'We'll do it in less than that,' declared Daniel. 'Get a sling rigged up for Victoria, Sam. I'd prefer to be taking her to a European doctor, but anything's better than sitting here and watching her die. I'll set the Mashonas breaking up camp.'

The Mashonas seemed unusually reluctant to move. Not until Jandu stepped in did they make any real effort to prepare for the day's march.

'They are afraid that Chiminuka will be angry if they go uninvited to the Great House of the Chiefs,' explained Jandu. 'I had to convince them that the anger of Mzilikazi would be equally great and the consequences even more certain.'

Once on the move they found the going easier than before, the countryside being much flatter than the hills of Matabeleland. A mountain range loomed high in the distance, but only the occasional hill rose from the dusty, wooded plain on which they now travelled.

They had been on the move for three hours when Daniel first saw a group of tribesmen watching them silently from the slopes of one of the isolated hills. A mile further on, he looked back to see that the tribesmen had left the hill and were following at a distance of a couple of hundred yards. Leaning forward, Daniel released the strap securing his rifle.

'You will not need your gun,' Suliyana said quietly. 'Those men are Rozwis, the guardians of the Great House of the Chiefs. They do not harm those who come to them in peace.'

She pointed to where a solitary figure could be seen running ahead of them. 'See? They send a runner to say we are coming. It is their duty to keep the White Mondoro informed of all strangers. If we were a raiding party his guards would take him and hide him until it was safe once more.'

'You seem to know a great deal about this place,' commented Daniel. 'I thought your lands were still many miles from here?'

'They are, but the White Mondoro is known to my people.'

'This Mondoro. Why is he called "white"?'

'Because that is the colour of his skin . . . but he is not like you.' Suliyana gave Daniel a gentle smile. 'Be patient. You will soon see him for yourself. We are very close now.'

They entered a more thickly wooded area, and through the trees Daniel could see that their escort had increased in size. The silent warriors now moved on either side of them and fear oozed from every pore of the Mashona porters' bodies.

Suddenly they broke clear of the trees and Daniel reined in his horse, his mouth dropping open in sheer astonishment. In front of them was an incredible stone-built, fort-like building. Circular in shape, it was at least two hundred feet in diameter and had walls thirty feet high. Daniel had never seen anything like it before. Beyond the stone structure was a rocky, steep-sided hill on which similar stonework had been used to reinforce natural borders, creating a second, almost inviolable fortress.

Daniel had time for no more than a glance at these remarkable building achievements. Advancing towards him was a grizzle-haired old man flanked by an escort of warriors. Other spear-carrying warriors emerged from the trees about the new arrivals and took position beside the old man.

Daniel was nervous, but the man held up his hands, palms forward, in a gesture of peace. Then, to Daniel's surprise, he spoke to Suliyana first.

'Greetings, Suliyana, daughter of uTshwebe, Queen of the House of Rozwi. Our home is your home, as always. You and your friends have been expected and are welcome.'

At the old man's words, Jandu started violently and a look of awe crossed his face. In answer to Daniel's question, Jandu whispered, 'She is the daughter of uTshwebe . . . and a Rozwi!'

Before he could say more, Suliyana walked towards the old man, arms held out in greeting. But this was a Suliyana Daniel had not seen before. A new, confident girl who accepted the old man's deference as her due.

'Thank you, Pamire, Keeper of the Great House of the Chiefs. We have one with us who is very sick. She has been bitten by a snake – a boomslang.'

'When?'

'Yesterday. She has been bled and I gave her soup made from the poison of the same snake, but still she does not wake.'

Pamire nodded. 'You have done enough. She will not die. Bring her to my hut.'

Turning away, the old man walked off without a word of greeting to Daniel or the others. While they waited uncertainly, Suliyana called for the Mashonas to bring Victoria, then she followed Pamire. The Mashonas had also heard Pamire's respectful greeting and hurried to do Suliyana's bidding.

'Who is this uTshwebe?'

Daniel asked Jandu the question and the Matabele licked his dry lips anxiously before replying.

'uTshwebe is a chieftainess . . . but she is more than that too. Many men swear she is a goddess. They say she can walk upon water – like the bird after which she is named. She also has two hearts, and my people know this to be true. Many years ago a tribe of Zulus came far from the south to the lands of the Manica, who for hundreds of years had been ruled by the

46

Rozwi tribe, a people favoured by the gods. uTshwebe was captured by the Zulus and taken before their Chief. She refused to marry him and he became angry. He ordered one of his strongest warriors to plunge a spear through her heart. This he did and uTshwebe fell to the ground. A moment later she rose to her feet once more. Although bleeding from the wound which should have killed her, she spat in the face of the Chief. He immediately fell to the ground and died. His warriors fled. I have heard no one talk of seeing her since that day.'

Jandu gave Daniel a wide-eyed look of apprehension, 'What manner of people have we fallen in with? A woman who is the daughter of uTshwebe, a people who live in a great stone house . . . and a White Mondoro!'

Daniel remembered the night Suliyana had spent in his store at Khami. He wondered what would be happening to him now had he shared his bed with the daughter of a 'Goddess'.

Before Daniel could pursue this line of thought further, a warrior came to lead them to more modest accommodation than the Great House of the Chiefs. They were taken to huts in the valley, a hundred yards away. Here Daniel was given a hut of his own, Sam Speke being led away with the promise that he was being taken to Victoria. Food and milk were brought for Daniel, but when he tried to leave the hut to discuss what was happening with the others, he found his way barred by a spear, wielded by one of Pamire's warriors.

Daniel remained alone in the hut until darkness fell and the drums in the sprawling village about the great stone fortress began pounding out their rhythm, setting the night air throbbing.

Without warning, the blanket hanging over the open doorway was brushed aside and a warrior entered. Curtly ordering Daniel to follow him, he turned on his heel and ducked out of the hut.

Daniel stepped into the night and hurried after the uncommunicative warrior. Skirting the village, he was taken to the river. Here, in the light of half-a-dozen flickering torches, he saw Sam Speke and Jandu bathing under the watchful eyes of Pamire.

'I am sorry you have been left alone all day,' Pamire apologised. 'Chiminuka had to be told of your arrival and the woman made well. Now you will be taken to the Mondoro.'

'Victoria is all right? But . . . her arm?'

'She will always remember that she was bitten by a boom-slang, but I have healed worse cases. Now, join your friends in the river. You must wash the dirt of other places from your body before you enter the house of the Mondoro.'

The water of the river was cold, but Sam Speke delightedly splashed water at Daniel, behaving as though he were a young boy. When Daniel remonstrated, Sam Speke retorted, 'Daniel, I'd have plunged into iced water, aye, and fire too, for Victoria. If this god of theirs wants us to be clean when we meet his Mondoro, then that's the way we're going to be. I tell you, it was a miracle. They first forced a mixture of herbs down her throat, bled her from the arm a little, then tied this black stone over the wound. Twice they took it off and washed it in some evil-smelling potion. The third time they did it, Victoria came to. She complained that her arm hurt, and she had a headache, but you'd hardly think she'd had more than a heavy sleep. It's a miracle, right enough. I'll tell the world that.'

'I see Pamire has impressed you with his healing skill.' Suliyana had approached quietly. She walked into the river until the water rose above her knees. Then, quite unself-consciously, she removed the belt of beads about her waist, together with its attendant brief apron. Plunging deeper into the river, she swam away from them. The only man to show any embarrassment was Jandu.

When Suliyana turned and swam back to them, Sam Speke said, 'You've just left Victoria . . . she's still all right?'

Suliyana shook water from her short, tightly curled hair. 'I have washed her with water brought from the river. She will need help, but she is eager to visit the White Mondoro. Come now, before Chiminuka sends his lightning to move us.'

Before coming to the river, Sam Speke had fetched clean clothes for himself and Daniel from their saddlebags. As they dressed, he continued his eulogy of these people who had cured Victoria so rapidly.

Victoria was waiting in the village, borne between two of Pamire's warriors on the makeshift litter on which she had been brought to the Great House of the Chiefs. She held out a hand to Daniel and he gave it a reassuring squeeze before the procession got under way, accompanied by a great many torch-bearing warriors.

Once clear of the village the procession began to climb steps cut in the side of the huge rocky hill overlooking the great stone building. Behind them, voices joined the drums in a strange haunting chant unlike anything Daniel had ever heard in Africa. Its deep notes reminded him of an ancient Hebrew song that Aaron sometimes hummed as he worked in the Khami store.

When the first of the torch-bearers reached the top of the steep steps, Daniel was able to take a closer look at the walls, cleverly built to lock into the giant boulders strewn about the crest of the hill. As the party passed in through a low doorway and began twisting and turning along a narrow passageway, sometimes no wider than a man's shoulders, Daniel wondered even more about the origins of the two fortresses.

Ducking under a final low overhang of rock, Daniel found himself in an enclosure that was almost completely surrounded by giant, rounded boulders. Here was a flimsy shelter, no more than a flat roof of hides, backing on a low wall.

Beneath the shelter squatted a frail-looking man, a brightly patterned blanket wrapped about his shoulders to protect him from the chill of the night. He was younger than he appeared at first sight, but he was much lighter skinned than any African Daniel had ever met. It was not until the man raised his head and the torchlight fell upon his face, showing his opaque, pink eyes, that the truth was revealed. The White Mondoro was an albino. He was also totally blind.

Beside Daniel, Jandu recoiled in horror. An albino was abhorrent to the Matabele people. They were unnatural, imperfect beings. Any born to Matabele women were either killed at birth, or cast out of the tribe at the earliest opportunity. Now here was one who, it was claimed, was the medium through whom the spirit of the great god Chiminuka spoke to his people.

The White Mondoro's first words shook not only Jandu, but startled the whole party. As if his sightless eyes had been able to read Jandu's mind, he said; 'One of the strangers draws back from me. Is it because he is a slayer of our people and fears a

49

blind man's revenge? Or perhaps it is because he does not wish to hear the words of Chiminuka?'

The Mondoro's chuckle was that of an infirm man who spent his days and nights huddled too close to the lung-searing smoke of an ox-dung fire. 'Trouble not, son of Mzilikazi, I have neither the teeth, claws . . . nor yet the roar of a lion. I have only words. You will one day be a great man among your people. As a child you were once known as "The Scatterer". You will have that name again, but it will not be your enemies you cast to the winds. It will be your own people, the Matabele. They will be scattered and lost because of your deeds. You will not live to see it happen, Scatterer, and neither will I, but one day it will be the Mashona who rule all the peoples who now bow before Mzilikazi. The sons of your sons, and those of others here will witness the fulfilment of my words . . . and they will remember.'

The Mondoro had appeared to grow in stature as he spoke. His voice, loud and strong, carried to every corner of the enclosure. When he stopped speaking there was a long silence during the course of which he once again became a slight, sick man, chin sagging on the blanket about his chest and the breath in his throat heavy with spittle.

'Go!' the Mondoro croaked at last. 'Chiminuka will not speak again in your presence. It will take more than water to wash away the blood that will stain your hands.'

Pamire gave a peremptory nod of his head and four Mashona warriors closed in upon Jandu. Daniel started forward, but Suliyana put out a restraining hand to stop him. 'They will not harm him. We are all under Chiminuka's protection here.'

The Mondoro said nothing until Jandu had been led from the enclosure, then he once more raised his head. 'Chiminuka would speak to the white trader. Come, sit before me.'

Feeling extremely uneasy, Daniel walked to the shelter and squatted on the ground. The Mondoro reached out a hand and when he felt nothing, beckoned to Daniel. 'Come closer, I wish to touch you.'

Daniel moved forward until his knees almost touched those of the African medium. There was something eerie about sitting here in the ruins of what Daniel realised must be a very ancient building, with a blind albino who claimed to speak with the voice of a spirit god. Daniel did his best to remain completely rational, but knew he was not quite succeeding.

The Mondoro put out a hand and his fingers ran rapidly over every inch of Daniel's face. Then the fingers felt the material of Daniel's cloth shirt, and finally took hold of his hand.

'You do not understand, trader. You are afraid?'

'We came to you because we were in trouble. You and your people have saved the life of my friend's daughter. Why should I fear you? I am among friends.'

In spite of his words, Daniel had difficulty in maintaining an outward impression of calmness. In surroundings such as these a man could be tricked into believing anything. Daniel did not want to accept that he was in the presence of anything more sinister than a clever albino who had somehow survived native prejudice and achieved a position of importance among his people.

The grip on Daniel's hand tightened until it became painful. When the Mondoro spoke again it was with the voice that had foretold a grim future for Jandu.

'You have made your home among the Matabele. I see you going through life touching hands with many of them and they bow their heads respectfully to you. It is good, but it will not always be so. I see another hand stretching towards you – and it holds a spear. It is a day of much wind . . . there are many spears pointing at your people. The spears and the wind sing together. You hear the song and your heart weeps . . . but the tears are not for yourself—'

The voice broke and dropped to a whisper. 'As your heart weeps, so you will remember the words of Chiminuka's Mondoro.'

The Mondoro's hand slipped from Daniel's grasp and Daniel rose to his feet. He was perturbed at the other man's words, but he was still not certain.

'Trader,' Daniel had to lean forward to catch the words. 'Chiminuka spoke of what must be. Do not try to run from your destiny.'

'I will live my life as I think it should be lived . . . Madala.' Daniel added the courtesy title used when addressing tribal elders.

Sam Speke did not share Daniel's casual acceptance of the

Mondoro's words. 'Don't let anything he's said upset you, Daniel,' he hissed when Daniel returned to his place. 'There's half-a-dozen of these Mondoros scattered about Mashonaland. They all claim to speak for Chiminuka – Mwari, or some other such god—'

He broke off as the Mondoro said loudly, 'Where is the girl who was bitten by the snake? Bring her to me.'

Sam Speke had scornfully dismissed the Mondoro as a fraud, yet he was unhappy at the thought of him talking to Victoria. But before he could prevent it, Victoria had been carried forward by two warriors and set on the ground before the albino.

Daniel saw her recoil in revulsion as the Mondoro's hand explored her face then traced the lines of her slender neck down to her shoulders. Next the Mondoro took the arm that had been bitten by the snake and smoothed the wound with his finger, nodding in apparent satisfaction. 'It is good, the wound will heal well.'

Releasing her arm, he asked, 'What is your name?'

'Victoria . . . Victoria Speke.'

'We are much alike, you and I, Victoria.' The White Mondoro spoke with his own voice and it contained much sadness. 'I am of my people – yet am not one of them. You are born of two peoples – but are not of either. It is hard, child . . . but now Chiminuka would speak.'

The Mondoro's voice gained in power once again, 'For you there are bad times to come. You are a thread that joins white with black, yet you are not strong enough to pull them together, so you must break. One day, perhaps, there will be many such as you. The threads must join together to make a strong rope . . . but such a time is far, far away. Do not look for happiness, child, happiness is not within you – but you will seek it among your own kind—'

'What nonsense is he trying to feed her?' Sam Speke rose to his feet angrily, but one of Pamire's warriors barred his way with a spear. Only Daniel saw Victoria's stricken look as she turned at the commotion.

Victoria was carried back to her companions and Sam Speke put a comforting arm about her, grumbling all the while about 'stupid men who frighten young girls.'

Pamire asked the Mondoro whether Chiminuka would speak to Victoria's father.

'No. Chiminuka speaks only of the future. There is none for the father of the girl.' Daniel was glad that Sam Speke was too busy reassuring Victoria to hear what had been said.

Pamire signalled to his warriors and, one by one, Daniel and his companions were led away through the narrow passage-way that led to the steps outside the hilltop fortress.

At the low, overhanging rock, Daniel paused to look back. Suliyana sat cross-legged before the Mondoro, both her hands held in his, her head bowed low as she listened intently to his words.

CHAPTER FIVE

Daniel and his party set off from the Great House of the Chiefs the next day. Daniel suggested it might be better if Victoria were allowed to rest in the Rozwi village for a while longer, but Sam Speke would not hear of it. The Mondoro's words to Victoria the previous evening had greatly upset her. He was determined she would not spend another night among his people.

Victoria was a very different girl to the one who had set off from Khami with such high hopes. She was strong enough to ride a horse today and showed no physical after-effects of her close encounter with death, but she was withdrawn and morose. Nothing Daniel said could jolt her out of her mood of apathy and, eventually, he left her alone and rode off to look for game.

Victoria improved slowly over the course of the next few days, but the warmth she and Daniel had always shared had somehow gone from their relationship. Daniel put her strange mood down to the pain she must still feel in her arm, even though Victoria insisted it no longer troubled her.

After spending a pleasant night camped by a hot spring, they began to ascend the mountains that had dominated the skyline for so many days, and now they caught glimpses of an ever higher range far to the east.

There were people here in the mountains, but they never came close. Daniel thought it unusual that they did not possess sufficient curiosity to come and meet the newcomers to their land.

When he mentioned it to Suliyana, she replied, 'They have learned their wisdom through the years. Men with horses have been to these mountains before – to take slaves. They still come, but see few Manicas, and fewer Mashonas. They have learned how to hide.'

Soon after noon, Suliyana directed them through a series of

deep valleys, tucked between well-wooded hills. Eventually they came out into another valley that must have been three miles wide, extending into the distance for as far as they could see. Ahead, no more than five miles away, was a very large kraal. The smoke from cooking fires hung over it like a hazy, blue cloud.

'That is Chena, my home . . . the village of uTshwebe, my mother.' She gave Jandu a sidelong glance. 'Does the thought of meeting uTshwebe fill you with fear, Matabele?'

Since setting out from Khami, a very easy relationship had developed between Jandu and Suliyana. He gave her a somewhat sheepish smile. 'Not unless she too speaks with the voice of Chiminuka.'

Suliyana's smile vanished. 'My mother hears many voices that are not heard by others, but when Chiminuka speaks all men should listen.'

'Talking of Chiminuka – you never did tell us what the Mondoro said to you after we had left,' Daniel said.

'It was a message for my mother,' Suliyana replied evasively. 'It will be known to you in due course. For now, you have other things to think about. There is a river between us and my village. The crossing-place is narrow, no wider than a man's shoulders. You must be careful.'

They reached the river soon afterwards – and suffered the first fatality of the long trek.

It came with a suddenness that took Daniel by surprise. The first few Mashona porters had reached the far bank and the remainder were strung out in a loose file across the river. As Daniel led his horse into the water there was a sudden commotion in mid-river and the glistening dark grey bulk of a three-ton hippopotamus emerged from the water.

The great animal had been making its way down the river, below the surface. Reaching the ford it surfaced, intending to cross the bar and continue on its peaceful way. Its sudden appearance caused consternation among the Mashonas. Deserting the pack-horses they beat the water to a frenzy in an attempt to escape. The hippopotamus was as surprised and frightened as they were and tried to leap over the bar to deeper water. Unfortunately, one of the Mashonas was in its path. The great jaws opened and closed upon the unfortunate man, the great yellow teeth almost cutting him in half.

Daniel's rifle cleared its scabbard while the tribesman's scream still lingered on the air. Both barrels were discharged into the hippopotamus's body just before it reached safety, the dead Mashona dangling from its cavernous mouth.

The bullets struck the animal just behind the left shoulder, narrowly missing its heart.

As Daniel hurriedly reloaded, standing waist-deep in the river, the Mashonas already ashore shouted that the hippopotamus had turned and was coming back towards the ford. Their observations were based on the bloody bubbles racing to the surface of the churned-up water as horses and men fought their way up the muddy river bank.

The hippopotamus erupted from the water not three yards from Daniel with a speed that belied its bulk. It was looking for someone to pay the price for the pain burning deep inside the huge body. Fortunately for Daniel its attention was diverted to the Mashonas shouting on the far bank and it charged at them in a series of ungainly leaps that threw water back over Daniel as he fired off another two shots. He placed them in almost the same spot as before, the shots echoed by the rifles of Victoria and Sam Speke.

The hippopotamus was dead before it hit the river bank, but its speed sent it skidding for twelve feet through mud and earth, bowling over three of the Mashonas along the way.

With the danger past, the Mashonas screeched their noisy relief, rejoicing at the vast supply of meat that lay before them. All concern for their more unfortunate companion was forgotten.

Grabbing the reins of his own horse and driving a couple of pack-horses before him, Daniel gained the bank where the others stood.

'That could have been much worse,' commented Sam Speke as he extended a hand to help Daniel ashore.

'Tell that to the man who died,' replied Daniel, grimly. 'But it looks as though our shots have stirred up the villagers. I hope they're as friendly as Suliyana promised they would be.'

Warriors could be seen pouring from the entrance to the Manica kraal. From this distance they reminded Daniel of bees leaving a smoked-out hive.

As the warriors drew nearer, sunlight glinted on the many spears and when the men formed a long battle line Daniel looked anxiously to where Suliyana stood.

Smiling reassuringly, Suliyana went out to meet her countrymen – the effect was dramatic. When the Manica warriors moved close enough to recognise her they stopped in their tracks. Those behind continued to advance, then they too recognised her. Moments later the line of warriors became a series of disjointed groups and Jandu clicked his tongue against his teeth in noisy disapproval. Then, as Suliyana continued to walk towards the army of her people they began to back away from her, muttering anxiously among themselves.

It needed only one man to break and run and the whole of uTshwebe's army would have turned tail and fled. Then Suliyana called, 'Do the warriors of uTshwebe run from women now? Or have the memories of her people grown so short that even Chibisa fails to recognise his own sister?'

One of the warriors stepped from the ranks of the army hesitantly. 'My sister Suliyana was killed by the Matabele.'

Suliyana snorted derisively. 'I was taken prisoner to the village of Mzilikazi, the Matabele. Now I return to show white men the way to the sea. I also bear a message from Chiminuka for uTshwebe, my mother.'

Chibisa advanced slowly and cautiously, still not certain. Then, when he was closer, Suliyana grinned at him and suddenly all his fears disappeared. He ran forward and embraced her, shouting excitedly. The remainder of the warriors surged forward, most of their attention directed at Suliyana – but a few were equally excited at the sight of the dead hippopotamus.

'It is the first hippopotamus seen in this river for longer than anyone can remember,' explained Suliyana when she brought her brother to meet Daniel. 'It is a good omen for your arrival at Chena.'

Daniel thought it was a strange mischance that the lost Mashona should have been in the path of the only hippopotamus seen in the river for so long – but his fellow tribesmen already seemed to have forgotten him. They were cutting up the dead animal, reluctantly apportioning a share to the

Manicas. Leaving them to their bloody task, Daniel rounded up the pack-horses and, with the others, followed Suliyana and her brother to the village.

Messengers had run ahead to tell of the return of Suliyana. Queen uTshwebe, ruler of the tribes of the Manica valley came from the kraal to meet them. Tall and regal, she wore a cloak of civet skins about her shoulders and Daniel thought she was an artist's dream of an African queen. One of the last survivors of the once powerful Rozwi people, she was a benevolent ruler to her Manica people – but today she was a mother greeting the daughter she had thought dead.

When the emotional reunion had run its course, Suliyana introduced Daniel and his party. The Queen welcomed them all warmly – until Suliyana called Jandu forward.

Queen uTshwebe rounded on Daniel. 'You dare to bring a Matabele into my land?'

'King Mzilikazi has sent his own son with us to ensure that we pass safely through the lands of those chiefs who pay him homage.' Daniel hoped fervently he was choosing the right words. If he failed to satisfy Queen uTshwebe his journey to the Indian Ocean would end right here. 'He comes in peace, as do we.'

'Peace? No Matabele knows the meaning of the word. Mzilikazi least of all.'

Returning her attention to Jandu, uTshwebe said, 'You stare at me, Matabele. Is it because of the stories your people tell of me? You think they lie, perhaps? Then look here.'

Unfastening the neck of her cape, uTshwebe let it fall to the ground and stood naked to the waist. Cutting through her left breast was an ugly scar, the width of a man's hand – or an assegai blade.

'Look well – and remember, Jandu, son of Mzilikazi. When you return to your father tell him you have seen the scar borne by uTshwebe. Remind him that when the spear struck home it was the chief who ordered the blow who died, not me. I want no more Matabele raids upon my villages.'

'There will be no more raids,' promised Jandu, looking away from the mark of the spear that should have killed the Rozwi Queen.

'Good. Now you will be shown to your huts. Suliyana, you

have a message from Chiminuka. Come, I would hear his words.'

That night a celebration was held to mark Suliyana's return to her tribe. Cattle and goats were roasted and the Manica men and women took full advantage of the occasion, singing, dancing and eating their fill at the expense of their ruler.

Squatting on the ground close to a roaring fire, Daniel was filled with a sense of well-being. He enjoyed watching tribal dancing, especially when there were no undertones of war or violence to detract from his enjoyment. Unlike the Matabele, these were settled people who had lived in these same mountains and valleys for hundreds of years. Their lives had been untroubled by others until the breakaway elements of the Zulu nation began their journeys northward from Natal.

At the height of the celebrations, Daniel was summoned to sit beside uTshwebe. As he took his place the Queen handed him a gourd of beer, having first taken a polite swig to assure her guest it was not poisoned.

'You saved the lives of Suliyana and the other Manica women. I am pleased. You will always be welcome in my land.'

It was the opening for which Daniel had been waiting.

'Your words make me happy, uTshwebe. I make this journey to establish a trade route between Matabeleland and the sea. It is good to know your people will look on me as a friend.'

'You will need guides to take you through the Portuguese country – and porters. You will take Manicas. We are known to the tribes you will meet. Your Mashonas can stay here until your return.'

'Will Suliyana come with us?'

uTshwebe shook her head. 'No, there are slave-traders in the Portuguese lands. My daughter has escaped from captivity once. She might not be so fortunate again.'

uTshwebe nodded to where Victoria sat with her father, 'It will be better for the Mambari girl to remain here too. She would fetch a good price. I can send only a few warriors through the lands of others. Such a small party travelling with a valuable Mambari girl . . . ?' The Rozwi Queen left the remainder of the sentence to Daniel's imagination.

Daniel looked to where Victoria sat staring morosely into

the fire, seemingly oblivious to the noise and laughter about her. Her mood worried Daniel and he was pleased that uTshwebe's words gave him an excuse to leave her behind in Chena. A few weeks spent resting in a peaceful and secure village might restore her to full health. But how should he tell her? Daniel decided it was a problem that would wait until the right opportunity arose.

An hour after her conversation with Daniel, Queen uTshwebe retired to her hut. Daniel and the others followed suit soon afterwards. It had been a busy and eventful day.

After a while, only Jandu and Suliyana remained seated beside the dying fire. A few dancers were still performing in a small group on the far side of the kraal, but the majority had followed the example of their Queen. Soon the light from a liberal sprinkling of stars in the night sky took over the task of illumination from the many fires that now burned low in the kraal.

'Are you still frightened of uTshwebe, Jandu?' There was a glint of white teeth from Suliyana as she asked the question, but Jandu took it seriously and carefully weighed his reply.

'I have heard the stories of my people and with my own eyes have seen the scar she bears. But I have also talked to her and watched her when she is with her family and her people. I believe uTshwebe is a woman ... but one who has the protection of the gods.'

'And me, Jandu? Am I a woman?'

'You are truly a woman, Suliyana.' Jandu felt the stirrings of his body. He had heard such half-teasing questions before, put to him by hot, eager young girls around the fires of Matabele villages. But Jandu was unprepared for Suliyana's directness.

'You would like to share my blanket tonight?'

Jandu wanted her. Yet even as his desire became a fever, innate caution held him in check. One did not form a casual liaison with the daughter of a Queen – especially one such as uTshwebe.

'I would take you as a wife, Suliyana.'

The words came from his mouth as though uttered by someone else. Of course, Jandu had toyed with the idea of marriage with the Rozwi girl, from the moment he had learned she was the daughter of uTshwebe. It would be a good marriage. Certain to meet with the approval of Mzilikazi. It would also enhance Jandu's prestige in his own tribe . . . but Jandu had not intended putting his thoughts into words quite so soon.

Suliyana rose to her feet and extended a hand to Jandu. 'There will be time for marriage talk tomorrow. Come.'

Much later that night, when the drums had stilled and only the muffled sounds of the surrounding bush-veldt disturbed the night, Suliyana sighed contentedly and eased the weight of Jandu from her. His hands reached for her again, but she wriggled from his grasp.

'Wait, Jandu! You spoke earlier of marriage. Is such a thought still with you . . . now you have known me?'

'More than ever,' Jandu replied eagerly. He had never before enjoyed such a woman as the daughter of uTshwebe.

'I am not a village girl who can be bought for six cows. uTshwebe will ask a high bride-price for me.'

'I will pay whatever is asked. You will be able to hold your head high among the women of my people.'

'There is one other thing. I must always be your "great wife" – no matter how many women you marry.'

Jandu propped himself up on one elbow. 'You will always be the head of my household – but only a King has a "great wife".'

'One day you will be King, Jandu. It was told to me by the White Mondoro. I want my son to rule the Matabele. Only the first son of a "great wife" can be undisputed King. I must be sure, Jandu.'

'You have my promise, daughter of uTshwebe. You will become my "great wife", and you must give me many sons.'

Jandu reached for her again and this time she came to him eagerly. Chiminuka's prediction would be fulfilled.

The silence maintained by Victoria after her meeting with the Mondoro ended abruptly when Daniel told her she was to be left behind in Chena while he pushed on to the coast.

Angrily, she shouted, 'Had I wanted to sit around in some native village I could have stayed in Khami – among friends. Why must I stay here? I can keep up with the rest of you – and it's not my fault I was bitten by a snake. No, I'm not going to be left behind. The going is much easier now and we're only a few days from the sea.'

When Daniel tried to explain the reasons put forward by uTshwebe, Victoria brushed them aside with a petulance that he remembered from her childhood days, but which she had been careful to hide from him in more recent years.

'Don't try to fob me off with excuses, Daniel Retallick. You want me out of the way so that you can be alone with Suliyana. I should have realised that at the very beginning . . . after you'd spent the night together in your precious store.'

As soon as he was able to halt her angry flow of words, Daniel told Victoria that Suliyana would also be staying behind in the village.

Only slightly mollified, Victoria continued her tirade until she realised that Daniel would not be moved. She then lapsed once more into a sulky silence. After trying unsuccessfully to talk her out of it, Daniel went in search of her father.

Sam Speke was as reluctant as Victoria to remain behind in the Manica village, and for similar reasons. Sam Speke had known Daniel since he was a three-year-old child and Daniel was as a son to him. It was Sam Speke's dearest wish that one day Daniel and Victoria should be married. It was to help Victoria to achieve this end that he had set out on the journey that had almost cost Victoria her life. He was determined that her suffering would not prove in vain. She *would* get the man she loved – no matter what an albino witch-doctor might say to the contrary, but romance could not pursue its course if Daniel and Victoria were hundreds of miles apart.

However, common-sense eventually prevailed. Sam Speke reluctantly agreed to remain behind at uTshwebe's village while Daniel and Jandu pushed on for the coast.

For the remainder of that morning Daniel was busy organising the onward trek, with little opportunity to worry himself about Victoria's moods. He was aware of Jandu's presence as he loaded the packs, but it was not until Sam Speke went off in search of Victoria and Daniel was alone that Jandu told him of the decision to make Suliyana his wife. In the absence of his father, Mzilikazi, Jandu asked Daniel to negotiate the 'lobola' – the bride price, on his behalf.

The request took Daniel completely by surprise. He had been so wrapped up in his own problems he had not noticed how much attention Jandu and Suliyana were paying to each other.

'Are you quite certain of this, Jandu? Have you discussed marriage with Suliyana?'

Jandu nodded. 'It will be a good marriage. Suliyana thinks so too. She says it is the will of Chiminuka.'

'Then I'll be pleased to negotiate for you – and congratulations, Jandu. You're a lucky man. But before I go to see uTshwebe we'd better decide how many cows you're prepared to give for her.'

'As many as it takes. Agree to whatever uTshwebe asks. The important thing is to convince her that I will be a good husband for her daughter.'

Daniel was impatient to be on his way to the coast, but for such a reason as this he was happy to postpone his departure for a few days. The negotiations for a marriage between a son of Mzilikazi, and the only daughter of uTshwebe could not be hurried. It would provide the foundation of a powerful alliance between two great tribes – and ensure continuing friendship from them both for Daniel and his trading company.

uTshwebe received Daniel in the private enclosure that surrounded the royal household. As he sat opposite her he thought once again that she was a very handsome woman. Suliyana had told her mother that Jandu wished to marry her and uTshwebe was fully aware of the purpose of Daniel's visit, but she opened the conversation by making polite conversation. The Queen asked him about his family and the people of South West Africa where he had lived for so long, his trade, the state of his business.

In return, Daniel praised the kindness of uTshwebe's tribe and the beautiful country in which they lived and promised he would bring the Manicas and their Queen many gifts from the coast.

Finally, when he judged the time was right, Daniel broached the subject of the proposed marriage. Following the traditional pattern of such negotiations, Daniel began by praising Jandu, his father and his family. In view of the recent raid by the

Matabele into Manicaland Daniel was obliged to choose his words very carefully. He succeeded in a manner that brought a smile of delight to uTshwebe's face.

'Truly, trader, you are a man who thinks well before he speaks. I wish you were one of my own advisers – but you are here to speak for Jandu. Will he make a good husband for Suliyana? Would she be happy in the land of the Matabele, far from the hills of Manicaland?'

'She will be the envy of every Matabele woman. Jandu is one of Mzilikazi's favourite sons, and a brave warrior. He will be a good husband.'

'I have known many brave warriors . . . but few to whom I would entrust the future of my daughter.'

uTshwebe gave Daniel a sudden warm smile that broke the tension that had crept into the discussion. 'Suliyana told me of the night she spent in your store. Perhaps I should demand lobola from you and make her *your* bride.'

'It would be a great honour,' Daniel replied, adding hastily, 'but I am not yet ready for the responsibility of a wife and family.'

uTshwebe gave Daniel a shrewd look. 'Do not repeat those words to the Mambari girl. She is used to having the things she wants . . . and my eyes tell me she wants you.'

'She's a young girl and has met few men of her father's people,' explained Daniel. 'One day we'll probably marry, but not just yet.'

uTshwebe had her own thoughts on the matter, but she made no comment. Instead, she brought the talk back to the proposed marriage of her daughter with Jandu.

The bride-price was eventually agreed at one hundred prime cattle. It was extremely high, but if Suliyana wished to command the respect of the Matabele women among whom she would live it could not be less.

When Daniel returned to tell Jandu of the success of his mission, the Matabele was overjoyed – but the high bride-price created a problem. Protecting a herd of one hundred head of cattle on a journey from Khami to Manicaland would require a large escort of Matabele warriors who would spread fear and alarm along the route. There was also the possibility that the herd would include a number of cattle recently stolen from the

Manicas. It would be an inauspicious beginning for future relations between the two tribes.

Daniel suggested that he leave behind enough trade goods to purchase a hundred head of cattle. Sam Speke could conduct this aspect of the negotiations. It would give him something to occupy him while he awaited Daniel's return.

CHAPTER SIX

Daniel and Jandu set off from Chena with an escort of fifty Manica warriors. Jandu looked upon the light shields and throwing spears of the Manicas with barely concealed scorn. These were not warriors of the calibre of the Matabele. In battle the Manicas would throw their spears away, leaving themselves defenceless, then run for their lives. The short handle and wide blade of the Matabele assegai ensured that it could not be thrown. The warrior who held it had to stand his ground and engage an enemy in hand-to-hand combat. Developed by Mzilikazi himself, this was the tactic that made the Matabele warriors the most feared of all African tribes.

Wisely, Jandu said nothing of his thoughts, but he found it difficult to hide his contempt.

The first day's march was a gruelling slog over mountains higher than any Daniel had ever seen. He thought they must have been at least eight thousand feet high – but the view from the summit gave promise of better things to come. The land dropped away sharply to a green plain covered in lush vegetation. Unfortunately, as they descended so the temperature rose. By the second day they were in a steamy, unhealthy area that abounded in flies and biting insects.

Among the flies there must have been the feared tsetse. On the third day one of the pack-horses began to hang its head and stumble along so unsteadily that Daniel was obliged to remove the pack from its back and redistribute the contents among the other animals. That same night the horse lay down and died.

This was only a beginning. The next day Daniel's riding horse and two more of the pack animals collapsed. By the sixth day all the horses were dead and the disgruntled Manicas were complaining bitterly about having to carry the loads formerly borne by horses.

It was Jandu who eventually shamed the reluctant porters into silence. Shouldering the pack of one of the warriors who was protesting particularly loudly, Jandu set off at a cracking pace and kept it up all day. When they stopped to make camp he dropped the bundle at the feet of the Manica warrior without saying a word. That night the other Manicas berated their companion for giving Jandu the opportunity to dictate the pace of the day's march. The following morning the disgruntled warrior was the first to take up his load – and that same day they reached the sea.

Their sudden arrival at the coast came as a complete surprise to them all. They were following a faint, overgrown path through dense bush when the undergrowth ended abruptly and they were on a ridge of grass-tufted sand. On the far side of the ridge was the beach, sloping gently down to the sea not more than three hundred yards away. The sea was extremely shallow here, extending towards the far horizon for almost a mile before a change of colour indicated deeper water.

It was a moment of great excitement and the Manicas threw down their loads and dashed into the water, whooping in joy when they discovered a number of large spider crabs. Gathering them up in great scratching armfuls they carried them up the beach in anticipation of a feast.

Jandu had never before seen crabs. They had the appearance of large, hairy-legged spiders and he watched the antics of the Manicas with disbelief.

More to Jandu's liking was the rhinoceros which appeared unexpectedly from the thick undergrowth not fifty yards from the impromptu camp and stood sniffing the air suspiciously. The short-sighted animal was aware of unusual activity on the beach, but was unable to locate the cause. As it turned broadside on to the suddenly silent men to investigate a new and imagined sound, Daniel took careful aim and fired.

The front legs of the rhinoceros collapsed and the powerful animal's foremost horn dug into the sand, supporting the one-and-a-half-ton weight for a few seconds. A dying shudder upset the precarious balance and the rhinoceros crashed sideways to the ground.

With both fresh meat and sea food so plentiful, Daniel knew there would be no shifting the Manicas now. A camp was set up close enough to the rhinoceros for the men to stagger to the cooking fire with their loads of meat – yet far enough away to ensure they would not be bothered during the night with the quarrels of the scavengers.

It was one of the most pleasant camps Daniel could remember. Occasionally he woke to look up at the stars, listen to the whispering of the sea upon the beach and think of life. He hoped Victoria was making a good recovery and wished he could share this night with her.

Daniel's only concern was the fact that he had contracted a mild fever. It was no doubt a recurrence of the malaria from which he had suffered for many years. It returned intermittently, but had never been serious enough to really trouble him.

Daniel's happy frame of mind was rudely shattered soon after dawn. The Manicas were busy cooking as much meat as they could pile on the fires before the heat of the day became unbearable, when a shot rang out from the undergrowth. It was quickly followed by two more and one of the Manica warriors stumbled forward a few paces before pitching face downward on the sand.

'Get down – quickly!' Daniel called the warning as he himself dropped to the sand behind the scant shelter of a small, wind-shaped sand dune. Jandu and the Manica warriors followed his example more slowly, uncertain what was happening and another of their number fell to the ground with a musket ball lodged in the flesh of his thigh.

A thick cloud of black smoke seeped through the bushes from whence the shots had come and Daniel triggered the contents of one barrel of his rifle low into the undergrowth. He was rewarded with a cry of pain, but it did not fell the attacker and he could be heard crashing away through the bushes.

Daniel could not think who might want to attack him and his party in such a manner, but one of the Manica warriors muttered to his companion about 'Pombeiros', and Daniel knew they were being attacked by the half-caste Portuguese rebel traders.

More shots were fired at their vulnerable position on the beach, but the attackers had now moved further back to the shelter of some trees and the musket balls pattered harmlessly on the sand in front of Daniel and the Manicas.

The situation was a stalemate – but the advantage would be

held by the Pombeiros when the hot sun rose above the beach.

Aware of the danger of being pinned down on the beach in the full heat of the day, Jandu picked up his short assegai. Calling on the Manicas to follow him, he leaped over the low dune and sprinted towards the undergrowth.

After only a moment's hesitation, about twenty Manicas sprang to their feet and followed him. They may not have been willing porters, but they were enthusiastic warriors. The remainder of the Manicas would have charged after their companions had Daniel not shouted for them to remain with him. He would need them to protect the trade goods should the unseen attackers break from the cover of the undergrowth.

For a few minutes after the last of the Manicas had disappeared from sight there was a nerve-racking silence. Then a single shot was followed by the excited cries of the Manicas. Suddenly, a man dressed in dirty and ragged European clothing ran from the bushes clutching a musket. A flurry of spears followed him and Daniel saw two of them strike home. As the man fell, Daniel could see a red stain spreading wide over the man's shirt from an ugly wound in his left side. Jandu had already been in action with his broad-bladed assegai. The Pombeiro had been mortally wounded before the spears of the Manicas struck home.

There were no more shots now, but the unseen Manicas still called excitedly to each other from different parts of the dense undergrowth.

It was another half hour before Jandu returned to the beach with some of the Manicas. The antipathy between them had disappeared. For a while they would share the excitement and cameraderie of a battle in which men had died.

One Manica warrior lay dead and two had been shot. Neither of the wounded men were seriously hurt, although both would always bear scars that would be the envy of their companions. Two of the Pombeiros had also been killed, the second body being dragged from the undergrowth by the returning Manicas. He had been hit in the leg by one of Daniel's shots and, unable to keep up with the retreating bandits, he had been abandoned by them and hacked to death by uTshwebe's warriors.

Dressed in the ragged style adopted by natives in the habit of hanging around European towns, Daniel saw with a sense of shock that his features were as finely chiselled as his own. His skin much lighter than any African's.

'He's Portuguese.'

One of the Manicas shook his head. 'No, he is a Pombeiro. There are many in this country. They steal and kill as a way of life.'

'Then we'll do well to keep to the beach. They'll probably attack us again.'

'They have gone,' declared Jandu. 'They had horses not far away. We will not see them again. Unless the tsetse fly kills their horses too.'

Although Jandu was probably right, Daniel took his party northwards along the firm sand close to the sea's edge. Not only was it safer, but they would make faster time. The Manicas were not certain where they were but Daniel believed the Portuguese port of Sofala lay not many miles from where they were.

That night they camped on a narrow headland, setting a guard against a surprise attack by any enterprising Pombeiros. The night passed peacefully enough, but Daniel's fever flared up alarmingly. He woke with an illusion that the whole landscape was advancing upon him, then as rapidly retreating.

Dosing himself with quinine, Daniel kept going until noon, aided by a concerned Jandu. Then one of the Manicas who had been foraging ahead called excitedly from a small hill that he could see a big kraal with stone huts.

Daniel staggered his way to the top of the hill. When the world swirled less wildly about him, he caught a glimpse of an indifferent village at the water's edge, about a mile away. There was a church, a tumbledown fort, a couple of stone houses and an empty quay.

It was the last thing Daniel was to remember for a long time. As he watched, the village distorted grotesquely, the whole merging in an ever-growing cloud that rose to envelop Daniel and he pitched unconscious to the ground.

The dilapidated state of Sofala had been brought about by a series of raids made on the once great seaport by Pombeiros and migrating tribesmen during the past few decades.

For this same reason, the sight of fifty armed warriors

descending upon the village sent the remaining residents into a paroxysm of fear. Most ran to collect their valuables, in preparation for flight to the surrounding heavily wooded terrain. A few primed their guns, prepared to defend their ramshackle village against the approaching enemy.

Much to the relief of everyone, not least the would-be defenders, the bulk of the advancing warriors halted outside the town and laid down their arms. Only three men came on. One was a white man, being carried by the other two.

Most Portuguese spoke the language of the Manicas and they listened to their story with quickening interest, especially when the newcomers spoke of inflicting a defeat upon the Pombeiros. Only a few days before, Sofala had been treated to a rare visit by a troop of Portuguese soldiers. They had ridden all the way from Quelimane, on the trail of the Pombeiros who had attacked Daniel's party. A villager was immediately despatched to ride after the soldiers and inform them of this latest sighting. In the meantime, Daniel was carried to the stone-built house owned by an important official who was in the village on a visit from his estate in the interior of the country.

The next few days were an unreal nightmare for Daniel. During this time he was unable to distinguish waking moments from the dreams that appeared to haunt his sleep. Perspiration escaped from every pore of his body as he tossed and turned in a frantic effort to escape from the animals and unknown creatures that lurked in every corner of the room. There were blood-lettings and foul medicines, and faces . . . many faces. One in particular kept recurring. Light-skinned, with dark eyes, and a frame of long, black hair, this face alone brought him peace.

Then, one morning, Daniel opened his eyes and became aware of the world once more. He found he was in a bed in an unfamiliar room. A room with furniture, and the feel of silk beneath his fingers. He turned his head to where a welcome breeze ruffled the curtains at the window. Puzzled, he tried to sit up, but he was too weak. The slight effort involved left him like a newly landed fish, gasping for breath.

Daniel tried to remember what had happened. What he was doing here, but his mind was no more functional than his body. At that moment, the door opened and a girl came in. She had the face of the one who had come to him in his fever.

Seeing his eyes open, she smiled in delight. The smile transformed her moderately attractive features into a face of great beauty. 'Ah! Louvar a Deus, Senhor.'

Observing Daniel's blank expression, the girl smiled, 'Pardon, Senhor. I forget. You are not Portuguese. I thanked God for your recovery. I am very happy that your fever has passed. You are fome . . . you are *hungry*, perhaps?'

Daniel nodded. He was gathering his thoughts now. He remembered who he was. What he had been doing before he became ill.

'Where am I? How long have I been here? Where are the others?'

'So many questions for a man who has just stepped back from the grave!' Placing a soft hand on his forehead, she said, 'You must not tax your mind too much yet. You are in Sofala. In the house of Senhor Pedro Carlos e Costa Farrao, Captain General of the North West District and Commandant of Sena. You have been here almost a whole week. The tribesmen who were with you have returned to their village – all except the Matabele. He alone refused to believe you would die.'

'Jandu! Where is he now?'

'You will see him soon enough. He comes every day . . . but no more questions. You must save your strength if you are to get well soon. I will bring soup.'

The girl turned to go. but when she reached the door, Daniel called, 'Wait! What's your name?'

She smiled. 'Elvira e Costa Farrao. This is my father's house.'

As the door closed quietly behind her, Daniel lay staring up at the plank ceiling of the bedroom for a long time. When the Manica warriors reached their village they would say that he was already dead. They could not risk incurring the Queen's wrath by admitting they had deserted him when he was desperately ill. He wondered how Victoria would take the news? He would have to send word that he was alive, before she and Sam Speke decided to return to Khami. But who could he ask to make such a journey? He would have to return himself. But he was not fit enough yet. How long would it be? A week? Perhaps two . . . .

His thoughts were interrupted by the return of Elvira. Her father was with her. Senhor Farrao helped his daughter to prop Daniel up on the pillows, then he beamed genially down at him, 'You are looking better, my young friend. It is good. For a while I and "O Medico" thought you would die. He told us so. Elvira . . . ? She said you would live. She has worked very hard to prove she knew best. Day and night she has been here with you. I told her to rest, we have other women to sit by your bedside. But no, she stayed.'

Senhor Farrao shrugged in an exaggerated manner. 'What daughter obeys her father when a handsome young man demands her attentions?'

Elvira chose to ignore her father, but Senhor Farrao put an arm about her shoulders affectionately. 'You did well, Elvira. I am proud of you. Now, feed your young invalid while I sit here and bore him with my talk.'

Daniel protested that he was able to spoon the soup to his mouth without assistance. He learned better when Elvira allowed him to try. His hand shook so much he dared not raise the spoon from the bowl.

'There,' declared Elvira decisively. 'No more argument, if you please. I will feed you.'

The soup tasted better than any food Daniel had ever taken. He felt the first spoonful travel all the way down to his contracted stomach. The mere thought of it was enough to put new strength in his body.

He was so engrossed in eating that it was a moment or two before he became aware that Senhor Farrao was talking to him.

'. . . our soldiers found the place where you had fought the Pombeiros – and discovered what remained of their bodies. You and your Manicas did better than the Portuguese army. Our soldiers galloped this way and that for days. They lost half their horses to tsetse fly and two soldiers were bitten by snakes, but they saw nothing of Pombeiros. In spite of this they claim to have chased them inland for twenty miles. They also say it was Mariano and his men. If they are right then no soldier could have caught him. Mariano knows Mozambique from end to end. He will be inland now, taking slaves. It is not so dangerous as trying to rob young English traders, eh?'

Senhor Farrao chuckled to himself for a few moments. Then he leaned closer to the bed. 'I have been talking to your Matabele . . . a most interesting native. Fascinating. The first of his tribe I have ever met. He is most concerned for you. He tells me you are here to seek a route to the sea for the goods you trade with his people. I know little of the lands beyond the Manica mountains, but I am surprised you chose to come across country to Sofala. It is very unhealthy between here and the mountains.'

Daniel gulped down the last spoonful of soup and leaned back into his pillows gratefully as Senhor Farrao continued.

'Forgive me, but I have inspected your goods. Indeed, I have them safely locked away in my own store. You have some excellent ivory – and those ostrich feathers! They are beautiful. What price are you expecting for them?'

'Forty pounds sterling for a pound of feathers.' Daniel felt drowsy now and he kept his reply brief.

'Forty pounds? Um . . . .' Senhor Farrao made some rapid mental calculations. 'That would be two hundred dollars . . . a good price. I will buy them all. If the price you ask for the rest of your goods is equally fair I will buy everything. But if you wish to have a regular trade with me you must bring your goods to Sena. It will be better for you, I think. The route will be healthier.'

'I don't know of Sena. I've been taking my goods to Whalefish Bay, in South West Africa, but the tribes are warring there.'

'South West Africa? You have actually crossed the African continent? From coast to coast?'

'I lived in South West. Then Mzilikazi invited me to his kraal,' Daniel yawned wearily; he felt very tired. 'It's a long story—'

'And one that will wait,' interjected Elvira firmly. 'You will sleep now. Father, it is time for you to leave.'

With her father's assistance, Elvira settled Daniel down in the bed and left him to sleep. Outside the room she chided her father. 'You wearied him with your talk. He must rest, he has been very ill.'

'Yes . . . yes, of course,' Senhor Farrao replied, abstractedly. 'But you heard what he said. This young man has journeyed from west to east across Africa. He knows the tribes of the interior – and he is here with us. He could help to realise the dream that every Portuguese man of vision has had for centuries. A colony extending from Angola in the west to Mozambique in the east. Such a belt across Africa would prevent England from expanding beyond her present territories. It could herald a new greatness for Portugal.'

'You forget that *he* is English. Why should he help *you*?'

Senhor Farrao put an arm about his daughter's shoulders and kissed her on the forehead. 'My dear, when he is fully recovered he will be filled with gratitude towards us for saving his life. You must nurse this adventurous young man well. I wish to take him to Sena with us.'

When Daniel awoke again it was evening. Through the window the sky over the sea was already darkening. Daniel was aware of someone else in the room and he thought it was Elvira. But then he saw the figure of Jandu standing motionless beside the door.

'Jandu! It's good to see you. Are you being looked after well?'

The big Matabele crossed the room and his relief was evident as he looked down at Daniel. 'They treat me well, my friend, and all the men are anxious to talk to me.' Jandu smiled. 'Indeed, it seems these people do little else but talk. When their soldiers returned from their unsuccessful search for the Pombeiros they boasted as though they had fought and won a great battle. In truth, the only enemies they saw were the bodies of the men we killed. They claim to have pursued the Pombeiros for twenty miles. I do not believe they left the beach. I look around this place and see houses in ruins after a raid. When I ask I learn that the raid took place ten years ago! The Portuguese do not move with any speed. I have seen only the woman of this house busy. She has taken good care of you. But for her you would not be alive now.'

'There are those at uTshwebe's village who will have been told that I died many days ago.'

Jandu snorted. 'Hah! The Manicas are not warriors but women. They talked of crops, and ground that needed to be tilled. Once out of sight of their village they begin looking over their shoulders ... but is it for the Mambari girl you are concerned? The daughter of your friend and his Herero woman?'

Daniel nodded. 'Yes, she'll be upset.'

'Perhaps – but she is less of a woman than the daughter of this house.'

Daniel bit back the retort that he did not want to hear Jandu's opinion of Victoria. Jandu was by nature a close-mouthed man, not in the habit of expressing opinions of others.

'Your friend Speke is very proud of his daughter and she knows this well. Anything she wants – he will give to her. She is accustomed to taking without giving in return. Because of this she has learned to think only of herself.'

'I hadn't realised that you'd studied her so closely, Jandu? Certainly not enough to have taken a dislike to her.'

'I neither like nor dislike her. I tell you only what I see. Others would tell you the same.'

'Oh? And do you have an opinion about Elvira Farrao?'

'The daughter of this house? *She* cares for others. It would have been easy for her to become as selfish as the Mambari girl, had she not had to look after her father. Now she puts others before herself. Her father, you – even I. She works hard and there is a fire inside her. *This* is a woman indeed, my friend.'

Daniel smiled. 'Thanks for your advice, Jandu ... and I realise I owe her my life. I must think of some way to repay her. But for now it's very important that I get word to Sam Speke. If I don't he's likely to return to Khami and give Mzilikazi news of my "death". After finally reaching the Indian Ocean I don't want to get back to Khami to find my trading company has folded up.'

The two men discussed the problem of sending news to uTshwebe's village. They were no closer to an answer when Elvira came into the room to light a lamp and order Jandu out.

'Jandu is very impressed with the way you've worked to nurse me back to health,' said Daniel when the lamp had been lit and placed on a table close to the bed. 'I owe you my life, I know. Saying "Thank you" just doesn't seem enough, but I'm saying it anyway. I am very grateful to you.'

Elvira was ridiculously pleased at his words, but she shrugged them off. 'I have had to nurse many people. My father, grandmother . . . and many of the servants at Sena.'

'What of your mother?'

'She died when I was very young. I never knew her.'

'I'm sorry. Tell me about your home and Sena. Is it very far from here?'

'Far enough. A day's voyage by sea to the mouth of the Zambezi River. Then perhaps five days travelling upriver – it depends on the time of the year. Sometimes, if there has been much rain, the current flows stronger than at others. You will see it for yourself. The ship has arrived to take us to the Zambezi. There will not be another for some months. We must leave in a day or two. You are not well enough to remain here. You will come with us.'

'That's impossible! I haven't yet said I *will* trade with Sena. Besides, I need to get back to u Tshwebe's village. My friends are there and believe me dead.'

'If you attempt to go to them before you are fully recovered they will be right . . . and it will not be safe for you to remain here after we have gone. There is much bad feeling in Mozambique towards the English. It has been that way since your country took over Natal and began pushing its borders northward from the Cape Colony. It is said you are trying to take over the whole of southern Africa – including those places where the Portuguese flag was first seen more than three hundred years ago. Some men say you want even Mozambique itself.'

'I know nothing of the ambitions of Great Britain,' replied Daniel. 'But I doubt whether any of it is true. Mzilikazi and the Matabele nation hold the country between Mozambique and South West Africa. South of Matabeleland are the Bechuanas and the Boers of Transvaal. The only Englishmen I know who are trying to come north are lone hunters and prospectors – and Mzilikazi will not even allow them to enter his country.'

Elvira shrugged. 'I tell you only what is said and believed by my countrymen. You will not be safe here.'

She looked at him from beneath long, dark lashes. 'Does the thought of travelling with me to my home distress you so much?'

'Of course not. But I must get word to my friends that I am still alive. They will be very upset.'

'One of these friends . . . is a girl?'

'Yes. She and her father came with me to Manicaland.'

Elvira's manner became suddenly brisk. 'I think it is better for this girl . . . and her father, to remain upset without cause. Try to go to them before you are well and you will throw away your life. But you must do as you wish. It is nothing to me. Now I have other things to do. I cannot stay here talking to you.'

Elvira swept from the room without a backward glance and Daniel wondered what he had said to make her so angry.

CHAPTER SEVEN

The following day, Daniel's fever returned. It lasted for only twenty-four hours, but at the end of that time he received tragic news that was to change all his plans.

The luggage and goods that Senhor Farrao and Elvira were taking home to Sena were loaded on the Portuguese merchantman. Now, while the captain fumed at the delay, father and daughter were doing their best to persuade the weak but determined Daniel to take passage with them.

Daniel wanted to remain in the Farrao house until he regained his strength and then return to uTshwebe's village with Jandu. He argued that it might take a week – certainly no more than two.

There appeared to be little chance of the Farraos overcoming Daniel's stubbornness when from outside came the boom of the signal cannon in the village square. As the sound rolled away men began shouting excitedly while women's voices were raised in near-hysteria.

'Wait here,' Senhor Farrao gave the order to his daughter before running from the room. Ten minutes later he returned with two heavily perspiring Portuguese.

'A large war party of natives is advancing towards Sofala. There are at least five hundred warriors. It must be another rebellion. We cannot hope to fight such a number off. Including the ship's crew we can muster no more than forty men and perhaps a hundred native militia. It is chaotic in the streets already. Every native for miles around is in Sofala, seeking the protection we cannot give them.'

Senhor Farrao rapped an order to the two men. Drawing back the sheet covering Daniel, they lifted him clumsily from the bed.

'What are you going to do? Where are you taking me?'

'To the ship,' replied Senhor Farrao. 'It is our only hope of escape. Elvira, you go on ahead . . . quickly now.'

'Wait!' Daniel struggled feebly against the two men holding

him. 'It might be warriors of uTshwebe's tribe, come to take my "body" back with them.'

The idea sounded stupid as soon as he had made it. uTshwebe would not send a veritable army to recover the body of an almost unknown white man. Senhor Farrao too knew it was most improbable, but he gave new instructions to Daniel's hot and unhappy bearers.

'You can see the road into Sofala from the window of my bedroom,' he explained. 'But we must be quick. The ship's captain is nervous. If we delay too long he will leave without us.'

Daniel was hurried to the spacious bedroom of the owner of the house and the men held up Daniel so that he could look out from a window.

For a few minutes the glare of the afternoon sun blinded him. Then, as his vision improved, he saw the advancing warriors and knew immediately who they were. With their high, plumed head-dresses of ostrich feathers, and shields as tall as the men who held them, there could be no doubt. The sight of Jandu hurrying from the village to meet them was ample confirmation. A full Matabele regiment was advancing upon Sofala.

Daniel passed on the astonishing information to his companions and Senhor Farrao listened to the news in disbelief. 'A Matabele raiding party here in Mozambique? No, you must be mistaken. Perhaps it is another migration of Zulu tribes from the south—'

'They are Matabele,' insisted Daniel. 'See?'

The Induna leading the impi had seen Jundu and recognised him instantly. Halting his regiment, he advanced alone and saluted Jandu with assegai raised high in one hand, shield in the other.

Jandu acknowledged the salute and as both men met and embraced, Senhor Farrao's astonishment grew.

'This Jandu . . . who is he that his tribe should send an army hundreds of miles to find him?'

'He is a son of Mzilikazi.'

The expression of incredulity on the faces of Senhor Farrao and his daughter told Daniel that the reputation of the Matabele King was well known, even here.

'Something must have happened. Take me outside.'

'That will not be necessary,' said Elvira. 'Jandu is returning.'

Through the window, Daniel saw that Jandu was hurrying back towards Sofala. Meanwhile, the Induna returned to his men and they lowered their shields to the ground and squatted wearily beside them. It was apparent to the most nervous occupant of Sofala that this was no raiding party, intent upon murder and pillage.

'I think Daniel can go back to his bed and await the news from there,' said Elvira, firmly.

Ignoring Daniel's protests, the two men carried him to his sick room and dumped him unceremoniously on the bed as Elvira clucked in disapproval at the rough handling he was receiving from the nervous bearers.

Jandu entered Daniel's room a few minutes later and his expression was grave. 'I have sad news, trader. My own impi awaits me outside the village. They have come to tell me that the great mountain of Matabeleland has fallen. Mzilikazi, my father, is dead.'

Daniel was shocked. 'I'm sorry, Jandu . . . deeply sorry. I've lost a wise and great friend. But my grief is as nothing compared to that of you and your people.'

'Every man, woman and child of my people has lost their father,' declared Jandu. 'Before Mzilikazi there was no Matabele nation. I fear that unless a successor is found very quickly there will once again be no Matabele nation. I must return home immediately.'

'Of course. I wish I could come with you, but . . . .' Daniel shrugged helplessly. 'My thoughts go with you, Jandu.'

Jandu nodded. 'I will inform the spirit of my father that I carry with me the respects of his friend. He would understand. He was fond of you, trader.'

'And I of him . . . .' Daniel choked on his words. The illness that had laid him low had left him totally unable to cope with such an emotional crisis.

Jandu turned to leave, but Daniel called, 'Wait! You will call at uTshwebe's village?'

'Of course. I have a wife to take to Khami and share my sorrow. I will tell your friends where they might find you.'

* * *

At the wide, featureless estuary of the Zambezi River, the Portuguese sailors transferred their three passengers to Senhor Farrao's own river paddle-steamer, *Bartolomeo Dias*. Overland trekking with all its accompanying discomforts was not for the Captain General of Mozambique's North West District. His cabin on the river boat was fitted out with all the luxury that was possible in nineteenth-century Africa.

Daniel had a comfortable bunk in a deck house, but during the day, when the churning paddles of the shallow-draught vessel were driving *Bartolomeo Dias* further inland through green and evil-smelling swamp, he spent his time on deck. Relaxing beneath an awning that was stretched over two-thirds of the deck area, he enjoyed what little breeze there was.

For the first two days the paddle-steamer chugged between low mud banks choked with mangrove trees, the grotesque, tangled roots of which reared high above the water line at low tide. There was lush green grass here too, and rushes high enough to conceal a standing man.

Gradually, the estuary became a river. Still more than a mile wide, it was laced with ever-narrowing channels that could only be negotiated in daylight. At night, the silence was broken by the shrieks of animals and night-birds, and the sound of crocodiles and hippopotami slipping into the water all about the travellers.

This was an unhealthy area, notorious for striking men down with malaria. At Elvira's insistence they all took a dose of quinine three times a day until the boat left the swampland behind and steamed noisily up to the quay of the small, fortified village of Shupanga. News of their approach had travelled ahead of them and the small garrison was drawn up on a riverside lawn to salute the Captain General.

That night was spent ashore, in the stone house of the garrison commander. Daniel was welcomed courteously enough by the Portuguese officer and his half-caste family, but their greeting lacked warmth. The Zambezi had served as the highway to the interior of the province throughout its long history. The Portuguese hereabouts had seen many Englishmen pass along its braided waterways. They had come in pursuit of knowledge, converts to the gospel, or self-glorification. Few had bothered to hide their contempt for the half-hearted manner in which the Portuguese had developed the African colony. Those who survived to make the return journey hurried off to send despatches to the British government of the day, urging it to ignore the territorial claims of their recent hosts and send an army to occupy the rich and fertile region. Such conduct, coupled with Great Britain's alarming rate of expansion in southern Africa had soured traditional Portuguese hospitality towards their ancient allies.

As the evening wore on and it was ascertained that Daniel spoke no Portuguese, wine freed tongues usually tied by the rules of hospitality. The hosts questioned Senhor Farrao's wisdom in bringing Daniel so far up the Zambezi and making him welcome, instead of ordering him from the country.

When the arguments became more heated, Daniel realised from the furtive and occasionally hostile glances cast in his direction that the conversation was about him. He excused himself from the company, pleading his recent illness as an excuse to make his way slowly towards his sleeping quarters.

It was a cool night and, once outside on the wide balcony that stretched the whole length of the single-storey house, he paused to admire the full moon, riding high in the night sky. He decided he would sit here and enjoy a pipe of tobacco before turning in for the night. He filled his pipe and lit it, shielding the light with cupped hands against the light breeze, blowing inland along the river valley.

'You should be in bed, Daniel. The night air is too chill for an invalid.'

Elvira's voice from the shadows on the verandah startled Daniel. He had not seen her seated on the bench seat.

'Come, sit beside me. The smoke from your pipe will chase away the mosquitoes.'

Daniel accepted her offer and seated himself close to her. When the tobacco was well alight, he took the pipe from his mouth and said, 'Why are you out here all alone?'

'I have no wish to be in that room listening to the ill-mannered talk of my countrymen . . . or in the kitchen with their African women.'

'I know nothing of their women, but the men don't seem to welcome strangers – or is it just Englishmen they don't like?'

'You understand what they say?' Elvira put the question sharply.

'I don't speak your language, but it isn't difficult to follow what they are saying. They don't want me here and are going to no great lengths to hide their sentiments.'

'They are concerned for their estates, and the way of life they have enjoyed for so many years. During the past few years we have seen more Englishmen than Portuguese this far up the Zambezi. They come here with such arrogance that the prazeros – the owners of the river estates – feel sure your country must be planning to take Mozambique from them.'

'You keep speaking of Britain as my country. I have told you before that I've lived in Africa since I was three years old.'

'I know. No doubt my father will tell this to the prazeros, but they are simple men. In Portugal they tended the land for a master, owning nothing. They came here because they were promised land of their own. It is a hard life for them, but they now have more than they can ever hope for anywhere else in the world.'

'You and your father are not simple people, Elvira. What are you doing here . . . and where did you learn to speak English so well?'

'Are you seeking mysteries, Daniel? If so, I am afraid you will be disappointed. My father is the youngest son of one of Portugal's greatest families. He loves Portugal and was often outspoken against the excesses of the ruling family, the Braganzas. After publicly challenging one of them to a duel, it was thought best that he be sent to an overseas colony. He chose to come here, with my mother. Publicly, of course, it was an "official appointment". He was given a grant of land and the post of Captain General of North West Mozambique.

'My father accepted that any future he had must lie here, in Mozambique. He settled down to the life of a prazero. I was born here . . . and my mother is buried on the river bank at Sena. I do not think we will leave now. As for my English . . . when my mother died there was a serious rebellion and I was sent to school in your Cape Colony. I remained there for a number of years, until I was able to persuade my father to let me return.'

Having reduced her life and that of her father to a few

minutes of conversation, Elvira began questioning Daniel in an attempt to fill in the details of his own life. Daniel was unused to talking about himself and she found it hard going. But, gradually, she learned of the foundering of the ship on which he and his parents were travelling when Daniel was three years of age. He told her of their desperate trek along the Skeleton Coast of South West Africa, of their unexpected rescue by Bushmen, and of the life that followed in a Herero village.

It took even more patience on Elvira's part to prise from Daniel the story of his love for Hannah, daughter of his trading partner, Aaron Copping. It was a story he had never before put into words for anyone. Elvira's hand found his when he told her in a hoarse voice of Hannah's suicide after she had been raped by a Boer trader. It was this tragedy that had brought him eastwards to Matabeleland, away from the painful memories of South West Africa.

'What of the other girl? The one you left behind in the Manica village?'

'Victoria? Her father was one of the seamen who survived the shipwreck with my parents. He married a Herero woman. They came to Matabeleland with me. Sam helps me to manage my trading store.'

'She is beautiful, this . . . Victoria?'

'Yes, I suppose she is,' Daniel replied. He had never really thought about it a great deal. Victoria had always been . . . well, just 'there'.

'You and she are to be married?' Suddenly his hand was empty once more.

'Nothing has ever been said in so many words,' said Daniel, choosing his words carefully. 'We have both assumed that one day we will marry, I suppose. Victoria is . . . well, she's a nice girl.'

'Ah! But she is not a *wonderful* girl? A girl who takes your breath away whenever you think of her? She is just a "nice" girl?'

'Yes.' Daniel felt he was being disloyal to Victoria and went on the defensive. 'She's a *very* nice girl. Is there anything wrong with that?'

'No, Daniel. There is nothing wrong with that at all. Come now, you have had a very tiring day. You must rest.'

*　　*　　*

The remainder of the voyage to Sena passed uneventfully. Once, a group of Pombeiro rebels came to the water's edge as the paddle-steamer passed, but they did no more than brandish empty muskets and shout equally empty threats. They were as ragged and careless of their dress as the Mashona tribesmen of the far interior, and hardly less black. A single shot above their heads from Senor Farrao's musket was sufficient to send them fleeing for the cover of the nearby tropical forest.

The paddle-steamer made hard work of the final thirty miles of river before Sena, but eventually it wheezed its way alongside the wooden jetty, steam escaping from a dozen loose joints as the engineer closed the steam valve and the boat came to a halt with a near-human sigh of relief.

Sena was hardly more imposing than Shupanga had been, but considerable effort had been put into making it secure against attacks from rebel tribesmen and marauding Pombeiros. The village had been built along the river bank and was surrounded on the land side by a double wooden stockade more than a mile in length. Inside was a fort, several stone houses, and a noisy native kraal. The finest house belonged to Senhor Farrao and had close-cropped lawns slipping away to the water's edge. From here there was a fine view to the north, where distant hills began crowding in upon the river.

Their arrival created even more of a stir than it had at Shupanga. The garrison, a motley collection of half-a-dozen Portuguese soldiers, a handful of half-castes and about a hundred Africans, were all well armed. They were also drilled better than their comrades down river.

As the Captain General stepped into the sunlight from his cabin, a couple of ancient 12-pounder cannons fired a welcoming salute.

The effect of this harmless cannonade was extremely gratifying to the gunners. The noise struck terror into every living creature within a mile of the landing stage. Animals fled in panic and birds took to the air with a noisy clatter of wings. In the native kraal, naked babies who a moment before had been playing happily in the dust, fled screaming to their mothers.

Senhor Farrao stepped ashore, acknowledging the salute of his garrison, then waited politely for Elvira and Daniel to step from the boat.

Elvira was assisted ashore by a young Portuguese officer dressed in a clean, white, linen uniform. His black hair glistened with a perfumed hair-dressing that assailed Daniel's nostrils when he was still six paces away. When Elvira stood safely on the bank, the dapper young officer raised her hand to his lips, holding it there as he bowed low. When Elvira smiled at the officer, Daniel frowned in sudden, unreasonable jealousy.

The young officer was introduced to Daniel by Senhor Farrao as Lieutenant Francisco St Anna of the Portuguese army, 'sent here to make soldiers of my farmers and their natives', explained the Captain General. 'And to tell me where I have been making mistakes in running my own militia for so many years.'

Lieutenant St Anna's bow to Daniel was no more than a perfunctory nod of the head. 'Senhor Farrao is too modest. He has built excellent defences here. If he has a fault at all it is that he is over generous . . . both to his friends and to strangers.'

Once again Daniel realised he was faced with the thinly veiled hostility he had encountered at Shupanga.

'There must be many who take advantage of such generosity,' he agreed amiably, before turning away to follow Senhor Farrao and Elvira along the path to the house.

That night Daniel sat down to eat in a style he had never before experienced. The table was set with fine silver and porcelain from the most renowned potteries of Europe. The food, excellently cooked and served, was accompanied by wine of a quality to delight the most critical connoisseur.

As the evening wore on, the talk turned to Mzilikazi's death and the impact it would have upon the Matabele. Daniel was surprised at the lack of knowledge the Portuguese possessed of the interior. Both Senhor Farrao and the young lieutenant appeared to believe that the Matabele lands were adjacent to Manicaland, the tribal area that spread along the Mozambique border.

They looked sceptical when Daniel told them that Matabeleland was five hundred miles from Sena, situated on the far side of the lands of the Mashonas. Lieutenant St Anna went so far as to accuse Daniel of deliberately misleading them, adding that such talk was calculated to fool the Portuguese and allow Britain to drive a wedge between their colonies of Angola and Mozambique.

Daniel patiently told the young officer that Mzilikazi kept *all* Europeans south of the Limpopo River, thus effectively preventing such a 'wedge'. Lieutenant St Anna refused to accept his explanation, dismissing the idea of a tribal leader who could successfully dictate to Europeans.

'Not that it matters in the least. All the lands of the interior belong to Portugal,' he declared sweepingly. 'It was given to us by the Monomatapa, almost three hundred years ago.'

The Monomatapa was an ancient African ruler of the lands now called Matabeleland, Manicaland and Mashonaland.

'It was later taken back again by one of his successors,' corrected Daniel, grateful to the missionaries at Khami, who in a rare moment of friendly generosity had loaned him a number of books on the history of southern Africa. 'There was not a Portuguese left alive away from the coastal areas by the beginning of the eighteenth century. The Matabele have never seen a Portuguese — and I doubt very much whether the Mashona have met more than one or two. No, Lieutenant, I don't know where you set your borders, but Central Africa — from the Zambezi south to the Transvaal — belongs to the Matabele. Neither your army, nor ours, will ever take it from them.'

Lieutenant St Anna stood up a trifle unsteadily and said, 'I cannot speak for the army of Britain . . . we have seen nothing of it here, in Africa, but I can assure you, sir, that a Portuguese soldier will fight to the death for what is his.'

Ostensibly, Lieutenant Francisco St Anna was talking about the fighting ability of the Portuguese army, but Daniel was left in no doubt that he was being warned off Elvira.

Bowing stiffly to his host and to Elvira, Lieutenant St Anna left the room on legs that behaved as though they were carrying the Portuguese officer up a steep hill.

Senhor Farrao smiled benignly. 'Francisco is a passionate young man, Daniel. I beg you to forgive his bad manners. He is honest, and a first-class soldier. We all sleep more safely in our beds since he came to Sena to take charge of our garrison.'

'Perhaps,' said Elvira. 'But "poor Francisco" must be quite certain where his responsibilities begin — and where they end.

Like Portugal, if Francisco tries to claim what is not his he might receive an unpleasant surprise. Now I too will retire to bed. Good night, Daniel. Good night, father.'

Elvira swept from the room, leaving Senhor Pedro Carlos e Costa Farrao with a worried frown on his face. He had hoped that bringing Daniel to Sena might help Portugal to gain a rich empire in Africa. He had never considered that he might lose a daughter in the process.

CHAPTER EIGHT

After his arrival at Sena, Daniel made steady progress towards good health. By mid-August he was out riding with Elvira and beginning to make plans to return overland to Matabeleland.

Senhor Farrao had generously told Daniel he could take half-a-dozen of his best horses with him to Khami. These were the mounts that were usually sent to a farm near Quelimane, clear of all danger from the tsetse fly for the hot, wet months of summer. Inland, the threat faded as the coastal plains gave way to the healthier uplands.

One day Daniel and Elvira rode to the top of a hill, about six miles from the Sena stockade. Here, Elvira set out a picnic for them while a bored Portuguese soldier and twelve militiamen maintained a guard from a discreet distance.

For more than an hour they sat on the hilltop, admiring the lush country on all sides while Elvira pointed out places of particular interest. Daniel commented that it was a great pity no determined effort had been made to cultivate such a fertile and well-watered area.

'A determined effort *was* made,' replied Elvira. She pointed out a number of large clearings where there were no trees, only lush, green vegetation. 'My father persuaded the government in Portugal to send out a number of peasants, offering them good land along the river. They became prazeros. All they could cultivate became theirs. It was a great opportunity for them – but the scheme failed. The peasants had been used to having their lives organised for them by a *patron*. Here they not only had to work for themselves, but also to *think* for themselves. It was necessary to plan crops and manage native labour. It was too much for them. They were peasants, not prazeros. They grew dissatisfied and lazy. Some left Mozambique for Brazil. Others returned to Portugal. When the Pombeiros struck in this area it was the final blow to my father's great experiment. Those "prazeros" who were not killed moved into our kraal. Now they work for my father and are once more content. He has become their *patron*.'

'I sometimes wish I had someone to do my thinking for me,' said Daniel. 'I might have avoided a great many of the mistakes I've made in the past. But I've grown too used to working things out in my own way. I couldn't change now.'

'You have thought out for yourself that you must leave us soon?'

'I have a company to run.'

As they talked they had begun to walk slowly along the bush-covered crest of the hill, leaving their escort lounging in the ground behind them.

'Have you decided where you will bring the goods you trade from Matabeleland?'

'No. I don't know what the country is like between here and Khami – and the distance is more than to Sofala.'

It was a lie. Daniel had already made up his mind to trade with Senhor Farrao at Sena – but he wanted to know how Elvira would react if there was the chance she would not see him again. It had become very important to him.

Elvira lapsed into an unhappy silence and Daniel said, quietly, 'Unless the route is quite impossible I'll be bringing my goods to your father, here at Sena.'

'Even though it is further than to Sofala?'

'Even if I find it's twice the distance,' he admitted.

The next moment Elvira was in his arms, her face against his chest and she was trembling violently. Lifting her chin gently, he brought his mouth down hard upon hers. She responded to him immediately, then suddenly she pushed him away.

Looking up at him, she pleaded, 'Please, Daniel . . . don't kiss me unless it means something to you too.'

It took him a moment to realise the full implication of her words. Saying nothing, he pulled her to him. Her eyes were still searching his face, but as he kissed her once more they closed. Her arms went about his neck and her body moulded to his.

They were interrupted by the sound of the Portuguese guard clearing his throat noisily nearby. Elvira broke free and Daniel turned to see the soldier leering at Elvira.

'What do you want?' snapped Daniel, angrily. It was doubtful whether the soldier understood, but he stopped leering and rattled something off in Portuguese to Elvira, at the same time gesticulating towards the distant river.

'A boat is coming,' explained Elvira.

Scanning the winding course of the Zambezi, Daniel finally made out a faint plume of smoke rising above the trees that hid much of the river from view.

'Our boat is not due back here for at least another two weeks,' said Elvira. 'Something must have happened.'

Minutes later they were cantering the horses down the hillside towards Sena. The Portuguese soldier was not a good horseman and he bounced awkwardly in his saddle far behind them. Further back, the militiamen ran as fast as they could in a vain attempt to keep up with the riders.

They arrived at the landing-stage to find that the whole village had turned out to meet the unexpected steamer, brought from their huts and houses by the vessel's hoarse steam whistle. It had been sounding continuously from the moment it had come within view of Sena.

It was not the *Bartolomeo Dias*. This was a stern-wheel paddle-steamer never before seen on the Zambezi. As the craft hugged the bank nearest the jetty, it could be seen that the deck was crowded with blue-uniformed Portuguese soldiers.

Shouted questions and answers began as soon as the vessel came within hailing distance, but as the shouted conversations were in Portuguese, Daniel did not understand a word. With everyone shouting at the same time it was doubtful whether those on the bank were any the wiser.

As the steamer bumped against the wooden jetty a man in civilian clothes pushed his way through the noisy, gesticulating soldiers. With a sudden shock, Daniel recognised Sam Speke. But this was not the cheerful, one-time sailor Daniel had left at uTshwebe's village. Sam Speke looked ill and tired, his eyes dark-circled and his normally chubby face gaunt and unshaven.

Daniel pushed his way through the crowd on the river bank and reached the boat as Sam Speke jumped ashore.

Clasping his friend's hand in both his own, Daniel asked, 'Sam! What's happening? Did you get my message from Jandu?' Daniel searched the faces on the boat. 'Where's Victoria?'

The grip of Sam Speke's hand tightened involuntarily, 'That's why I'm here, Daniel. She's gone . . . run off with a Pombeiro. A murdering, thieving scoundrel named "Mariano".'

When Daniel left uTshwebe's village, Victoria was very unhappy, and unsettled. True, much of her unhappiness stemmed from the prophecies of the White Mondoro, but Victoria was honest enough with herself to admit that it went back further. To her return from South West Africa, in fact. She had been away from Daniel for many months, living in a country ravaged by war. During the long days there she had hugged to herself a dream of Daniel. Gradually, she had weaved her hopes of a future with Daniel into a tangled fantasy that helped to keep the tragedy of day-to-day life among the warring Hereros at bay. By the time she left South West Africa the fantasy had become as real to her as life itself and she fed it on the long homeward journey with thoughts of a dramatic and romantic reunion.

When the reunion finally took place it came as a bitter disappointment. Daniel was not the besotted lover of her imagination. He was the man he had always been, rather reserved, his mind filled with the problems of running a trading company in the heart of a primitive continent.

The disappointment had remained with her until the snake bite resulted in her being given a bleak vision of the future by the Mondoro.

But there was something else. Something that hurt even more than the Mondoro's foreboding. It was the grotesque albino's declaration that she too was an outcast — set apart from those she loved.

Victoria had never before thought seriously about her mixed parentage. She accompanied her father everywhere, accepted by Daniel and the few other white people she met, and made welcome in their homes, or about their camp-fires. She had always regarded herself as one of them without question — until the Mondoro spoke to her.

Victoria was both hurt and confused. She needed to talk to someone . . . to Daniel. Unfortunately, before an opportunity arose, Daniel went away.

Suliyana could see how unhappy Victoria was and she did her best to be kind, but Victoria could not bare her heart to the

Manica girl. Suliyana had absolute faith in Chiminuka's spokesman. She would not say the words Victoria wanted to hear. Neither could she tell her father what was troubling her. He would have taken the blame for her hurt upon himself. There was no alternative for Victoria but to keep the problem bottled inside her. It was a heavy burden.

Not until the returning Manica warriors told a stunned Victoria and her father of Daniel's death from fever did grief drive away all other emotions. At first she refused to believe the news, but the men all had the same story to tell. The expedition to the coast had gone through 'bad' country. The horses had died. Daniel had contracted fever and they had been attacked by Portuguese dissidents. uTshwebe's men swore they had fulfilled their mission faithfully. They had, they said, carried the dying Daniel to the white man's kraal by the sea, so that he might die among his own people.

Reluctantly, Victoria had to accept that they were telling the truth. The only discrepancy in the warriors' stories concerned the whereabouts of Jandu. Most of the Manicas insisted he had stayed at Sofala. Others said he had returned to his home without bothering to come with them to Chena. When questioned further, the returning warriors merely shrugged their shoulders and looked surly. What did it matter? Jandu was a Matabele, not one of them. What he did was his own business.

When Sam Speke pointed out that Jandu had paid the full lobola for Suliyana and would hardly return home without his bride, they became even more evasive. Jandu had made it quite clear he had a low opinion of the Manicas as men, why should he have more regard for one of their women? The bride-price had been paid with Daniel's goods. Now Daniel was dead. What had the Matabele lost?

Sam Speke was of the opinion that the Manica warriors had killed Jandu somewhere on the return journey from the coast, but Suliyana was confident he would return to her. It was Chiminuka's will. It was probable that Jandu had tired of the company of the Manicas – or believed they meant him harm, and slipped away from them.

Before the village had time to recover from the excitement of the return of their warriors, it received another visit, one that caused a great stir. The newcomers were men of the Matabele impi carrying news of Mzilikazi's death – and they sought Jandu.

The quaking Manica warriors were brought before the Induna of the impi, and this time they did not lie. Jandu had been left behind at Sofala. He was, they assured the Induna, alive and well.

The Matabele impi was in a huge Manica kraal containing more than three thousand warriors, all of whom hated the Matabele and envied them their reputation as great fighting men. uTshwebe could have called on ten times that number from the surrounding mountains, yet the Induna was as contemptuous of the Manica warriors as Jandu had been.

'I hope your tongues have fed on the truth,' he told Jandu's late travelling companions. 'If you have lied I will return and cut them out before I raze this village to the ground. Even that will not be the end. If Jandu has died by your hands the spears of the Matabele nation will point at you. Our armies will come and we will not return home until the name of Manica is no more.'

There were angry shouts from those warriors who had not been on the journey to the coast until uTshwebe stepped forward and demanded silence.

To the Induna, the Rozwi Queen said, 'If my warriors have lied they will answer to me. Jandu has paid the bride-price for Suliyana, my daughter. He is my son. There will be no more talk of war between us.'

The Matabele Induna refused the offer of huts in which his warriors might rest. Since leaving Khami they had averaged fifty miles a day through difficult and unknown country, sending out small advance parties to capture elusive local tribesmen and so learn the route taken by Jandu and the others. The impi would not be allowed to rest until it had accomplished its mission. The Induna asked uTshwebe only that he and his men be given a hot meal and reliable directions to Sofala. He refused the offer of a Manica guide, declaring that the man would not be able to keep up with the impi.

As the warriors ate, Sam Speke talked with the Induna. He asked whether Jandu was being sought because he was to become the next King of the Matabele.

The Induna shook his head. It was dangerous to be drawn

into speculation on such a subject. If he intimated support for the wrong man he would not survive the coronation.

'I seek Jandu because he is the King's son, and we are Jandu's impi. Mzilikazi has many sons eager to take his place. Kanje is favoured by many. Others say that only Kulumani, the son of Mzilikazi by his chief wife, must become King. But no one has seen Kulumani for very many years. Some say he lives in a white man's house in the Cape Colony. Others whisper that he was killed by Mzilikazi because he tried to take the King's place too soon, when our tribe first came to Matabeleland. The selection of a King is not in my hands. I am concerned only that if Jandu does not return to Khami quickly his enemies will say he thought ill of his father and is afraid to greet his spirit. Once such talk begins even his friends will be afraid to support him against his brothers.'

'Will you be returning this way?'

The Induna nodded, 'Jandu has married uTshwebe's daughter. It is a good marriage, one to please the Council of Elders. They will name the new King. Jandu will want to take her to Khami with him. If Jandu is dead . . . but we will not think of that. It will be better for you to remain here and come to Khami with us. When the news of Mzilikazi's death reaches the tribes of the amaHoli they will suddenly become brave. The land will not be safe for travellers.'

The Induna used the all-embracing derisory word 'ama-Holi', meaning 'men of no account'. He was referring to the vassal tribes who dwelled about the borders of Matabeleland, but the term was used to describe anyone who was not a Matabele.

When the Induna set off on his journey to Sofala, Sam Speke travelled with him for half a day. He left filled with admiration for the men of the impi who maintained a mile-consuming trot for hour after tireless hour.

It was dusk by the time Sam Speke got back to uTshwebe's village and he was surprised to see a number of unfamiliar tribesmen camped outside the kraal. Dressed in ragged European clothing, they were all armed with ancient muskets. Nearby, four thin and bony horses grazed on the sparse grass.

Entering the village, Sam Speke saw more strangers seated about his own camp fire. But these were not natives – they were

Pombeiros. Six of them, they had travelled through tsetse fly country, losing all their mounts but the four Sam Speke had seen. These men too were well armed, but in common with their followers, the guns were a motley collection of aged muzzle-loaders.

Victoria was seated at the fireside with the men. Her cheeks flushed, she was having an animated conversation with the man who appeared to lead the Pombeiros. Sam Speke took an instant dislike to the half-caste Portuguese. The lightest-skinned man of the group, he sported a moustache and scrubby beard and his long, dark hair was tied behind his head in a style that had been fashionable in Europe more than half a century before.

When Sam Speke reached the fireside the Pombeiro stood up and gave him a shallow bow. He snapped an order at his companions and they too rose to their feet, with varying degrees of reluctance.

'Happy to meet you.' The Pombeiro extended a hand to Sam Speke. 'My name is Mariano. I am a trader – as you are too, I believe?' Unused to speaking the language, Mariano's English was thick with accent.

'I trade in merchandise. What's your speciality – slaves?'

Mariano's ingratiating smile left his face for only a fleeting moment. 'I trade in whatever gives me a living. If white men want ivory, I get ivory. If they cannot get black women for themselves, then I take slaves. We Pombeiros have to earn our place in the white man's world.' Mariano gave Victoria a sidelong glance. 'It's not a thing you white men boast about, but we make lovely bastardos, don't we?'

Sam Speke's anger flared and the rifle he was holding arced through the air, the butt striking Mariano just below his cheekbone, knocking him to the ground. As the Pombeiro scrambled to a sitting position and snatched at the knife tucked in his belt he found himself looking into the barrel of Sam Speke's rifle. The click of the hammer being drawn back sounded ominously loud.

'Choose your words more carefully when you speak of my daughter. You may be a bastard . . . she's not.'

Mariano's hand dropped away from the knife. With the rifle barrel following him, he rose slowly to his feet. Behind him his

companions fingered their muskets nervously, unable to interfere while Sam Speke kept his finger on the trigger. All about
the campfire uTshwebe's tribesmen edged quickly away,
anticipating trouble.

Mariano dusted himself down carefully and when he spoke
only his eyes betrayed the anger he felt. 'Your daughter is
fortunate to know her father. That is to your credit – but if you
ever strike me again I'll kill you.'

Turning away, Mariano signalled to his companions and
they followed him silently from the camp fire.

Sam Speke eased down the hammer on his rifle with relief.
He knew he had come very close to death. His relief was
short-lived. Victoria, fists tightly clenched at her sides and with
tears starting from her eyes, sprang to her feet and glared at
him furiously.

'What did you do that for? Why did you hit him?'

Sam Speke was taken aback by the vehemence of his daughter's words. 'You heard what he said? I'm not having some
Portuguese half-caste talk about you like that—'

'*I'm* a half-caste – or had you forgotten? Would you have hit
a white man for saying what Mariano did?'

'I'd hit anyone who spoke about you in such a manner . . .
but why are we quarrelling? You're not the same as that . . .
that – trash.'

'I'm *exactly* like him. Don't you remember what the Mondoro said? He told me that my future lies with my own kind.'

Half-blinded by her tears, Victoria turned and fled towards
her hut, ignoring her father's calls for her to return.

'Damn! damn! damn!' Sam Speke cursed the Mondoro,
Mariano, and the whole disastrous expedition that had
brought them to uTshwebe's village.

Sam Speke would have liked to devote the whole of the next
day to restoring good relations with his daughter, but he had
promised uTshwebe he would hunt down a leopard which was
playing havoc with the goat herds of a village some miles away.
Before he left, he went to Victoria's hut to say goodbye to her.
She was quieter than usual, but to his great relief she no longer
seemed angry with him. Sam Speke left her with a promise that
he would return with a leopard skin as a gift.

It was a promise that proved easier to make than to fulfil.

For three days Sam Speke and the Manica hunters stalked the leopard without having a single sighting. Each night it proved it was still in the area by forcing a way inside a goat pen and slaughtering the helpless creatures as they ran about in close-packed, bleating terror.

Sam Speke decided a change of tactics was called for. He built a platform six feet high in the largest goat pen and on this precarious perch kept watch for the killer cat.

His first night's vigil was an utter waste of time. He heard the deep, throaty cough of the leopard as it circled the thorn barrier about the pen, but the animal made no attempt to come inside to where Sam Speke waited.

Nevertheless, the following night Sam Speke resumed his vigil. There was a bright, three-quarter moon and the goats settled down to sleep, reassured by the presence of a human in their midst.

Sam Speke waited and watched for hours without incident and began to think this night's watch too was doomed to failure. He dozed off, but suddenly jerked fully awake, aware of a disturbance among the goats in the pen beneath him. Sam Speke listened intently, hoping to hear the leopard's cough from somewhere outside the pen. He could hear only the terror-stricken bleating of the goats.

He contemplated dropping from the platform and patrolling the inside perimeter of the pen, when suddenly he saw a movement in the shadows, not more than fifteen feet away. It was on the *inside* of the pen!

At that moment the nerve of one of the more timid goats snapped and it fled from beneath the shelter. The sudden movement stampeded the remainder and they poured out from beneath the flimsy platform, the fleeter animals attempting to leap over the backs of their slower companions.

The platform jerked and shuddered alarmingly as the panic-stricken goats pushed and jostled against the supporting posts. One goat, brought face-to-face with a post, turned. It was immediately jammed against the wooden pole while those behind, anxious not to be left by the others, charged on.

Their weight proved too much for the temporary structure. The platform gave a mighty lurch and tilted alarmingly. Sam Speke clutched at the side – and missed. Before he could save himself he was thrown to the ground, falling beneath the sharp little hooves of the last few goats.

Choking in the pall of dust kicked up by the goats, Sam Speke rose to his hands and knees, bruised and scratched. During a momentary lull in his own coughing, he realised with a sudden thrill of horror that the sound was being echoed from somewhere close at hand – but thorn fences did not throw back echoes!

During the fall Sam Speke had lost his gun and for a few moments he came close to panic. The hooves of the frightened goats might have kicked it yards away from him. Still on hands and knees, he began groping about him frantically. The coughing of the leopard became a growl and the terrified goats set off for another corner of the pen, bleating pitiably.

Sam Speke was hardly aware of the goats now. He had detected a movement in the shadows nearby. The moonlight caught a green reflection in the leopard's eyes as it slunk into the light, belly low, tail twitching spasmodically.

At that moment Sam Speke's fingers touched the butt of his rifle. Even as the leopard sprang he threw himself to one side in a desperate dive. His finger found the trigger of his gun and he rolled over, using the rifle to ward off the leopard's attack. The great cat tried to cuff the muzzle aside, but Sam Speke's finger squeezed the trigger and the gun fired with a muffled 'Crack!'

Sam Speke smelled burning fur. A fraction of a second later two hundred pounds of screaming, spitting leopard fell upon him.

Instinctively, Sam Speke covered his head with his arms and rolled away, oblivious of the claws that etched two bloody lines down his back. Suddenly he was clear, although the screaming of the leopard continued. Scrambling gratefully to his feet, Sam Speke watched the death throes of the beautiful animal as it threshed about in the moonlight. Shot through both lungs, the leopard snarled in pain and anger, tearing at the place where the bullet had entered its body. After only a few minutes of torment, the leopard collapsed on its side, blood bubbling from its mouth and nostrils as it lay panting its life away.

When Sam Speke recovered his gun, he found the butt had

been broken in two. He levered a cartridge into the breech and the leopard raised its head to look at him.

Hunter and prey gazed at each other for half a minute before a bullet from the shattered rifle ended the animal's misery.

The shots had roused the village and soon men came running to the pen. When the light from their spluttering torches fell upon the dead leopard they crowded around Sam Speke, pointing in awe to his dishevelled condition and the broken rifle. The village headman expressed the heartfelt gratitude of the Manicas and tried to persuade Sam Speke to adjourn to his hut and celebrate the success of his night's vigil. But Sam Speke had enjoyed enough excitement for one night. There was a bright moon high in the sky, and uTshwebe's village was no more than a few hours ride away.

He had promised the leopard skin to Victoria. Asking the headman to have it skinned right away, he limped off to prepare his horse for the night's ride. As he went he became aware that he was aching in every limb.

Sam Speke reached uTshwebe's village just before dawn. A few women were already abroad, sleepily building up cooking fires for the first meal of the day. His arrival did much to awaken the remainder of the village as the dogs got scent of the bloody leopard skin he carried on the saddle before him.

The cooking fire before his own hut was no more than a low heap of faintly smoking ashes. Sam Speke paused to throw on some twigs and poke it into life before going on to Victoria's hut and presenting his daughter with the hard-won trophy.

As he straightened up from the fire he thought he saw someone slip from the doorway of Victoria's hut and disappear into the shadows.

'Victoria . . . is that you?'

There was no reply. Frowning, Sam Speke strode to the hut. He could see no one, but he distinctly heard the sound of footsteps running away in the darkness.

Quickly, Sam Speke returned to his fire and thrust a dry piece of wood into the low flames. It took only seconds to burst into flame and, carrying the crackling torch to Victoria's hut, he ducked inside.

'Victoria, are you all right?'

Naked, Victoria grabbed for her clothes. She was far too

alert to have been woken up by his call. As Sam Speke put a light to a candle and doused the rough torch, Victoria looked at him with wide-eyed apprehension. She shrugged her way into a shirt, but not before he saw the bite, as big as a man's thumb-print, on her neck just beneath the collar bone.

Sam Speke stared at his daughter in horrified disbelief. He knew now he had not been mistaken. He *had* seen someone leaving Victoria's hut. He knew who it must be, yet he was not willing to believe the overwhelming evidence of his own eyes.

'Victoria . . . not with Mariano? Please God . . . not with him?'

She could not meet his eyes and he knew the worst.

'Why? Why? So soon after Daniel—'

'Daniel's *dead* and I'm alive – although you don't seem to realise that. I'm a *woman* now, not your little girl. Where will I ever find a man in Khami? Or do you want me to marry a Matabele? Yes, I slept with Mariano – and I'll do it again and again, because he's the only chance I'll ever have of getting a man.'

Sam Speke struck Victoria across the face with the back of his hand and sent her reeling across the hut, 'Then you'll need to learn to live without one . . . because I'm going to kill him.' Beside himself with anger, Sam Speke stumbled outside.

In his own hut he found a spare musket. It was an old, muzzle-loading percussion gun, but it would serve until he had repaired the stock of his own Wilson breech-loader. It would kill a man. Impatiently, Sam Speke searched for his powder-horn and ready-made musket balls. Loading and priming the gun carefully, he slung the powder-horn and shot pouch across his shoulders and ducked out through the doorway of his hut.

Greeted by the restless lowing of the Manica cattle, the dawn was streaking the eastern sky with thin layers of light as Sam Speke headed for the Pombeiro camping area. His earlier rage had now been replaced by a cold determination. He was setting out to kill Mariano. He should have warned him off in no uncertain terms when he first came to the Manica village. He would, had he believed that his daughter was foolish enough to become infatuated with a thieving Pombeiro slaver.

Sam Speke winced at the memory of striking Victoria. He should not have done that. But she would understand why when things were back to normal again. When the memory of Daniel's death no longer clouded her judgement. They would return to Khami as soon as possible. Today. Along the way they would discuss the future. They would move on from Khami. He would take her to Whalefish Bay . . . or somewhere else where Victoria could meet respectable young men.

At the edge of the village, Sam Speke brought his gun to the ready. The camp fires of the Pombeiros were burning low, but there was enough daylight now to make out the forms of the sleeping men who lay nearby. He picked his way carefully between them, searching for Mariano. The Pombeiro would not be asleep, but he might be shamming.

There was no sign of the half-caste Portuguese – or the other Pombeiros. The men about the camp fires were the armed slaves Mariano had brought to Manicaland with him. Sam Speke kicked one of them awake and asked where Mariano was sleeping. His question was greeted with a blank stare. Most of these slaves came from well to the north of the Zambezi River, speaking a different dialect to the southern tribes. A few of them spoke Portuguese, but Sam Speke understood neither language. Eventually, by constantly repeating the name of Mariano, he made himself understood.

Shivering in the chill morning air, one of the slaves led Sam Speke towards a camp fire set apart from the others. When he reached the spot, the slave stopped in surprise. Running to one of his companions he shook him into wakefulness and pointed towards the Pombeiro's fire, gesticulating and shouting in his own language.

The words needed no translation. Mariano and his companions had gone – but they had not left empty-handed. Dawn came rapidly in the Manica mountains and it was now light enough to see that the gate of the pen where horses were kept stood wide open. Not only were the Pombeiro horses gone but Daniel's pack-horses, Victoria's riding horse and the one just set loose by Sam Speke.

Angrily Sam Speke strode back to the village. Victoria must have warned Mariano. By her foolishness she had lost their horses.

He burst into her hut, determined that on this occasion he would not be easily placated by his wilful, spoiled daughter.

The hut was empty. Victoria's gun and a few hastily gathered items of clothing had gone too.

In that moment, on a chill Manica morning, Sam Speke's world collapsed about him. Sinking to his knees, he put his face in his hands and wept for Victoria.

CHAPTER NINE

When Sam Speke arrived at Sena, he had been searching for Victoria for six weeks. At first he was accompanied by a large party of Manica warriors, sent out by uTshwebe. When it became clear that Mariano and his party were heading for the unknown country of northern Mozambique, the warriors insisted upon returning to their home village. Here Sam Speke received the first good news that had come his way for weeks. Jandu had passed through the village to claim his bride, leaving word that Daniel was alive and had been taken to Sena by Senhor Farrao.

With only two Manica guides, Sam Speke followed Daniel's route to Sofala, then travelled in a small fishing boat along the coast to Quelimane. Rumour was rife here of a rebel band led by Mariano terrorising the populace of the interior. An army was being assembled to set off after the Pombeiro. When the general commanding the Portuguese army in Mozambique heard Sam Speke's story, he sent him upriver in the army's stern-wheeled paddle-steamer, newly arrived from Portugal. With him went a full company of regular Portuguese soldiers.

That evening, Sam Speke related the full story of events at uTshwebe's village. He told it to Daniel and Elvira as they stood on the balcony of Senhor Farrao's house, looking down the sloping grass lawns to the river, its muddy water dull, unpolished gold in the moonlight. In the house behind them there was the sound of ribald laughter from the newly arrived Portuguese officers as one of their number shared a joke with his host.

'I'll find her, Daniel. I'll find her if it means staying here in Mozambique for the rest of my days. All I ask is that you tell Mary what I'm doing . . . and look after her for me.'

'We'll go back to Khami together,' declared Daniel, firmly. 'When we've found Victoria.'

'You are not a fit man,' said Elvira gently. 'Please, leave this to our soldiers.'

'The army will be out to kill Mariano,' replied Daniel. 'They'll not concern themselves with a . . . a girl who has gone off with Mariano willingly.'

He had almost referred to Victoria as a 'half-caste'. The realisation both shocked and dismayed him. It was as though by joining Mariano she had stepped over a barrier he had never before realised was there.

One of the Portuguese officers – and there were a great many of them with the small force – came on the verandah with a glass in his hand and put an arm across Sam Speke's shoulders.

'Hello, my friend. Don't worry, Mariano will soon stand in front of a firing squad, and your daughter will be home where she belongs.'

As other Portuguese officers left the heat of the house, bringing the noise and laughter to the verandah, Elvira stepped down to the path and made her way towards the river. Daniel caught up with her as she passed through the shadows cast by a clump of bauhinia trees.

'Why did you rush away so suddenly?'

Elvira countered with a question of her own. 'Why are you going off with the soldiers? Why not stay here and wait for their return?'

'Sam Speke is my friend. He needs my help.'

'Mariano is his daughter's man. When the choice had to be made between him and her father she chose Mariano. Do you think she will have changed her mind, already? Or is it that you believe she will return for you?'

'I don't know,' said Daniel honestly. 'I only know I must try to get her away from Mariano. He's a murderer and a thief. She deserves better.'

Elvira turned on him fiercely. 'Your Victoria slept with her man because that was the only way she knew to keep him. Is that what I must do to keep you, Daniel? Is that the way things are done among the Matabele – and all those other tribes you have lived with?'

'You don't have to do anything to keep me. If you are sure you want me, I'll be back.'

'I want you, Daniel. More than anything in my life I want you.' Elvira spoke with all the desperate passion of an eighteen-year-old, in love for the first time.

From the verandah of Senhor Farrao's house, Sam Speke saw the two shadows beside the trees merge into one. He realised that, although Daniel was alive, his own hopes for Victoria and Daniel had died at Sofala.

A week later, the Portuguese army was still at Sena. One delay had followed another. The senior officers continually made detailed plans for the campaign, only to cancel them within hours. It seemed to Daniel and Sam Speke that the whole expedition was doomed to end here at Sena in utter chaos. Then refugees began streaming into Senhor Farrao's stockade from upriver, fleeing from Mariano and his Pombeiro rebels.

When villagers arrived from Chemba, no more than twenty miles away, such panic erupted inside the Sena stockade it was as though the Portuguese soldiers had heard of Mariano's attacks for the first time. Now, finally, the Portuguese commander made a determined attempt to bring some organisation to his small expeditionary force. Calling all his men together, he told them they would be leaving the stockade to fight for the glory of Portugal. Upon their return to Quelimane, he promised that they would be hailed as heroes. History would record their names on its pages as the soldiers who had rid Mozambique of the scourge of Mariano and his Pombeiro rebels.

The cheers that greeted the Colonel's stirring speech were all that a commanding officer could wish for. With 120 men such as these, he felt confident of carving a path across Africa, if need be.

The majority of the soldiers and all the officers travelled upriver on board their stern-wheeled paddle-steamer. The under-powered vessel could make no more than two knots against the sluggish Zambezi current, but its low speed and frequent grounding on hidden mud banks suited those soldiers who marched along the river bank, grumbling at the comparative comfort of their more fortunate comrades.

Marching with the regular soldiers were Lieutenant St Anna and his native militia. The young Portuguese officer had pleaded with the Colonel to give his militiamen the opportunity to put their months of hard training to the test. Airily, the Colonel had agreed, stipulating that Lieutenant St Anna must keep his natives out of the way of the professional soldiers when the actual fighting began.

To Daniel, used to the workmanlike preparations of the Matabele army, there was something farcical about this expedition. Only Lieutenant St Anna's militia displayed any degree of discipline. The regular soldiers marching with them straggled along a mile of river bank, while their officers sat on the deck of the paddle-steamer, swigging red wine and deploring the heat of the day.

Daniel and Sam Speke travelled on the boat for the first day and night, but then they asked to be put ashore, unable to endure the noise on board any longer. There was a constant clank and splash of the great paddle, the rumble and hiss of steam – but above all, the babble of voices raised in never-ending complaint or argument.

Once ashore, Sam Speke stayed with the main body of the army while Daniel, impatient of their slow progress, forged a mile or two ahead with a small scouting party of St Anna's militia.

There was little fear of ambush here. The grass, trampled down by the hooves and feet of an abundance of game animals, lay brown and lifeless all about the gaunt, leafless trees. The whole Zambezi valley waited for the rains that would transform the parched landscape.

At first there was little to be seen to account for the mass evacuation of the local populace to the safety of the Sena stockade. The mystery deepened when Daniel and the scouting party entered Chemba. The village was exactly as the inhabitants had left it. Evidence of their hasty departure was everywhere. Cooking pots stood on the cold, grey ashes of dead fires. Chickens strutted about the village, pecking at imaginary seeds, or breaking into a high-stepping run in pursuit of any insect careless enough to alight within their view.

There was even a bewildered, bleating, young goat who ran towards the new arrivals, pitifully pleased to discover that the human race had not vanished entirely from the face of the earth. The young animal would have been wiser to remain in hiding. One slash of a militiaman's knife ensured that the advance party, at least, would not go to sleep hungry that night.

When the main body of the Portuguese expeditionary force arrived, it was decided to spend that night at Chemba, with the steamer tied alongside the bank. The Colonel called a conference to discuss the little army's next move. He was of the opinion that the villagers of the area had been frightened by nothing more serious than unsubstantiated rumour and was in favour of returning to Sena until proof of Mariano's presence in the area was forthcoming.

Most of the Portuguese officers were against such a swift return. They argued that the force should continue upriver for another few days, at least. The Portuguese Colonel eventually agreed, but with a bad grace. He had anticipated a swift and not too serious engagement with the rebels, followed by a triumphant return to the comfort of his villa and mistress at Quelimane. He had even composed the self-congratulatory report that would be sent on to Lisbon. Senior promotions were made from such reports – they were not the result of weeks spent perspiring in discomfort on some filthy river that few officials in Portugal had ever heard of. After all, he had attained the rank of colonel without ever setting foot on a battlefield. Now was not the time to change the habits of a lifetime.

The next morning, Daniel once again set out ahead of the main army, in company with St Anna's scouts. There were a number of small kraals along the bank and, shortly before noon, the leader of the scouts halted Daniel with a gentle touch on his arm. He could not speak English, but his attitude, nose in the air, told Daniel as clearly as words why he had stopped. Daniel too could smell something new. It was the faint scent of wood-smoke hanging on the air.

The small party moved forward cautiously and now another, less palatable smell reached their nostrils. Not more than a hundred paces ahead, around a bend in the riverside path, they arrived at the edge of a village . . . or what had once been a village. Now not a hut remained standing. Charred circles on the ground indicated where they had once stood, with here and there a tumbled frame skeleton of charred wood.

That was not all. This village had not been evacuated and the occupants had been slaughtered where they were caught. It was difficult to say how many victims the Pombeiros had claimed because the scavengers had moved in when the renegades left. Hyaena, wild dog and jackal had all taken advantage of the Pombeiros' ferocity.

Sickened, Daniel turned away from the scene of carnage and destruction, but the leader of the scouts was picking through the wreckage, examining the bodies of his unfortunate countrymen. When he was satisfied, he held up two fingers to Daniel, 'Anteontem' – 'The day before yesterday'.

Daniel accepted that the mutilated bodies had lain in the razed village for two days, but his concern now was for a Senhor Alvara. According to Senhor Farrao, Alvara, with his brother and their families, farmed some miles beyond Chemba. The farm could not be far from here.

Daniel mentioned the name to the leader of the scouting party. The African pointed ahead, to where the track followed the river bank. He said something in Portuguese to Daniel and shook his head, but when Daniel set off along the track, the militiaman shrugged and set off after him.

Daniel and the scouts passed through two more tiny settlements, both put to the torch. Then, in the distance, he saw a long, low, stone house surrounded by a stout wooden stockade. The house was built in a good defensive position on a small hill and for a few moments Daniel's hopes soared. Then he saw that the stockade gate stood open.

The two Alvara brothers lay dead in the first room Daniel entered. Both had been stripped of their clothing. Beyond them, in the bedrooms, lay the bodies of the Alvara women, their two African wives and three daughters. Two of the girls lay spread-eagled on the bed, their throats cut. The others lay naked on the floor, shot dead by the men who had raped them there.

Daniel felt ill. Going outside the house, he leaned against the stone wall and sucked in great gulps of air. At this moment he felt he hated the Pombeiro, Mariano, more than any man he knew. Standing there, he remembered that Senhor Farrao had told him the two brothers operated a ferry service across the river – but Daniel could see no sign of a boat.

Not until he hurried to the river bank did he see what he was seeking. The ferry lay half-submerged on the far side of the river. The Pombeiros must have crossed the river and sunk the ferry to prevent any pursuit.

Daniel was still standing on the river bank when he heard the roar of a cannon. It sounded as though it had been fired about a mile downriver. As the men of the scouting party ran from the Alvara house, where Daniel suspected they had been looting, there was another cannon shot. This time it was accompanied by the distant crackle of musket fire.

Daniel set off along the path at a trot, the scouts on his heels. By the time they reached the scene of the massacre at the first kraal they had found, they could see what was happening. Mariano had set a clever ambush for the paddle-steamer carrying the Portuguese officers and men. Just beyond the village, the main channel of the quarter-of-a-mile-wide river took a wide sweep to pass within fifty yards of the opposite bank. When the asthmatic little steamer arrived at this spot it had been fired upon by a well-concealed small cannon. The ancient gun, brought upriver from the ancient fort at Quelimane had stood outside the door of the Alvara brothers' house until twenty-four hours ago. Now it was being used against the army of the nation it had served for more than two hundred years.

The range at this spot was so short that even the inexperienced Pombeiro gunners could not miss their target. To make things even easier for them, The Portuguese pilot on board the steamer had run his craft aground on a mud bank when the first six-pound cannon ball struck home. The boat and its occupants were sitting targets for the Pombeiros who raked the vessel with musket fire between cannon shots.

By the time of Daniel's arrival the deck was littered with dead and dying soldiers. A few had abandoned the helpless vessel and screamed for mercy as they floundered waist-deep in mud, caught in the musket fire of the Pombeiros. The only mercy they were given was a swift end to their terror. A few soldiers made a determined attempt to reach the safety of the south bank, where their companions yelled useless encouragement to them, but the mud held them fast until they too were picked off by the gleeful Pombeiro marksmen.

Lieutenant St Anna's militiamen, terrified by the booming of the cannon, milled about adding to the confusion, ignoring St

Anna's shrill orders to form up and return the Pombeiros' fire. Only a few of those regular Portuguese soldiers who had been marching with them were kneeling down and returning the fire of the rebels hidden across the river.

'Aim for the cannon when you next see it fire,' called Daniel, and commenced to set an example. His gun was far superior to those used by the Portuguese soldiers and, when Sam Speke joined him, they were able to place their bullets in the thicket from whence smoke poured after every cannon shot.

Their firing brought quick results. After some initial commotion in the bushes across the river, the cannonade ceased. It resumed again some minutes later from a spot further along the river bank, but the accurate shooting of Daniel and Sam Speke had unsettled the aim of the gunners. The cannon balls now fell harmlessly in the mud of the river.

When Daniel, Sam Speke and the Portuguese soldiers began firing at the new position, the rebel gunners decided they had seen enough action for one day and abandoned their stolen cannon. Nevertheless, the success of the ambush had exceeded all Mariano's expectations. The Portuguese army's newly acquired stern-wheeler was settling to the bottom of the Zambezi River – carrying with it the bodies of some of Mozambique's most senior army officers. Only five soldiers succeeded in floundering through the glutinous mud to the safety of the river bank.

Lieutenant St Anna's militiamen located two dug-out canoes at the edge of the nearby village and launched them in the main channel of the river. They managed to get on board the steamer before it slid off the mud bank and sank, but only eleven men, all wounded, were found alive.

Using the same canoes, the militiamen and the remnant of the expeditionary force were ferried across the river to search the surrounding undergrowth for Mariano's men.

They found the abandoned cannon and two dead rebels, but Mariano and his men had left the scene of their remarkable victory. Not until late that evening, when the last of the militiamen had been ferried across the river did one of the scouts who had accompanied Daniel, discover a live rebel. He was one of Mariano's slave-warriors. Wounded and abandoned by his companions, the unfortunate Bemba tribesman had hidden himself beneath branches and dried grass, hoping to crawl away when night fell. Abducted from his village north of the Zambezi when no more than a boy, he was an unwilling rebel, but that made no difference to his captors. When Daniel arrived on the scene he was being pounded insensible by the butts of the militiamen's muskets.

Knocking the guns aside, Daniel threatened to shoot anyone else who touched the wounded man. His action was not taken through any sense of compassion. He wanted information, and the Bemba might be able to provide some answers.

With Lieutenant St Anna acting as interpreter, Daniel asked whether Victoria was with Mariano. The reply was in Portuguese, but Daniel feared the worst when the tribesman shook his head.

'She was taken ill with fever,' explained St Anna, to Daniel's relief. 'Mariano left her at Chief Vumba's kraal.'

'Where's that?'

Lieutenant St Anna put the question to the Bemba, who inclined his head in a vague, westerly direction.

'He knows only that it is inland, many days' march away.'

'Is that where Mariano has gone now?'

The Bemba's reply caused consternation among the militiamen, who had been following the questioning with a surly lack of interest until now. Lieutenant St Anna snapped a question back at the rebel, but this time the reply came as no more than a faint nod.

Lieutenant St Anna stood up abruptly, his face pale, 'He says that Mariano is on his way to attack Sena.'

It was impossible to set off immediately. Dusk was already falling, and this side of the river was unfamiliar country to everyone.

After a sleepless night, Daniel, Sam Speke and Lieutenant St Anna set off just before dawn with the few able-bodied Portuguese survivors and the bulk of the militia. The remainder would return to Sena at a slower pace, bringing the wounded.

First, they had the frustratingly slow task of recrossing the river, being uncertain of crossing places further downstream. Once across, they set off at a pace that would have done credit to a Matabele impi, making much better time than when the slow-moving steamer had dictated their pace. Even so, when they found the shallow river crossing used by Mariano and his men they learned from the signs that they were a full day behind the rebels.

At nightfall there was a brief discussion among the men. The Portuguese regular soldiers were in favour of camping for the night. They had spent a gruelling couple of days and were exhausted – but the militiamen had families at the fort and they had seen what Mariano and his Pombeiros could do. It was agreed that they should march through the night.

They travelled much more slowly than before, caution being very necessary along the bank of the river. Every wild animal for miles around came here to drink during the night. At about midnight the moon rose over the horizon like a great pumpkin lantern. Now the militiamen were in country they knew well and the pace increased once more.

Sena was reached about half an hour before dawn. The stockaded village was so quiet that Lieutenant St Anna whispered hopefully that they might have passed the rebels during the night without seeing each other.

Daniel would have given much to believe him, but Mariano must have known the survivors of the ambush would follow his trail and eventually guess at his destination. He would have wasted no time in falling upon the almost defenceless village.

One of the militiamen was detailed to scale the palissade and learn what the position was inside. He returned as the first traces of dawn lightened the sky above the flat lands to the east. The militiaman brought the grim news that Mariano had attacked shortly after dusk and was in possession of most of the stockade – including Senhor Farrao's house. Senhor Farrao himself was in the stone-built fort which served as the arsenal for the militia, where he and a few men were still holding out against the rebels.

'Is Elvira in the fort with him?' Daniel asked anxiously.

'I don't know,' came Lieutenant St Anna's whispered reply. 'My man got his information from an old woman. She could not tell him much – but come, we must get inside the stockade before it is light if we are to surprise Mariano.'

Half a dozen militiamen were sent over the pallisade, with

orders to open the gate. They did their work well and silently, using knife and spear to silence the dozing guards. With the gates standing open to them, a plan was hastily agreed upon. About a third of the militiamen would move on their own village while Daniel and Sam Speke led a handful of militiamen against Senhor Farrao's house. Meanwhile, Lieutenant St Anna and the remainder of his men would take on the Pombeiros and their followers who were besieging the fort.

The plan was a simple but sound one and might well have spelled the end for Mariano and all his men had not one of the militiamen seen something move on his way to the village and fired before the others were in position. The shot was a good one and killed an early rising pig. It also woke everyone within the stockade.

Cursing the stupidity of the militiaman, Daniel made for the stone house at the run, Sam Speke lumbering along behind him.

Two Pombeiros broke from the house when Daniel was still some distance away. He fired both barrels of his rifle at them and had the satisfaction of seeing one fall to the ground. But the other paused to return the fire and a musket ball passed uncomfortably close to Daniel's ear. Afterwards, Daniel was to swear it had been Mariano himself, but at the time he was less certain. Shouting for one of the militiamen to pursue the fleeing man, Daniel continued his run towards the house, sliding new cartridges in his rifle as he went.

Hurling himself through the doorway, he fell over a body. It was one of Senhor Farrao's servants. Another lay a few feet inside the room. It was dark in here and when a white shadow appeared in a doorway leading off the room, Daniel called out a challenge, hesitating to shoot lest it was one of the household. The reply came in the form of a musket flash and a militiaman to one side of Daniel grunted in sudden pain.

Daniel's first shot dropped the man in the doorway and Sam Speke shot the man who took his place. Then they heard a crash of splintering wood and glass from the rear of the house as another Pombeiro dived through a window and made his escape.

Stepping over the bodies in the doorway, Daniel entered the

first bedroom cautiously, his rifle held before him. His eyes were becoming accustomed to the gloom now and he saw it was empty. Militiamen were in the second bedroom and he left them to search there. In the third bedroom there was the aroma of a perfume he had smelled before. This was Elvira's room. It was also the room from which the Pombeiro had jumped through the window. Daniel was relieved to find the room apparently empty.

Then he heard a faint sound and thumbed back the hammers on his rifle quickly. He waited for the sound to be repeated. When it came it sounded as though a small puppy was whimpering for attention. Something stirred in a corner of the room and Daniel moved towards it cautiously.

When he was no more than two paces away, a light breeze wafted a curtain free of the shattered window and Daniel saw the figure in the corner of the room was that of a crouching woman – a naked woman. His throat suddenly went dry.

'Elvira . . . ?' He hoped – he *prayed* it would not be her. When she turned her face up to him it was battered and misshapen from a severe beating.

'Oh my God!' Daniel dropped to his knees beside her, but she squirmed away, trying to burrow further into the corner.

'Go away . . . Please . . . ! Please!'

Daniel breathed again. It was not Elvira, but her maid. Gently, Daniel put his arms beneath the sobbing girl. Lifting her, he carried her from the room.

Daniel found Senhor Farrao in the fort where Elvira lay wounded. She had been hit in the stomach by a long-distance shot from a Pombeiro musket when they first stormed the stockade. Lying in bed in Lieutenant St Anna's room in the fort, she looked close to death.

Wringing his hands in anguish, Senhor Farrao looked down at his daughter and called on the Blessed Mother to be merciful to her. It was doubtful whether Elvira even knew he was there and taking the stricken man's arm, Daniel led him from the room.

'Elvira needs medical attention,' he said. 'Is there a doctor nearby?'

For a moment it seemed Senhor Farrao's grief would prove

too much for rational thought, but he made a great effort and gained control of himself. 'I . . . . I'll send for Senhora Lopes, if she still lives. She is not a doctor, but she always treats our wounded.'

Senhora Lopes was indeed alive. The daughter of a Portuguese father and a Manica woman, she was now married to a Portuguese – and she was a very capable and resourceful woman. During the brief occupation of the stockade by the Pombeiros, she had hidden herself and her daughter in the hayrack of a small building occupied by an evil-tempered pedigree bull, owned by Senhor Farrao. It was the only place outside the stone fort to escape the attentions of Mariano's men.

Brought to the bedroom, she made sympathetic noises over the still form of Elvira, then promptly ushered Daniel and Senhor Farrao from the room.

There was nothing Daniel could do here and he did not feel inclined to listen to any more of Senhor Farrao's lamentations. Desultory fighting was still in progress as the militia flushed the last of Mariano's men from the makeshift huts of the refugees from the river valley villages. Snatching up his rifle, Daniel went to assist St Anna's men.

By the time Daniel reached the scene, the brief but fierce battle was over. Lieutenant St Anna's militiamen had finally proved their worth and Daniel found the young Portuguese officer flushed and happy, proud of his men. But one look at Daniel's haggard face told him this was not the moment to solicit praise.

'I have heard about Elvira,' he said. 'Is she very bad? She will live?'

'She's alive, but unconscious . . . there's nothing we can do at the moment. Let's see if we've got Mariano.' Daniel desperately wanted to be doing something . . . anything. If he stopped he would think of Elvira . . . .

The bodies of the Pombeiros and their followers were brought to the ground in front of the fort and laid out for all to see, but Sam Speke confirmed that Mariano was not among them. Nevertheless, it was the end of the legend of invincibility that Mariano had built about himself. For ten years he and his men had terrorised the country without suffering a single defeat. It had even begun to be whispered that the Gods were fighting with him. Now, with thirty Pombeiros and two hundred rebel tribesmen lying dead, word of Mariano's great defeat would spread faster than he could ride – and Mariano was riding hard. He had left horses in a thorn corral outside the stockade for just such an emergency as this and at this very moment he and two of his lieutenants were riding away from Sena as fast as they could go.

Back at his house, as servants cleared up about them, Senhor Farrao explained what had happened when Mariano launched his night attack. The Pombeiros had been heard approaching, but it was thought they were men of the Portuguese army returning. No one imagined that Mariano would have the audacity to attack Sena while he was being hunted by the largest expeditionary force ever seen in this part of the country. Instead of manning the walls of the stockade to fight him off, the Pombeiro had found the gates thrown wide to welcome him! Called from his dinner table, Senhor Farrao had himself gone to the jetty with lamps, to guide in the expected steamer.

The ghastly mistake that had been made was realised when the Pombeiros charged through the gates, shooting those who had turned out to welcome them. Senhor Farrao had run to the house to fetch Elvira and she was shot as they came out through the door. Assisted by one of the servants they had barely made the safety of the fort ahead of Mariano and from here had conducted a successful defence against the Pombeiros' surprise attack.

Now it was the turn of Lieutenant Francisco St Anna to tell the Captain General the story of the Portuguese army's disastrous defeat at the hands of the Pombeiros.

Although it was not voiced aloud, everyone in the room knew that, had the rebels not been so decisively defeated at Sena, the débâcle on the river would have resulted in Senhor Farrao being stripped of all his offices. The Portuguese government was notorious for selecting scapegoats to take responsibility for its overseas failures.

When Daniel told of the capture of the Bemba rebel and his news of Victoria's whereabouts, Senhor Farrao surprised everyone by exclaiming, 'Vumba's kraal? I know it well. I went there many years ago on an official visit. Vumba is a chief of the northern Manicas. I negotiated a treaty of friendship with him.'

'This treaty is still in force?'

'Of course . . . but you are not going there?'

'I am, if you'll tell me where it is. I can do nothing for Elvira by remaining here. I'd rather be doing something positive to capture Mariano – and I'm certain Mariano will go to Vumba to lick his wounds. There's nothing left for him here. Will you give me a translation of your treaty – and have as many impressive-looking seals attached to it as you can find.'

'It will be ready by morning. Take the best of my horses . . . take all my horses. Kill Mariano and everything I own is yours.'

'You will need my militiamen with you,' declared Lieutenant St Anna. 'A treaty decorated with many seals is very impressive, but you will find a hundred well-armed men far more comforting if Chief Vumba wishes to forget his promise of friendship and side with Mariano. No doubt the chief has many reasons to fear Mariano, but he has seen no Portuguese soldiers in his lifetime – who do you think he should fear most?'

Daniel could see the wisdom of Lieutenant St Anna's argument, but he also remembered how reluctant the Portuguese expeditionary force had been to move off on the journey upriver.

'It's a kind offer,' he said diplomatically. 'But speed is more important than a show of force. I intend leaving tomorrow. If your men are ready, they can come along. If not, Sam and I will take our chances.'

Lieutenant St Anna was taken aback by Daniel's ultimatum, but going inland to Chief Vumba's kraal had become a matter of honour, 'We will be ready.' He bowed to Senhor Farrao. 'If you will excuse me. I have much to do.'

When Daniel looked in upon Elvira that night, Senhora Lopes was sitting with her. Putting a finger to her lips, Senhora Lopes ushered him from the room and followed him outside. Closing the door carefully behind her she reached for Daniel's hand and dropped something into it. When he looked down he saw it was a musket ball.

'You took this out? You operated on Elvira? Does Senhor Farrao know?'

'Would he have said "yes", had I asked his permission?' Senhora Lopes smiled. 'It was better this way, Senhor. Do not worry, she will live.' The smile left the woman's face. 'I cannot say whether she will ever have children, but she *will* live.'

Daniel looked from the lead ball in his hand to Senhora Lopes and she smiled again. 'I have taken musket balls from a great many wounded men. I am not a doctor, but few of my patients have died. Go now, Elvira sleeps and must not be disturbed. You can see her in the morning.'

Daniel returned to the fort the next morning, shortly before he and Sam Speke were due to set off with Lieutenant St Anna's militiamen.

The curtains in Elvira's room were closed, but there was enough sunlight seeping through for Daniel to see Elvira's face on the pillows and, as he looked down at her, she opened her eyes. The pain in them tore him apart, especially when she tried to smile at him.

Daniel stooped over her and kissed her cheek. 'I'm glad I am able to speak to you before I go.' He saw the dismay on her face and added quickly, 'I'll be back, I promise you. I want you to remember that, whatever happens.'

'Must you go?' It came out as a whisper.

'Yes, but I'll be thinking of you every minute I'm away. I love you, Elvira.'

'You're not just saying that because I'm ill. To make me feel better?'

'I'm saying it because it happens to be true. I didn't want to leave Sena without telling you.'

'I love you too, Daniel.'

Daniel took her hand and gripped it as tightly as he dared. 'Then you can be absolutely *certain* I'll come back to you.'

Bending over the bed again, he kissed her on her lips. As he straightened up and tried to pull his hand from hers, her fingers tightened and she held him fast.

'You . . . you're not going after Mariano again?'

'I must. We think we know where to find him. Victoria is ill with fever at a Manica kraal. Mariano will be on his way there now.'

'Is it for Mariano, or for Victoria you go, Daniel? I can understand Senhor Speke's eagerness to find his daughter . . . but you?'

'I want them both. Victoria because she is my friend's daughter — and Mariano because I'm going to kill him for what he's done here.'

CHAPTER TEN

Lieutenant Francisco St Anna's militiamen marched off from Sena with a jauntiness that was in marked contrast to the army that had set off upriver a week earlier. They had won a notable victory against the Pombeiros and their spirits were high. Lieutenant St Anna was convinced he now commanded a formidable fighting force. Hopefully, his faith in the militia would not be put to the test on this occasion, but no one could be certain. They were venturing into little-known territory.

There was another reason for the brisk pace maintained by the part-time native soldiers. Far away, above the sea to the east of Mozambique, the brilliant hue of the dawn sky had lately been dulled by wispy cloud. It quickly dispersed as the sun rose higher, but each day would persist for a little longer until great banks of storm cloud formed to dominate the whole sky.

Each morning the eyes of every tribesman and woman turned to the east to check on the progress of the build-up. It was almost time for the most crucial few months in the African calendar — the rainy season. This was the season when the Gods decided whether they would grant life or death to their peoples. If the rains came, it was life. If not, then death would stalk a drought-ridden continent.

Either way, it was a time for a man to be at home. The militiamen would follow Lieutenant Francisco St Anna and complete the annihilation of Mariano and his Pombeiros – but only because he had promised to bring them safely home to Sena before the first drop of rain fell.

The journey proved to be much easier than Daniel had anticipated. A day away from Sena they began climbing gently in a country of wide wooded valleys and great sweeping hills, topped with granite outcrops. By keeping to the slopes of the hills they made excellent progress. Daniel, with a good trader's eye, realised it was first-class trekking country. Oxen and wagons could negotiate these hills with little difficulty.

On the fourth day from Sena, the hills suddenly reared up and became mountains, but there was nothing here that Senhor Farrao had not described in detail. A short detour brought them to a pass that wound its way between crags towering to a height of eight thousand feet on either side.

On the fifth day they left the mountains behind and entered a huge valley with spectacular views that faded only with the mauve haze of distance. Here they found Vumba's kraal.

A couple of miles short of the Manica kraal, Lieutenant St Anna had his men form themselves into a passable marching formation. Then, with the Portuguese flag fluttering at the head of the column, they set off on the last leg of their journey to visit Chief Vumba, declared 'friend' of the Portuguese.

The force of a hundred men had seemed large when they set off from Sena, but so vast was the canvas of nature spread out here, that they were no more than a mere speck of movement on the valley floor.

They were expected. Indeed, there was no way for strangers to approach Vumba's village without being seen. Many Manica warriors were in evidence about the kraal, but Daniel noticed that they were careful not to bunch together in large enough groups to cause the Portuguese any concern. Before the militiamen entered the village, Daniel and Sam Speke took a ride around its perimeter to check on possible escape routes that might be taken by the Pombeiros. They returned just as Chief Vumba came out to the Portuguese officer and his small militia army.

The Manica chief was not pleased to see them. Through his interpreter, he asked St Anna why he had brought armed men to the lands of the Manicas. Had he come to fight?

Lieutenant St Anna expressed surprise that the Chief should entertain such bad thoughts about his friends. Why, he had even brought gifts to the Chief of the northern Manicas. A percussion musket, shot and powder and two rolls of calico were produced and laid on the ground before Vumba. Then St Anna produced the copy of the document of friendship, liberally adorned with the very impressive seals of the Captain General of the North West District of Mozambique. He read it first in Portuguese, then had it translated by one of his militiamen who spoke the Manica language fluently.

Chief Vumba looked uncomfortable, then said something to St Anna through the interpreter, at the same time pointing across the valley.

'He says no Portuguese have been to see him for so many years that he has found a new friend. A white man who came to him from the west. A man who stays with him and even now is working in the rocks, just a little way along the valley.'

Lieutenant St Anna began to ask Vumba about this new-found friend, but Daniel interrupted him impatiently. 'Save the diplomatic wrangling for some other time. Tell him we've come for the girl who has been recovering from fever in his village . . . and ask whether Mariano is here with her.'

Chief Vumba looked even more unhappy when the questions were put to him and his reply was accompanied by a great many gesticulations.

'He knows nothing of any girl, and there are no Pombeiros here.'

'He lies,' said Daniel. He nodded towards the cattle pen, about a hundred yards from where they stood. 'There's a small pen just the other side of the cattle with half-a-dozen horses inside – most of them stolen from me.'

Lieutenant St Anna nodded, but when he spoke he was careful not to show his feelings. 'It is regrettable, but I fear that Chief Vumba of the Manicas is not a man to be trusted. He needs to be taught a sharp lesson.'

Calling forward one of the militiamen, St Anna spoke to him at some length in a low voice. The militiaman looked frightened at first, but finally nodded his agreement and St Anna explained his intention to Daniel.

'I have told my man to shoot one of the cattle in the large pen . . . the chief's pen. I want to impress upon Vumba the destruction that one *hundred* men might do if he continues to lie to us.'

Daniel frowned anxiously. A chief's cattle meant more to him than any living creature. More than any member of his family with the exception of his eldest son. Lieutenant St Anna was taking a great gamble. Chief Vumba *might* decide it was time to tell the truth. On the other hand, he could order his warriors to fall upon the arrogant Portuguese officer and his men. If that happened they would be quickly overwhelmed by the sheer weight of numbers. There were at least a thousand spear-carrying Manicas in the crowd at Chief Vumba's back.

Lieutenant St Anna barked an order at his marksman. The man dropped to one knee, took quick aim – and fired.

A hundred yards away, one of Chief Vumba's cows collapsed at the knees and dropped to the ground without so much as a twitch, a well-aimed musket ball in her heart.

Chief Vumba's howl of protest brought angry mutterings from the assembled Manicas, but all sound ceased as St Anna's militia took up firing positions with well-practised precision.

'Tell Chief Vumba the choice is his,' said Lieutenant St Anna to his interpreter. 'We'll see if his love for a marauding, thieving Pombeiro is greater than his love for his own cattle.'

There was a confused babble of sound from the Manicas when St Anna's words were translated, but Chief Vumba's answer came hastily enough.

'Do not shoot any more cattle. He will give you the Pombeiro – and the girl.'

Before any more could be said, a heavily bearded man galloped up to the village from the direction of an area of broken rocks not far from the village. At first glance Daniel thought he was a Pombeiro, but Pombeiros did not sport heavy black beards, and the skin beneath the new arrival's unbuttoned shirt was as white as Daniel's own.

'What the 'ell's going on here, man? Who's doing the shooting – and what's the idea of this Portuguese flag, eh? Portugal has no jurisdiction here, it's too far inland.'

It was an accent Daniel had heard many times before. The thick, throaty intonation of a man who was more used to speaking Dutch than English. The newcomer was Andreus Van Niekerk, a Boer, descendant of the Dutch settlers who had colonised the Cape of Good Hope two hundred years before.

'We'll argue about who owns the country later. Right now we're after a Pombeiro named Mariano.'

'The half-caste Portuguese?' The Boer spat in the dust at his feet. 'Don't tell me you're risking a war over him? You'll find him drunk in his shack, with his woman. That's his place over there.'

He nodded towards a hut that was in need of new thatch, not thirty paces from where they were standing.

Lieutenant St Anna responded to the information swiftly. Ignoring Chief Vumba, he sent his militiamen to surround the hut, ensuring that no one could escape. To make doubly certain, he sent four of his men to guard the pen where Daniel had seen the horses, just in case Mariano had already left his hut.

Next, Lieutenant St Anna advanced to within a few feet of the low, blanket-covered doorway of the hut and called upon Mariano to come out and give himself up. The reply was a musket shot that left a smouldering hole in the blanket, the lead ball singing through the air only inches from St Anna's head.

The Portuguese officer ducked away quickly and called out an order to his men. The dozen or so militiamen stationed before the entrance to the hut put their guns to their shoulders. Before they could fire in through the doorway, Daniel called, 'Wait!'

Before St Anna could argue with him, Daniel ran forward to take up a crouching position beside the hut doorway.

'Victoria . . . are you inside?'

Daniel received a similar reply to the one given to Lieutenant St Anna, but this time the musket ball punched a fist-sized hole through the mud and wattle wall of the hut and shattered a hard-clay milk gourd standing in the shade of a hut twenty yards away.

Through the thin wall Daniel could hear the sound of a hoarse, whispered argument. Then Victoria called, 'Who . . . who is it?'

'It's Daniel.' Daniel crouched low, anticipating another shot, but it never came.

'Daniel! But I . . . we, were told you were dead!'

'You were told wrong – but come outside and let's talk.'

There was a quick movement inside the hut, then a man's voice called, 'No. She's staying here. If you attack she dies with us.'

'Victoria.' Sam Speke had run to Daniel's side and now he shouted to his daughter. 'Try to persuade them to give themselves up. The hut's surrounded by the Portuguese army. There's no escape.'

'Either we are *all* allowed to leave together, or we die

together,' shouted Mariano. 'Tell the soldiers to go back to Mozambique. This is not Portuguese territory.'

'Mariano, let my girl go, for God's sake! You do that and I'll do what I can to persuade the Lieutenant to allow you to go free.'

Mariano gave a short derisive laugh. 'Do you really expect him to listen to you after what we did to his army on the Zambezi River? Of course he won't – but he's going to have to come in after us, and Victoria will die with her own. There will be no more talk now. Go, or I shoot again – this time to kill.'

Sam Speke would have stayed to argue with the Pombeiro, but Daniel pulled him away and half-dragged him to where Lieutenant St Anna crouched beside another hut with a few of his troops.

He listened to Daniel's report of the conversation with Mariano impatiently. 'I expected nothing else. Mariano knows he will not leave Vumba's kraal alive.'

St Anna snapped an order to his men and two of them hurried away.

'What are you going to do?' Sam Speke watched the two men until they went out of sight between the huts. 'You can't attack, my daughter is in that hut.'

'So are the Pombeiros,' stated St Anna briskly. 'None of them are there against their will. However, I will not order my men to shoot into the hut until I have tried to drive them out by other means. Get back now, things will happen very quickly.'

At that moment, Daniel realised what Lieutenant St Anna had planned. The two men he had sent away suddenly appeared behind Mariano's hut and each of them carried a lighted torch. Creeping close to the hut they tossed the torches high in the air to land on the thatched roof. One torch rolled off to splutter harmlessly in the dust, but the other clung to the thatch and seconds later the tinder-dry roofing ignited with a mighty roar.

Sam Speke started forward, his daughter's name on his lips, but Daniel held him back. 'Wait, Sam. St Anna's idea might work.'

As they watched, thick choking smoke began to pour from the hut, around the sides of the blanket hanging at the door and the militiamen moved forward cautiously. A full minute passed and Daniel thought that he and St Anna might have underestimated the determination of Mariano and his men. Then the blanket was wrenched from the doorway and Victoria staggered from the hut, coughing and retching.

Sam Speke broke from Daniel's grasp and reached his daughter's side just as five Pombeiros burst from the hut. Their eyes streaming from the acrid black smoke, none of them could see where he was going, but each of them had a gun in his hand and they ran out firing wildly.

Sam Speke staggered and, as Victoria screamed, he fell to the ground in front of her. One of the militiamen was also hit and he sat on the ground clutching his stomach, screaming in agony and fear.

Daniel reached Sam Speke just as the militiamen, obeying Lieutenant St Anna's order not to shoot, began clubbing the Pombeiros to the ground with their rifle butts.

The Pombeiro bullet had struck Sam Speke in his side and it was immediately apparent to Daniel that it was a mortal wound. The ex-seaman knew it too. With Daniel supporting him in his arms and Victoria kneeling by his side, he tried desperately to speak to his daughter but the sound was choked off in his throat as blood welled up and dribbled from both corners of his mouth.

Three times Sam Speke tried to say something to Victoria before he finally accepted that the words were not going to come. Reaching out, he took her hand in his and died, looking up at her face.

Daniel was stunned at the sudden death of the man who had been his friend for as long as he could remember, sharing dangers and troubles across the breadth of Africa.

But his death was an even greater tragedy for Victoria. It had happened so quickly that, at first, she was quite unable to comprehend what had happened. When realisation finally came that her father was dead, she looked up at Daniel in horror.

'This is my fault, Daniel . . . . I killed him!' Suddenly she scrambled to her feet and turned as though she was going to hurl herself into the blazing hut.

Daniel grabbed her and held on as she struggled to get away.

'Let me go – Daniel, please let me go!'

'Get a grip on yourself. We came here to take you home. Do you want me to tell your mother that Sam died for nothing?'

Still struggling in his arms, Victoria began to scream. She did not stop until Daniel released one of his arms and slapped her sharply across the face. The sharp blow had an immediate effect. Victoria collapsed against him and began sobbing uncontrollably. Meanwhile, all about them, excited Manica tribesmen were working frantically to prevent the flying sparks from igniting the whole of the village.

At the insistence of Lieutenant St Anna, Daniel led Victoria away from the Manica village, leaving two of the militiamen to carry off Sam Speke's body. Pushing the badly beaten Pombeiros along before them, the remainder of St Anna's force retreated from the village and set up a defensive camp at the foot of a nearby hill, close to a spectacular waterfall that tumbled in a series of cataracts a hundred and fifty feet down the steep face.

For a couple of hours there was feverish activity in the Manica village and the anger of Chief Vumba and his tribe at the actions of the Portuguese militia was an almost tangible thing.

Just before dusk fell, Andreus Van Niekerk came to the camp leading a riding horse and two pack animals.

'You've stirred up a hornets' nest down there,' he declared angrily. 'Vumba's village is no place for a white man tonight – and you'd better keep a good guard posted. Vumba's warriors are just wild enough to want to give you a damn good fight.'

'If he allows his warriors to attack us Chief Vumba will learn the penalty for breaking a treaty of friendship.'

'Good. You teach a good, hard lesson, General. It will save me trouble if he learns it from you. I have a treaty with Chief Vumba too – and it's one he's not going to wriggle out of in a hurry.'

'*You* have a treaty?' Lieutenant St Anna looked at the Boer suspiciously. 'Vumba is a tribal chief in Portuguese territory. You have no right to come here and make a treaty with anyone.'

'More right than you, I'd say. I came here at Chief Vumba's invitation . . . I'd hardly say the same for you. Chief Vumba swears he *isn't* in Portuguese territory. I agree with him. So does the Government of Transvaal – and the British Government at Cape Town too, I reckon. You *might* have some jurisdiction along the Zambezi River – although from what I hear that's no more than a matter of opinion. You certainly have none here.'

'The Portuguese flag was planted here before the first Dutchman – or Englishman, had ever sighted the coast of South Africa.'

'You might as well have planted potatoes,' retorted Van Niekerk insultingly. 'This is free territory and that's just the way it's going to stay . . . for a while, at any rate.'

'What sort of a treaty have you made with Vumba?' Daniel asked Van Niekerk the question in a bid to head off an even more serious argument between the two men.

'I've got the sole mining rights for the whole of Manicaland on behalf of the Cape Mining Company,' replied Andreus Van Niekerk, proudly. 'Here, look at this.' He thrust his hand into a pocket and pulled out two irregular shaped objects that gleamed dully in the faint light that remained. 'They're gold nuggets. I picked them up in a stream not a mile from here. By this time next year there will be fifty miners working in these mountains.'

'How will you get that many men here?' asked Daniel sharply. 'They'll need to come through Matabeleland. Mzilikazi's policy has always been to keep white men out—'

'Mzilikazi's dead,' interrupted Andreus Van Niekerk. 'And the Matabele can't make up their mind who's going to take his place . . . not that I care, mind you. I've already got all the permission I need.'

Van Niekerk opened a pouch at his belt. Taking out a many-folded piece of paper, he handed it to Daniel.

Walking to the fireside, Daniel read the document in the light of the flames. Short and to the point, the note gave permission for Andreus Van Niekerk and employees of the Cape Mining Company to pass through the lands of the Matabele, and those of their vassals. It was signed, 'The Reverend Farewell Loveday, acting on behalf of Umnombati, Regent of the Matabele Nation.'

Daniel finished reading the permit and handed it back to Van Niekerk, shaking his head in disbelief. 'Farewell Loveday must be mad!' he exclaimed. 'How many of these has he issued?'

The Boer replaced the document in his pouch and shrugged his shoulders. 'I don't know . . . about fifty, or sixty, I suppose. What does it matter? The sooner this country is opened up, the better.'

'The better for whom?' retorted Daniel. 'Certainly not for the Matabele. To allow Europeans to enter Matabeleland right now is dangerous folly. Mzilikazi must have at least thirty sons who have a good claim to the throne. Each of them has his own impi, ready to back him. The whole country could erupt in bloodshed at any moment. Any white men in the country would be caught right in the middle of the fighting.'

'I'll look after myself, they'll need to do the same,' said Andreus Van Niekerk indifferently. 'Besides, the deaths of a few Englishmen might be all the excuse the British Government needs to send an army to Matabeleland and take over the country. That should suit you. If they're not up to it I'm quite sure the Government of Transvaal will be happy to do the job for them.'

'Such a move will unite the Matabele as nothing else could,' declared Daniel. 'Anyone who tries to move in can expect to be opposed by a well-disciplined army of at least thirty thousand men. It will be a blood bath.'

Andreus Van Niekerk looked slyly at Lieutenant St Anna, who frowned as he listened to both men discussing territory to which Portugal also laid claim. 'We could always call on the General's kaffirs to come and rescue us.'

Daniel ignored the Boer's sarcasm. 'With all that's happening in Matabeleland, the sooner I get back to Khami the better.'

'You're travelling to Khami? So am I.' Van Niekerk looked to where Victoria sat huddled in a blanket by the camp fire. 'Is she coming too?'

'Her mother is there. She's all the family she's got left now.'

Andreus Van Niekerk looked at Victoria speculatively. 'Um! I'd have preferred the company of another man. One who could handle a gun, but she'll help time to pass more quickly. It will take us ten days to reach Khami. By the time we get there I might have forgotton she's got a kaffir mother and has opened her legs to that son of a kaffir whore, Mariano.'

Andreus Van Niekerk rose to his feet and went off to unload his horses. Daniel watched him go, swallowing his anger. He would have preferred not to have the Boer's company to Khami, but he knew it would save him a great deal of time. Van Niekerk knew the route. All the same, Daniel thought the Boer was one of the most obnoxious men he had ever met.

That night a strong guard was placed about the camp. Lieutenant St Anna feared a surprise attack from Chief Vumba's Manicas, but when trouble arrived it came from *inside* the camp.

Daniel woke with a start as shots were fired from somewhere nearby. The shots were followed by excited shouting and Daniel snatched up his rifle. By the time he reached the scene of the disturbance the excitement was over. When torches were lighted from a low-burning camp fire, it became apparent that Mariano and his Pombeiros had made a determined bid for freedom. One Pombeiro and a militiaman lay dead on the ground. The other Pombeiros were being handled roughly and tied by their angry guards.

'How did they get free?' Daniel asked St Anna. When he had seen the Pombeiros shortly before he lay down to sleep, they were trussed so tightly he was concerned that the ropes would cut off the blood supply to their limbs.

'I thought of putting that question to *you*. They used this.'

Lieutenant St Anna tossed a razor-sharp skinning-knife through the air. Catching it by the handle, Daniel recognised it as his own. Kept in a sheath at the back of his belt, it had been on the ground beside him as he slept.

'Victoria!' he said quietly. She had been sleeping only a few feet from him.

'Who else? I should have anticipated such a rescue attempt. However, the death of another of my soldiers makes the decision I have to take easier than before. Go back to sleep now. There will be nothing more to disturb you tonight.'

Back at his own fire, Daniel threw on more wood, hoping Victoria would sit up and say something. But she lay still and gave no indication that she could hear him when he spoke softly to her. Tucking the knife and belt beneath the boots he was utilising as a pillow, Daniel lay down to sleep once more.

He was still awake when the first rays of the sun stirred the camp into life.

Lieutenant Francisco St Anna convened a court for the purpose of trying Mariano and his fellow Pombeiros on charges of insurrection and murder. The proceedings were both simple and brief. St Anna was prosecutor, the only witness – and the judge. He did not deem it necessary for the Pombeiros to have the benefit of a defence counsel. After listing the crimes of which the accused were charged, he pronounced sentence of death upon them – and wasted no time in ordering the sentence to be carried out.

Victoria knew nothing of what was happening. Crouching dejectedly at Daniel's camp fire, she waited for the coffee pot to come to the boil. When a great cheer rose from the assembled militia, she looked up to see her lover and his three companions twitching their lives away at the end of ropes hanging from two nearby trees.

Victoria started to her feet and began to scream, but Daniel was quick enough to intercept her as she tried to run to the scene of the executions.

'No . . . Victoria . . . . There's nothing you can do now.' He held her until the struggles gave way to a grief that was worse than she had shown for the death of her father.

Victoria had managed to gain control of herself by the time Andreus Van Niekerk strode angrily across the camp to Daniel. He had been remonstrating with Lieutenant St Anna. His anger was not because of the irregular and arbitrary nature of the Pombeiros' trial and execution, but because Mariano had managed to steal the Boer's horse during the escape attempt and it had been shot dead from beneath him.

After making a rough cross to mark Sam Speke's grave beside the waterfall, Daniel, Victoria and Van Niekerk were ready to depart for Khami. The Boer was still grumbling about having to ride one of his pack-horses. His mood was not improved when Daniel went to Vumba's village to reclaim his own horses and gave the best of them to Victoria to ride.

Chief Vumba was also unhappy. He had hoped to make the horses his own property, but the sight of the four bodies dangling from the trees made him disinclined to argue. When

Daniel presented two of the horses to him in return for the right to bring trade wagons through his territory, his humour improved.

Lieutenant Francisco St Anna's farewell to Daniel had a warmth about it that Daniel would not have thought possible when they had first met, only a few weeks before.

The Portuguese officer smiled when Daniel voiced his thoughts. 'Much has happened since then, Daniel. We have stood together in battle. At such times one learns the worth of a man very quickly. We will meet again, you and I, at Sena. I will convey your affection to Senhorita Farrao and will guard her with my life until you return for her. You look surprised. Did you think, perhaps, your feelings for her were a well-kept secret? Oh no! When you first arrived at Sena I realised I had lost any chance of gaining Elvira for myself. For that reason we could not be friends then. Now I know you better I am happy for her . . . and for you.' Shaking Daniel's hand warmly, Francisco St Anna strode away to attend to the breaking-up of his own camp.

Andreus Van Niekerk had not finished repacking his saddle-bags. Leaving him to catch up with them, Daniel and Victoria rode off slowly, alone for the first time since their unhappy reunion. As they rode past the dead Pombeiros, Victoria averted her eyes, biting her lower lip fiercely as she struggled to keep a firm grip on her emotions.

'Had it not happened here, the end would have been just as certain somewhere else,' said Daniel, as gently as his own feelings would allow. 'Mariano was no good. For what he and his men did at Sena I would have tracked him down and killed him myself.'

'Because of the girl the Portuguese officer was talking about . . . Elvira.'

'Partly . . . but there were other girls there who suffered more than gunshot wounds.'

'Who is this girl, Daniel?' Victoria chose to ignore what Mariano had done at Sena.

Daniel gave Victoria an outline of the way he and Elvira had met, telling of their journey together to Sena and the weeks he had spent there.

'Are you going to marry her?'

Daniel knew that Victoria wanted him to lie to her, but he could not. 'Yes, if she'll have me when I return to Sena.'

They rode in silence for a long while. Then, in a voice choked with emotion, Victoria asked, 'What will happen to me now? I . . . I feel as though I'm caught up in some unbelievable nightmare. When uTshwebe's warriors returned and said you were dead I didn't know what to do. I couldn't think straight. Every night I cried myself to sleep. For a while I . . . I thought I'd die too. It would have been better if I had,' she added bitterly. 'Instead . . . Mariano came along.'

Victoria gripped the pommel of her saddle so tightly her knuckles gleamed white against the worn, brown leather, 'I've made a complete mess of my life. Dad is dead because of me. He warned me against Mariano, at uTshwebe's village. Oh God! Why didn't I listen to him? How am I going to face ma . . . ?'

Daniel wanted to comfort her. He felt deeply sorry for what had happened to her, but there were some things he could not forget. 'Blaming yourself isn't going to bring Sam back. You've got to forget what's happened. It won't be easy, but for your own sake – and your mother's, you've got to pick up the threads of your life again.'

Victoria suddenly raised her head and looked directly at Daniel. 'If things had been different. . . . If you hadn't fallen ill and met Elvira, and I hadn't got mixed up with Mariano – would you ever have married me?'

'It's a question I've asked myself many times during these past couple of weeks. The honest answer is – I don't know.'

Victoria gave him a wan little smile that made him suddenly remember her as she had been when she was a small girl. 'That can only mean "No", Daniel. You made your mind up quickly enough once you'd met Elvira. It makes things easier for me, really. It means that I haven't lost you because of my stupidity. You were never mine to lose.'

'There'll be other men, Victoria. Some day the right one is going to ride in, take one look at you and carry you off to the nearest preacher.'

It was a half-hearted attempt to bridge the wide gap that had opened up between him and Victoria, but it failed miserably.

Victoria looked away from him before she spoke again, 'He'll need to be a very understanding man, Daniel. I'm carrying Mariano's child.'

CHAPTER ELEVEN

Andreus Van Niekerk soon proved himself to be quite as objectionable as Daniel had anticipated. After inquiring in the crudest manner into the relationship that existed between Daniel and Victoria, the Boer used every means short of actual physical force to persuade Victoria to share his blanket at night. He became so persistent that Daniel threatened to knock the Afrikaaner down if he did not leave her alone. Andreus Van Niekerk grumbled that it was none of Daniel's business. He uttered vague threats, but saved his advances for the occasions when Daniel went hunting, or rode off to find a detour more suitable for an ox-wagon laden with trade goods.

Eventually, Victoria put a stop to the Boer's amorous hopes in a way that made a deep and lasting impression upon him. With the Manica mountains three days behind them they were now on the edge of the Mashonaland plateau, close to the headwaters of the Sabi River. When Daniel sighted a herd of buffalo grazing in open bushland under the watchful eyes of a muscular young bull, it was agreed that buffalo meat would make a wonderful evening meal for the three travellers.

'The Lord could almost have laid the table for us,' said Daniel, sliding from his horse and pulling his rifle free from the saddle holster.

'From this range?' Van Niekerk was sceptical. 'That herd's four hundred yards away. Fire a shot from here and all you'll have for supper is a mouthful of dust.'

Daniel was about to prove Van Niekerk wrong when Victoria reined her horse in front of him, spoiling his aim. She carried the rifle that had belonged to her father. Without dismounting, she raised the weapon to her shoulder, took careful aim – and fired. To Daniel's delight and Andreus Van Niekerk's astonishment a fat buffalo cow on the edge of the herd took an involuntary step forward, then pitched on her side in the red dust.

The crack of the rifle-shot startled the herd, but they had

never before encountered gun-carrying hunters and did not associate the horses and their riders with the death of the buffalow cow. While they milled about, snorting their bewilderment, the herd-leader raised his great head and tested the air to the north, east, south and west. He was utterly confused. Advancing to where the dead cow lay stretched on the ground, his nose caught the scent of blood. He backed off in alarm, but the fear passed quickly. Death was as much a part of the bush veldt as the aged, balancing rocks, the gnarled thorn trees and tall dried grass. Three minutes after the echoes of the shot died away, the buffalo herd was grazing as though nothing had happened.

It took Andreus longer to recover. He had not believed such a shot possible – and had said so. To be forced to eat his words was bad enough, but to be proved wrong by a coloured *woman* . . . . !

'If you think that was a lucky shot I'll down another,' said Victoria, mockingly. Behind her, Daniel grinned at Van Niekerk's discomfiture.

'It was a good shot,' Van Niekerk conceded grudgingly. 'But it's easy to look clever when you've got a better gun than anyone else. Now I'll show you what hunting is really about.'

Van Niekerk pulled his own gun free from the saddle holster. It was a large-bore muzzle loader. Capable of punching a hole right through an elephant, it was notoriously inaccurate and far too heavy and clumsy for professional hunters. Swinging down from his horse, Andreus Van Niekerk set off at a crouching run through the long dry grass towards the buffalo herd.

Daniel's smile changed to a frown as he watched the Boer move closer to the herd. 'We'd better go and help him. The damn fool's so eager to prove he can shoot a buffalo he's likely to kill himself in the attempt.'

Mounting his horse, Daniel kneed it forward, rifle in his hand. Flicking the reins of her own horse, Victoria fell in beside him.

Meanwhile, so determined was Andreus Van Niekerk to down a buffalo that he had thrown off all reasonable caution. Closing in upon the herd he ignored the wind that blew from him towards the animals. His scent was caught first by a scarred old bull, the recently deposed herd-leader. He moved instinctively to put himself between the cows and the calves he had sired – only to be stopped by the young bull. The well-muscled younger animal had caught Van Niekerk's scent too and his grunt of alarm swiftly alerted the cows. They began calling their offspring as the bull turned to face the unseen threat.

At that moment, Andreus Van Niekerk rose to take up a shooting stance and he and the young herd-leader stared at each other, separated by no more than fifty yards of rough-grassed veldt.

The Boer brought the heavy rifle slowly and carefully up to his shoulder, but made no attempt to fire off a shot until the young bull turned to drive his herd away from the offensive smell of man. For a moment he stood broadside on to the Boer hunter – and Van Niekerk squeezed the trigger.

The big-bore gun threw high. Instead of penetrating the big bull's heart, the musket ball struck it just above the shoulder. With a bellow of pain, the wounded bull rounded on Van Niekerk as he desperately poured black powder down the barrel of his gun from the leather powder-horn hanging at his belt.

As the old bull took over the familiar task of ushering the herd clear of trouble, his wounded successor lowered his head and charged – and a three feet spread of curved horns bore down on the Boer hunter.

While Van Niekerk was still frantically ramming home the heavy lead musket ball, he realised the buffalo would reach him before he was ready to fire again. He looked about him desperately for somewhere to take refuge, but there was no tree within a reasonable distance that might take his weight. By the time this realisation came to him it was too late to run. He jumped to one side as the buffalo bull reached him, but a side swipe of the horns sent him tumbling heavily to the ground.

The bull slithered to a halt in a cloud of red dust and wheeled about, hot-eyed and angry. Andreus Van Niekerk's rifle, ramrod protruding from the barrel, lay where it had fallen, ten feet away. The Boer raised himself on one knee, aware that he was at the mercy of the enraged animal and could do nothing to help himself. The bull lowered its head once more, but before it could charge two rifles fired in unison. The buffalo's legs buckled and it fell dead to the ground.

When Daniel and Victoria rode up, the dust was beginning to settle. It had been Andreus Van Niekerk's intention to deny he was ever in danger, but as he slapped the dust from his clothing, his shaking hand betrayed him and the lie died on his lips.

'That was a damn fool thing to do!' Daniel exclaimed. 'You'd have got away with shooting a cow . . . any cow. But to go for a young bull . . . the herd leader at that! It was madness.'

'Yes, I know. I should have known better. I . . . I'm not the world's best shot either. You saved my life . . . both of you. I'm grateful. Very grateful.'

The Boer spoke the words looking at Victoria and Daniel's anger left him. Andreus Van Niekerk had swallowed a great deal of pride in acknowledging that he owed his life to a girl – and one with African blood in her veins.

To Daniel's surprise, Victoria suddenly threw her rifle to Van Niekerk, who caught it before it hit the ground. 'Here, take this. Learn how to use it properly and you'll have no need to poke a gun into a buffalo's ear before pulling the trigger. It's all right,' she added, as Van Niekerk opened his mouth to protest. 'That was my dad's gun. I've got one of my own.'

Abruptly, Victoria tugged at her horse's reins and the animal trotted briskly to where the other ponies stood with drooping reins, cropping at the coarse, dry grass.

Perplexed, Andreus Van Niekerk looked from the modern rifle in his hands to the departing girl. He turned to Daniel for an explanation, but Daniel shook his head. He was as baffled by Victoria's quixotic gesture as was the Boer. Van Niekerk had certainly not behaved in a manner to deserve such generosity . . . but Daniel accepted that Victoria was wiser in the ways of men than he was.

'She's quite a woman,' said Andreus Van Niekerk, grudgingly. 'She shoots better than a man.' He gazed admiringly after Victoria and Daniel knew she would have no more trouble from the Boer.

'You'll be needing cartridges for that gun. I have plenty, but you'll pay for them at trade rates. Now, give me some help with these buffalo we've killed, or there'll be no supper for anyone.'

During the night a fierce storm raged over the high hills to the north and although they enjoyed a dry camp where they were, they suffered from the effect of the distant rain the following day. They reached a river and found it swollen. It meant they would need to make a wide detour, following the swift-flowing river towards its source until they found a shallower crossing-place.

It was only a beginning. The next night the storm returned again. This time the rain fell over a far wider area and washed out their camp.

For days the travellers zig-zagged their way across the high plateau on which they now were, the storms adding many miles to their journey. Then, one bright, crisp morning, after they had suffered the nightly downpour, Daniel saw something that made all the additional hardship well worthwhile.

They had made camp the night before enveloped in thick grey rain cloud that laid an amorphous blanket over the whole land reducing visibility to a few yards.

Now it seemed the whole world was laid out before them in a panorama of breathtaking beauty. Only a few hundred yards from their camp the ground dropped away steeply to a valley that must have been ten miles wide and about twenty long. The valley ended, not in another range of hills, but with a further drop to lowland that extended to the southernmost borders of Mozambique, four hundred miles beyond the horizon.

A small river wound through the valley, fed by a dozen mountain streams cascading via moss-hung steps from the surrounding hills. The valley floor was not flat, but undulated gently, with here and there a small, round-topped hill and thick clumps of trees. Among them Daniel recognised the attractive Bauhinia, and the purple-flowering Citamusi.

The blue sky, lush green of the grass and the purple-flowering trees painted a picture on Daniel's memory that he would always remember. He had never seen a more beautiful place.

Daniel would have liked to spend time exploring the valley,

but Van Niekerk was impatient to reach Khami and send his report to the mining company for whom he worked. Daniel had to be content with entering the valley upon the map he was compiling, circling the area for future attention.

That afternoon, the travellers had an encounter that drove all thoughts of the valley from Daniel's mind for a while. They met up with a Matabele impi, heading eastwards to teach a sharp lesson to a Mashona village Headman. The vassal headman had sought to take advantage of Mzilikazi's death by withholding the annual payment of cattle, made to the Matabele to ensure immunity from their raids.

Heading the impi was Kanje, Mzilikazi's younger son. It was immediately apparent that Kanje had not forgiven Daniel for spoiling his homecoming celebrations. Ignoring Daniel, he put his questions to Van Niekerk, asking him for details of their journey. While the two men talked, the Matabele warriors of the impi began examining the loads carried by Daniel's pack-horses. It was mostly foodstuff, although there were also a certain amount of trade goods, as much as Senhor Farrao had been able to gather together at short notice.

The Matabele were a naturally inquisitive people and it was not unusual for a traveller to have every one of his possessions taken from the wagons and pack horses and held up for general inspection. Daniel was fully aware of this. He also knew that under Mzilikazi's rule every single item would be accounted for when Matabele curiosity had been satisfied. Such was not the case today.

Warriors began to move away, arms laden with the contents of the saddle-packs. Daniel unsheathed his gun and thumbed back the hammers, the double click sounding ominously loud.

'Tell your men to put back my trade goods, Kanje. I've not brought them this far only to be robbed by my friends.'

Kanje glared angrily at the gun pointing at his middle, not certain how far Daniel was prepared to go in defence of his property. They were anxious moments. A number of Kanje's men were armed with new muskets and were no doubt eager to use them. It appeared that someone believed Kanje would be the next Matabele King and was staking a claim to future trade concessions.

'Have the Matabele been reduced to stealing since they lost

their King – or is it only your regiment that has turned to scavenging?'

Kanje barked an order to his impi. Their expressions surly, the men about the horses moved away, those who had taken goods dumping them to the ground.

'You are carrying trade goods, yet you have no permission to trade.'

'My permission came from Mzilikazi. Is his memory already so dim that his word means nothing now?'

Kanje scowled. He did not enjoy bandying words with Daniel in front of his own men. 'You have no permit to be in our country. You must leave.'

'My home is at Khami. Come there with me and tell me in front of Mzilikazi's Council of Indunas that I am not welcome in your country. I'll get a permit, if one is necessary – *when* I reach Khami.'

Kanje's scowl grew deeper. At any other time he would have killed Daniel and his companions on the spot, taking a chance on being found out. But with the Matabele throne almost within his grasp there was too much to lose. He had laid his plans well – but he relied heavily on European backing. He would not alienate them now by killing Daniel. There would be time enough for that later.

'Go to Khami, trader . . . but you would be unwise to remain in our land. When there is a new King you will not be welcome among my people.'

'I'm aware there'll be no place for me if *you* become King, Kanje – but you are not the ruler of your people yet.'

Daniel threw the last few words after Kanje as he turned his back and walked away.

'You've made a bad enemy,' said Victoria, beside him. 'Kanje is very popular with the Mahaja – the young Matabele warriors.'

'Fortunately, the *Elders* will decide who is to become King. Kanje would tear the Matabele nation apart.'

Andreus Van Niekerk had been listening to their conversation with some surprise. Now he said, 'You mean there's some doubt about who'll become King? Kanje is already promising concessions. I've committed my own company pretty heavily as a result.'

'Then you'd better do something to cut your losses quickly,' suggested Daniel, unsympathetically. 'I'd give a dozen of Mzilikazi's sons a better chance than Kanje – and it's the senior Indunas who'll decide. You upset them and your company won't have a hope in hell of gaining a foothold in Matabeleland.'

Andreus Van Niekerk pressed Daniel to tell him more about the possible succession to the Matabele throne, but Daniel was in no mood to be helpful. Van Niekerk's declared aim was to bring a great many white miners into the country. Daniel held the conviction that an influx of white men would result in a conflict between the two races and have a disastrous ending for the people with whom he had made his home.

That night Daniel made camp in an ancient stone fortress that was a miniature version of The Great Home of the Chiefs, where Chiminuka spoke through his albino medium. Daniel could see that Victoria was affected by the similarity, but neither of them spoke of it. For his part, Daniel was relieved that they had been able to find a secure place in which to spend the night. He feared that Kanje might change his mind and return with his warriors to attack them.

Kanje did not return, and although Daniel was awakened in the night by what he at first thought to be gunfire, it turned out to be nothing more serious than thunder. He lay awake for an hour watching lightning scribbling on the sky far to the east. As the thunder rolled from hilltop to hilltop and grumbled against the stout stone walls of the ancient fortress, Daniel wondered what the future held for himself and the Matabele nation. Probably it was his surroundings that caused him to remember the predictions of the Mondoro and what he had said about Sam Speke having 'no future' to see. That prediction had proved to be tragically true. Daniel pondered upon the remainder of his words, but fell asleep before he had arrived at any conclusion.

The next day they had been travelling for less than an hour when they were intercepted by yet another Matabele impi – but this one was led by Jandu, and it was no chance meeting.

After he had greeted Daniel warmly, and answered questions about the health of Suliyana, Jandu explained the reason for his presence.

'I heard you were on your way to Khami and knew my brother, Kanje, would be in this area. He has taken on many of the airs of a King, but none of the responsibilities. I feared he and his impi might find you and do you harm.'

Jandu's words and manner were in marked contrast to those of his half-brother. Jandu spoke with a natural authority that was totally lacking in Kanje. Daniel hoped it had been duly noted by the elders of the Matabele tribe.

'I am pleased to see you have rescued the daughter of your friend Speke . . . but where is he?'

Daniel told Jandu of Sam Speke's death, without going into detail and the Matabele expressed his sympathy to Victoria, '. . . he was a good friend to my people. He will be greatly missed.'

Victoria's eyes immediately brimmed with tears and, in a bid to change the subject, Daniel asked whether the Matabele Council of Indunas had met to discuss the question of a successor to Mzilikazi.

Jandu made a gesture of frustration. 'They have met many times, yet my people are still without a King. Many Indunas insist that my father's true heir is Kulumani.'

'What does Umnombati say?'

Umnombati, the present Regent, was the oldest of the tribe's Indunas – and the most powerful. He alone of Mzilikazi's contemporaries had survived to enjoy old age and had been the Matabele King's friend and confidant to the very end. If any one man could influence the choice of the future Matabele King, it would be Umnombati.

Jandu gave a short laugh. 'When they talk of Kulumani, Umnombati holds his tongue – and with good reason. Many years ago word was given to the tribe that Kulumani had been sent to a small Zulu tribe many hundreds of miles to the south. It was a not uncommon custom to protect the King's heir from his enemies. Umnombati knew the truth. Acting upon my father's orders, he had taken Kulumani only as far as the river. There he strangled him and threw his body to the crocodiles.'

Daniel looked at Jandu in disbelief, 'Why? Why should Mzilikazi kill his own son – your brother?'

'To find the answer to this you need to know the story of my people, trader. Mzilikazi's father – my grandfather – once led the Kumala clan, in the land your people now call Natal. He was falsely accused of treachery and executed by Zwide, paramount chief of the Kumala and many other tribes. Mzilikazi never recovered from the shock of his father's death. He eventually became chief of the Kumala clan himself and a great warrior in Zwide's army. Zwide was so pleased with him that he gave him two of his own daughters to be his chief wives. One of them bore him a son – Kulumani. But Mzilikazi had never forgiven Zwide for killing his father.

'When the opportunity arose, he joined with Shaka, Zwide's enemy and together they killed him. Yet still that was not enough. Mzilikazi was determined that no grandson of Zwide would ever rule the Matabele. Besides, Kulumani posed a very real threat as long as he lived because his mother also had her father's death to avenge! Kulumani was killed and Mzilikazi was able to rule his people without looking over his shoulder to see who waited at his back with a knife. So, you see, Umnombati is forced to sit and listen to the other Indunas calling for Kulumani to be found – and he can say nothing. He is old but he still values his own life.'

It was a horrific story, but Daniel had long ago ceased to be shocked by the ruthlessness of Mzilikazi. 'Umnombati is not too old to sell permits to anyone who wishes to enter Matabeleland, either.'

Jandu shrugged. 'Umnombati does no more than make two lines that cross each on a piece of white man's paper. Who is to say that these lines are his – and those are not? The Council of Indunas decided that the missionary, Farewell Loveday should write the permits for those men to whom Umnombati grants permission to enter Matabeleland. I am not an Induna of the Council. If I were I would want to know why for every permit signed by Umnombati, five men enter Matabeleland.'

'Are you certain of this?'

'As certain as I am of trouble when a new King is named. The impis are unhappy that the Council is doing nothing to prevent white men from trampling our land, shooting all the elephant and digging holes in the ground for gold. They will expect the new King to turn the white man out of our country. If he does not the impis will rebel against him. If he does, the white men will be angry.'

Jandu smiled ruefully. 'Your missionaries say they have come here to teach my people a wonderful new way of life, trader. If it is so wonderful, why do so many white men turn their back upon this way of life in their own lands and come to Matabeleland?'

As Daniel struggled to think of a convincing reply, Jandu said, 'But you have had many problems of your own. We will have time to talk of other things when we reach Khami. For now you must tell me of the things that have happened to you since we parted at Sofala. How is the daughter of Senhor Farrao? I am surprised you did not discover her worth for yourself and bring her back as your wife . . . .'

CHAPTER TWELVE

In Khami, Daniel could smell uncertainty in the air. It showed on the faces of the people and in the dejected demeanour of the normally proud Matabele warriors. Without a King they lacked a focal point for their fierce loyalty. In a desperate bid to keep the army together, their Indunas led them on an ever-increasing number of raids against surrounding tribes. But such diversions were not sufficient to prevent a number of bloody clashes between impis led by rival royal sons. One solution would have been to send each impi to a different region of the country until a King had been chosen, but the sons were reluctant to leave the capital for anything other than a morale-boosting raid against the Mashonas.

Daniel was quick to perceive the problems of the Matabele, but his first unhappy task was to return Victoria to her mother and inform the Herero tribeswoman that her husband was dead.

It was a difficult duty. Mary Speke had never felt at home among the Matabele. Now, with her husband gone, she felt her isolation more keenly than ever before. Daniel promised to guarantee her future, whether she decided to remain in Khami, or return to her native village in South West Africa, but it was doubtful whether the distraught widow listened to his words.

Her howls of grief quickly drove him from the house and he left Victoria to comfort her mother and tell her as much, or as little, as she wished of the events leading to Sam Speke's death.

Daniel found his partner in the store. Aaron had heard from Andreus Van Niekerk of Sam Speke's death and the news cast a pall over the success of Daniel's trip to the east coast. Eventually, the conversation turned to other matters and Aaron told Daniel of the difficulties he had been facing since the death of Mzilikazi.

'Difficulties, I say? Daniel, you wouldn't believe me if I told you the half of them. Things have changed here – and nothing for the better. The Matabele are edgy. Their concern is understandable. Some of the Europeans in this land have spent years behind bars. They'll be in prison again if the British or Transvaal authorities ever catch up with them. I'm not sure we did the right thing when we moved here, Daniel. Oh yes! I know we've made money from trading – good money too. But if things go on the way they are we'll lose the lot – our lives too. The country is fast becoming an unofficial penal colony.'

In spite of Aaron's pessimism, Daniel quickly learned that the shrewd old Jew had still succeeded in making a handsome profit on all their trading transactions during Daniel's absence. There was competition now, where there had been none before, but the new traders usually arrived with no more than a wagonload of goods to sell. Permits were being issued to whoever was able to pay the standing fee of fifteen pounds sterling, a bag of black gunpowder and a box of percussion caps, but the Indunas were adamant that the newcomers must not build houses, or even huts for themselves. All their business was being conducted from wagons.

Trading was bearable in the warm, dry, winter months, but with the rainy season at hand, all but the hardiest traders had called it a day and returned to more civilised parts. Aaron had bought up the stock of four such fair-weather traders, purchasing their wagons at bargain prices. These would be sold to ivory hunters next season – at a handsome profit, of course.

Later that night, as they enjoyed a drink together in the store and the rain beat a vigorous tattoo on the roof, Daniel told Aaron of Elvira. It was not easy. As he spoke, it seemed that the smiling ghost of Hannah, Aaron's daughter crept into the room to haunt them both, as she had haunted Daniel for so many years.

When Daniel told Aaron that he intended marrying the Portuguese Captain General's daughter, the old trader rose to his feet and hugged Daniel. There were tears in his eyes as he said, 'What can I say, Daniel? I am as happy for you as though you were my own son. She sounds just the girl for you. It's not good for a man to be alone for so long. A few more years and you'd grow to be like me. My Hannah would never have wanted that for you. I must meet this Elvira of yours. If we can find someone trustworthy to leave in charge of the store I'll come with you when you return to Sena.'

Talking about Elvira brought her closer to Daniel, but he knew it would be many months before he was able to return to Sena. Until the rains ended, the rivers would be swollen and impassable, while the short, dry grass of winter would soon be as tall as a man, its razor-edged stems sharp enough to lay open a man's arm, or a horse's leg. Until the dry season returned it was doubtful whether a messenger would get through with news of Elvira's recovery from her bullet wound.

The next day Daniel was summoned to the mission station outside the kraal by the Reverend Farewell Loveday.

When he walked into the little room used by the missionary as an office, Farewell Loveday was seated behind an elegant rosewood desk. Incongruous in its present setting, the desk had once enhanced the study of an East Anglian Bishop's palace. The missionary had been waiting for Daniel and he came straight to the point. 'It's been brought to my notice that you don't have a permit to be in Matabeleland.'

'No . . . and I don't intend applying for one. When I came to Matabeleland the only permission a man needed was the King's word and every man knew it had been given. If you were found in the country without it you were killed. That's the way things were when you came to Matabeleland too, remember? You asked me to use my influence with Mzilikazi on your behalf.'

The Reverend Farewell Loveday had the grace to look embarrassed, but it was a fleeting emotion.

'There was a despot on the throne then, Retallick. Now he's dead. We have a golden opportunity to bring some order to this land. To teach these poor people the advantages of progress and religion.'

'Perhaps you'll teach me at the same time,' Daniel retorted. 'From what I hear, all you've done is to put the Matabele at the mercy of the sweepings of the world's prisons.'

Farewell Loveday flushed angrily. 'I doubt if such an opinion was expressed by a Christian. Come to the mission church any Sunday and you'll meet the "sweepings of the world's prisons", as you call them. With their more enlightened Matabele brethren they will be praising the Lord's name – and it's only a beginning. Now that Kulumani's been found . . . .'

'Kulumani found? I thought he was dead.'

'So did a great many people. I'm pleased to say he's alive and well. Kulumani has been working for Theophilus Shepstone, Secretary for Native Affairs in Natal. What's more, he's had the benefit of Christian teaching.'

Armed with the information Jandu had given to him, Daniel was inclined to greet Farewell Loveday's news with some scepticism. However, Umnombati was an old man. He might well have been romanticising about his part in an event that would have been on the tongue of every tribal rumour-monger when he was a young man.

'Kulumani will need more than Christian teaching if he's to rule the Matabele and survive. He'll need the strength of his father and will have to become skilled in the politics of both the Boer and British governments, as well as those of his tribe. At least he'll have the advantage of speaking English. What's his job with Shepstone, interpreter?'

Farewell Loveday looked suddenly ill-at-ease, 'No . . . . he's a garden boy.' Aware of Daniel's expression of astonishment, he added quickly. 'But he *is* Kulumani. Shepstone is quite certain . . . .'

'Of course he is!' Daniel laughed out loud. 'By God, Loveday, I've got to admire your nerve . . . yours *and* Shepstone's. What could be more convenient than to have a Matabele King who's used to taking orders from his European masters? Surely you and Shepstone could have given him some semblance of dignity? A garden boy . . . . ?'

Daniel's laughter ceased and he leaned across the desk to look down at Farewell Loveday. 'Do you take the Matabele for fools? Or are you deliberately setting out to cause trouble? You try to put your garden boy on Mzilikazi's throne and you'll start a war that will spill the blood of both Christian and heathen, and set back your "progress" fifty years. Is this what you want?'

'He *is* Kulumani,' insisted Farewell Loveday, doggedly. 'You'll see for yourself before many more days have passed. The Reverend Pugh-Williams went to Natal to bring Kulumani home to his tribe. He should be here soon.'

Daniel looked surprised. 'But I saw Mrs Pugh-Williams outside.'

'She didn't go with her husband. She hasn't been well.'

Farewell Loveday made the statement sound so aggressive that Daniel was immediately reminded of the Matabele rumours concerning Loveday and Helena Pugh-Williams. It helped to convince him that Farewell Loveday's plans for Matabeleland were not entirely theocratic. The missionary had ambitions that extended beyond the narrow confines of his church.

'We still haven't settled the matter of your permit. If you intend to remain in Matabeleland you'll need to have one—'

'You can give me one when your garden boy is crowned King of the Matabele,' said Daniel. 'Until then I'll go about my business as I've always done.'

On his way back to the store from the mission station, Daniel pondered on his next move. It was evident from the advanced stage of Farewell Loveday's plans that they had been carefully thought out. No hint that their long-lost 'Prince' was on his way to Khami had been given to the Matabele. The missionary must have been confident of Kulumani's imminent arrival, or he would not have broken the news to Daniel now.

Timing was important for the success of such an audacious scheme. The news of the coming of the new King had to be leaked so that the excitement of his 'subjects' would reach its height when he arrived. Riding the wave of popular acclaim, his coronation could be rushed through and the Natal garden boy proclaimed King before doubts could be aired about the authenticity of 'Kulumani's' claim to the throne of Matabeleland.

Daniel was particularly concerned about the British Government's involvement in the plot. He did not believe Theophilus Shepstone would have submitted his garden boy's claim without their approval. It could mean that the British were prepared to send troops to assist the garden-boy King if his authority were seriously challenged. No doubt such an eventuality had been considered – based, of course, on Farewell Loveday's derisive assessment of the Matabele as a fighting nation.

If such assistance were forthcoming, Daniel believed the British army would suffer their greatest defeat in African history. He shuddered at the thought. Somehow, the claimant to the Matabele throne had to be prevented from entering the country until his dubious credentials were thoroughly checked.

There was only one man who could do this.

Daniel reached Umnombati's kraal late that afternoon, after a difficult ride through the worst storm of the rainy season. Hilltop was joined to hilltop by jagged lightning, and the crashing echoes of thunder had Daniel's mount dancing with fear, it's ears twitching as peal followed noisy peal. For the whole of the journey rain fell in torrents that turned the countryside into a slippery quagmire.

Daniel was shown into Umnombati's hut immediately upon his arrival, the old Induna commenting that a man who rode through such a storm must be on a very urgent mission.

Daniel was wearing a cape, but so heavy was the rain that it had found its way inside, soaking every item of clothing he wore. The old Induna clicked his tongue in distress at Daniel's condition and called two of his wives to the hut to dry the visitor. One wife was almost as old as Umnombati himself. The other was a recent acquisition, and very young. Ignoring Daniel's protests, the aged Induna ordered the women to strip off his wet clothes and rub him dry before wrapping him in a blanket by the fire, with a giant-sized gourd of beer beside him.

As the two women carried out their task, the senior wife, aware that her age put her beyond any scandal, kept up a constant stream of ribald remarks. The younger woman allowed herself only an occasional giggle, but more than once she gave Daniel a bold glance that went further than the senior wife's bawdiness.

Umnombati was aware of both glances and remarks, but his only response was an occasional amused chuckle. When Daniel was seated comfortably close to the fire that glowed cheerily in the centre of the circular hut, Umnombati waved his womenfolk out.

Once they had gone, Daniel repeated what Farewell Loveday had told him, and Umnombati listened in silence. When Daniel had ended, the Induna gazed into the fire for so long that Daniel feared the old man's mind had wandered elsewhere. Then Umnombati turned expressionless eyes upon Daniel.

'Did the missionary tell you what this . . . "Kulumani" looked like?'

'No. Do you think he lies?'

'I *know* he lies.'

Through the smoke from the fire, Umnombati looked at Daniel but he was seeing another time. Another place.

'I knew Mzilikazi for more years than any other man. In all that time I never once failed him. That is why I lived when all others close to the King died.' Umnombati held out two bony hands, palms upward. They shook like corn in a wind. 'These two hands killed Kulumani. It was Mzilikazi's order. Afterwards I threw the body in the river and watched the crocodiles fight over it. If anyone says Kulumani lives he is a liar.'

'But what can you do? You can't tell the Tribal Council that you killed Kulumani. Too many Indunas are jealous of your power. They would have you executed.'

'Death is a young man's enemy, trader. I have walked beside him for too many years to have any fear left. If a man is coming here claiming to be Kulumani, I *must* tell the Council what I know . . . but it has not come to that yet.'

Umnombati looked at Daniel speculatively. 'Why have you come here to warn me of this? If the man who calls himself Kulumani is made King he will owe a great debt to the white man. Have you spent so long with the Matabele that you have become one of us?'

'Perhaps. It's a question I've asked myself many times. I think the answer is that when I first came to Matabeleland Mzilikazi gave me his hand in friendship. In return I have given my heart to his people.'

Umnombati nodded his head approvingly. 'I know this to be true, trader. Mzilikazi told me many times that you are the only white man whose word he never doubted. Because you are also a man whose thoughts go deep you will know that a false King would bring great trouble to our country – for both Matabele and the white man.'

'I know this, Umnombati. If there's anything I can do to help—'

'There is. I need to meet this man who says he is Kulumani, but I am too old to walk and I cannot sit a horse. You have a wagon?'

'Of course, but it will be slow going.'

Umnombati snorted. 'Time is not important. You have ridden here through the rain. If the false Kulumani is on the other side of the Shashi River he will not be able to cross for days. If he crossed before the rains then he would already be in Khami. I will send a messenger to have your wagon sent here. You shall come with me.'

Theophilus Shepstone's ex-garden boy had not crossed the Shashi River. When Daniel's wagon swayed down the slope to the river bank, 'Kulumani' and the Reverend Arnold Pugh-Williams were huddled in a damp camp on the far bank of the swollen river, together with a retinue of disgruntled Bechuana porters. The porters had been reluctant to undertake a trip to the land of the warlike Matabele in the first place. The sight of Umnombati's fifteen-hundred-strong impi – the largest in the Matabele army – setting up camp on the opposite bank of the river proved too much for them. Most of the Bechuanas stole away in the night, forfeiting their pay and stealing only what they could carry off.

It was two more days before the river dropped sufficiently to allow Umnombati to cross the river, borne on the shoulders of one of his strongest warriors. Daniel went with him.

Arnold Pugh-Williams was, for once, genuinely sick. He had a fever and stood on the river bank in his damp and crumpled clothes, shivering uncontrollably. Only the realisation that he had almost accomplished an historic mission kept him on his feet. He believed that Umnombati, as the senior Induna of the Matabele nation, had come to welcome the new King, bringing an impressive impi to escort him to the capital.

'Kulumani' was not so certain. He hung back, staying close to the fire. He had no fever, but he was shaking almost as much as the missionary. 'Kulumani' was not an impressive man, certainly not cast in the mould of the man whose son he claimed to be. Not more than five feet six inches in height, he had only one eye. The real Kulumani was known to be blind in one eye, too, but Umnombati declared that it was an affliction the Royal Prince had suffered from birth and that both his eyes had been intact at the time of his murder.

Set down on the river bank, Umnombati appeared frail and

vulnerable. He stood and looked at the pretender to the Matabele throne for long minutes, which did nothing to put 'Kulumani' at his ease. Then the aged Induna said he wished to speak to 'Kulumani' alone.

For the first time, Arnold Pugh-Williams realised that this was not the welcoming party he had thought it to be. He looked from his protégé to Umnombati in sudden dismay.

'Umnombati wants to be certain it *is* Kulumani,' lied Daniel, feeling sorry for the inept missionary. He was certain Pugh-Williams had been unwittingly drawn into the conspiracy to put Shepstone's garden boy on the Matabele throne. 'If he's satisfied, your man will be allowed to go on – and he'll have an impressive escort.'

'*If* he's satisfied? Theophilus Shepstone has said he's Kulumani. Are you doubting his word?'

Daniel shrugged. 'Shepstone is nothing to the Matabele. They are the ones who have to be convinced. I suggest you and I leave Umnombati alone with Kulumani. You look as though you could do with a strong dose of quinine and a dry bed.'

Arnold Pugh-Williams was in the habit of taking daily doses of quinine, in the belief that it was a preventative as well as a cure for fever. Unfortunately, his return journey to Natal had taken him a month longer than estimated and he had used up his supply. He was pathetically grateful when Daniel swam his horse across the river to return with quinine and a dry set of clothes.

His pleasure was short-lived. Even as he emerged from his tent wearing the borrowed clothing, the meeting between Umnombati and 'Kulumani' came to an end. Ignoring the missionary, Umnombati said to Daniel, 'We need remain here no longer. I wish to return to Khami and speak to the Council of Chiefs.'

Daniel glanced over the Induna's head, to where Pugh-Williams' protégé sat staring dejectedly into the cooking-fire. 'What of "Kulumani"?'

Umnombati spat on the ground at his feet. 'Kulumani, indeed!' He raised a hand to point towards the imposter. 'He is no King. He is not even a Matabele – although before he learned to dig in the ground for a white man, he was a child prisoner of the Zulus for many years. Ask him, he is eager to tell the truth now.'

Daniel looked for the missionary's reaction to the blunt statement – and leaped forward in time to catch Pugh-Williams as he slumped senseless to the ground.

Umnombati looked down at the unconscious figure. Dryly, he said, 'I don't doubt that the white man's God is as all-powerful as is claimed, trader – but I will never understand why he chooses men like this to fight his battles.'

'I'm afraid Pugh-Williams is a born loser,' agreed Daniel, as he laid the missionary on the ground and called for one of Umnombati's warriors to fetch a blanket from the mission-ary's tent. 'But how did you persuade "Kulumani" to change his story?'

Umnombati chuckled wickedly. 'I said I would take him to the river where I had thrown Kulumani's body to the croco-diles and tell my warriors to throw him in too. When he walked from the river unharmed I would kneel at his feet and swear that he was the true King. After all, can a crocodile eat a man twice? It was then he remembered his name is Charlie and that he should be in Natal, digging the ground of his white master.'

Umnombati arrived in Khami to scenes of great excitement. Believing the arrival of the new 'King' to be only days away, Farewell Loveday had released the news of his coming.

The inhabitants of Khami, eager to get a first glimpse of their new ruler swarmed from the town to meet the old Regent's wagon. They quickly learned the truth from the men of Umnombati's impi. Their first reaction was one of anger. But as the full story of the pretender's background emerged, the mood of the crowd changed to one of amusement that the missionaries could have believed such a man to be the missing Kulumani. In their naïvety they believed the missionaries had been duped. Umnombati was happy for them to accept such a story. Had they suspected it was part of a European plot to foist an imposter on them, not a white man would have been safe in the land.

On the way to Khami, the wagon halted to allow Arnold Pugh-Williams to be carried inside his mission house and placed in the bed where he had spent so much of his mission service. While Helena Pugh-Williams put on a great show of anxious concern, Farewell Loveday tackled Daniel. His anger was hardly in keeping with the humility attributed to those who spread the Lord's word among those in need of example.

'This is your doing, Retallick,' Farewell Loveday spat the words out, his face pale with subdued rage. 'You put Umnombati up to warning Kulumani off.'

'Umnombati makes up his own mind about such matters,' commented Daniel, amiably. 'I think he knows enough about the real Kulumani to realise that your man was an imposter.'

'You'll pay for this, one day. I'll make certain there isn't a European in the country who doesn't know that you've deliberately thrown away the best chance there will ever be to give them a secure future in this land.'

'You can say what you like . . . but I'd look to your own future. Arnold Pugh-Williams may be a poor specimen of a man but he's not a complete fool. He was delirious for much of the way here and seems to have it on his mind that there's something between you and his wife. I gather he's voiced his suspicions to the Bishop in Natal. I suggest you forget about Matabele politics and try a bit of praying.'

Daniel's warning alarmed Farewell Loveday. It was doubtful whether the mission authorities could prove anything against him, but they might withdraw him from the Khami mission station — and Farewell Loveday had too much at stake to leave Matabeleland now. He was convinced that the country would soon come under the protection of the British government. When that day arrived an Administrator would be needed who was familiar with the country and acceptable to its people. Farewell Loveday was determined to be that man.

His ambitions suffered a setback the following day. Umnombati called a meeting of all Indunas, both political and military. When Farewell Loveday put in an appearance, complete with bound notebook and pencil, there was a rumble of resentment from the military Indunas, always more ready to voice their opinions than their political counterparts.

Farewell Loveday explained that he was taking notes for the Queen of his own country, the 'Great White Mother', in order that she might better understand Matabele law and customs.

Umnombati declared that the Indunas had nothing to hide from any man — or any Queen. The missionary was welcome to remain and make his notes.

The Indunas sat in a great, loosely packed circle and listened as Umnombati told how he had spoken to the man who called himself Kulumani. He had satisfied himself beyond all doubt that the man was an imposter. He then spoke of the danger of allowing the Matabele nation to drift along without a King. As things stood at present, the nation had no sense of purpose, or direction, it's impis being free to raid and plunder at will. The old Induna declared that the Matabele must forget Kulumani. He was assuredly dead. They must elect a King from among Mzilikazi's many sons who had remained with the tribe, and whose ways they knew well.

There were those who disagreed with him. They stubbornly insisted that it must be Kulumani, or no one. However, the vast majority of the Indunas agreed with Umnombati. They realised that the Matabele were a young nation with few tribal traditions to fall back on. They needed a King to give the people guidance and put the heart back in the Matabele people.

The arguments raged back and forth for hours, until it began to emerge that the vast majority were swinging to Umnombati's side.

Finally, a satisfactory compromise was reached. A King should be chosen now. If Kulumani were not found within one year from the end of the rains, the new King would be confirmed in office.

Umnombati looked around the circle from man to man, his gaze not moving on until he had received a nod of agreement.

'Good!' Umnombati was well pleased. He had expected much stronger opposition to his idea. 'Now it only remains to choose which of Mzilikazi's sons shall take his father's place.'

A ripple of amusement ran through the gathering of Indunas at Umnombati's words. With so many sons eager to become King, this would undoubtedly be the hardest task of all.

First there came the process of elimination. This one would not suit because he had not yet proven himself in battle. That one because he favoured his mother's tribe. One of the first son's to be nominated was Mangwane, one of the elder Princes. Umnombati disclosed that Mangwane was at that moment being sought for execution, having been caught sleeping with one of the late Mzilikazi's young wives. According to Matabele law this was a crime akin to incest, the vilest of tribal crimes. The unfortunate widow, together with every one of her family, had already suffered the fate that awaited Mangwane.

As the merits and demerits of each candidate were discussed, two names recurred time and time again. It soon became apparent that the Matabele crown would pass to one of them. The names were Kanje – and Jandu.

This was the moment of truth. Both men were present and were fully aware that before the meeting broke up one of them would inherit the most powerful nation in Central Africa. The disappointed son could either pledge allegiance to his half-brother, or get as far away from Khami as he could in the shortest possible time. With the final choice of the tribe so finely balanced, the loser would pose a threat to the other for as long as he lived. The King-elect could not afford to rest until he was dead.

The issue was still not decided when Umnombati rose to his feet and began to relate the history of the Matabele nation. He began with Mzilikazi's break with Shaka, his Zulu overlord, forty years before. He described how Mzilikazi had led the Matabele to the land between the Shashi and Zambezi rivers, and reminded his listeners that in those earlier days victory was assured in battle for the leader with the most powerful army. North of the Orange River a man with a strong army was free to roam the face of Africa at will, harassing and conquering weaker tribes and settling wherever the land suited him. Since then the African way of life has changed dramatically. It was now the gun and not the spear that decided battles. Personal bravery and iron discipline were not enough. The new King must arm his armies to take their place in the changing world. He himself needed to be able to get along with the white man and gain his trust and friendship. Whether the Matabele liked it or not, the white man was moving in strength ever closer to Matabeleland's borders and would play an increasingly important part in the country's future . . . .

As Umnombati spoke, the sun sank beneath the rim of the

western hills. The flickering light from the fire illuminated faces that epitomised the vanishing Africa of which Umnombati was talking. This was a great indaba – a meeting of tribal Elders. A meeting at which they, and they alone, would decide the future of their own people. The power to make such decisions had already been taken away from many of the tribes to the south.

Only one man was insensitive to the poignancy of the historical moment . . . Farewell Loveday. He listened in increasing annoyance as Umnombati declared that the Matabele people needed a ruler who was aware of the changing pattern of Africa. A man so experienced with life that his head would control his heart. A man who had travelled beyond the borders of Matabeleland and seen the white man in his own home.

It soon became apparent that Umnombati was talking of Jandu. Farewell Loveday became dismayed at the increasing number of Indunas who nodded their agreement. Jandu was Daniel Retallick's friend. The missionary had pinned his hopes on Kanje being made King of the Matabele. Finally, he could keep silent no longer.

'Before you make up your minds you must consider that Jandu is an older man, already set in his ways. Kanje is young. Aware of the needs of his people. He knows many of the white men in your country now . . . . British and Afrikaans. He's respected by them.'

The icy silence with which his interruption was received finally registered with Farewell Loveday. He realised he had committed a grave breach of protocol. 'It's a personal point of view . . . a white man's opinion. I thought you would like to know.'

Umnombati turned his head first one way, and then another before he spoke.

'Has a dog come to play in our kraal and disturb a meeting of men? Surely not. It must have been the yapping of a jackal.'

Farewell Loveday burned with anger at the old Induna's insults.

'I should have asked permission before I spoke—'

'There it is again,' said Umnombati. 'My old ears caught the sound that time. It is nothing. No more than a white man's mule breaking wind. He has not the stomach for Matabele fare. But a mule cannot be taught good manners. Move closer to the fire and it will probably go away.'

Chuckling at Umnombati's insults, the Indunas moved to form a more tightly knit circle about the fire, leaving Farewell Loveday outside. Red-faced and angry he rose to his feet and stalked away, the bound ledger clutched tightly beneath his arm.

Kanje left the circle of Indunas at the same time. He was equally angry, but he concealed his feelings more successfully than Farewell Loveday. Only a few Indunas noticed him leave the fireside. One of them was Jandu. The King-elect had hoped that his half-brother would accept him as King. Now he knew he would one day have to fight and kill him.

CHAPTER THIRTEEN

Daniel heard the news of the Indunas' choice of Mzilikazi's successor the next morning and hurried off to congratulate Jandu. He found the King-elect inside the enclosure of his house. Shielded from prying eyes by a high, reed fence, Jandu was having his early morning bath, aided by Suliyana. About them relays of female slaves brought wooden buckets filled with water which they poured over the head of their master.

'I'm happy for you and the Matabele people,' said Daniel. 'The Indunas have made a wise choice. Now they have the leader the nation has been waiting for.'

He meant every word. It would be more than a year before the ceremony that would officially make Jandu King, but he would begin guiding the nation's destiny long before then. His advice would be sought by the Council of Indunas and no important decisions would be taken without his express approval.

'I suppose that now I am to be a King you will expect me to honour my debts, trader? I owe you a hundred head of cattle for Suliyana. She can hardly become my chief wife until I have paid the bride-price.'

Jandu was in a jovial mood and Daniel responded in similar vein. 'Perhaps you should wait until you're certain you'll keep her.' There was little fear of the remark causing offence. It was evident to everyone that Jandu and Suliyana were very happy together. She would become Chief Wife, and, as such, hold a powerful position in the land. Ruler of the King's household, she would organise the busy daily routine, maintaining a firm control over the other wives and be at the heart of all affairs of state. Daniel had no doubt at all that the daughter of uTshwebe would perform her duties well.

'Jandu will keep me,' said Suliyana, confidently. 'I will give him many sons. The Matabele will never be in any doubt about their next King.'

His ablutions completed, Jandu said, 'Come with me and

choose your cattle, trader. You will need herd boys – and grazing land. Do you have any place in mind?'

Daniel remembered the valley he had seen on his return journey from Sena. It was no more than two days ride from Khami. He told Jandu about the valley, adding that it was the most beautiful place he had ever seen.

Jandu nodded his understanding. 'My country is full of such places. I have seen many of them and never fail to marvel at such beauty.' He made a snap decision. 'Come, we will choose your cattle now and I will find you some Matabele herd boys. Then you and I will take the cattle to this valley you have found. No – it is not a matter for argument. When I am King I will rarely go beyond the bounds of my royal enclosure. I must make the most of the time I have left to me.'

When Daniel told Aaron he would be away from Khami for a few days, Aaron muttered that he might as well be trading on his own again. There was some justification for his complaint. A surprising amount of trade was coming in for the time of year. Many hunters had been taking full advantage of the present easy-to-come-by pass system in the belief that it would come to an end when a new King took the throne. Unable to ship their ivory and ostrich feathers out of the country because of high rivers and impassable roads, they were happy to sell them to Retallick and Copping.

'Look at these tusks,' said Aaron, pointing to a pile of first-class ivory. 'Each of them weighs at least eighty pounds. Should I have to move them by myself? Better I should have a sleeping partner. At least I could wake him when things get busy – but don't you worry about me. You go off and play with cattle in your valley. I'll wear myself out to see that we still have a trading company when you return.'

In spite of his grumbling, Aaron enjoyed haggling with the hunters. He also appreciated the good fortune the company would enjoy now that Jandu had succeeded his father. Had it been Kanje, Retallick and Copping would have been loading the contents of their store upon wagons, bidding farewell to Matabeleland for ever, leaving Boer traders to fight over their business.

Daniel selected a hundred prime cattle from Jandu's herds and purchased a fine, deep-chested bull to run with them. The

Matabele herd boys had been personally selected by Jandu and were aware of the honour accorded them. Twenty in number, they were accompanied by thirty captured Mashona boys. This small force would be expected to guard Daniel's cattle against thieves and predators – sacrificing their own lives if the need arose.

To his consternation, Daniel learned that the whole of Jandu's impi would accompany them to the valley, although he was quick to appreciate the necessity for such a large escort. Kanje and his supporters would dearly love to put Jandu out of the way. Only a large escort would deter them. As Jandu explained rather sadly to Daniel, his days of travelling alone, or with only a close friend, were over. He was now the most important person in the land, his every word and deed observed and commented upon by the Matabele people.

When they arrived at the valley Daniel had chosen for his cattle, Jandu was able to relax somewhat. After posting look-outs on the surrounding hills, he and Daniel set out to explore the valley. Jandu agreed immediately that it was a most attractive spot. 'This is a garden of the Gods, trader – an "Insimo" indeed.'

Daniel liked the name. It exactly summed up the feeling he had for the valley – the Insimo Valley.

That night they set up camp close to a waterfall. The water tumbled down a near vertical cliff-face to a clear, rock pool, surrounded by flowering trees and shrubs, the scent of which filled the evening air. It was a beautifully sheltered spot, yet from here one had a view that encompassed the whole of the valley and the panorama of the low-veldt beyond.

Daniel lit his pipe and stood watching the colours of the landscape darken and merge one into another as night advanced over the continent of Africa.

'You think deep thoughts, trader?' Jandu spoke the words softly as he stood beside Daniel.

'Not so deep. I was wondering what more a man could want if he had a house here and could gaze out upon this view every night?'

'He would find something more to seek . . . but such a man would indeed have much to envy. Tell me, when do you marry your Portuguese girl?'

'I hope to return to Sena as soon as the rains cease. If she is well enough and her father agrees, I will marry her then.'

'Her father will accept you as a son.' Jandu placed a reassuring hand on Daniel's shoulder. 'But it will be many months before you bring a wife to Matabeleland. Use that time well, my friend. Build a house for her . . . here, on this very spot. You have fallen in love with the valley – I give it to you. From hill-top to hill-top. It is yours for as long as I am welcome in your house. You will rule this valley, just as I rule the remainder of Matabeleland.'

Daniel found it difficult to grasp that he had just been given two hundred square miles of land, 'But . . . but I'm a trader, not a farmer.'

Jandu pointed to where the hundred cattle were being driven inside a hastily erected thorn-bush pen. 'By this time next year you will have twice as many cattle and you will be as concerned for them as though they were your own children. Tell me then that you are only a trader. You have a partner who can run your store. Where would you rather bring a young wife? To Khami, or to this valley? No, you have no need to answer. Build a splendid house, give her many women-servants to keep her company while you are away from home and she will stay happy.'

Daniel was overwhelmed by Jandu's great generosity, but when he tried to stammer his thanks, Jandu said simply, 'Friends do not need to express gratitude as do other men. Giving is all part of friendship.'

Before Daniel could think of an adequate reply, Jandu turned and walked off into the night.

On the return journey to Khami, Daniel's mind was full of thoughts and plans for the valley Jandu had given to him, but he found an unexpected matter awaiting his attention when he arrived at the store.

Andreus Van Niekerk was in the back room with Aaron. Both men were drinking, but the Boer was not drunk. When he spoke he was surprisingly subdued and polite.

'I'm sorry to trouble, you, Daniel. There's a little matter I'd like to discuss with you. It's . . . rather personal.'

Aaron took the broad hint. Downing his drink he stood up, a trifle unsteadily, Daniel thought.

'All right. All right. I'm just going. Oi! What sort of part-nership is this? He goes . . . I have to stay in the store. He sets foot in the store again and has hardly bid me "Good day" before I'm told I'm not wanted – and that by a brandy-swilling Boer who's sat here for two days emptying bottles without paying me a penny piece. Perhaps one day my partner will sit down with me and we'll talk about business together.'

Daniel stood to one side as Aaron made his way to the door with exaggerated care. Aaron was no drinker . . . neither was he used to spending time trading over a store counter, his evenings taken up with compiling ledgers and making labo-rious lists of shortages and future trading requirements. Most of Aaron's life had been spent in an ox-wagon. It had been his home, his shop, and his passport to wherever trade and the whim took him. Aaron was a true descendant of his biblical namesake. He was a wanderer who would never find his promised land. His pleasure was in the seeking. He had remained at Khami for many months during Daniel's journey to the east coast and he was restless to be on the move.

It was the first time Daniel had seen his partner even slightly drunk and he spoke to Van Niekerk more abruptly than he intended. 'What is it you want? Couldn't it have waited until I had time to come home and sort out my own business?'

'I'm sorry. I know I'm being a damned nuisance, man, but it really can't wait. I should have left here two days ago, but I've stayed to see you first. You see, I've had a letter from the manager of my company. He's told me to forget the gold mines in Manicaland. It seems the Portuguese are raising a fuss. They claim it's their territory and my company aren't prepared to argue. Instead I'm to go straightaway to Tati. Gold has been found there and some prospectors have already struck it very rich. I'm to prospect and peg claims on behalf of my company.'

Tati was a few miles on the Matabele side of the Shashi River. Although claimed by both the Matabele and Bechuana, the area was not considered to be worth fighting over. As a result, it had become a 'no-man's land'. The discovery of gold might well change all that.

'I wish you luck,' said Daniel. 'But what does this have to do with me? I don't care where you prospect.'

'I'll be taking Victoria with me,' Van Niekerk said. 'I hoped you might speak to her mother for me. See if there's anything she wants ... I mean, I know she's only a kaffir, but I understand she was properly married to Victoria's father. With his death and Victoria going off with me I thought things might be hard for her. I'd like to help, if I can.'

Andreus Van Niekerk's news and his confusing mixture of emotions took Daniel by surprise. It had been no secret on the journey from Manicaland that Van Niekerk fancied Victoria, but she had shown only contempt for the Boer – or had she? Daniel remembered how she had given him her father's gun at the very moment when she might have thoroughly humiliated him. Daniel thought, not for the first time, that he would never understand women. As for Van Niekerk's concern for Mary Speke—! It was so out of keeping with Daniel's assessment of the Boer's character that he could only believe this meeting was one of Victoria's conditions for going off with Van Niekerk.

'What do you want me to tell Mary Speke? That you're taking her daughter to live in a camp full of prospectors, every one of whom will look on her as easy meat – just as you did on the way from Manicaland? Or perhaps you're going to marry her?'

'I can't marry her, you know that. I'm a Boer, my home is in Transvaal – and she's a baster. But I won't have any jaapies hanging round her. I'll look after her well, man. That's a promise.'

Daniel knew that Van Niekerk's promises would fade with every mile he put between himself and Khami. He was not happy at the thought of Victoria going off with the Boer to the goldfields of Tati. He could abandon her whenever he wished. But anything Daniel said to either Van Niekerk, or Victoria, would be wasted. If they had both made up their minds he could exert no pressure on them.

'I'll speak to Mary,' he said. 'But she's in no need of anything. Sam was a careful man. He's left enough behind to keep his family for the rest of their lives. When are you and Victoria setting out?'

'In the morning. I've been all packed ready to move for two days.'

'I'll see you before then, but don't expect me to bring you Mary Speke's blessing. Victoria is her only daughter.'

Daniel met Victoria coming out of the Speke house. She was red-eyed, as though she had been crying, but she looked at Daniel defiantly. 'If you're here to try to talk me out of going with Andreus to Tati, you can save your breath.'

'I realise that. I'm here to talk to Mary. To see if there's anything she wants. It's Van Niekerk's idea – but his concern doesn't extend to wanting her for a mother-in-law.'

'If it did she'd be asking him for lobola . . . .' Victoria fought against tears as she struggled to regain her composure. 'It's no good talking to her, Daniel. She's in there sitting on the floor in a corner of the room, singing a Herero mourning song. She's been like it ever since I came back from Manicaland. I can't stand it any more. It's as though she's never been married to a white man. I think she really *has* forgotten what chairs and tables and beds are for. I've asked her a hundred times a day what she wants and I get the same answer every time. She wants to go back to Hereroland. Once there she'll be able to forget Dad, forget she's ever had me and live like a tribeswoman until the day she dies.'

'I'll see she gets home,' Daniel spoke more gently to Victoria 'But do you think it's right to leave her now? When she's like this?'

'What would you like me to do? Go back with her and live like a Herero woman myself? Marry some old man and dig his fields and clean his pots with nothing to look forward to but the night when it's my turn to have him in my bed? Is that what you want for me, Daniel? If it is then you should have thought about it years ago – you and Dad. Instead of letting me come with you both wherever you went. Letting me ride horses and shoot guns. Allowing me to believe I belonged to your world. Treating me as though I were a white girl—'

Victoria choked on her words and now she could no longer control her tears. She turned to run but Daniel caught her arm and pulled her to him. With his arms about her, she clung to him fiercely, sobbing as though her heart would break, for many minutes.

When he thought she could hear him, Daniel said softly, 'You don't have to go to Hereroland – or to Tati with Van Niekerk. I'm building a place in a valley only two days ride from here. Come and live there. You'll be able to lead the life you've always known, with as much riding and hunting as you want. It's a wonderful place, Victoria . . . we saw it on the way to Khami, remember? You'll have a good life.'

Victoria pushed herself away from Daniel reluctantly. 'Your Portuguese bride will be there too, won't she? Do you think I could ever be happy watching you together? No – and I doubt whether she'll want to be tripping over me and my bastard all day.'

'Elvira will welcome your company. It's a beautiful place, but lonely. Think about it, Victoria . . . please.'

Victoria shook her head sadly. 'You really *don't* understand, do you? Only a few months ago I would have gone with you anywhere in the world. Things are different now – we both know that. I'm going with Andreus to Tati. Be sure to call on us if ever you're that way.'

'What does Van Niekerk say about the baby?'

The tears had been wiped away now, and Victoria looked at Daniel defiantly. 'He doesn't know. When it comes I'll tell him it's his.'

'You'll do that? He'll never believe you.'

'He'll believe me. I made certain of that on the way back from Manicaland . . . while you were off hunting.'

The admission shocked Daniel. For a few moments, while she was crying in his arms, he might have been holding the girl he had known since childhood. But this was not the girl he thought he knew as well as any sister. Victoria had changed.

'You couldn't have known anything about Van Niekerk going to Tati, not before we reached Khami.'

Victoria shrugged. 'No. I was hoping he'd take me to Cape Town with him. Oh, I know Andreus Van Niekerk isn't the greatest catch in the world and I'm not going to keep him for ever, but he maintains *some* of the standards I'm used to. He'll do for now.'

Daniel opened his mouth to speak, but Victoria cut him short. 'There's nothing more to be said . . . and I have a lot to do.'

She suddenly stood on tiptoe and kissed him briefly on the mouth. 'Goodbye, Daniel.' She gave him a thin, controlled smile. 'Forget what I've just said. Remember me as I was before I met Mariano – and before you met your Elvira.'

Victoria turned away abruptly and hurried to the enclosure where the horses were kept, leaving Daniel staring after her.

His thoughts were no clearer when he left Mary Speke. As Victoria had said, it was as though Sam Speke had never come into her life and talking of Victoria meant nothing to her. It was as though her daughter had never been born. Her mind had blotted out the happiness she had known for half a lifetime. Unable to cope with the tragic loss of her husband, Mary had turned instinctively to the familiar pattern of Herero life. She wanted to go back to Otjimkandje, the Herero village in South West Africa, where she would be among family and friends. Daniel promised her she would be taken home as soon as was possible.

Daniel and Aaron were discussing the matter that evening when Andreus Van Niekerk came back to the store. Aaron looked at him questioningly. 'I thought you were in a hurry to rush off to your goldfield? What do you want of me now? I should go for a walk – or pour you a brandy?'

Andreus Van Niekerk had not been blessed with a sense of humour. 'You can stay . . . but I'd like a drink.'

Van Niekerk appeared agitated and, when he had downed half the glass of brandy handed to him by Aaron, he blurted out his reason for coming to the store. 'You've been good to me, so I've come to warn you. You'd better get out of Khami, while you have the chance. There's going to be trouble.'

'What sort of trouble?' Daniel frowned, wondering whether Van Niekerk had been drinking before coming to the store.

'Big trouble, man! There's going to be a war. Kanje is going to kill Jandu and take over the Matabele tribe. A Boer commando of about fifty men and some Griquas have come up from Transvaal to help him. You'd better get out with whatever you can carry, while there's still time.'

Daniel eyed Andreus Van Niekerk suspiciously. 'How do you know about this?'

'Jan Potgieter is leading the commando. He's a cousin of mine. He's sent someone to warn me and to ask how many Boers are in Matabeleland. He wants them to join him. The messenger left Khami not half an hour ago.'

Now Daniel believed the Boer. 'What did you tell him?'

'I told him not to be a fool. That most white men in Matabeleland are English, like yourself. He'll get no help from anyone here.'

Andreus Van Niekerk downed the second half of his drink. 'Jan won't listen. He's from my mother's side of the family. Once they get an idea in their heads it takes the kick of a horse to shake it loose.'

'Where's Potgieter now?'

'Somewhere in the Matopos Hills, that's all I know.'

The Matopos was an area of massive, granite hills and deep valleys, a few miles south of Khami. There were also huge caves and forests where an army might hide without fear of detection. It was a good place from which to launch a surprise attack on Khami. It was also ideal country in which to set an ambush.

Leaving Aaron to replenish Van Niekerk's glass, Daniel hurried away in search of Jandu.

CHAPTER FOURTEEN

When Daniel rode into the valley camp of Jan Potgieter soon after daybreak two days later, there was consternation among the newly awakened Boer adventurers. They had chosen their camp-site well. In the very heart of the Matopos, the valley was steep-sided and had only one narrow entrance, easily guarded from the heights on either side.

'Who are you? What are you doing here?' The questions were in Afrikaans and a squat, thick-set man stalked to where Daniel slid easily from his horse. 'I should have known better than to leave two Griquas on guard together. They'd go to sleep if you fired a musket three feet away from them.'

Daniel doubted whether the Griqua sentries would hear a cannon fired alongside them now. They had been silenced by Jandu's men before daybreak.

'I heard you were on your way to help Kanje against his brother. I've come here to suggest you change your mind.'

'You've come? Who are you?'

'Daniel Retallick. I live in Khami.'

Jan Potgieter spat his contempt on the ground at Daniel's feet. 'I've heard of you. You're a kaffir-boetje.'

The term was a Boer insult, intimating that Daniel loved natives more than his own people. It had been levelled at Daniel on more than one occasion by disgruntled Boers.

'You've worked to keep us out of Matabeleland for years and now you've thrown in with Kanje's brother, eh? Well, you're out of luck, Retallick. Kanje is going to take over the Matabele tribe and he'll be helped by Transvaalers. You English have moved as far north as you're going.'

'All you'll succeed in doing is stir up a war that will spill over into the Transvaal. Jandu has been elected King of the Matabele by the full Council of Indunas. He's backed by an army of more than thirty thousand men.'

The gasp of incredulity from the listening Boers told Daniel that they had not been given a true picture of the situation in Matabeleland before they left Transvaal.

Jan Potgieter scowled. 'You're lying. Farewell Loveday agrees with Kanje. The army will come over to his side when they see that we're backing him.'

The mention of the Reverend Farewell Loveday made it clear that this was more than a desperate attempt by Kanje to seize the leadership of the Matabele nation. It was a plot that went much deeper than the personal jealousy of half-brothers. No doubt, before Farewell Loveday had put forward the idea, he had ensured that it was backed, unofficially or otherwise, by the unsophisticated Boer government of the Transvaal.

Jan Potgieter cleared his throat and spat at the ground again. 'Agh! What does it matter. There's going to be a fight between two kaffirs. One is friendly to me, so I help him. Who's going to complain about that, eh?'

Instead of replying, Daniel drew his rifle from the saddle holster and fired a single shot in the air. At the sudden noise, the Boer horses, tethered nearby, whinnied in fright, tugging on the long slip-rope to which they were all attached.

'What do you think you doing, man? If that's some form of signal—!'

'It *is* a signal. I thought you'd like to see a small part of the army that will fight Kanje – and you, if you support him. Take a look up at the ridge.'

'Jesus Cristus!' The oath came from one of the Boers and there were gasps of disbelief from the others. The next moment there was a rush for the muskets scattered about the camp. On the hills all about the valley, Matabele warriors had appeared, carrying shields and weapons. At very short notice, Jandu had still been able to muster four impis, a total of about four thousand men. They now occupied every ridge about the valley, deliberately deployed to achieve the maximum dramatic effect.

At a raised-arm signal from Jandu, the impis began beating their shields with the knobkerries each man carried. The sound bounced off the steep valley walls, echoing and re-echoing in a rising crescendo.

'These are only a few of Jandu's warriors,' Daniel was grim-faced. 'The rest are on their way here to fight you . . . and they're backed by every white hunter in the country.'

'Hell, Jan, we didn't come here to take on the whole

Matabele nation by ourselves,' one of Jan Potgieter's men voiced the opinion of his companions.

'Shut up!' Potgieter rounded on the man, but he too had been shaken by the sheer numbers of the Matabele on the hill-tops. He had only fifty Boers and about eighty Griquas. The secure valley in which he was camped had suddenly become an indefensible death-trap. If the Matabele attacked down the steep valley slopes their very momentum would carry them through the Boers. But they had no need to risk their own lives. They could sit up on the ridge and pick his men off as though they were rats in a bran tub.

Turning to Daniel, Potgieter said, 'All right. You're calling the tune. What do you want us to do?'

'Pile your guns in the middle of the valley, then ride out of here and don't return. If you do, the Matabele army will chase you all the way back to Transvaal – and beyond. You've got homes and womenfolk there, think of them.'

'You're sending us out through the Matabele without guns? Man, they'll slaughter us.'

'They'll slaughter you if you stay. Do as I say. I'm giving you Jandu's promise of safe conduct to the border. You'll live to tell your grandchildren how a "kaffir" keeps his word.'

Reluctantly, Jan Potgieter ordered his men to throw down their guns. When Jandu saw what was happening, he held his shield high in the air. Immediately, the drumming ceased and the silence that followed was more awesome than the earlier din.

Without their weapons, the tough Boers felt denuded. They lost no time in forming up and following Potgieter out of the valley. Only the Griquas looked fearfully over their shoulders as they went.

Daniel watched them ride off with a sense of great relief. Jandu had won the first battle in the Matabele war of succession without a shot being fired. Of even more importance, the immediate danger of Boer involvement had receded. But something would have to be done about the Reverend Farewell Loveday, before he plunged the whole country into a war that would have repercussions far beyond the borders of Matabeleland.

To Daniel's surprise, when he suggested to Jandu that he

should close the mission station, the Matabele King-elect shook his head. 'I cannot do this. My father permitted your people to build a mission in my country. He gave his word to Loveday that he might stay in Matabeleland as long as he wishes. Can I break the word of Mzilikazi?'

'No, but you can follow Mzilikazi's example. He allowed the missionaries in, but refused to allow them to preach to the Matabele people. You could make life so difficult for Farewell Loveday that he would have to pack up and go.'

Jandu smiled. 'You are my friend, trader. I too have thought of this. When I am King my first order will be to move my kraal many miles from here. The mission, of course, was given permission only to come to Khami. I will not order them to go, but they will see no Matabele. Only empty hills and the scavenging animals who take over deserted kraals.'

'That's an astute move, Jandu. Worthy of Mzilikazi himself. But first we have to keep you alive until you are proclaimed King.'

For a while, it seemed that Kanje's challenge to Jandu had ended with the ignominious retreat of Jan Potgieter's commando from Matabeleland. Kanje took his dissident impi off to the unhealthy swampland about the upper reaches of the Zambezi river, on Matabeleland's northern border. From here he harassed the Makololo tribes across the great river, and occasionally led his men against the northern villages of the Mashona.

The problem of Farewell Loveday also came to a temporary halt. The politically ambitious missionary was recalled to Cape Town to answer to the charges brought against·him by Arnold Pugh-Williams. Incongruously, accuser and accused, together with Helena Pugh-Williams, the subject of the inquiry, all travelled southwards together in two ox-wagons. Arnold Pugh-Williams had not recovered from the bout of malaria that had laid him low, and had to be carried to his wagon to begin the twelve-hundred-mile, bone-jarring journey to the Cape.

With immediate problems out of the way, Daniel was impatient for the end of the rainy season. He wanted to return to Sena. In the meantime he supervised the building of a substantial stone house in the Insimo valley, and also bought in a record amount of ivory and ostrich feathers.

Aaron took a great interest in Daniel's valley home. At his suggestion, Daniel incorporated a store behind the house. Aaron would not be at Khami to see the project reach completion. He had volunteered to make the long journey to South West Africa with Mary Speke, taking half the trade goods with him. He set off many weeks before the rainy season came to an end. Travelling westwards, across the arid Kalahari Desert, any rain he encountered would be a blessing, not a disaster.

With Aaron gone, Daniel became more impatient than ever to leave for Sena. The house was well on the way to completion. The roof was on and only the fitting out of the interior remained.

At the end of February one of the herd boys came to Daniel and reported that a lion had attacked his cattle, killing a cow that was heavy in calf and dragging her body away to the long grass close to one of the small rivers that flowed off the hillside.

When Daniel asked why the herd boy and his companions had not driven the animal away before it was able to charge in among the cattle and make its kill, the herd boy turned around with some pride. Three deep, bloody furrows were gouged in his back, extending from shoulder to waist.

The young herd boy, no more than eleven years of age, had been with an older boy guarding the cattle when a lioness rose from her hiding place and made a bold charge into the midst of the cattle.

The older boy turned and ran, but the younger boy was made of sterner stuff. Armed with only a lightweight spear he struck at the lioness as she tore at the cow's windpipe.

The spear glanced off a bone in the great cat's rear leg, but it diverted her from her gory task for a moment. Turning on her young attacker, she dabbed a paw at him in reproach and, much as a cat gathers in a doomed mouse, pulled him to her.

Fortunately, at that moment the badly injured cow made a desperate attempt to struggle to her feet. The lioness turned on her once more, leaving the dazed herd boy to crawl away with the memory of a lion's hot breath on his face, and three scars on his back to proclaim his bravery.

After the young herd boy had shown him the place where the

attack had taken place, Daniel sent him back to Khami with a note for Jandu. The note would be read and translated by one of the Europeans staying there. In it Daniel detailed the bravery of the boy and suggested he should be rewarded by being taken into one of the Matabele training regiments, an ambition the boy might not otherwise achieve for another three years.

When the boy had left him, Daniel followed the spoor of the lioness through the lush grass. The trail was not hard to see, the cow had bled profusely. A few hundred yards from the scene of the attack, the trail led to a thick clump of undergrowth in the shadow of a tower of balancing rocks.

Daniel scouted all sides of the rock tower without picking up the trail of the lioness again and he knew the animal was still in the undergrowth – probably watching him at this very moment! The thought of it sent tingles up the back of his neck, but he could not allow the lioness to escape now. She had learned how easy it was to kill cattle. She would feed on nothing else until his hundred cows were gone. She had to be killed.

To go into the undergrowth was suicidal. Daniel decided that the only hope of seeing the lioness was to climb the rocks and look down on the area that was in shadow.

Climbing the rocks presented no problem. Carefully and silently, Daniel scaled them from the far side of the undergrowth. Once at the top he crawled out along a huge, flat rock until he was over the thick, tangled bushes. To his annoyance, he found that due to the overhang of one of the lower rocks he could see no more than half the area of undergrowth.

Daniel decided he must go lower. He climbed down until eventually he was no more than nine feet from the ground – no height at all to an attacking lioness!

Gingerly, he edged his way along the rock until he could see down into the undergrowth – and almost immediately below him he saw his dead cow. She had been ripped open and meat taken from the belly.

No sooner had he made this discovery than he became aware of a sound that had been present all along, but which he had erroneously dismissed as the drone of insect noises along the nearby river. It was a deep, regular, happy sound – the purring of a contented lioness!

Daniel froze. The lioness had to be close . . . very close, yet he could not see her. He scanned the undergrowth inch by inch until finally he came to a spot immediately below him that appeared to be a patch of dry grass in the deepest shadow. He was standing on a narrow ledge of rock, no more than twelve inches wide and was actually looking between his feet at the 'grass', when it moved and a pair of languid tawny eyes looked up at him.

With a grunt of disbelief the lioness scrambled to her feet and for a brief moment hesitated before springing. In that instant Daniel fired. Leaning forward in an attempt to make as accurate a shot as was possible. The kick of the rifle knocked Daniel sideways. He shifted his feet hurriedly in a bid to keep his balance, but the next moment he was treading air.

He crashed to the ground beside the quivering body of the lioness and took a rolling dive away from her, only to be brought up short by the body of the partly eaten cow. He expected to feel the jaws of the lioness close about his neck at any second, but no attack came and, looking over his shoulder fearfully, Daniel saw the lioness quivering from head to tail in her death throes. She would never kill another cow. His bullet had penetrated her brain. She was dead, but the taut nerves of her hunter's body had not yet accepted death.

Daniel put another bullet through her heart before ejecting the empty shell cases and reloading his gun.

As he took the bullets from his gun belt, he saw that his hands were covered with blood. It might have come from the lioness, or from the cow she had killed. He needed to wash his hands. Leaving the shadow of the balancing rocks, he made his way to the river.

The water was shallow and fast-running here and icy cold from a spring on the hill high above. The temperature meant there was no fear of crocodiles and, stripping off his shirt, Daniel plunged his head and arms in the river.

He came up blowing hard. Reaching for his shirt, Daniel dried his face on it. Suddenly he stopped short. Something beneath the surface of the water had caught his eye.

Reaching in elbow deep, he pulled out a round object the size of a musket ball that gleamed dully as he held it in the palm of his hand. Carrying it up to his mouth he tested it between his teeth. The give was just enough to tell Daniel he had found a nugget of pure, alluvial gold. A rapid search of the shallow river bed quickly provided three more — one of them larger than all the others put together.

Not only did Daniel own a beautiful valley — he also had a fortune in gold!

CHAPTER FIFTEEN

Victoria and Andreus Van Niekerk took a fortnight to reach
Tati, a journey usually accomplished in four or five days. Van
Niekerk's wagons had lain unattended in Khami during his
expedition to Manicaland and sun and rain had taken their
toll. Each broken axle cost them an extra day, and once a
wheel collapsed and had to be rebuilt completely.

Victoria took full advantage of each delay to go off hunting
by herself, keeping her and Andreus and their Kalanga porters
in meat.

Because of the constant delays it was not a happy party that
outspanned each evening. Victoria had quickly learned that
Andreus Van Niekerk was not the strong, hard Boer he had
appeared to be when she and Daniel had first met up with him.
He complained about the laziness of the porters, but never
gave them firm orders. If they did something he particularly
disliked, he would bluster and berate them ineffectually. As a
result, the mood of the Kalanga porters was one of surly
truculence. When they had difficulties in crossing one swollen
river, they were for abandoning the accident-prone Boer and
returning to Khami. It was left to Victoria to bully and cajole
them to heave the wagons through mud and wheel-high
channels to the far bank. From that day, she took command of
them, her knowledge of their language ensuring that there was
no mistaking her orders.

On the fourteenth day after leaving Khami, the Van Niekerk
wagons creaked through the mud of Tati's main 'street'.
Africa's newest boom-town was an unprepossessing place.
The majority of the buildings sprawled on either side of the
muddy approach and most were constructed of mud and
thatch. Beyond the town, the tents of the miners perched on
and about the mountains of mine-waste. Here and there
smaller mounds of gold-bearing quartz awaited crushing. The
discovery of gold in this hitherto unknown corner of central
Africa had attracted adventurers from many parts of the

world. The accents of England, Transvaal, Ireland and Australia could all be heard on the streets here.

An option for much of the land where gold was to be found had been taken by a large British company, The London Goldfields Development Company. It was a grand-sounding name and the Tati operations were being directed by a personage of no less distinction – Sir William Ballard.

In a time and a place where men grew as rough and tough as their surroundings, Sir William Ballard stood out as a shining example of all that they had abandoned. Always formally dressed, he traversed the rough tracks between diggings riding in a neat, two-wheeled gig, drawn by a high-stepping horse of impeccable pedigree. When he was obliged to travel any distance from his Tati headquarters, Sir William was fortified by one or two crates of champagne, stored carefully beneath the high seat of his light gig. It was said that he could be tracked through virgin bushveldt by following the *Chocolat Menier* labels he scattered along the way. It was even rumoured that he bathed *every* day, although such an unlikely story was less widely believed.

Soon after his arrival, Sir William Ballard made a determined attempt to bring law and order to the isolated mining community. His first attack was upon the high incidence of drunkenness compounded by the local Bechuana tribesmen who made a good living from the sale of their home-brewed 'kaffir beer'. When it became apparent that this particular crusade was doomed to a far-from-dismal failure, Sir William displayed the business acumen that had put him at the head of his company's African ventures. He had two wagonloads of gin rushed up-country from Natal and opened the town's first gin shop, quickly taking back much of the salary his company paid to its hard-working miners.

Sir William also founded Tati's first Town Council, with himself as its chairman. The other serving members were the town's men of substance, storekeepers, transport owners, the gold assayer, and the manager of Sir William's gin shop. Together they formulated laws for their town, producing a penal code that listed crimes ranging from theft to murder. The punishments ranged from a whipping, for simple crimes, to shooting by firing-squad for murder.

In truth, Tati and its committee were in a unique situation. The area in which the town stood was claimed by no European power and remained the subject of a half-hearted dispute between Matabele and Bechuana tribes. In short, it was truly a 'no-man's land'. The only laws in force were those made by the men who lived there.

Early in 1869, only a couple of months before Victoria and Andreus Van Niekerk arrived, the first two European women reached the town. The wives of two shopkeepers, they formed the nucleus of Tati society. Under their influence the first permanent houses and a church were built.

This was the town to which Van Niekerk brought Victoria. The Boer represented a large mining concern which hoped to establish operations in the Tati area and it was made immediately apparent to him that he had committed an unpardonable blunder. He had brought a coloured girl to a white community. One in which there were white women and an embryo social structure. Van Niekerk had been prospecting for so long that he had almost forgotten the deep division between whites and non-whites – but he was given a swift reminder. Spurred on by the indignation of the town's ladies, Sir William Ballard sent for Andreus Van Niekerk.

The unfortunate Boer was informed bluntly that if he and his 'lady' stayed in Tati, Van Niekerk's company would lose every square inch of land in which it hoped to dig for gold. The displeasure of the two European ladies was no doubt heightened by Victoria's beauty, and the fact that she was an intelligent girl. They showed far less concern for the presence of the Bechuana girls who sat on the wooden sidewalk outside the gin shop selling their bodies in the bushes behind Sir William's house for beads and trinkets.

Andreus Van Niekerk set up his camp on the river bank, two miles outside Tati. It was only a temporary solution of his problems and no one was more aware of it than Van Niekerk himself. He spent much of his time in and about the town, prospecting, pegging claims and supervising the building of splendid offices for his company.

Victoria, the child inside her growing larger every day, found riding uncomfortable and rarely left the camp, spending her days with only a couple of surly Bechuana servants for company. Unused to talking to anyone during the day, she found it difficult to carry on enthusiastic conversation with Andreus when he returned full of his importance as the representative of the second largest mining company in Tati. The developing life inside her body made it equally difficult to respond to the bedtime demands of Andreus. Arguments between them became more frequent and soon he was spending less and less time at the camp with her, preferring the company of card-playing miners.

But Andreus Van Niekerk was no more successful at gambling than he was at any other pursuit. He began to lose more than he could afford. Food became short at the riverside camp. The Bechuana servants, fearing they would not be paid, disappeared one morning, carrying off Victoria's two best blankets with them.

That night Andreus Van Niekerk stumbled back to the camp at midnight – but he was not alone. Victoria heard the whispering outside her tent. When she called out to Andreus, the whispering ceased abruptly.

More curious than angry, Victoria rose from her bed. Scraping a light to a candle, she was about to go outside the tent when the flap was suddenly thrown open. Swaying alarmingly, Andreus Van Niekerk lurched inside. With him was a heavily bearded fellow Boer. Both men were red-eyed from drinking Sir William Ballard's cheap gin.

Blinking at her as she stood clutching the lighted candle, the newcomer rounded on Van Niekerk angrily. 'What sort of a crooked deal is this you've given me? You didn't tell me she was heavy with child.'

'Heavy . . . ? Heavy . . . ?' Andreus Van Niekerk mumbled drunkenly. 'She's not more than four or five months gone. She can't be.'

'What's all this about? Andreus, who is this?'

Both men ignored her.

'She's seven months if she's a day!' Andreus Van Niekerk could only blink stupidly as the words were roared at him. The newcomer peered more closely at Victoria in the candle-light, 'Um! She's good-looking, ja – but not worth the money you owe me. Agh! We'll argue about it in the morning.'

'You!' He jabbed a finger at Victoria. 'Put on some clothes and come with me.'

'I'll do no such thing! Who are you? Andreus! Will you tell me what this is all about?'

The heavily bearded Boer took her arm roughly. 'You can forget about Andreus. I'm Uiys du Toit. Andreus put you up against the money he owes me. You may not be worth much, but it seems you're all he has left.'

Victoria shook herself free. 'First of all, I'm not his to give away like some Bechuana girl. Get out of here – now!'

Uiys du Toit's eyes were dark and angry in the candlelight. 'You're forgetting your place, girl. It'll do you no good putting on airs and graces. You're mine, that's all there is to it. Hell! By the time I get you to my shack half the night will have been wasted. I'll have you here tonight and take you with me in the morning.'

Du Toit turned Andreus Van Niekerk about and propelled him outside. 'We won't need you. I'll have words with you in the morning. You'd better hope she's good to me, man.'

As Andreus Van Niekerk stumbled away from the tent mumbling drunkenly to himself, Uiys du Toit switched his attention back to Victoria. She pinched out the candle and attempted to slip past him in the darkness. He was too quick. His arms went about her and as she kicked and struggled, he wrestled her to the bed. When they fell to the ground together he was on top. His arms tightened about her and Victoria gasped noisily for breath. Still she kicked and struggled. Then, as his hairy face brushed against her lips, Victoria lunged forward and bit his cheek as hard as she could.

Uiys du Toit hooted in pain and released her. But before she could break free from him, his fist swung through the air and exploded against the side of her head. For a few moments she was dazed. It was time enough for him to pull her nightdress up about her waist.

Victoria's rifle was on the far side of the tent, but before she had gone to bed she had been doing some mending. The scissors were on the ground not far away. Feeling about her she located them and her fingers closed on the looped handles just as Uiys du Toit shifted his weight from her body to fumble with the top of his trousers.

Victoria stabbed him once . . . twice . . . three times. At the first blow his grunt was a mixture of surprise and disbelief. When the second blow was struck he shouted. As the scissors struck home in his side for the third time, he screamed in pain and rolled away from her.

The continuing screams of his countryman sobered Andreus Van Niekerk. Hurrying back to the tent, where Victoria had relit the candle, he leaned over Uiys du Toit and saw the blood spreading across the blankets beneath him. Du Toit's breathing was ragged and shallow and flecks of blood came up at Andreus Van Niekerk from the foam forming about the wounded man's lips.

Andreus Van Niekerk dragged du Toit from the tent by his ankles and somehow got him across the saddle of a horse. Then he led horse and burden away into the night, heading for Tati, but Uiys du Toit was dead long before the town doctor was wakened to tend him.

When Sir William Ballard led a party of grim-faced miners to the riverside camp to arrest Victoria at dawn the next morning, they found her writhing in labour. Her screams were more dreadful than any uttered by Uiys du Toit in his dying moments.

It was not one baby, but twins. A boy, spindly and sickly, and a girl. The desperate struggle put up by Victoria the previous night had done nothing to improve their chances. The boy child fought bravely for three hours and then died.

Victoria refused to relinquish her hold on the surviving baby and mother and child were carried to a wagon and taken to Tati. There they were locked in a windowless hut together.

Three days later, her baby still clutched tightly in her arms, Victoria went 'on trial' for the murder of Uiys du Toit. Sir William Ballard presided over the proceedings, determined to make an example of Victoria. She helped him by refusing to say anything in her own defence. However enough of the truth emerged to ensure an acquittal on the charge of murder. Indeed, there was a great deal of sympathy for her and the baby among the miners. A conviction would have resulted in wholesale rioting.

Sir William Ballard, well aware of popular feeling, gave

Victoria a long homily on the evils of loose-living. Then, ordering her from Tati, he released her.

In her weak state, with a baby to care for, the order to leave the mining town was a harsh and unchristian act, made as a sop to the outraged feelings of the town's European women.

Victoria left Tati with only the clothes she had worn in the town's mud-floored gaol. Yet, somehow, she and her baby survived the first night in the bushveldt.

The following day they were taken in by the wife of a leprous Bechuana tribesman. The unfortunate couple, themselves cast out by their people, had built a new life for themselves in a lonely part of the bushveldt, far from the eyes of their fellows.

With the simple family who had learned to cope with a tragedy far greater than her own, Victoria gradually learned to be a mother. She delighted in watching the baby she had named Therese grow stronger with the milk it took from her own body. But the respite and her new-found contentment were short-lived.

She had lived with the Bechuana couple for a month and was working in the small vegetable patch they had carved out of the virgin bush, when a European, Henry Swilley, came riding by. One of a group of three men who had a mining camp beside the river some distance from Tati, Swilley went to town only to bring back supplies of gin. Otherwise, he and his companions kept well clear of the town's social activities – and Sir William Ballard's administration.

The three men were referred to as Tati's 'Australian Miners' because they had spent many years working in the gold mines of New South Wales. In fact, the three were convicted English felons, carried in chains to Australia during the last years of Transportation. All had served their sentences in full. Swilley's crime had been one of highway robbery, for which his accomplice had been hanged. Swilley himself had been spared only because of his age. He was eleven years old at the time.

On the transport ship and during the long period spent in the Australian penal colony, Swilley had learned many things. First and foremost among these lessons was how to take the things he wanted from life . . . and still survive. The successful application of this knowledge had taken him from the gold-fields of Australia, to the more remote gold-mining areas of

South Africa, and finally to Tati. Here, in their camp, beyond the limits of the town's jurisdiction, Swilley and his companions lived their lives untrammelled by the standards of behaviour set by other men.

When Henry Swilley saw Victoria, he wanted her. She had not heard his approach and was bending down to her tasks, the ends of her long skirt tied up about her waist, exposing her thighs as she worked. Swilley watched her for some minutes before making his presence known.

'Well, well! What have we got here?' Swilley urged his horse forward. 'That's no work for a pretty girl. Do you speak English?'

Victoria straightened up and looked at the miner, taking in at a glance his unkempt and disreputable appearance. 'I speak English better than you, by the sound of it. Now, go away. I have work to do.'

Henry Swilley was taken aback by both her command of English, and her disdainful manner, but he was quick to recover.

'You're bright, girl. Far too bright to be bending your back in some kaffir's garden. I've got two mates upriver. We're working a claim . . . a good claim. We need someone to do the cooking and manage the chores for us. How d'you fancy that for a job, eh?'

Swilley's offer appealed to her. Victoria was grateful to the Bechuana couple for giving her a home and taking care of her when she desperately needed help, but she longed for the company of Europeans. She did not particularly like the look of this man, but if there were three of them in the camp she should come to no harm. Victoria had only limited experience of white men and, despite her recent treatment at the hands of Andreus Van Niekerk she tended to judge them by the standards set by her father and Daniel. However, she did not want to appear too eager to accept Henry Swilley's offer. Turning her back on him, she said, 'I've got a job here, thanks. Besides. I've got a baby to think of.'

Frowning, Henry Swilley brought his horse closer, trampling the half-grown stalks of maize, around which Victoria had been weeding. The Bechuana woman had seen Swilley's arrival and watched apprehensively from the door of the hut as he talked to Victoria. Now, seeing her precious corn trampled into the ground by Swilley's horse, she emerged from her hut and began berating him in a shrill, angry voice.

The miner's answer was to yank at the rein of his horse, causing the animal to execute a tight turn. The horse's rump caught the Bechuana woman and sent her crashing heavily to the ground.

The woman's cry of pain brought her deformed husband limping from the hut, the stumps of his leprous fingers gripping the haft of a hunting spear.

Swilley saw him as he ducked through the doorway of the hut. Before the stricken tribesman could even straighten up, Swilley drew a heavy, Colt Dragoon revolver from his belt and put two .44 bullets through his head from point-blank range.

The Bechuana woman rose from the ground screaming hysterically at her husband's killer. Henry Swilley turned the gun on her and a heavy lead bullet tore a gaping hole through the fragile muscle wall of her heart.

Victoria snatched up her baby and looked at Swilley in speechless horror. He looked at her and shrugged matter-of-factly, 'I did them both a favour. He was dying a lingering death and she would never have been accepted back in her tribe. I reckon it's solved your problem about staying here, too. There's nothing to keep you now.'

Henry Swilley still held the revolver in his hand and Victoria knew that if she refused to go with him, or tried to escape, he would shoot her too. She protested that she wanted to bury the bodies of the two Bechuanas who had befriended her, but Swilley curtly ordered her to leave them where they were. Bodies buried in the ground could always be dug up and a cause of death established. Left where they were, the scavengers of the bush would get to work immediately night fell. By morning there would be nothing left in the small clearing but an empty hut and a deserted patch of kaffir corn.

Victoria's life with the three miners in their isolated camp was a continuous nightmare from the very beginning. Away from the eyes of their fellow men, the thin veneer of civilised behaviour had fallen away from the ex-convicts. Their camp was a squalid disgrace. They lived like animals – but abused

Victoria as no creature would have used one of its own kind.

For the first few days, Victoria suffered every kind of degradation in silence, fearing that her baby's life might be in danger if she remonstrated. Each night she prayed that she would awake in the morning and remember this only as a terrible nightmare that had been brushed away by the dawn's light. She would once more be the spoiled daughter of Sam Speke and would have only to walk a few yards from her home in Khami to be given a friendly smile from Daniel.

But the awakening never came. The nightmare went on and on. Victoria gave up her body to whatever demands the three miners made upon her, thankful that they ignored Therese, unless the baby cried too much. The good nights were the ones when they allowed her to drink with them and she could drink herself insensible, oblivious to whatever was happening to her.

Meanwhile, in the world that lay beyond the river-bank mining camp, word of the goldfields of Tati spread from coast to coast. The richness of the strike was much exaggerated. Rumour had it that gold was lying about in exposed reefs, just waiting for some fortunate miner to come along and collect enough to make him rich beyond his dreams.

The Matabele and Bechuana resurrected their respective claims to the area and their raiding parties met and fought within view of the terrified residents of Tati. The incident provoked an urgent plea from Sir William Ballard. He called for Great Britain to annexe the area in the name of the Crown – before another nation stepped in.

Sir William Ballard's warning was a valid one. The Boers of neighbouring Transvaal, in desperate need of funds with which to prop up their ailing, infant republic, were casting envious eyes upon the goldfield so tantalisingly close to their vaguely defined borders.

Although the Portuguese had no clear idea of Tati's geographical position, they too were determined not to be outmanoeuvred by the territorial ambitions of their newer colonial neighbours. The Governor of the Portuguese East African territory of Mozambique sent a strongly worded warning to the governments of both Great Britain and Transvaal. Buried beneath the wealth of flowery language was a reminder that all lands north of the Limpopo River were the sole property of His Most Faithful Majesty, King Luis I of Portugal.

It was a preposterous claim. Portuguese adventurers and conquistadors *had* passed through Mashonaland many centuries before. They had been followed by Jesuit missionaries who lived precariously in the northern part of what was now Matabeleland. But the tribes had soon tired of the stern-faced men who taught a joyless religion and promised only hellfire and damnation at the end of their unhappy lives. They turned on the Portuguese, massacring them in the shadows of their giant crosses. That had been during the last decade of the seventeenth century — and far to the north of the Tati goldfields. Two centuries of unrecorded history had passed since the language of Portugal had been heard on the high plateaus between the Zambezi and the Limpopo. Yet now the ghosts of the ancient conquistadors were being stirred into life by the gold finds at Tati.

Laughable though the Portuguese claim was, it brought death and violence to the area — in the shape of the Pombeiros. As was usual in the Portuguese province of Mozambique, any rumour that promised gold found its way to the ears of the half-caste rebels. Around more than one isolated campfire the discussion turned to the easy pickings to be won in a rich gold-mining area, unaccustomed to organised banditry.

One evening, the three miners in Henry Swilley's camp were beginning their evening meal, heaping abuse upon Victoria for keeping them waiting. As Swilley reached for the coffee pot, bubbling on the fire, he saw a movement along the riverside track leading to the camp. A moment later twenty mounted men rode slowly into view. Slumped untidily in their saddles, they presented a picture of apathy and indolence.

Henry Swilley spat contemptuously at the fire, 'Griquas. They won't trouble us.'

The Griquas were the misfits of Central Africa. A mixture of white and black blood in their veins, they had gathered together to form a loosely knit tribe. Quarrelling incessantly with their neighbours they were ever ready to serve the white men of any country, especially in time of war.

The mounted men followed the river-bank path, passing no more than fifty paces from the camp. As though suddenly seeing the three miners for the first time, the line of horsemen came to a ragged halt and the first three men urged their mounts in the direction of the camp fire.

'Those Griqua bastards are coming up here to beg some victuals from us,' grumbled one of the miners.

'Then they'll leave faster than they came,' declared Henry Swilley loudly.

As the three men rode casually up the slight slope from the river, they talked among themselves and Victoria's heart began to beat faster. The men were talking Portuguese. They were not Griquas – but Pombeiros.

The leader of the three Pombeiros stopped well short of the camp and nodded affably at the men who sipped their coffee about the fire.

'Good evening, Senhors. We are on our way to Tati. We have travelled far. I wonder if you might spare a cup of coffee?'

'You need wonder no more. You'll get no coffee here – nor anything else. Keep going upriver and you'll reach Tati. You might be lucky and scrounge a cup of coffee there . . . but I doubt it. You'll be no more welcome than you are here. Tati's a white man's town.'

There was something very familiar about the Pombeiro, but not until his eyes found hers did Victoria realise what it was. He bore a striking resemblance to Mariano!

'You're not so particular about the colour of a *girl*'s skin, eh?' The Pombeiro spoke to Swilley without taking his eyes from Victoria.

'We'll have less of your cheek,' said another of the ex-convicts. 'Get on your way before I kick your arse out of our camp.'

The Pombeiro's eyes glittered angrily, but he tugged on his horse's reins as though he would do as he was told.

'Wait!' The cry came from Victoria.

The Pombeiro pulled his horse to a halt.

'Take me with you . . . please!' Victoria had been with Mariano for only a few brief months and her Portuguese was far from perfect. She desperately hoped that the Pombeiro would understand her.

He did. Smiling in derision, he replied in the same language, 'What would I want with a white man's whore? The world is full of unbedded girls, just waiting for a Pombeiro to come along.'

The other Pombeiros smiled broadly at their leader's words. But Henry Swilley called, 'What the hell's going on? What language is that you're speaking, you coloured slut?'

Victoria snatched up her baby from the blanket on which she was lying. Holding her up to the Pombeiro, she said, 'This is the daughter of Mariano. Her twin brother is dead. Killed by white men such as these.'

The smiles disappeared from the faces of the three mounted men.

'You bore my brother's son? You must be . . . Victoria?'

Victoria nodded. 'And you are Philippe. He spoke of you often. Help me, please.'

'What do you want me to do?'

'Victoria, come here . . . right now, if you don't want the hiding of your life.'

Henry Swilley rose to his feet as though to carry out his threat there and then.

Victoria placed Therese on the ground quickly. 'Throw me your gun,' she hissed at Philippe.

Slipping his rifle from its holster beside the saddle, Philippe tossed it through the air to her.

Catching it clumsily, Victoria turned to face Henry Swilley. The ex-convict stopped and stared at her in disbelief. 'Don't be stupid, girl—'

They were the last words he ever uttered. The rifle was a large-bore, over-and-under hunting rifle and the bullet from the first barrel slammed into Swilley's chest, knocking him four feet backwards before he dropped to the ground.

One of Swilley's companions dived towards the tent where the guns were kept, but the bullet from the second barrel sent him face downwards in the stony earth.

The third miner died as he rose to his feet with arms raised in surrender, shot by one of Philippe's companions.

'Yes, you are Victoria.' Philippe's thin smile expressed his admiration. 'I heard you could shoot like a man. Now I believe it. Come, bring your child, we will leave this place.'

'Wait a moment.' Victoria ran to Henry Swilley's tent and returned dragging a heavy wooden box behind her. With no sign of emotion, she removed a bloody key from a string about Swilley's neck and returned to the box. Opening it, she took out twenty-five small, hard-packed bags and threw them to Philippe and his two companions.

'Swilley's been bragging that there were four hundred ounces of gold in here. There's little sense leaving it for someone else to steal.'

It was a sizeable fortune and represented the total output of Swilley's mine. Victoria had effectively bought her place in the Pombeiro band of Philippe, brother of Mariano.

Before the disappearance of the three 'Australians' came to the notice of their fellow miners, there were three more unsolved killings in the vicinity of Tati.

First to die was Andreus Van Niekerk, shot by a marksman's bullet as he staggered drunkenly through the ill-lit streets of the gold town in the early, dark hours of morning.

The others were Sir William Ballard and his unfortunate Bechuana driver, shot just outside Tati in broad daylight, as the director of the London Goldfields Development Company returned from an inspection of his company's outlying mines.

No assassin was ever apprehended for any of the killings. Not long afterwards, the failure of the mines in the Tati area left the town an empty shell, peopled by the ghosts of men who had once walked its streets, the town ordinances long-forgotten.

Meanwhile, three hundred miles away, Philippe, the Pombeiro was earning the appellation, 'The scourge of Mozambique'. It was a title that had been vacant since the death of his brother, Mariano.

CHAPTER SIXTEEN

Daniel was not able to set off for Mozambique until the end of March. The rains had ceased in Matabeleland, but in the uplands of Mashonaland, through which he would have to take his wagons, heavy cloud hung low over the hills and rain persisted for longer than in any other season the Matabeles could recall. For a month, while his trek oxen grew fat on the lush green grass of the Insimo valley, Daniel chafed at the unexpected delay. His wagons were loaded with a fortune in ivory – and he wanted to see Elvira again.

It was about three hundred and fifty miles from Insimo to the Portuguese settlement at Sena, but Daniel planned to make the long trek in a month. Much would depend on how well he remembered the route through Mashonaland and Manicaland, on the height of the rivers – and on the mood of the tribesmen he met along the way.

He would be travelling without a Matabele escort. A secure trade route was of great importance to Jandu too, but Kanje's men posed a constant threat to him. He needed all his warriors at home. The best Jandu could do was arm a hundred Kalanga tribesmen and send them to accompany the wagons. The Kalangas were vassals of the Matabele, used by them for menial tasks, and were scorned as warriors. However, their presence might make other tribes think twice about attacking Daniel.

At last, Daniel's patience ran out. Although dark clouds still brooded over the Mashona hills, he fancied they were lifting – and he was not prepared to wait any longer. He sent to Jandu to 'ask for the road'. It was an unnecessary courtesy, and the request was granted immediately.

On the day of departure, the Matabele King-elect rode into the Insimo valley, at the head of an impi. His horse was one Daniel had presented to him some months before, a highly valued 'salted' horse – one which had survived a bout of horse sickness and was now considered to be immune from further sickness. Jandu had become fond of riding and used the animal whenever possible.

Jandu and his impi travelled with Daniel until the sun was directly overhead and they reached the first river. The river was only a small one, but the rainwaters of the high Mashona plateau drained into it and it erupted from the hillside in a spectacular waterfall that cascaded down the rocky slope in a series of giant leaps, weaving rainbows into the lacework of spray that rose high in the air. Here Jandu announced he would have to return to Khami.

Clapping his hands together in the traditional gesture of friendship, he then clasped Daniel's hand in a spontaneous show of warmth. 'Goodbye, and take care, my friend. Be sure to bring your bride back in time to see me installed as King of the Matabele.'

'I'll be back long before then,' Daniel promised. Jandu's coronation was set for early 1870 – a year ahead. Daniel hoped to have established regular trade with Sena by then.

Daniel's trek to Sena went almost exactly to plan, although it was not without incident. The rains retreated eastward ahead of him, but the rivers were still dangerously swollen and he lost one wagon. It capsized in a strong river current and swept over a waterfall, disappearing in a deep chasm gouged in the Manica hills by the rushing waters of centuries of rainy seasons. Fortunately, the wagon had been only partly loaded, much of the ivory being portered across the river to lighten the wagons.

Three of the Kalanga tribesmen were also lost. One was taken by a crocodile, when drinking from a river. The other two were killed by the Mashonas in a daring attack on a foraging party.

This attack so enraged the remaining Kalangas that they forgot for a while they were a subject people, scorned and despised by their overlords. Led by their headman, they made a vengeful foray into the surrounding hills, firing every kraal they found and killing the Mashona occupants. When they returned to the wagons, the Kalangas had become warriors and it was in this mood that they continued the journey to Sena.

Not willing to put the new-found confidence of his escort to a further test, Daniel directed the wagons well to the north of Vumba's kraal. No doubt the Manica chief would think twice about incurring the displeasure of the Portuguese authorities once more but Daniel was taking no chances.

The long journey took only a few days longer than he had allowed and Daniel came within sight of the stockaded village on the first Sunday in May. It was usual for the Portuguese and their families to gather in the tiny mud and thatch church beside the fort on Sundays. Here, three or four times a year, a visiting priest would come from the coastal area to celebrate Mass for the isolated community. For the remainder of the year they had to make do with Bible reading and prayers conducted by Senhor Farrao.

On this Sunday the prayers remained securely locked in the hearts of the men and women of Sena. Days before, news had reached Senhor of the approach of armed men. Remembering the earlier raids of the Pombeiros, the populace of the surrounding countryside poured into Sena's stockade. The stout wooden walls were manned day and night by armed soldiers and militia, all nervously fingering the triggers of their ancient muskets. One evening, at dusk, an unsuspecting and short-sighted rhinoceros wandered absentmindedly from the cover of the thick bush, five hundred feet from the stockade. Immediately, a wild fusillade of shots rang out and musket balls pattered like hail among the leaves of the trees about the startled animal. Not one of them so much as grazed its tough hide but, confused by the soft sounds about him, and the crackle of exploding powder from the stockade that was too far away to see, the rhinoceros turned and trotted back to the safety of the bush.

Daniel knew nothing of this. Riding beside his lead-wagon as it lurched from the trees to open ground, he looked up to see the green and red flag of Portugal hanging limply above the fort of Sena and knew the long journey was over.

Flinging his hat high in the air, Daniel let out a yell that startled his horse and caused the Kalangas to rush to the head of the column, fearing something was amiss. The reaction from the stockade was far more dramatic. High on the wall of the fort there was a flash of igniting gunpowder and a large boom echoed along the river as a cannon was fired.

Brought up from Quelimane during the summer months and never before fired, the gun was badly layed. The cannon ball crashed harmlessly among the trees, well to one side of the wagons. Nevertheless, the shot terrified the Kalangas, who had never before heard cannon-fire. They promptly fled back to the safety of the bush. Daniel was alarmed. If a shot fell among the wagons the oxen would also bolt, overturning wagons and scattering his goods across miles of Portuguese territory.

Digging his spurs into the flanks of his horse, Daniel galloped towards the stockade, shouting for the Portuguese to hold their fire. He was too late to prevent a second shot but, fortunately, the gunners' aim was no better than before.

Daniel was recognised before a third shot could be fired. As he slid his horse to a halt before the stockade entrance, the heavy wooden bolts were slid back, the gates swung open and the slight, dark-haired figure of Elvira ran out.

Daniel leaped from his saddle and the next moment Elvira was in his arms. 'Daniel . . . Daniel!' Her voice was caught between tears and laughter. 'It's been more than half-a-year. I was beginning to believe you would not return—'

'You should have known better. I have a trading arrangement with your father.'

Daniel knew the joke had misfired when she turned a dismayed face up to his. 'That is the only reason you have returned to Sena? Because of your trading?'

When she saw his smile she shuddered violently and clung to him. 'Don't tease me about such things, Daniel. I have dreadful nightmares about you not wanting me.'

Pushing away from him she took his hand. After he satisfied himself that the Kalanga warriors had come out of hiding and were bringing on the wagons, they walked inside the stockade together. As they walked, she turned to him in a sudden gesture of sympathy. 'I am very sorry about your friend, Samuel. When Francisco returned and told us what had happened—' Her earlier uncertainty returned to her. 'Your friend's daughter . . . Victoria? You returned her safely to Khami?'

Some of Daniel's happiness left him and Elvira feared the worst.

'Yes, I returned her to Khami. But she didn't stay there long.'

He told Elvira about Andreus Van Niekerk. How the Boer

had taken Victoria to the Tati mines while Mary Speke had returned to South West Africa. '. . . So, you see, the Speke family has gone out of my life after being a part of it for as long as I can remember.'

'It must be very sad for you, Daniel. I am sorry.'

Elvira's expression belied her words, but by now they were at the fort and were quickly surrounded by Portuguese traders and soldiers who remembered Daniel from his earlier visit. Senhor Farrao was among them – and *Captain* Francisco St Anna, newly promoted as a direct result of his successful campaign in Manicaland. As Elvira explained, he was newly married too. When Daniel offered congratulations and asked about his wife, he was hastily informed that St Anna's wife was not well enough to leave Portugal just yet.

Sensing a mystery, Daniel said nothing. Later he learned that St Anna's marriage was the result of a scandal. The brilliant young army officer, fresh from battle, had succumbed to the charms of the passionate young daughter of a high government official. Her determination to hold nothing back from the young hero who was the toast of Portuguese society had brought the reward she sought. A hasty marriage had been arranged and she would come to Mozambique when their child was born.

The greeting given to Daniel by Senhor Farrao and Captain St Anna was courteous enough, but Daniel imagined it lacked warmth. He broached the subject that evening when he and Francisco St Anna were standing on the verandah, enjoying a drink and Elvira and Senhor Farrao were busy in the house.

'I've been looking forward to this particular drink throughout the whole of the trek, but I get the feeling I'm not particularly welcome in Sena.'

'No! No, that is not true, Daniel.' St Anna was full of concern. 'Senhor Farrao would be deeply hurt if he heard your words. His house is your house. It will always be so – he has said this to me many times. You must understand that Senhor Farrao finds himself in a difficult situation. He and Elvira both have a deep affection for you, but Senhor Farrao is an important official of the Portuguese Government. He is Captain General of the North West District of Mozambique, and very proud of the honour his country has bestowed upon him. He takes his duties very seriously. Unfortunately, the area of his jurisdiction has never been accurately defined. On one side it is bounded by the Quelimane district, but on the other . . . ?'

Francisco St Anna spread his arms wide in a gesture of helplessness. 'Our government in Portugal knows nothing of Mozambique. They insist that the lands taken by our conquistadors are still rightfully ours. They have received disturbing reports about the intentions of your country – and the Transvaal Republic, in the interior. Why, you can understand this. You are established in Matabeleland – and we both heard Van Niekerk's boast of bringing fifty miners to Manicaland. Orders have been received by all Captain Generals. They are to re-establish a Portuguese presence in the interior. Of course, it is quite impossible. We in Mozambique have neither the troops nor the resources to implement such an order.'

'You can forget about Van Niekerk and his fifty miners. His company has abandoned its plans for Manicaland and he's been sent to the goldfields, at Tati.'

'Ah yes . . . Tati! It is claimed that Tati is *also* Portuguese territory. A protest has been sent to your government, and that of Transvaal, demanding that the miners be withdrawn from Tati immediately.'

Daniel smiled, thinly. 'From what I hear, neither the British nor the Boers have any more jurisdiction over Tati than the Portuguese. The miners will tell them all to go to hell – and good luck to them.' He looked at St Anna quizzically. 'You can't seriously believe that Portugal has any claim on a place at least five hundred miles from the Indian Ocean? Why, apart from one or two villages like Sena, on the Zambezi, you've hardly colonised Mozambique to a depth of more than five miles from the coast!'

Captain St Anna grunted noncommittally. 'I keep my beliefs to myself, as all ambitious soldiers should. I am merely passing on the official attitude – as a friend.'

The discussion ended when Senhor Farrao came from the house to join them. Soon afterwards the three men and Elvira sat down to a dinner that would not have been out of place had the smoking tallow lamps and the humid, semi-tropical surroundings been exchanged for chandeliers and the paved steets of Lisbon.

Senhor Farrao managed to produce a mood to match the meal. Had Daniel not talked with Captain St Anna, he would have told himself he must have imagined Senhor Farrao's earlier reserve. Not until Daniel mentioned the valley given to him by Jandu did the guarded look appear again.

'This valley. It is many miles to the west of Sena?'

'Yes, a little over three hundred and fifty miles due south west – why?'

Senhor Farrao shook his head. 'Curiosity, no more.'

Inwardly, Senhor Farrao breathed a sigh of relief. He had recently paid a visit to the Governor of Mozambique, at Quelimane. After a long meeting the two men had agreed that they should urge their government to make a more realistic approach to the border question. The furthermost Portuguese settlement along the Zambezi River was Zumbo, four hundred and fifty miles inland. The Governor would suggest to his government that the border of Mozambique be set a few miles beyond Zumbo. Extending southwards, it would curve in to exclude the high Mashonaland plateau. Much of the land so claimed would undoubtedly be disputed by the British – and the Boers, but it should be possible to settle their differences without going to war. Senhor Farrao had just ascertained that Daniel's valley lay beyond the proposed border. There need be no quarrel between them.

Soon the conversation turned to trading. Senhor Farrao had inspected the goods brought by Daniel from Matabeleland, and was well pleased. He kept in close touch with the prices prevailing in Quelimane and knew he would make a handsome profit.

This knowledge, coupled with the excellence of the meal, mellowed the Captain General. He leaned back contentedly in his chair as brandy was poured in large, pot-bellied glasses, and blue tobacco smoke drifted upwards to hang in a flat, wispy cloud just beneath the ceiling.

'You will, of course, remain in Sena for a few months?'

'No. The truth is, I'd like to make one more trading trip before the next rainy season.'

Senhor Farrao raised his eyebrows, 'Indeed? Business is so good in the land of the Matabele?'

Daniel was not listening. He had seen the dismay on Elvira's face when he mentioned leaving again soon. He cleared his throat nervously. 'There's one other thing. I'd like to marry Elvira before I go – and take her with me.'

The words came out much faster than Daniel intended, tumbling over themselves in their hurry to be said.

There was a gasp of surprise from Elvira and Senhor Farrao stared thoughtfully at his glass as he lowered it slowly to the table. He was aware that Daniel and Elvira were very much in love and that the question of marriage had been discussed between them. But . . . so soon? However, Senhor Farrao was an observant man. He too had seen Elvira's dismay – and he had watched it become concealed joy when Daniel declared that he wanted them to be married quickly.

'This valley of yours – it is a safe place to have a home, a wife?'

Daniel nodded. 'I have already completed a stone house. It's a good house, Senhor Farrao. Elvira will not be ashamed of living there, and the valley is a present from Jandu. An attack on me there would be an attack on Jandu himself.' Even as he spoke the words, Daniel thought uncomfortably of Kanje, but now was not the time to entertain such doubts. 'Why not come and see the house for yourself?'

Why not indeed? Senhor Farrao's mind worked quickly. By claiming that one of their senior officials had travelled as far as Matabeleland, it might be possible to successfully push the border still further westwards . . . . Then Captain General Farrao looked again at the eagerness in his daughter's eyes. He remembered the time, many years before, when he had come to Mozambique with a young and starry-eyed bride. They had arrived with a dream. Together they were going to make a home in their own part of the Zambezi valley. Land that no man would take from them. It was to be a small private empire at the heart of the wilderness, just such a place as Daniel's own valley.

Senhor Farrao sighed. 'I would love to see this valley of yours, Daniel, but it is not possible. Perhaps one day things will be different and I will be able to come to visit my grandchildren, eh?'

'Then you'll let us marry? Before Daniel returns to Matabeleland?' Elvira's happiness was something Senhor Farrao had seen too little of in recent years. Such happiness was rare in Africa's harsh environment. Only the most unfeeling man would dare to shatter it – and Senhor Farrao was not such a man.

'If I say "no", I believe Daniel will carry you away with him anyway. Then I will have lost both my daughter and a valued trading partner. You have my blessing. I only wish your dear mother were here to share my joy for you both.'

Senhor Farrao had at first intended bringing the Bishop of Quelimane to Sena to perform the marriage ceremony, but when he put the idea to his future son-in-law, Daniel objected strongly.

Daniel remembered the total lack of organising ability shown by the senior officers of the Portuguese army. If the same incompetence extended to the church it would be many months before the marriage could take place.

But it was another argument put forward by Captain Francisco St Anna that eventually persuaded Senhor Farrao to abandon his plans for a grand wedding. The soldier suggested it might be better if the wedding of the Captain General of Mozambique's North West District to an *Englishman* were a more discreet affair.

Daniel and Elvira were married in July 1869 in Sena's tiny chapel. The ceremony was performed by a missionary priest from the garrison town of Tete, a hundred and fifty miles upriver. It may not have been a great occasion in the calendar of Mozambique's provincial society, but the day was declared a holiday in Sena and villagers, tribesmen, and Portuguese prazeros flocked to the stockaded village from the surrounding area. They brought presents for the young couple that ranged from bead purses and live chickens, to an antique, solid gold, christening cup.

After the ceremony, Senhor Farrao laid out a feast that was more than enough to fill the belly of every man, woman and child there. The wedding feast was followed by tribal dancing. Later still the nostalgic music of Portugal was sung and played by men and women, many of whom knew the home country only from the romanticised memoirs of fathers and grandfathers.

When it became clear that the celebrations would continue all night, Daniel and Elvira slipped away to the little honeymoon cottage especially prepared for them at the river's edge. Temporarily vacated by Captain St Anna's quartermaster and his small family, it had been newly decorated and furnished for the occasion by Senhor Farrao.

Daniel was about to slip into bed alongside Elvira, when the boom of the fort's signal cannon boomed forth, shaking the walls of the cottage. As its echoes died away, the voice of the look-out called out excitedly.

Elvira sat up quickly, drawing the sheet about her body.

'What is it? What's he saying?' Daniel asked.

'There's a fire, from either the de Souta or Nunes houses. Both are no more than two miles from here.'

At that moment the look-out called that he could see yet another fire, and among the cries of the crowd outside, Daniel heard a word that he recognised.

The word was . . . Pombeiros.

Daniel reached for his clothes, but Elvira stretched an arm from the bed and gripped his hand.

'Please, Daniel. Don't leave me. Not tonight.'

Daniel hesitated. Then he remembered another night, and a girl cowering in a corner of Elvira's room as Pombeiros fled to safety. His clothes dropped to the floor and a few moments later he was holding Elvira to him and her trembling had nothing to do with thoughts of Pombeiros.

Some hours later Daniel eased himself from Elvira's arms and slid quietly from the bed. Standing at the window he could see the flames of a fire licking skywards from yet another house. This one was on the slopes of a hill, many miles from the original fires. The Pombeiros were having a busy night.

There was a sound from the room behind him as Elvira slipped from the bed and joined him at the window, still naked. Putting an arm about his waist she rested her head against him and they gazed together through the window at the burning house. Suddenly, Elvira shuddered, and Daniel pulled her closer to him.

'I'm sorry Daniel. Looking at that fire, I remembered another night. I pray that no one is suffering as they were made to suffer then. Not tonight.'

The flames in the distant house reached the gunpowder store and it exploded with a flash that lit up the night sky, the sound of the explosion rattling the cottage windows seconds later.

Elvira moved from the window and as he followed her towards the bed she turned and clung to him fiercely. Their desire for each other grew stronger and Elvira whispered, 'Daniel . . . come back to bed now. I want you to love me. Ah! My marido, I want you . . . .'

CHAPTER SEVENTEEN

Daniel and Elvira left Sena with their wagons a week after the wedding. It was considered that the Pombeiros must be far away by now, but Senhor Farrao took no chances. Captain Francisco St Anna, with a large force of militia accompanied the newly-weds and their Kalanga tribesmen until they were well beyond the Manica mountains.

It was not far enough. Three days after the departure of St Anna and his troops, the Pombeiros struck.

Daniel was asleep in the living-wagon with Elvira when a faint sound woke him. It was not yet fully dawn, but a pale light seeped through the taut canvas above him. He listened and caught the soft jingle of metal upon metal. Such a sound as harness makes when a horse shakes its head. Daniel sat up hastily. The only horses accompanying the wagons were those belonging to Elvira and himself. They were tethered in a thorn-bush pen – without bridles.

He slipped quietly into his clothes, not wanting to waken Elvira at this stage. After checking his rifle, he unlaced the wagon flap and peeped outside.

What Daniel saw in the faint light filled him with dismay. There were many horsemen milling about the wagons. Some were herding the Kalanga tribesmen in one large group, the sleepy tribesmen behaving like docile, frightened sheep.

The horsemen were moving methodically from wagon to wagon and there must have been at least twenty of them, probably more. Dark though it was, Daniel instantly recognised them as Pombeiros.

'Elvira, wake up,' the words were whispered, but they were loud enough to waken her.

Startled, she opened her eyes and her lips parted to speak, but Daniel hurriedly clamped a hand over her mouth. 'Don't make a sound. Pombeiros – they're searching the wagons.'

Above his hand, Elvira's eyes widened in apprehension.

'Hurry and get dressed.' He put a loaded rifle on the wagon floor beside her. 'When you're ready I'm going to jump from the wagon and try to draw them away. As soon as you hear shooting pick up this gun and run for the thick bush beside the river. Hide there until the Pombeiros go – then head eastwards. Try to get back to Sena. It's a long way, but it's your only chance.'

He removed his hand from her mouth and snatched up a second rifle, easing a cartridge into the breech before laying the cartridge belt beside Elvira's gun.

'Wha . . . what will you do?' Still wide-eyed, Elvira asked the question in a hoarse, fear-tightened whisper as she shrugged a dress down over her body.

'I'll try to lose the Pombeiros in the bush. It shouldn't be hard in this light. They won't want to follow me far, the grass is too high.'

Daniel hoped she would not recognise the lie. He doubted whether he would reach the shelter of the nearest patch of long grass before the Pombeiros shot him down. His hope was that it would create sufficient diversion to enable Elvira to make good her own escape.

'I'll come with. We will live or die together—'

'There's no time to argue.' Daniel had heard a shot from one of the searching Pombeiros. They had found the crates of wine, a present from Senhor Farrao. They were stored in the wagon outspanned ahead of the living-wagon.

Throwing back the wagon-flap, Daniel vaulted to the ground – and found himself in the path of a Pombeiro who was riding towards the living-wagon. The Pombeiro shouted a warning and urged his horse forward. As Daniel scrambled to his feet, the rebel's horse bowled him over.

Daniel looked up to see the Pombeiro's rifle raised to gun him down. A shot rang out, but it left Daniel unscathed and it was the Pombeiro who slumped from his horse.

On the box-seat of the wagon, Elvira struggled to release the breech of her rifle, but it had jammed and as Daniel reached for his own gun, other Pombeiros fell on him and he was quickly pinned to the ground.

Another Pombeiro jumped from his horse to the wagon seat. Disarming Elvira, he threw her roughly to the ground. With a whoop of delight, two of the half-caste rebels leaped upon her. Shouting for them to leave her alone, Daniel struggled violently with the men who held him.

The two men manhandling Elvira had ripped her dress from throat to waist before the Pombeiro leader rode up and ordered them to release her.

One of the Pombeiros was reluctant to relinquish his prize. The leader spurred his horse forward, the short, rhinoceros-hide whip in his hand cracked and the Pombeiro staggered back from Elvira, a bloody weal etched diagonally across his face from ear to mouth.

Shaking off the men who held him, Daniel went to Elvira, his own face bloodied and bruised. He pulled the torn dress up about her shoulders and she put up a hand to hold it in place. Her other hand found his and he squeezed her fingers in a futile bid to reassure her.

'What a very touching scene,' said the Pombeiro leader mockingly, as he looked down at them from his horse. He spoke in English, although his next words proved that he knew Elvira was Portuguese. 'We have captured a rich prize indeed. A fortune in trade goods *and* the daughter of a Provincial Captain General! You are far from home, Senhorita Farrao – ah! My apologies. Senhora Retallick. Your wedding was a day to remember – for all of us.'

'What do you intend doing with us?' asked Daniel.

'With *us*, trader? You are nothing to me. I have your wagons and your goods. I also have your wife . . . and Senhor Farrao will pay generously for her return, I think.'

'He will pay for my husband too,' said Elvira quickly.

The Pombeiro shook his head and smiled without humour. 'No, we will ask a *very* high price for you. He will not be able to afford more. Besides, it is a long ride to Sena and my men will need to guard you closely, day and night. Of course, they will expect you to reward them for taking such care of you.'

Spreading his hands in an apologetic gesture, the Pombeiro added, 'It would embarrass you to know that your husband was a witness to your "gratitude", would it not? It is better that you say goodbye to your husband now, Senhora, then you will forget him.'

He called an order in Portuguese and Daniel was seized by

two of the nearest Pombeiros. Elvira began screaming and jumped at the men, but she was quickly dragged away.

'Stop!' The cry, in a woman's voice went unheeded, but when a rifle shot rang out, much of the excitement about the two prisoners died away. Held fast by Pombeiros who had been securing his wrists with rope cut from one of his own wagons, Daniel looked on in disbelief as Victoria walked towards him, smoke trickling from the barrel of the rifle she held.

'Let them go,' she snapped.

When the Pombeiros were slow to respond Victoria raised the gun to her shoulder. Immediately, they leaped away from Daniel and those about Elvira stepped back hastily. They had been present when Victoria shot the two Australian miners. There had been others since. Victoria's ruthlessness was already a legend among the Pombeiros of Mozambique.

Victoria moved to release Daniel's wrists, but he slipped off the ropes without her aid and went to help Elvira. Shaken and dishevelled, Elvira held on to all the dignity she could muster. She knew who this Pombeiro girl must be and was determined that Victoria would not see her reduced to tears.

'What are you doing?' The demand came from Philippe as he confronted Victoria. 'What is this white man to you?'

'We were brought up together. His father and mine were friends.'

Philippe looked at Daniel with more interest than before. 'He does not seem eager to remember old friends now he moves among the Portuguese aristocracy. After all what is a poor Pombeiro girl compared to the daughter of a rich Portuguese Prazero?'

Daniel spoke to Victoria for the first time. 'Have you forgotten how your father died? Does his memory mean so little that you seek the company of these thieves and murderers?'

Daniel spoke quietly, but the words reached Philippe. The Pombeiro leaned forward in his saddle and he glared angrily at Daniel. 'You have married into a Portuguese family, yet you speak of *us* as thieves and murderers? When the Portuguese first came to this country they marched beneath a bloody cross. They massacred whole tribes in the sacred name of their "bountiful" God, and his "Mother of Mercy". Since then they have robbed the people of this land of everything they ever possessed – including pride. And you call Pombeiros murderers and robbers? Mother of God! The same words mean different things in each of our mouths, white man.'

Philippe jerked the reins of his horse savagely and the animal pranced in a full circle, snorting in pain as Philippe waited to hear Victoria's reply.

When she spoke, Victoria's voice was cold and controlled, 'These "thieves and murderers" are my people, Daniel. They always have been . . . but you and Dad forgot to tell me. There were many things you forgot to tell me. For instance, you led me to believe men treated women with chivalry. I had to find out for myself that chivalry is only for white women. I learned it in the goldfields of Tati, where a coloured girl is something to be won or lost in a game of cards. Or used like an animal by drunken miners. Oh yes, Dad's memory means something to me, Daniel! I have him to thank for bringing me into this world. For making me someone who belongs neither to Africa, nor to Europe. Can you imagine what it means not to belong anywhere? No, of course you can't – but the White Mondoro does. He told me to find my future among my own. Well, I have. I'm a Pombeiro. They are all the things you've called them – and more. But I don't wake up each morning filled with shame as I did in Tati.'

'Van Niekerk did this to you?'

'He and others – but forget them. They are all dead.'

Turning from Daniel, she spoke to the Pombeiro leader, 'I want you to set Daniel and his wife free, Philippe.'

Philippe opened his mouth to argue, but he could see by Victoria's strained expression just how important this was to her.

'All right.' He shrugged nonchalantly. 'I wasn't looking forward to a journey to Sena with the girl, anyway.'

Daniel's relief threatened to overwhelm him – but his business instincts came to the fore. 'What about my wagons?'

'Don't push me too far. I am a thief, remember? However, you are a friend of Victoria . . . and a trader, so you are almost one of us.' Philippe grinned. 'My men will take only what they can carry away. The rest, together with the wagons, are yours.'

'And the Kalangas?'

Philippe sighed. 'You ask for too much. Your Kalangas are young and strong. The French pay good money for such men. I will leave you enough to drive your wagons, no more.'

'I *have* to accept that. I'm not so sure the Matabele will. The Kalangas are their vassals.'

'I will discuss the matter with them, if ever the Matabele come to Mozambique,' Philippe retorted. Dismissing Daniel from his mind, he turned to Victoria, and his expression changed. 'Now I must explain my soft-heartedness to my men. It may be necessary to remind them I am still their leader. Bring your rifle and watch them closely while I am talking.'

Victoria nodded. She stood looking uncertainly at Daniel for a few moments. 'We've moved into different worlds, you and I, Daniel. For you it is better that I've gone from your life.' She inclined her head towards Elvira. 'You will never have to apologise to anyone for being married to her.'

'I have never apologised to anyone for you, and I never will,' declared Daniel quietly. 'Today you've saved our lives. There will always be a place for you in our home. You'll find it in the valley we saw, two days ride from Khami.'

Victoria nodded. 'I remember the place. Thank you for the offer, Daniel. I have a child. I may send her to you one day.' She looked to where the Pombeiros had one of the crates of wine on the ground and were inexpertly smashing off the necks of the bottles against nearby rocks. 'Inspan your wagon and leave quickly. I'll make sure your Kalangas follow with the remainder of the wagons as soon as the Pombeiros accept what's happening.'

Victoria joined Philippe as he rolled a cigarette and eyed the Pombeiros. 'Where's the baby?' He spoke without looking at her.

'With one of the men, in the bush.'

Philippe inclined his head. 'Why did you not want the white man to see your child?'

He looked at her quickly, catching her sudden confusion.

'I . . . I thought there might be shooting. Therese is safer where she is.'

'I see,' he saw only too well, but made no comment. 'Come. If my men drink too much they will leave nothing for your friend and his new wife to take home with them.'

Daniel and Elvira inspanned their oxen as quickly as they could. As the wagons creaked excruciatingly slowly from the camp, the voices of the Pombeiros rose in argument behind them.

'I hope Victoria knows what she's doing,' muttered Daniel, cracking the twenty-feet long bull whip as the oxen heaved the wagon through a patch of thick, coarse grass. 'If Philippe changes his mind we'll never make it to Insimo—'

'He won't change his mind,' replied Elvira confidently. 'Did you see the way he looked at Victoria? He is very much in love with her. He will do whatever she wants.'

'I hope you're right . . . and for her sake I pray it lasts.' Daniel spoke through his teeth as he sawed on the long reins to turn the lead oxen towards more even ground. 'There'll be little happiness for her with the Pombeiros if ever he tires of her.'

'I am right,' Elvira assured him.

She did not add that she was less certain of Victoria's feelings towards her Pombeiro lover. To do so would call for explanations. Only a fool would tell her husband that another woman was in love with him.

CHAPTER EIGHTEEN

Victoria kept her word to Daniel and, six days after the incident with the Pombeiros, Daniel brought his bride to the Insimo Valley. He had been away for three months. In his absence the Mashona servants had scoured the valley for unusual and attractive plants, setting their discoveries about the house in a profusion of colour. Insimo was more of a garden valley than ever before.

It was love at first sight for Elvira. The valley, the house and everything she saw filled her with delight.

Leaving Elvira to supervise the unpacking of the possessions brought from Sena, Daniel made a quick tour of inspection. Because of the plentiful supply of water the grass everywhere in the valley was lush green. It would never wither and die as it did in other parts of Matabeleland. The cattle too looked well and the first calves had been born. Healthy and long-legged, they were captured by eager Matabele herd-boys and brought to him for his approval.

Assured that all was well in his valley, Daniel returned to the house filled with an unaccustomed sense of well-being.

That evening, Daniel and Elvira stood on the wide verandah of their house and looked down the length of the Insimo valley. The sun had disappeared below the rim of the nearby hills, plunging the valley into cool shadow, but it still shone brightly upon the low-veldt to the south. To Elvira it seemed as though she were looking out from a darkened window at a bright, new world. She leaned against Daniel and he put an arm about her, understanding something of her emotions. Many evenings like this, when the house was being built, he had stood here alone, overcome by the sheer magnificence of Africa, and longing for the day when he would share it with Elvira. With his wife.

'It's so ... so very beautiful, Daniel. A truly enchanted place. This is going to be a marvellous home in which to bring up a family and teach them about life. I am so happy. So very, very happy.'

The next few weeks were idyllic. Daniel busied himself about the valley, building paddocks to hold the additional five hundred cattle he had decided to purchase. He also had the Mashona workers till a couple of acres of land. Here he planted maize, the ubiquitous corn of the Matabele. Used by them in a variety of ways with every meal, maize was also the basic ingredient of their thick, intoxicating beer, a drink consumed by Matabele men and women in vast quantities.

Daniel took Elvira to see the gold in the stream that flowed from the hillside into the valley. In only half an hour of searching they found enough nuggets to cover the palm of Daniel's hand. They discussed the significance of the gold at some length and Elvira agreed with the decision Daniel had reached soon after the find. It should remain a secret for as long as possible, in order that the character of the valley should not change.

So pleasant was life in the Insimo valley that when the time came for another trading journey to Sena, Daniel persuaded Aaron to take his place.

Aaron had returned to Matabeleland a month after Daniel. Mary had been delivered to her family in the Herero capital of Otjimkandje and Aaron remained in South West Africa long enough to see her settle back in tribal life as though she had never been away. His attempts to barter his goods were less successful. The wagon-loads of ivory and feathers were delivered to Whalefish Bay and sold at a very high price to the trade-hungry dealers, but few ships now called at the isolated port. Aaron could buy no goods to bring back to Matabeleland.

Many of the merchants of Whalefish Bay had closed their premises and returned to their countries of origin. One or two had been bought out by Germans. The Germans alone, of all the trading nations, were taking advantage of the tribal wars, supplying arms to any tribe rich enough to pay for them.

After such an unsatisfactory trading experience, Aaron was eager to make a trek to Sena. Little trouble was expected from the Pombeiros now, but with Kanje safely out of the way in the northern swamplands, Jandu sent half an impi to escort Aaron to his destination.

Only one cloud darkened the horizon of Daniel's life in that warm and pleasant winter of 1869. Farewell Loveday had returned to Khami.

When the two missionaries had set out for Cape Town earlier in the year, poor, weak Arnold Pugh-Williams was a sick man. Two weeks later, after a lifetime spent nursing imaginary illnesses, he died uncomplainingly of malaria in the heat of a Kalahari afternoon.

Arnold Pugh-Williams was buried in a sandy grave at the edge of the trail that cut through a corner of the wide desert. Within a week, all record of the feeble missionary's existence had disappeared. The shifting sands of the Kalahari quickly swallowed up his grave and the rough wooden cross was reduced to ashes on a Bushman's fire.

The death of Pugh-Williams caused the mission authorities acute embarrassment. There was now no one to press the charges for which they had brought Loveday to Cape Town. In addition, his arrival with Helena Pugh-Williams set tongues wagging furiously.

Anxious to avoid a full-blown scandal, the mission authorities granted Helena Pugh-Williams a small pension and booked her a passage on the first available ship to England. The Superintendent of the Mission Society gave Farewell Loveday a long lecture on the virtues of discretion – and then informed him of his transfer to a remote mission station in the heart of Natal.

The posting was humiliating to a man with the Reverend Loveday's ambitions. It was also likely to prove extremely uncomfortable. The initial complaint about his conduct had been made by Arnold Pugh-Williams to the Bishop of Natal.

After a lengthy discussion with Helena Pugh-Williams, Farewell Loveday resigned from the mission society. Marrying the widow of his late colleague in some haste, he set off with her to return to Khami as a freelance missionary/trader.

His actions caused the biggest scandal the British community in Cape Town had ever known, but Farewell Loveday was unrepentant. Indeed, he turned the furore to his own advantage. Returning to Khami via Transvaal, he stopped at Potchefstroom where he had two days of talks with President Pretorius and other officials of the Transvaal Assembly. Loveday told the Boers that he was prepared to help them to gain a foothold in Matabeleland – but he also made it clear that he was willing to sell his services to the highest bidder.

When Daniel came to Khami after Farewell Loveday's return and heard the news, he was incredulous and not a little hurt that Jandu should have allowed Farewell Loveday, of all people, to trade in direct competition with Retallick and Copping.

Jandu was apologetic. 'I am sorry, but I am not yet King. The full Council of Indunas agreed that Loveday should be allowed to stay in Matabeleland, to serve your God and to trade with our people.'

Daniel looked at Jandu suspiciously. 'The full Council of Indunas met to discuss whether a man should be allowed to trade with the Matabele? There's more to this than you're telling me, Jandu. What's Loveday offering to trade – guns?'

'Will *you* sell us guns?' Jandu countered.

'I would sell them to you willingly, but neither the British nor the Portuguese will let me have guns in the quantities you need. They've both learned from bitter experience that sooner or later the guns will be turned against them. Farewell Loveday must be getting them from the Boers. No doubt they're selling them to Kanje too, just as they were a year ago. But even the Boers are hesitant about selling guns to the tribes – unless the price is one they can't possibly refuse. What are you giving in return for these guns, Jandu?'

Jandu shrugged, 'Nothing . . . yet. When I am King they want me to sign a treaty of friendship with them. Is that so bad?'

'It depends what conditions they put into their "peace treaty".'

Jandu smiled. 'By then I will be King and able to appoint you as my adviser of treaties. But not so serious, trader. You own a beautiful piece of my country and come to buy five hundred cows from me. You are a rich man with a new bride. Why should you be concerned with trade at all? Remain at Insimo with your wife. Raise many cattle and fine children. Now, when can I bring Suliyana to visit you? She has spoken of nothing else since your return . . . .'

For a while Farewell Loveday's trading activities hit Retallick and Copping very hard. The Matabele tribesmen fortunate enough to kill an elephant or ostrich still came to Daniel. So too did the occasional English hunter on a brief visit to Matabeleland, but the majority of ivory and feathers went to Farewell Loveday.

Aaron returned as the rains broke in November and the partners spent many of the wet evenings on the verandah of the house at Insimo, discussing the future of trade in Matabeleland. As Jandu had said, they really had no need to trade any longer. Aaron had been trading for a lifetime and had accumulated enough money to enable him to live in modest comfort for what remained of his life. Even so, he swore he would die of boredom within a matter of weeks if he had to stop working.

Daniel too could cease trading without suffering hardship. He was building up a vast cattle herd in the Insimo valley and had asked Senhor Farrao to arrange to have a couple of high quality bulls shipped by sea from the Cape Colony during the 'cool' season. He hoped to produce superior cattle to those bred by the tribesmen. Such animals would command a very high price from the Matabele, to whom cattle were the ultimate status symbol.

Daniel had also proved that the Insimo valley was an ideal spot for growing maize. He had planted enough at the beginning of the season to meet the needs of the whole population of Khami. Of course, if all else failed there was always the gold! But Daniel refused to contemplate gold-mining for the time being – and he was not going to let Farewell Loveday drive him out of business without a fight. He and Aaron went ahead with their trading plans.

The rainy season of 1869/70 was a disastrously short one, lasting barely two months. It made little difference to Daniel, water was plentiful in the Insimo valley. But the rains meant life or death to many of the villagers in the tiny communities scattered throughout the surrounding hills. Their headmen consulted the uGangas – the tribal 'witch-doctors' and for once they were all in agreement. The rains had failed because the traditional ceremonies offering tribute to the Gods had not been performed – and these could not be held until there was a King to lead the celebrations. The Gods were offended. They needed to be appeased in time for the great ceremony of Nxwala – 'First Fruits', traditionally performed soon after the cessation of the rains. Last year this great ceremony had not taken place and now the Gods were showing their displeasure.

The Council of Indunas met and agreement was swiftly reached. A reasonable time had elapsed for the missing heir to put in an appearance. Kulumani was declared to be officially 'dead'. No man must ever utter his name again. The time had come for Jandu to take his place as King of the Matabele.

Jandu was told to prepare himself and orders went out for the headmen and Indunas of the impis, strategically scattered throughout Matabeleland, to return to Khami and salute their new King.

The celebrations began at the end of January 1870 and the entire populace turned their faces towards Khami to witness the coronation of the new Matabele King. For the first time since Mzilikazi's death, the impis came together as a great army – but not *every* impi obeyed the call of the Great Council. As coronation day drew near, five impis remained absent. Among them was the crack regiment of which Kanje was the Induna.

A message was sent out to the recalcitrant Indunas, carried by senior members of the Council, in order that there should be no mistaking the authority of the call. One regiment wavered and was welcomed back into the loyal army of the King-elect. The remaining four impis withdrew into the swamplands of the Makololo tribes – and the tribal Elders sent to change their hearts were never seen again.

This was not the time for the Matabele people to raise their voices in anger against Kanje and his adherents. It was an occasion for rejoicing and celebration. A time to laud the new King – and enjoy his generous hospitality.

The tribesmen and their families gathered in tens of thousands about the capital, their campfires lighting the bush-veldt for many miles in every direction.

Daniel took Elvira to Khami in a horse-drawn wagon and they camped on a Kopje overlooking Khami, from which they would have a fine view of the whole coronation ceremonies. There were others here too, including all the Europeans who had gathered at the Matabele capital, hoping to gain concessions from a new and inexperienced King. Late arrivals on the kopje were Farewell Loveday and his wife. Helena Loveday was heavy with child and Elvira's heart went out to her as she struggled up the hill behind her husband. Elvira and Helena were the only two European women in the whole of Matabeleland, yet Helena Loveday acknowledged Elvira's presence with no more than a frigid inclination of her head, before turning away to talk with her husband.

As preparations for the coronation got under way, Jandu was taken to a small cluster of beehive-shaped huts, about two miles from Khami. Just before the actual ceremony began, he sent a message to Daniel, asking him to ride down to see him, bringing a spare horse. It seemed Jandu intended arriving for his coronation in some style.

Daniel reached the huts just as the Matabele army set forth from Khami to bring back their King. Dressed in ceremonial costume, each man's height was added to by a tall plume of feathers, rising eighteen inches from a band about his forehead. Across his shoulders, each warrior wore a cape of black skin, or feathers. A short skirt of skin hung from his waist, while arms and legs were decorated with bangles of beads.

In full battle array, the warriors were an awesome spectacle. Thirty-five thousand strong, they lined up twenty deep in the traditional 'head-and-horns' formation that their enemies had found invincible in the past.

In solid formation, a mile wide, the army advanced slowly across the space between Khami and the King's kraal until they were no more than a few hundred yards away. Then, at a given signal, their long shields decorated with two crossed spears were held in front of their bodies, forming blocks of different colours, each one representing a separate impi. Now the army moved more slowly, singing as they advanced and stamping their feet to the ground in unison, causing the earth to tremble before them.

Elvira thrilled as Jandu rode out from his kraal to meet his army, Daniel riding close behind him. A roar went up from the Matabele warriors as they swarmed about their King, enveloping the two horsemen in their midst. Moments later the ranks parted and Jandu and Daniel emerged, riding their horses at a slow walk. The great army fell in behind them, singing the praises of the King, who had himself served and fought in their ranks as a warrior.

Once he reached Khami, Jandu went forward with Daniel to meet the Great Council of Indunas, seated in the great cattle pen beneath the shade of the lone Indaba tree.

Jandu slipped to the ground to join the circle and as Daniel led the two horses away the coronation ceremony began. The senior Induna, Umnombati, related in a loud voice the reason why Jandu was undoubtedly the true heir to the Matabele throne, while lesser Indunas called out the praises of their new King. Meanwhile, hideously masked uGangas sprinkled specially prepared powders over their new ruler to cleanse him from all the impurities that might hamper him in his new role.

The first day's ceremonies came to an end when Umnombati pointed to Jandu and, in the loudest voice he could muster, cried, 'See him, warriors of the Matabele. Here is your King.'

That evening Daniel and Elvira went to Khami to spend the night in the store. The ceremonies and accompanying celebrations would continue for six days.

The next morning Suliyana came to the hut to take Elvira to the Royal enclosure to watch the proceedings in comfort, while Daniel was once again called upon to accompany Jandu.

This day's proceedings began with the ritual slaughter of black oxen, each one dedicated by Jandu to a named ancestor. Afterwards more cattle were killed, this time to feed the hungry warriors of the impis who pledged their loyalty to Jandu as they came forward to eat his meat.

So the daily ceremonies went on, often repetitious, but always colourful. On the final day Jandu was led away to a hill from which there was a panoramic view of much of Matabeleland. Here, his voice weak from six days of unaccustomed usage, the aged Umnombati made his final speech. Summing up all the dignity that his years had given to him, he slowly extended his arm and swept it in a wide arc to indicate much of the land about them.

'See, Jandu, there is the country of thy father. His cattle and his people are now yours. Take them and cherish them. Those who sin against your laws – punish. But those who obey – reward.'

Then the old man sank to his knees with some difficulty and banged his forehead on the ground at the younger man's feet. Jandu was now King of Matabeleland.

CHAPTER NINETEEN

After his coronation, it was expected that the new King would move to a new capital, as was the custom of his Zulu forefathers, and Indunas were sent out by the Council to choose a site. However, Jandu was in no immediate hurry to leave Khami. Suliyana was heavy with her first child and the present capital was pleasantly situated.

In the meantime, Jandu acquired sufficient muskets to arm two impis and he asked Daniel to train his warriors in the use of the unfamiliar weapons. The task was difficult, frustrating — and occasionally dangerous. The danger was due in no small measure to the poor quality of the guns supplied by Farewell Loveday. So bad were they that Daniel insisted that in future he be allowed to test every musket before it was accepted by the Matabele. The result was that two in three of the trade muskets were rejected as quite useless.

Alarmed by Daniel's actions, Farewell Loveday came to see him one day when Daniel was paying a visit to the Khami store. There had never been any pretence at friendship between them, but Loveday's manner was conciliatory — at first.

After admitting that rejection of two thirds of the muskets was playing havoc with his profits, Farewell Loveday indicated the goods piled up against the stone walls about the two men. 'You're a trader, Retallick. You know it's not possible to be too choosey about trade goods delivered this far from civilisation.'

'A good trader takes that into consideration when he sets his prices,' retorted Daniel. 'I'm testing guns as a friend of Jandu — not as a trader. Some of those I've sent back to you would have exploded in a man's face. As for the powder . . . !' He snorted derisively. 'It might have been brought to Africa by van Riebeeck!'

'The Matabele are given the same grade of powder as I sell to anyone else. I'm not an expert on gunpowder — and neither are you. Anyway, I have to take what I'm sent.'

'True. But Jandu doesn't. He'll take delivery of no second-rate goods while I'm around.'

'That may not be for much longer.' Farewell Loveday was stung into indiscretion. 'The Transvaalers have got your measure. They'll have you out of here so quick you'll be over the border before you have time to draw breath—'

Checking himself belatedly, Farewell Loveday gave Daniel a final glare before stomping from the store, slamming the door shut behind him. He left Daniel wondering what he had meant about the Transvaalers. They had no power here in Matabeleland and they would never dare to invade – or would they? Daniel decided he must pay more attention to the gossip of the few Europeans who came to his store. Someone had commented a few weeks earlier that there was a great deal of Boer activity in those regions of Transvaal closest to the Matabeleland border. Daniel had taken no notice of the remark then. Now he wished he had pressed the man to tell him more.

Before Daniel was able to look into the matter, Victoria entered his life once more. The end of the 1870 dry season was approaching and Daniel was at his Insimo home when one of the herd boys ran to the house to say that a rider was approaching along the valley.

Visitors to Insimo were so infrequent that Daniel and Elvira both hurried to the door. To their great surprise they saw Victoria nearing the house, riding a very weary horse. Slung in front of her was a young child, little more than a year old.

As Victoria pulled the horse to a halt she swayed in the saddle. Elvira ran past Daniel and accepted the child as Victoria swung it down to her. Victoria slipped from the saddle and Daniel stepped forward hurriedly to prevent her from falling.

'Daniel, I need help . . . Philippe is badly hurt.'

Victoria was obviously distressed, but Daniel found it difficult to summon up any sympathy for the Pombeiro.

'Troubles between the Portuguese army and Pombeiros are best left in Mozambique. Jandu can do without having them spill over into Matabeleland. What happened? Was there a fight?'

'It's nothing to do with the Portuguese.' Victoria clung to him as she pleaded. 'Daniel, I beg you to help him. There have been fights . . . too many. Captain St Anna has militiamen in every town and village. Their orders are to shoot coloured men on sight – whether or not they are Pombeiros. Philippe decided we must leave Mozambique and begin a new life together. We are on our way to Otjimkandje.'

'To thieve – or to fight for the Herero?'

Victoria was very, very tired. Her eyes filled with tears of defeat and she dropped her hands from Daniel in despair. 'He hoped . . . to trade. I said you might help him to make a new start. I should have known better. You have good reason to hate Pombeiros. You and your . . . wife.'

She reached out and took Therese from Elvira. As her thin shirt tightened against her body, Daniel could see how thin she was. Standing beside her horse with Therese in her arms she managed to muster some of her old spirit.

'You are wrong about Philippe. He *has* stolen – and killed, but he grew up knowing no other way of life. He had two older brothers who were Pombeiros. Both are now dead. Philippe is a much gentler man than they. He has been kind to me and has a great love for Therese. He is my man, Daniel. A *good* man, whatever the world may say. I would die for him. I *will* die for him.'

Before Daniel could reply, Elvira put an arm about Victoria and began leading her towards the house. 'Daniel will bring your man to our home. You will both stay here with the baby.'

Victoria stopped and looked hopefully at Daniel. He capitulated, grateful to Elvira for taking the decision from him. 'I'll go and fetch Philippe. Where did this accident happen? How badly is he hurt?'

'It was no accident. We were attacked by a Matabele impi, no more than ten miles north of here. Philippe was shot in the leg. We had only one horse but managed to escape, leaving the impi our wagon and the oxen . . . everything we owned.'

'A Matabele impi ten miles from here?' Daniel was startled. This was well off the beaten track for either a hunting party, or an impi raiding Mashona country.

'They were Kanje's men.'

'Are you certain? Quite certain?' Now Daniel was alarmed. Kanje's impi was supposed to be hiding in the Makololo swamps. They had been there since before Jandu's coronation.

'I lived with the Matabele for almost as many years as you, Daniel. The warriors carried shields bearing Kanje's colours. They were his men.'

'How long ago did all this happen. Are the impis heading this way?'

'I don't know. I don't think so. They seemed to be heading for Khami, but some of Kanje's men came after us. We were attacked just before dusk last night. We wandered around in circles in the darkness. By this morning Philippe was too weak to stay on the horse. I couldn't hold him and the baby. I left him in the shade of some overhanging rocks – about an hour's ride away.'

'You'd better come and show me the place. Elvira, give her food and drink while I organise some herd-boys to come with us.'

For a brief while Insimo was a scene of unusually hurried activity. Daniel issued muskets to some of his herd-boys and another was sent to ride to Khami to warn Jandu of Kanje's presence. Others were ordered to drive the herds of cattle to a high-walled side valley where they might be protected from Kanje's impi if the need arose. Most of the remaining herd boys were brought to the house and stationed with muskets behind heavily shuttered windows.

Daniel was grateful for the whim which had made him build the house so that it might be easily defended. The house could only be taken at the expense of massive loss of life on the part of the attackers – and Daniel believed Kanje had other plans for his warriors.

Daniel, Victoria and the mounted herd boys had travelled two miles from the house when, at the wide entrance to the valley, the youthful Matabele marksmen were called upon to put the training Daniel had given them to the test. Topping a small rise, they rode headlong into about fifty of Kanje's warriors, carrying guns in addition to their shields and spears.

With a cry of warning to the others, Daniel kneed his horse forward and charged through the ranks of the startled Matabele rebels, discharging both barrels of his rifle at the only warrior who retained sufficient wits to attempt to stop him.

Daniel's herd-boys and Victoria rode full tilt after him, firing as they came on and scattering Kanje's warriors.

When Daniel and his companions drew rein to reload, Kanje's men attempted an old-style Matabele charge. It became apparent immediately that the guns they carried were no more than morale-boosters. Four shots were fired at Daniel's party but the bullets went wide. The remaining warriors appeared to have little idea of firing a gun and one or two warriors threw them to the ground in disgust, trusting to their more familiar assegais.

The short, stabbing-spears were no match for the well-aimed muskets of Daniel's mounted party. When the first charge broke, seven men lay dead on the ground.

For fifteen minutes the one-sided battle followed the same pattern. Fire . . . and withdraw. Load, fire . . . and withdraw. It was so easy that long before the last few survivors threw down their arms and fled, Daniel was sickened by the slaughter he and the others had inflicted upon the foolishly courageous warriors of Kanje's impi.

Only the thought that they might go on to attack the house at Insimo kept him doggedly loading and raising the gun to his shoulder.

When all danger had passed, Daniel walked among the Matabele dead and picked up one of the rifles they had dropped. It was a brand-new Martini Henry breech loader, the moving parts still smeared with the grease put on by the manufacturers. It seemed that Kanje had access to a source of arms that was denied to his half-brother.

Mounting his horse again, he followed after Victoria and not long afterwards they reached the spot where she had left the badly wounded Philippe.

Delirious with pain and loss of blood, the Pombeiro tried to raise his gun and shoot Daniel as he leaned over him. He was so weak that Daniel simply plucked the gun from his hands and handed it to one of the herd-boys.

Daniel was horrified when Victoria changed the rough dressing she had left on Philippe's leg. One of Kanje's men must have been armed with a large-bore hunting rifle and been more skilled than his fellow-warriors. The heavy bullet had shattered the bone about four inches beneath Philippe's knee. He had lost so much blood it was a miracle he still lived. Victoria tied a fresh dressing about the leg, but they both knew the wound needed urgent and expert attention – and that would be difficult to find.

It was a slow return journey to Insimo. Daniel held Philippe before him on his own horse and it was merciful that the wounded Pombeiro was unconscious for most of the way. They met with no more of Kanje's warriors and Daniel guessed that the survivors of the brief battle had fled after the main body of their impi.

At the house, Elvira was busy feeding Victoria's young daughter, but she handed Therese to her mother and helped Daniel to get Philippe to a bedroom. The dressing had slipped from his leg during the journey and Elvira threw up her hands in horror when she saw the wound. Wrinkling her nose, she said, 'It smells as though gangrene has already set in. Philippe needs more help than we can give him if he is to live.'

'I'll have to go to Farewell Loveday, at Khami, he has some medical knowledge. But I can't see him coming all this way . . . not for a Pombeiro.'

'You must persuade him, Daniel. Philippe is no longer a Pombeiro – and he is Victoria's man. We must do all we can.'

'All right, I'll leave now and take two of the herd boys with me. Keep the others in the house until I return – and maintain a watch around the clock. I'll be back as soon as I can.'

'Take care, Daniel. Victoria is not the only wife who is concerned for her husband.'

It was now almost noon. By taking spare horses with him and riding hard, Daniel hoped to arrive at Khami soon after nightfall – if he did not meet up with Kanje along the way.

Dusk found him still twenty miles short of his destination. Leaving the herd-boys at a Matabele kraal, Daniel took the best of the horses and rode on alone.

He reached Khami at a time when most families were settling down after the main evening meal. He went first to Jandu at the royal enclosure, to ensure he had been given the news of Kanje's return to Matabeleland.

Surprisingly, he found the new King in a relaxed and cheerful mood, accompanied by a very heavily pregnant Suliyana and surrounded by female slaves.

'Yes, trader. I received your message. Kanje and his men have now swung to the south, moving through the hills of the

Matapos. He hopes to take me by surprise – but I know his every move. Each hour one of the men following him returns to tell me of Kanje's progress. The longer he skulks in the hills the better. Already I have gathered an army that is large enough to defeat him in battle, but more impis arrive all the time, all eager to take part in the defeat of Kanje. Seat yourself, trader. I am glad you have come to be with me when I set off to meet my brother.'

'I am here to find Farewell Loveday.' Daniel told Jandu of Philippe, and how he had received his wound.

Jandu frowned. 'This is the same Mambari who took the Kalangas as slaves?'

'Yes.' It was futile to try to lie to Jandu. He would learn the truth in due course. 'He has given up the way of life he led then. He is Victoria's man. They have a young daughter and are on their way to South West Africa to begin a new life. If they hadn't run into Kanje, you might well have been taken by surprise.'

Jandu nodded his agreement. 'True. A few Kalangas must not be allowed to sour my gratitude. Victoria's man is very sick?'

'I've never seen a worse leg wound.'

'Then he is fortunate to have earned my gratitude. A white doctor is visiting Khami. Tonight he eats with Farewell Loveday. His name is Henkel and he has been waiting for many weeks to be given permission to "hunt" in Matabeleland. I do not believe he is a hunter. He is a man who walks with his eyes always searching the ground and he examines many stones. The Bechuanas who came with him say he digs holes in a search for gold. Find this doctor. Tell him he is to go to the Insimo valley. If he cures the Mambari he has my permission to "hunt". If the Mambari dies the doctor would do well to leave my country very quickly,' Jandu smiled. 'I would speak to this Mambari. A man who steals the servants of my people and then dares to return to my country is either a fool, or a brave man. I would know which of these he is.'

As Daniel turned to go, Jandu called, 'Wait! Send the doctor to Insimo with someone else. I want you with me when I fight Kanje.'

Daniel knew better than to argue. He walked from the royal

enclosure musing that Jandu was beginning to behave as a monarch ... but perhaps he always had. One thing was certain, in spite of his earlier doubts about taking the throne, Jandu had slipped easily into the role of ruler of the Matabele.

Daniel found Henkel, the German doctor, in Farewell Loveday's house. He and his host were coming to the end of a substantial meal. Daniel was shown to the dining-room by a servant and the sight of so much food made his stomach contract in a sharp reminder that he had not eaten since breakfast time.

When Daniel repeated Jandu's words, Henkel looked uncertainly at Farewell Loveday, seeking his advice.

'Who is the wounded man?'

'His name is Philippe. He's from Mozambique.'

'Philippe the Pombeiro?' Farewell Loveday hooted the words loudly. His flushed face was evidence that the wine had been as plentiful as the food that evening. 'I've heard of him. He's a thieving, lying, half-caste. Why should Jandu care whether he lives or dies, eh?'

'The King is grateful. Philippe was wounded by one of Kanje's men. Because of it I was able to warn Jandu that Kanje is in Matabeleland.'

'Kanje?' Farewell Loveday paled, 'He's not supposed . . . . He's . . . . What is he doing here?'

'He's come to fight Jandu, I should imagine. I hope you haven't been selling guns to him too, Loveday. If you have you'd better get packed and ready to leave in a hurry.'

Daniel had long suspected that Jandu's half-brother had left Matabeleland only in order to re-arm and await an opportunity to challenge Jandu for the throne of Matabeleland. Seeing Farewell Loveday's concern made many things fall into place. The missionary-trader had been playing a dangerous game. Supplying Jandu with old, worn-out muskets and at the same time arming Kanje's warriors with modern weapons.

With a whole country at stake, Farewell Loveday had apparently thought the risk was one that had to be taken. In the eyes of many, Kanje had as much right to the Matabele crown as Jandu. If he succeeded in defeating his half-brother in battle, Kanje would be recognised as King in his place. He could be expected to show favour to those who had supplied him with arms — perhaps by throwing his country open to the white man.

Suddenly, Daniel realised that this was more than one man's bid to make a fortune. Farewell Loveday could never have raised the money to buy such rifles as Daniel had seen. It would require a sum such as only a government might provide — and there was one government with more to gain than any other by securing Matabeleland — that of the Independent State of Transvaal. They had for long sought a means of expanding northwards. With a ruler of their choosing on the throne, Matabeleland would be theirs before its people realised what was happening.

Daniel made another calculated guess. With so much at stake, the Transvaalers would not leave Kanje to secure his throne backed by only a couple of dissident impis. Jandu had thought that Kanje was heading for the Matopos Hills hoping to attack Khami from there and take him by surprise. It was far more likely that Kanje was going there to link up with a Boer force for a combined attack! Jandu had to be warned.

To the German doctor, he said, 'Well, have you made up your mind? Are you coming?'

'I will come. What time will we leave in the morning?'

'There's a bright moon, you'll leave tonight. I'll send someone to accompany you and make sure you don't get lost. Pack only what will tie behind you on a horse. You'll find anything else you need at my place. I'll see you there in a few days.'

Before Kurt Henkel could argue, Daniel had gone. There were urgent matters to discuss with Jandu.

CHAPTER TWENTY

Jandu set off from Khami at dawn with four impis – a little more than five thousand men. It was the same number of warriors as Kanje had in his own army. Two more royal impis had been despatched to watch the river crossings far to the south. Daniel had convinced Jandu that the latest developments, coupled with persistent rumours of armed Boer commandoes just across the border, indicated a Transvaal involvement. Now Jandu was on his way to confront Kanje while runners were sending more impis to take up positions between Kanje and the Transvaal.

The latest reports put the position of the dissident Matabele warriors as no more than twenty miles from Khami but Jandu and his impis moved much faster than Kanje's men, who had brought their women and cattle with them from the lands of the Makololo.

Jandu's scouts had carried out their task well. By midmorning they were arriving from the shadowed valleys ahead of the advancing impis with increasing frequency, pinpointing the position of Kanje.

The opposing forces led by Mzilikazi's two sons met on a wide hillside overlooking a beautiful, fertile valley, when the sun stood high in the sky. It was a battleground chosen by Kanje once he realised he was being pursued.

Even at this late stage Jandu was reluctant to join battle with his half-brother. He sent an Induna to Kanje, urging him not to set brother against brother. To accept the decision of the Council of Indunas and return with his warriors to the Matabele people.

Jandu's plea was so uncharacteristic of the Matabele's warlike nature, that Kanje mistook forbearance for weakness. The King's army was no larger than his own, and Kanje's warriors were well armed with their modern rifles. Only two of Jandu's regiments carried guns and these were a laughable mixture of flintlock and percussion muskets, with no more than a handful of breech-loaders.

Kanje's response was a typical example of Matabele humour in its crudest form. The ranks of Kanje's warriors parted to allow a number of women through. When they were no more than a hundred yards from the royal army, they turned their backs on the King. Bending over, they raised the flaps of their short leather skirts high. The insult brought howls of anger from Jandu's men and it was as much as Jandu and Daniel could do to prevent the royal army breaking ranks and falling upon the dissidents.

Jandu's continued restraint was once more misconstrued by Kanje. His men bunched up in the traditional head-and-horns formation and, shouting insults, charged the ranks of the King's army.

It was a disastrous tactic. Those men in the 'head' of the battle formation were so tightly crowded together that only a few in the front rank could use their guns. Those on the strung-out 'horns' of the advance were too far away from their enemies to shoot with any accuracy – had they been trained in the use of their weapons.

As Kanje's impis swept forward, firing haphazardly and erratically, Jandu's own musketmen held their fire. Not until no more than forty yards separated the two armies did Daniel shout an order for the front rank to shoot.

The result was devastating. Musket balls and bullets poured into the closely packed ranks, many passing through the bodies of more than one man. As the leading rank fell to the ground, those coming behind stumbled over them. They rose to take the full force of a volley fired by the second rank of Jandu's warriors.

By the time the third rank opened fire Kanje's impis had been thrown into utter confusion and the attack lost its momentum. Then Jandu's voice roared forth above the din, calling upon his warriors to fall upon Kanje's impis using assegai and shield.

Thrusting and stabbing with their broad-bladed, short-handled assegais, the loyal warriors drove the dissidents before them until they finally broke and fled, seeking refuge among the broken rocks of the hillside. Behind them they left two thousand bodies strewn upon the bloody slope.

The battle now became a slaughter as Jandu's men swarmed up the hill and fell upon the women and children.

Daniel watched this cruel finale ashen-faced. He had seen warfare in South West Africa and been involved in tribal battles there, but he had never before witnessed bloodshed on this scale. The stench of death and the howls of the blood-hungry Matabele warriors terrified Daniel's snorting and protesting horse and Daniel rode him back along the slope to calm the animal down. It was now he saw Kanje. Daniel did not recognise him at first. He was one of three warriors who broke from a dense clump of Msasa trees, fleeing from the fury of Jandu's warriors.

Daniel had witnessed enough killing for one day. He reined his horse to one side, to allow them to pass. Then one of the warriors stopped and raised a rifle and Daniel recognised Kanje.

The hatred in Kanje's eyes bordered upon insanity. Daniel's revolver cleared the holster and he fired from the waist a split-second before Kanje's finger tightened on his own trigger. The rifle shot went wide as a heavy revolver bullet struck Kanje in the hip, the force of it knocking him to his knees. For a few moments the two men looked at each other. Then a dozen Matabele warriors, led by Jandu ran down the hill towards them. They had seen Kanje flee from the scene of the battle and come after him.

The warriors paused beside Kanje, spears raised and looked to their King. This was his half-brother, royal blood ran in Kanje's veins.

Before Jandu could give an order, Daniel said quickly, 'Spare him, Jandu. He's been discredited. His impi's defeated. He'll never pose a threat to you again.'

Jandu raised his eyes and Daniel saw in them the same frenzied excitement that was on the faces of the Matabele warriors.

'I *beg* you, Jandu, your father granted me the lives of Kanje's captives once, remember? One of them was Suliyana, your chief wife. Give me the life of your brother.'

The half-crazed look left Jandu's eyes, but the coldness that took its place was even more terrible.

'He is my brother, trader, but I am King. When I was made

King I swore to punish those who broke the laws of my people. There can be few who have broken more tribal laws than Kanje.' He pointed towards the unsighted battlefield. 'Thousands of my people are dead, more than any enemy has ever killed. They are dead because of the ambitions of Kanje, son of Mzilikazi – the father of the Matabele. Yet, had he beaten me he would have stood before the council of the Indunas and declared he so loved the Matabele that he would be their King. Yes, he is my brother, trader, but the Matabele are my children now. For their sake there can be no mercy for Kanje – kill him!'

The raised assegais came down again and again and Daniel turned his head away quickly. Minutes later Kanje was dead. The last threat to Jandu's throne had been removed.

It was a week before Daniel was permitted by Jandu to return to his home in the Insimo valley. During this time, at a crossing on the Shashi River, a minor clash occurred between Matabele impis and Boers and Daniel hurried to the scene. When he informed the Boer leader that Kanje was dead and his army destroyed, the commando leader decided that he and his men had no business to pursue in Matabeleland. Much to Daniel's relief they withdrew to the Transvaal.

One or two of Kanje's lesser Indunas had survived the battle and saw no reason to keep the secrets of the dead pretender. The Transvaal government *had* supported Kanje and they implicated Farewell Loveday in the intrigue.

Daniel felt certain the missionary-trader would be expelled from Matabeleland this time, but yet again the incredible power of Mzilikazi stretched beyond the grave and saved him. The dead King, father of the Matabele nation had made a promise to the ambitious missionary. No Matabele would dare break that promise. Besides, Jandu reasoned that Loveday would never again have the confidence of the Boers. He had urged them to annexe Matabeleland and his scheming had failed.

Another important factor now took away the immediate threat of Transvaal expansion into Matabeleland. Diamonds were discovered at Kimberley – and at the same time gold petered out in the mines of Tati. The eyes of Africa were turned to the south. Men temporarily abandoned their ambitions in the lands of the Matabele and headed for the more tangible fortunes to be found in the blue clay of Kimberley.

One man, however, thought he had discovered his Eldorado where others had failed. That man was Doctor Kurt Henkel.

Daniel returned from Khami armed with the knowledge that he was in a stronger position than ever before. Farewell Loveday was to remain in Matabeleland – but as a missionary only. The right to trade had been taken from him. Retallick and Copping was once more the only trading company operating in Matabeleland – and he had Insimo.

After the bloody battle between Jandu and Kanje, Daniel had sent a message of reassurance to Elvira, but as Jandu's impis scoured the countryside in search of Kanje supporters, the hills of Matabeleland echoed to rumour and counter-rumour. Elvira's relief at having Daniel home again threatened to overwhelm him.

In answer to Daniel's question about Philippe, Elvira told him that the wounded man had lost his leg. Doctor Henkel had been forced to amputate it just below the knee. Daniel winced at the thought of what such a loss would mean to a man like Philippe, who had spent such an active life in the saddle.

Daniel went to visit Philippe at the earliest opportunity and found Victoria in the room with him. Much to Daniel's surprise, Philippe did not share his misgivings about the loss of his limb.

'No one need feel sorry for me,' he insisted. 'Thanks to you and Victoria I am here. To give up now would mean that you both risked your own lives for nothing. No, I shall do all the things I did before.' He gave Daniel a pain-filled grin. 'Perhaps I'll be slower, but that is all. Once, at Quelimane, I saw a sailor with a wooden leg. He was the mate of a ship trading between India and Portugal. He boasted he could do anything any other man could do – and do most of them better. I'll be the same, I promise you.'

'I believe you,' said Daniel. 'But where will you go?'

Philippe looked to where Victoria stood at the foot of his bed, holding a thumb-sucking daughter. 'We'll find somewhere.'

'My only trading rival in Matabeleland has just gone out of

business,' said Daniel, as though thinking of the idea for the first time. 'I'm going to be busier than ever before. I'll need someone to run things in this valley while I'm away. Do you think you could take it on?'

Victoria looked at Daniel in delighted disbelief, then her expression underwent a change. 'You're forgetting ... Philippe carried off those Kalanga tribesmen. If Jandu learns Philippe is in Matabeleland he'll have him put to death.'

'Jandu knows. Philippe made amends when he ran across Kanje's men and I was able to warn Jandu. My offer stands if Philippe's up to it – and providing he can remember the Matabele are friends, not enemies.'

'I'll remember. You won't regret your kindness.' Philippe grimaced. In his excitement he had changed position and knocked the stump of his leg.

'When you're well and are learning to walk we'll talk about this again. Now, where's that German doctor? I want to have a word with him.'

One of the herd-boys told Daniel with a smile that Henkel had been seen heading along the valley to the east soon after breakfast. The Matabele thought the German doctor mad because he was in the habit of wandering along the valley and up the hillsides, tapping the rocks with a little hammer. Daniel was less amused. Before leaving Khami he had learned that Kurt Henkel was more than a doctor of medicine and a keen hunter. The German was a renowned geologist – and his African travels were being financed by a London mining company.

Daniel intended bringing Henkel back to the house and sending him on his way to Khami before he found what he was seeking – but Daniel was already too late. He found the doctor on the bank of the stream where Daniel knew there was gold. Kurt Henkel was on his knees, hammering a stake into the ground. In the stake were carved the German's initials.

'What do you think you're doing?' Daniel asked, angrily.

Henkel was taken by surprise by Daniel's sudden appearance, but he faced him defiantly. 'I am staking a claim for this area. You will find a stake with my initials at each corner of the area I am claiming . . . Stop! You cannot do this . . . .'

Henkel shouted in dismay as Daniel pulled the nearest stake

from the ground and tossed it into the stream, where it was quickly carried away by the tumbling water. Complaining bitterly, he trotted behind Daniel as he located three more stakes and treated them in a similar manner.

'. . . I have staked my claim in a manner that is internationally recognised. Certainly it is accepted by the government of Transvaal – and I hold a prospecting permit from them.'

Daniel rounded on Henkel. 'What has Transvaal to do with Matabeleland?'

Henkel looked genuinely surprised. 'They have jurisdiction here, no? Soon they will occupy the land and appoint an administrator. Herr Loveday told this to me. He is a man of God, he would not lie—'

Daniel snorted. 'The Reverend Loveday's God has little more influence in these parts than the Transvaal government. Jandu rules this land – all of it. He gave me this valley. As far as I'm concerned that includes mineral rights – and every other right. If you don't agree I'll take you along to Khami and you can argue points of law with Jandu. If you're lucky he'll do no more than send you packing. In the meantime you can empty your pockets and give me any gold you've already found.'

When it became clear to Henkel that his protests were in vain, he handed over two small nuggets. Then he tried to reason with Daniel, promising to make him a rich man if he would join forces with the London mining company and persuade Jandu to allow them into Matabeleland.

Daniel looked at the German pityingly. 'Look around you, Henkel. All the land you see belongs to me. I have cattle, maize – and a house in the most beautiful setting in Africa. What more do you think you can give to me?'

Picking up a small knapsack containing Henkel's geological tools, Daniel swung it through the air to the doctor. 'You're still free to wander as you wish in my valley – but in future one of my herd-boys will be with you. As soon as Victoria is able to cope with Philippe I'll have you escorted to the Transvaal border. If you've got any sense you'll forget everything you've found here. Jandu will never allow miners to enter his country. Any who do get past him will be shot the moment they set foot in my valley.'

In September 1870, it seemed the prospects for peace in Matabeleland had never been better. The territorial ambitions of the Transvaal Republic had been thwarted and they would never again be in a strong enough position to invade Matabeleland. Indeed, so chaotic did the situation become in the sparsely populated Boer Republic, that Transvaal was itself annexed by Great Britain in 1877.

Jandu, hailed by his people as 'the scatterer of his enemies' took the accolade as his royal name, thus fulfilling yet another of the prophesies of the White Mondoro. 'The Scatterer', or 'Lobengula' as he will hereafter be called, was so distressed by the wholesale slaughter of the flower of Matabele manhood, that he moved his capital to the place of the great battle and named it 'Bulawayo' – 'the place of the killing'. Those who came after thought the name had been given in pride. Only Daniel knew that his capital had been so-called because it was here that the heart of Jandu died and Lobengula, the scatterer of his own people, was born.

But even as the labour pains of the Matabele people gave birth to Lobengula and a new and hopeful reign began, the final chapter in the story of their nation had already begun. On the first day of September, in that same fateful year, a sickly youth of seventeen years stepped from the gangway of the sailing-ship *Endora* to the dockside at Durban, port for Natal. This was the homeland of the Zulus and birthplace of Mzilikazi, first King of the Matabele.

The delicate young man was the fifth child in an English vicar's family of eleven children. Because of his status, his pile of worldly possessions took up very little space on the stone paved dockside. Those who noticed him observed his unhealthy pallor and shook their heads, declaring he would never survive the rigours of African life.

Yet, in a few whirlwind years, this same youth would become a diamond millionaire, be elected Prime Minister of the Cape Colony and redraw the map of Africa. His grandiose dreams of empire would allow no room for a tribal kingdom – such an anachronism needed to be put where it belonged: within the pages of the history books.

This then was the man. His name – Cecil John Rhodes.

BOOK TWO

Matabeleland
in the 1890s

Zambezi R.

Tete

MASHONALAND

MANICALAND

Umniati R.

Hunyani R.

Ft. Salisbury

Shangani R.

Sabi R.

Macequece
Ft. Umtali

MATABELELAND

Insimo

Ft. Victoria

Chena

Khami

Bulawayo

House of Chiefs

MATOPOS
HILLS

Shashi R.

Ft. Tuli

Limpopo R.

N

MILES

0   50   100   150   200

1871–87

The early years of Lobengula's reign brought expansion, prosperity and great happiness to the Insimo valley. Cattle multiplied and great herds grazed the valley. The slopes of the surrounding hills were covered with acres of golden maize. Insimo provided most of the food for the Matabele capital of Bulawayo and, in times of drought, Daniel's maize went further afield. He provided food for the inhabitants of the most distant kraals of Matabeleland and even the persecuted people of the parched hills of Mashonaland. The unmapped border of Mashonaland was not far from the Insimo valley and, timidly at first, then in increasing numbers, the Mashonas came to Insimo and were given work.

These were fruitful years for Daniel and Elvira too. In October 1877, their first son, Wyatt, was born. He was followed in 1880 by Nathan. Adam arrived in 1883 and the next year a fourth son, Benjamin, completed their family.

It gave Daniel a great feeling of pride and achievement to ride off along the valley with young Benjamin perched on the saddle before him, while the other children followed on their own ponies. Daniel and the Matabele herd-boys taught the young brothers to hunt and track game. From Elvira, they learned the good manners that set a Portuguese gentleman apart from his fellows.

The only sadness to touch the valley during these happy years was the death of Philippe. For many years he served Daniel well, taking care of things in the valley and occasionally making the journey between Insimo and Sena with Daniel's trade wagons. Philippe had been pardoned by the Portuguese authorities, who were relieved to be rid of the threat he and his Pombeiros had posed to them for so long.

Philippe died peacefully in his sleep, at home in the Insimo valley. He had been ill for many months, a victim of a tiny parasite that infested the slower-running rivers of Matabeleland. His death came as a hard blow to Therese. Brought up in the belief that Philippe was her true father, she adored him.

Therese had grown into a girl as attractive and vivacious as Victoria had once been. Her mother guarded her jealously, determined that her daughter would not suffer as she once had.

Lobengula's early years were good for the Matabele nation too. With no one to dispute his leadership, and absolute power in his hands, Lobengula devoted himself to the betterment of his tribe.

He ruled with restraint and wisdom. If his people never moved forward in step with the world beyond the borders of Matabeleland, they still commanded the respect they had earned with Mzilikazi as King.

Lobengula gathered many wives about him during his reign, but none of them achieved the status accorded Suliyana. She bore two sons to ensure the succession of her children to the throne of Matabeleland. The eldest, Nyamatakah, was born in the year his father became King. The second, Lundi, arrived within a week of Wyatt Retallick. The two boys became firm friends from the moment they learned to toddle together. Both were happy to spend days in the home of the other and Lundi so impressed his father with talk of life in the Retallick household that Lobengula had a house built of stone for himself.

Farewell Loveday remained in Matabeleland and still lived with his wife and their many children in the neglected and seedy old mission of Khami. It had become the rendezvous of the gradually expanding group of hunters and concession seekers who found their way to Matabeleland. These seekers and hunters came from many countries. Some had ridden 'up-country' from the Cape Colony. A few had travelled from Britain and Australia. Many had merely waded across the muddy river that separated Matabeleland and Transvaal.

The concession seekers, ridden by greed and uncertainty, were a squabbling, suspicious, constantly changing community, but, unlike Mzilikazi, Lobengula at first seemed to enjoy having white men about him. He took their presents and accepted their flattery, giving very little in return.

In time, Lobengula also grew very fond of the white mens'

drink. Brandy, gin – even crates of champagne found their way to his stone-built house.

During his often prolonged bouts of drinking, Lobengula's benevolence occasionally exceeded caution. An increasing number of unscrupulous white men staggered from Lobengula's presence in a woefully drunken state – but happy in the knowledge that they had obtained mumbled permission to explore his lands.

Eventually, in spite of all that Daniel tried to do to prevent it happening, heavy drinking took its toll on Lobengula's health, just as it had with his father. The fit, athletic warrior that had been Jandu, gave way to the gross, overweight man who was King. Daniel's concern occasionally resulted in Lobengula giving up heavy drinking for days – sometimes weeks, but as soon as Daniel left Bulawayo, the King was persuaded to return to his habits.

As his mental and physical state deteriorated, so Lobengula emulated Mzilikazi by adopting more and more of his excesses. His impis extended the range of their raids and undertook expeditions against the warlike Barotse, across the Zambezi River. They also continued to raid the unfortunate Mashonas, pursuing both with great ferocity.

By the middle 1880s there were equally bloody happenings at home. The scheming Indunas frequently manoeuvred their King into situations which resulted in the deaths of many of his closest friends and advisers, leaving Lobengula a lonely and suspicious man.

Farewell Loveday had become reconciled with the mission authorities and reported all these happenings to the mission headquarters in London, his reports being seized upon and avidly repeated in the newspapers throughout Great Britain. Laymen, arrogant with the power of Britain's greatness, advocated sending an army to put an end to Lobengula's bloody reign. In cathedrals, churches and chapels, men of God prayed that the Lord might send someone to carry the candle of enlightenment to the Matabele.

Unknown to them all, such a redeemer was already on the scene. One who would make a great impact on Southern Africa and change history in a manner to leave even the empire-building Victorians breathless with admiration. A man whom Daniel's instincts recognised as more of a threat to the Matabele way of life than all the concession seekers and renegades who warmed their hands at Lobengula's fire.

Cecil Rhodes was no longer the sickly young man he had been in 1870. Working in the new diamond diggings at Kimberley and financing his efforts by making and selling home-made ice-cream, Rhodes' determination and hard work paid off when Luck threw in her elusive lot with him. The toiling miners of Kimberley struck hard, blue bed-rock. Convinced that their claims had 'bottomed-out', they were happy to sell them off for the price of their fares home. For sums ranging from fifty to one hundred and fifty pounds, they unloaded them on the foolish young man who was mortgaging his future to his own intuition.

When Rhodes owned almost the whole of the Kimberley claims, he brought in his own experts. They announced that the 'bed-rock' was in fact blue, diamond-bearing clay. Soon afterwards the rains arrived and confirmed their diagnosis. The 'rock' became a soft, squelching putty that yielded a fabulous crop of diamonds.

Rhodes reaped a vast fortune from Kimberley – then went on to accumulate another in the gold fields of Witwatersrand. Now a multi-millionaire, the youthful Rhodes used his money to buy a seat in the Cape parliament – and immediately embarked upon a remarkable plan to expand the British Empire.

Within a few years, in a successful bid to thwart similar expansion plans made by the Transvaal Republic, Rhodes had engineered the annexation of half of Bechuanaland to the Cape Colony, proclaiming the remainder a British Protectorate.

A few years later, this remarkable man had Transvaal itself annexed by the Crown. This proved too much for the undisciplined Boers. Temporarily putting aside their own differences, they united to inflict a humiliating defeat on the British army and, in 1881, took back their land.

The Boers had set back Rhodes' dream of Empire, but his eyes were already upon the vast lands extending for mile upon fertile mile to the north. Rhodes realised he was involved in a race against time. The territory over which Lobengula held sovereignty was being squeezed unmercifully by larger and more ambitious nations. Portugal, Transvaal and the Germans, newly-arrived in South West Africa, were poised to take advantage of a savage and unsophisticated ruler.

Cecil Rhodes knew the time had arrived to take the initiative. In so doing he would change the lives of hundreds of thousands of men. Among them would be Lobengula – and Daniel Retallick.

CHAPTER ONE

In 1887, Daniel still owned the only trading company of any note in Matabeleland, but maintaining his monopoly had become increasingly difficult. Trade through Mozambique had slowed to a trickle, due to the current hostility of the Portuguese government towards all things British.

Southern Africa became jittery as it became apparent to everyone that the stage was being set for a showdown between the countries jostling for colonial expansion north of the Limpopo River.

At the moment, Great Britain would appear to be the favourite to gain the rich prize. They had already pushed their influence to the Matabeleland border, standing shoulder to shoulder there with the more militant, but far less organised, Boer Republic of Transvaal.

Portugal, historically the country with the soundest claim to the coveted lands, could do little more than stand on the sidelines, complaining impotently, her government and army in disarray. Nevertheless, the Portuguese authorities in Mozambique were able to make it very difficult for a non-Portuguese trader to bring his goods through their country. Only the powerful influence of Senhor Farrao kept the door to the Indian Ocean ajar for Daniel.

Fortunately, Daniel was able to open up a route to the sea through Transvaal, thanks to the efforts of a Boer named Uiys Toblin. Quietly spoken and sincere, Toblin was a trader and part-time hunter who had been allowed by Lobengula to shoot lion in Matabeleland for many seasons. When Toblin offered to put his resources in Transvaal at their disposal, in return for a share of the Matabele market, Daniel and Aaron were quick to agree. The arrangement worked very well, but the government of Transvaal refused to allow the partners to trade in the one commodity that Lobengula desperately wanted. Guns.

Two years before, Lobengula's impis had suffered their first defeat since the early days of Mzilikazi's flight from Shaka. It happened in humiliating circumstances. On an annual raid in neighbouring Bechuanaland, they attacked an inferior number of Bechuana tribesmen, only to discover they were a part of the Bechuana King's army armed with modern rifles, supplied by the British. The defeat of the Matabele impi was decisive, very few warriors escaping to tell Lobengula of the debacle.

Lobengula realised, there and then, that his warriors had to have the white mens' weapons if his tribe were to survive. He asked Daniel for his help, but the numbers that Senhor Farrao was able to obtain were hardly enough to equip Lobengula's personal bodyguard, let alone the forty other impis stationed about his kingdom.

The problem had not been resolved when Toblin brought his family to the Insimo valley early in 1887, to spend some months with Daniel and Elvira. The visit provided a wonderful interlude for Elvira who was always grateful for female company – but the visit was not without its problems.

One evening, Daniel came in early from the valley where he had been supervising the breaking-in of a number of young colts from his own horse herd. Sitting on the verandah he was enjoying a drink with Uiys Toblin and Jaconus Van Eyck, a grizzled old hunter employed by Toblin. With Van Eyck's son Jannie, the men had been on a number of successful hunting trips in recent days. Suddenly, Daniel saw a grim-faced Victoria heading for the house, leading her tearful and reluctant daughter, Therese, by the hand.

The years had mellowed Victoria – but not much. On many occasions, especially when she was angry, she showed the spirit of the younger Victoria . . . and she was angry now. Without a word of greeting, she strode on to the verandah and glared around her. Then, ignoring Daniel, she addressed her words to Jaconus Van Eyck.

'Where is he? It's no use trying to hide him from me. If I have to search for him I might have a gun in my hand when I catch up with him. If I do, I'll shoot him . . . .'

'Victoria, calm down! No one has the faintest idea what you're talking about. Where's who? Who are we supposed to be hiding?'

Victoria turned to Daniel and some of her anger died away. 'I'm sorry, Daniel. I had no right to come here like this.' She swung her attention back to Van Eyck. 'But he knows what I'm talking about. Ask him where his son is.'

Daniel began to understand. Therese was a very pretty eighteen-year-old with dark eyes and the vivacious ways of her mother. Van Eyck's son was of a similar age. A quiet, well-mannered boy. A good-looking boy . . . .

'I know where my Jannie is – but I'll not tell you while you're in your present mood. I suggest you control yourself, tell me what's happened. Then you and I will go and speak to him together.'

Almost as softly-spoken as Uiys Toblin, Jaconus Van Eyck's manner was mild, but his manner was deceptive. The hunter, now in his fifties, was a veteran of the Zulu wars in Natal. As a boy, he had survived an attack by Shaka's army on a Boer laager. He was a man whose courage needed bolstering by no bluster.

Victoria thrust Therese forward. 'Ask her what's happened. Perhaps she'll tell you more than she'll admit to me. What I do know is that she's been sneaking out of the house at night to see your son, when I thought she was in bed. I got the truth only today, after I overheard one of the Matabele herd-boys telling another that he'd seen Therese batheing in a pool up on the hill – with your son! I want to know what's going on. I know how the Boers treat coloured women – and I'm not having my daughter talked about by herd-boys. Neither do I intend being left with some Boer's bastard to look after, while he rides away scot-free.'

Jaconus Van Eyck looked seriously at the girl. 'Is there any likelihood that you're with child by Jannie?'

'No!' Therese's denial was emphatic and she looked at her mother in great distress. 'We've done nothing like that. I love Jannie, yes – and I think he loves me, but we've never done that together. Never—.' Suddenly she broke down and began sobbing. Daniel felt very sorry for the young girl having to endure such a humiliating ordeal.

'Love!' Victoria spat the word at her daughter. 'You're coloured. The daughter of a Pombeiro. A half-caste. Your precious Jannie is a Boer. Do you think it's *love* he feels for you? No, girl. You've led a sheltered life here. You've never been out of the valley . . . to the places where white men gather.

I have. *I'll* tell you about the 'love' you'll find with a Boer—'

Ignoring Victoria's outburst, Jaconus Van Eyck walked to Therese. Putting a finger beneath her chin, he gently brought her head up, forcing her to look at him.

'You say you think my Jannie loves you. Has he said so?'

As Van Eyck's finger dropped away from her chin, she nodded vigorously. 'Yes.' It came out as a defiant whisper.

Jaconus Van Eyck smiled wistfully. 'Then you can be certain you have the love of a very fine young man. Jannie doesn't lie.' Turning to Daniel, he said. 'Perhaps you will give Victoria a drink. I have a story I would like her to hear. It is something I would like you all to hear.'

Daniel poured a drink and handed it to Victoria. When she hesitated, Daniel said, 'Take it and sit down, for goodness sake – and stop playing the angry mother. Therese, you sit down too. I'll pour you a brandy. You look as though you have need of it.'

Reluctantly, Victoria sat down and the tearful Therese took the seat beside her.

Jaconus Van Eyck turned away from the others. As they waited, he looked out at the magnificent view that had first attracted Daniel to Insimo. For some minutes he stood with his back to them. Then he turned round and sighed, 'You know, this place reminds me of a valley I once found in the Drakensberg mountains. I had hopes of building a home there, one day. A home just like this . . . for Jannie's mother.'

A faraway look came into his eyes, but he shrugged it away and addressed his story to Therese.

'What I am going to tell you now is a story that only a few men know. Uiys is one, because he's more of a friend to me than any other man has ever been. Many years ago – more than twenty, I was riding northwards through the Transvaal, on my way from Natal to Matabeleland. I'd been hunting and was well away from any track or homestead. Riding through a valley I suddenly came across a covered wagon, outspanned beneath some trees. Nearby was a cow, a dog . . . and children. Ja! There were many children. Naturally, I rode over to pay my respects to whoever was living in this out-of-the-way place. I was met by a musket, held in the hands of a very determined woman. She told me in no uncertain terms that her husband didn't welcome strangers. That I'd best be well clear of the valley before his return. I didn't believe her. The whole place had that look that a home . . . any home, gets when there's no man about to do all the odd-jobs a woman just can't tackle.'

Jaconus Van Eyck smiled, and there was a pensive look in his eyes as he paused to light his pipe. Blowing blue, aromatic smoke high in the air, he continued, 'I can picture the whole scene as though it all happened only yesterday. The valley, midsummer dry and parched. The tethered cow, with more ribs than meat on its body . . . and the woman. Holding out that flintlock musket, she was scared to hell-and-gone, but was determined not to show it. Behind her, peering around the edge of the wagon were wide-eyed kids . . . so many I couldn't be sure whether I'd counted six, or seven. There was a baby too, crawling in the dirt around a broken wagon wheel.'

Jaconus Van Eyck shrugged his shoulders and sucked noisily on his pipe. 'I wasn't going to stay where I wasn't wanted. Whether she had a man or not was none of my business. I rode off.'

Elvira and Mrs Toblin had come from the house in time to hear the beginning of Van Eyck's story. Elvira was standing by Daniel and her hand found his as the Boer hunter re-lived his memories.

'Yes, I rode off and left them. Didn't even look back until I was half-a-mile away. Then I saw them all lined up, watching me go. The woman, a babe in her arms, and six young 'uns – all girls, standing around her. It's hard to describe the way I felt then. I'd been ordered out of the valley at gunpoint . . . yet I couldn't get rid of the feeling I was letting them down. Running away. Try as I might, that little family group wouldn't leave my mind.

'That afternoon I shot an impala. It wasn't a huge one, no more than a hundred pounds, but I'd only eat a fraction of it. The rest would be wasted. I thought of that family yet again . . . .

'When I got back to the wagon the woman had put away her gun and the youngest of the girls waved. I knew that whatever might be said, they were happy to see me again. Man, it was almost like a homecoming.

'I said to the woman, "I know your husband doesn't like

strangers around, but I shot this impala and it's too big for me."

'She looked me straight in the eye and said, "I didn't fool you. You know there's no man about the place. He got himself trampled by a rhino six months ago. He's buried beneath that tree over there. I suppose that's the only reason we've stayed here – not that we've anywhere else to go."

'I could see that she'd had enough. What with the children, and no man. I've never known what to do when a woman is close to tears, so I just let the impala slide to the ground and turned my horse to leave. She called me back. Told me the least she could do was to cook me a meal.'

Jaconus Van Eyck took the pipe from his mouth and made a loud noise of appreciation with his tongue. 'Man, that was a meal! With all due respect to your own fine cooking, Mrs Retallick, it was a meal such as I'd never tasted before. I sat beside that fire, with the stars overhead, surrounded by six little girls who looked at me as though I were some kind of god, and the baby – it was a girl too – gurgling in its mother's arms. I swear I was as happy as though they were my own.'

Van Eyck's pipe had gone out. Sucking at it absent-mindedly, he pulled a wry face, spat over the side of the verandah and knocked the ashes from it. He began to refill the pipe slowly, completely engrossed in his memories.

'What happened then?' Elvira prompted. 'After you had finished your meal?'

Jaconus Van Eyck delayed the reply until his pipe was crackling comfortably again. 'I never left them. I stayed around and repaired everything that needed fixing. Then I went off and bought some trek-oxen and we headed north west, looking for a place where we could settle. We searched for nigh on three years. Then I remembered the valley I told you about earlier. The one in the Drakensbergs. I turned the wagon in that direction – but we never made it. Funny, really. Martha had produced seven strapping daughters for her first husband, all born with no trouble. Then she ups and dies giving birth to a scrawny little boy who couldn't have weighed no more than five pounds. That was my Jannie.'

'Oh Jaconus! I'm so sorry,' Elvira was close to tears. 'But . . . but what happened to the girls?'

'I brought 'em up myself. Just as Martha would have done. Got them all married off too, choosing husbands that Martha would have been proud of. They were no trouble, and they helped me as though I were their real father. They were good girls. It was Jannie who was the difficult one, in those early days. He would have died if I hadn't met up with a family of Bushmen. One of the women had milk and while I shot meat for the family she breast-fed Jannie. He survived to become a son that any man might be proud to have.'

The long silence that followed Jaconus Van Eyck's moving narrative was broken by Victoria. 'I'm sorry about your wife . . . but it has nothing to do with what's been going on between your boy and Therese.'

Jaconus Van Eyck removed the pipe from his mouth and jabbed it in Victoria's direction. 'It has *everything* to do with it. Martha was coloured. Her father was a Boer, but her mother was half-English, half-Bechuana. It never bothered me, and it never troubled her first husband. Neither did it cause any difficulty for any of Martha's seven daughters. Two of them married coloured men, the other five married Boers and made very good wives. So, now that's out of the way we can decide what we're going to do about our two children. If you still want to run Jannie out of the Insimo valley, I'll take him. Not because he's done anything wrong, but because I'm a guest here and I'll cause no trouble for Daniel and Mrs Retallick.''

The pipe went back in Van Eyck's mouth and he spoke around it. 'On the other hand, if we're talking about your daughter's happiness and not your own pride we'd do better if I fetched Jannie and came to your house to discuss things there. Therese is a fine girl. I'd be proud to have her as my son's wife.'

Therese switched her gaze from Van Eyck to her mother and there was such pleading in her eyes that Elvira's heart went out to her.

Victoria stood up and, for a moment, Therese's hopes plummeted as she avoided looking at her. Then Victoria spoke to Jaconus Van Eyck in a strangely gruff voice. 'I'll be getting back to the house. We'll expect you and Jannie when you find him.'

The young couple wanted to marry immediately, but were

persuaded to wait for a few months. During this time Jannie was to remain at Insimo and build a cabin for his young bride-to-be. Once they were married, Daniel would employ Jannie to hunt game to feed the large numbers of Matabele and Mashona tribesmen who now worked in the valley.

Jaconus Van Eyck took his son to Bulawayo to discuss the wedding with the missionaries there and, much to Daniel's surprise, returned accompanied by Farewell Loveday.

Rumour about Lobengula's capital had it that Loveday was now a Rhodes man, but such a label meant nothing to the Matabele. Farewell Loveday, with his own almost eccentric blend of spiritual mysticism, coupled with sound business acumen, appealed to them. His acceptance by the tribe was matched only by Daniel's own.

It did not take Daniel long to learn that the rumours connecting the missionary with Rhodes were true. On the second evening of his visit, Farewell Loveday asked Daniel to ride with him to the brow of the hill at the back of the house. He claimed he wanted to witness a true, Insimo sunset.

Daniel took Loveday to one of the highest peaks for many miles around. From here there was a superb view along the valley to the lowlands, and over the broken hills to the north and west.

Farewell Loveday sat his horse, gazing about him with undisguised admiration. 'You are a fortunate man to live surrounded by so much God-given beauty, Daniel.'

'I think so,' Daniel agreed. He mistrusted Loveday – and believed this evening excursion was concerned with something more than the beauty of Insimo.

'Of course you do,' said Loveday, unctiously. 'But God created all this to be enjoyed by more than a mere handful of people.'

'The Matabele enjoy it. Lobengula himself agrees that it's one of the loveliest spots in his land.'

Daniel was being deliberately obtuse, waiting for Loveday to show his hand.

'The Matabele are heathens – and likely to remain so until we have enough good Christians in the country to teach them by example.'

Daniel snorted. 'They witness Christian example every day

in their own capital among the concession-seekers and jail-sweepings there. Their quarrelling, lying and whoring is notorious throughout southern Africa. I believe one of them recently brought the pox to Matabeleland and infected the women in Bulawayo. Is this the "example" you want to teach?'

Farewell Loveday flushed. 'All the more reason for civilisation to reach this country quickly and remind white men of their responsibilities. I talked to Mr Rhodes when I was in Kimberley, recently. He agrees with me.'

Daniel knew he was about to learn the real reason for Farewell Loveday's visit, and his willingness to come to Insimo to conduct the wedding ceremony for Jannie Van Eyck and Therese.

'I've heard a great deal about Mr Rhodes' plans,' he retorted. But Christian education for the natives has never been mentioned.'

'I don't know what you've heard, but I assure you that Mr Rhodes is a great man – and a great Christian. He is also an ambitious businessman.'

Farewell Loveday leaned closer to Daniel and lowered his voice as though someone might be listening in the vast emptiness about them. 'Rhodes wants to extend his influence north of the Limpopo. Not here, in Matabeleland – but in Mashonaland. He realises it would be most difficult for white men to live in peace under Lobengula's direct rule, so he's chosen Mashonaland. It's far enough from Lobengula's warriors to avoid trouble, but close enough for the Matabele to see for themselves the advantages of a well-run, Christian society.'

'Why Mashonaland? What's there for him?'

Behaving once more as though they might be overheard, Farewell Loveday said quickly. 'Gold. There's gold in Mashonaland.'

Daniel shrugged. 'Perhaps. But there's been little except rumour, so far.' He looked sharply at the other man. 'Why are you telling this to me?'

'Because between us you and I might change the course of Matabele history. The Indunas listen to me – but you are Lobengula's friend. He trusts you. If *you* suggest that Rhodes be given the sole concession to prospect and mine in Mashonaland I have no doubt it would be granted . . . . No, before you reject such a suggestion, hear me out. Rhodes isn't the only one after such a concession, as you must know. I'm not talking only of individuals who camp about Bulawayo. There is a great deal happening at international level. Transvaal trekkers are massing on the south bank of the Limpopo River. President Kruger is having difficulty preventing them from crossing and invading Lobengula's territory — if indeed Kruger *wants* to hold them back. The Portuguese have recently issued a map on which all of Mashonaland is shown as belonging to them . . . and much of Matabeleland too. In the north the Germans have pressed their claims as far as the border of Angola and are now disputing the Bechuana border with Great Britain. Very soon Lobengula will be forced to make a treaty with someone. His only choice will be . . . with whom? I suggest Rhodes is the obvious choice. I know him well and have always found him to be scrupulously fair. I would also point out that he has the might of Great Britain behind him.'

Daniel remained silent. Unpalatable though it was to him, much of what Farewell Loveday said made sense. He knew, as did Lobengula, that irresistible forces were building up about the borders of Matabeleland, squeezing the country ever tighter. Nevertheless, Daniel did not believe that Farewell Loveday had told him the whole truth about Rhodes' intentions.

'I'll give it some thought, but Lobengula doesn't like being forced into a corner any more than I do.'

'Nobody is *forcing* anyone anywhere,' purred Farewell Loveday, convinced his argument had won Daniel over to his side. 'I'm merely asking you to point out the facts to the King. You'll need money, perhaps, to win him over. With this in mind, Mr Rhodes has authorised me to put the sum of ten thousand pounds at your disposal, to do with as you will. I think you'll agree that he's being most generous . . . ?'

'Rhodes can keep his money,' retorted Daniel, angrily. 'I haven't said I'll help him — or anyone else, yet. You've given me something to think about, true — but that's all. When I reach a decision it will be in the best interest of the Matabele. Now, if you've had enough of the sunset, I suggest we return to the house and rejoin the others.'

Without waiting for a reply, Daniel reined his horse about and began the steep descent to the house.

CHAPTER TWO

Farewell Loveday returned to Khami without winning Daniel to his side, but after his departure Daniel thought long and hard about his words. He accepted that Lobengula might well be forced to give someone a concession, in order to safeguard the future of his country, but Daniel did not accept that Cecil Rhodes was the right man. True, Rhodes was one of the most influential men in southern Africa. He was also the richest. A member of the Cape parliament, it was hinted he would soon take over that country's premiership. But Cape Colony was a long way from Matabeleland. Other countries, Mozambique, Transvaal – and perhaps the Germans in South West Africa, were all within striking distance of Matabeleland.

Daniel felt Mozambique could be ruled out. The Pombeiros were active again. The Portuguese could not spare an army to occupy the interior. Daniel was less certain about the Germans in South West Africa, but from all he had heard they were fully occupied in their new colonial territory and were unlikely to risk losing all they had gained by taking on Lobengula and the Matabele nation.

This left only the Boer Republic of Transvaal – and Daniel admitted that it posed the greatest threat of all. Having recently regained their independence by defeating a British army at Majuba, the Boers would not hesitate to tackle the Matabele impis, no matter how awesome their reputation. Furthermore, the Boers suffered the same fears as Lobengula. That of being strangled out of existence by potentially hostile nations. For this reason alone they were unlikely to stand by and allow Lobengula to sign a treaty with any of the other parties.

Daniel gave the matter a great deal of thought before seeking Uiys Toblin and telling him of Farewell Loveday's proposition.

Toblin's initial reaction was cautious. 'Do you think Loveday really is Rhodes' emissary? Or is he trying to pull off a coup that he can sell to Rhodes, leaving the other concession hunters to go home and count their losses?'

'I believe he's Rhodes' man,' declared Daniel. 'To be charitable to him, I'm also convinced that Farewell Loveday believes the Church will gain by such a concession.'

Uiys Toblin snorted cynically. 'They might . . . but only if there's a long-term profit in it for Rhodes.' He looked at Daniel quizzically, from under lowered eyebrows. 'Why are you telling this to me? You must know that if I return to Transvaal and tell Paul Kruger what's in the wind he'll likely as not send his trekkers across the river – then send a Boer army to their aid if Lobengula attacks them. Kruger is a great believer in possession being nine-tenths of the law, Daniel. Even Rhodes would think twice about bringing an army this far up-country to dispossess him.'

'That's true, but it's a risk that has to be taken. I'm gambling on the fact that the Transvaal can ill afford a war at the moment. Kruger has as much land as can comfortably be administered and he's won a period of breathing space from the British. I'm certain he will forgo expansion for a treaty guaranteeing an independent but friendly country on his northern border – for a while, anyway.'

'If you can give him such a treaty I would agree with you – but why should you do this? You're English. Why should you throw in your lot with us Boers?'

'I have an English name, Uiys, but I've lived all my life in Africa and look upon the tribes as my people. I've carved out a good life for myself, here at Insimo. That life is secure only for as long as Lobengula and his heirs rule their own country. I don't trust Rhodes. I want things to remain exactly as they are. I believe this is the best way of ensuring they do.'

Uiys Toblin nodded. 'Perhaps. But will Lobengula agree to such a treaty?'

'After I've explained it to him, yes. The concession hunters have done their best to destroy him with drink, but Lobengula is still King of the Matabele. He knows instinctively what's best for his people. He'll sign.'

'Then I'll do the same on behalf of Paul Kruger and take the treaty to the Transvaal for his approval. When are you going to put this to Lobengula?'

'Right away, before Rhodes comes up with another plan that we'll know nothing about. We'll leave for Bulawayo in the morning.'

'Before we go I'll send Jaconus home to the Transvaal with my family. This treaty could stir up trouble with the concession hunters. I'd like my family well out of the way . . . just in case.'

Daniel agreed. As he had told Farewell Loveday, many of the so-called 'concession seekers' were, in reality, no more than fugitives from justice. They had found a safe and unexpected refuge from the law in Matabeleland. Few of them had any real interest in gaining entry to the interior of Matabeleland, or Mashonaland. They were quite content to remain at Lobengula's kraal, praising the King and enjoying the generosity of the unattached Matabele women. Any treaty concluded with one of the major powers would certainly contain a clause appertaining to the apprehension of fugitive criminals. For many it would amount to a death sentence. They would go to great lengths to prevent such a treaty being agreed.

As Daniel and Uiys Toblin approached Bulawayo it became increasingly apparent that all was not well. The Matabele capital was buzzing with excitement. Indunas hurried to and from the Royal Kraal, while armed impis trotted off in every direction.

With the two men were Wyatt, Daniel's ten-year-old son, and Lundi, second son of Lobengula and Suliyana. Lundi was returning home after having spent some months at Insimo.

As they entered the town, Lundi dug his heels into the ribs of his pony and galloped to head off a small impi led by a young and eager Induna. Moments later, Lundi rode back to the others, an expression of deep concern on his young face.

'What's happening? Are the impis out looking for someone?' It was a calculated guess on Daniel's part. Had there been danger from an invading army, the impis would be leaving Bulawayo in strength and all heading in the same direction.

'Yes,' Lundi answered Daniel's question, dark eyes wide. 'They are searching for Gamba. He and my sister, Hlomela, were found lying together in the hills. The impis have been ordered to kill him.'

Daniel gasped. The Matabele did not usually take illicit relationships between unmarried men and young girls too seriously, even when one was the daughter of the King, and the other the best known and most respected Induna in the King's army. But Hlomela had been promised as a bride to Umzeila, the Shangaan chief whose tribe extended across the far side of the Limpopo River and provided a useful buffer between the Boers and Matabele. Such a promise was as binding as the marriage itself. The amorous young couple were guilty of an act that was tantamount to adultery – and the Matabele punishment for this was . . . death.

Such a punishment inflicted upon a man of Gamba's standing was likely to cause a deep and lasting division in the Matabele nation. Gamba belonged to the small, but influential band of Matabele aristocrats, the 'abeZanzi', or 'Men from the south'. Of pure Zulu descent, their ancestors had advised and supported Mzilikazi when he broke with the Zulu nation and headed north. They were, in fact, more truly Matabele than Lobengula himself – for the King's mother had been a Swazi! Gamba's death would anger the abeZanzi and might raise again the long-forgotten issue of Kulumani, Mzilikazi's missing son. The resentment aroused could plunge the land into bloody civil war once more.

Such a situation required cool and dispassionate evaluation. Usually Lobengula excelled in handling such matters – but only if he were sober.

Leaving Wyatt to open the trading store and make Uiys Toblin comfortable, Daniel rode with Lundi to the King's kraal. Lundi was particularly concerned about Hlomela's fate. She was actually his half-sister, her mother being herself a woman of the Shangaan tribe, but Hlomela had always been closer to Lundi than any of the other children of the King. Daniel did his best to reassure the boy, although he knew Hlomela's only hope of surviving lay in the fact that she was also the favourite of Lobengula himself.

Daniel found the King pacing the long living room of his stone-built hut, issuing rapid orders to an Induna who kneeled before him, eyes averted from the face of his angry ruler.

Lobengula's eldest son, Nyamatakah, a tall, rangey youth of seventeen, stood scowling near the window. Nearby, Hlomela's mother sat on the floor, wailing noisily. A number of lesser wives were also in the room, eyes rolling nervously, afraid of showing any sympathy towards their unfortunate fellow-wife.

'Ah! You have heard the news, trader? Have you come to share the sorrow of a father whose honour means nothing to an ungrateful daughter?'

Lobengula waved his hand in an impatient gesture of dismissal and the Induna rose to his feet and backed from the room, relieved that none of the King's anger had spilled over him.

Daniel had heard the last few instructions issued to the departing Induna and he said, 'You intend making Gamba's family suffer for his indiscretion?'

'Indiscretion? It is an act of betrayal. His family will die, everyone whose blood runs in Gamba's veins. I will make Hlomela watch their deaths and she will listen to them curse her with their dying breaths. You do not agree with this?'

Daniel assumed an air of indifference. He needed to tread warily. If he upset Lobengula now there would be little likelihood of a treaty with the Boers. On the other hand, he could not allow Lobengula to make a disastrous mistake.

'It's none of my business whether I agree or not – but it's not one of your wiser decisions.'

'Not one of my—? Are you mad? The girl is promised to Umzeila, yet I now learn she is carrying Gamba's child! Very well, given the same circumstances, what would you do?'

'I'd think very carefully before I killed off Gamba's family. That's not going to bring back Gamba. Only the Boers could do that for you. He'll be travelling through their territory right now, heading for his father's people in Natal. He's quite likely to be able to whip up enough feeling there to have an army sent to Matabeleland to fight a war of revenge against you.'

Lobengula looked as though he was about to speak, but Daniel said, 'Hear me out. Such an army would have to come through Transvaal. It would anger the Boers and upset a plan I wish to discuss with you . . . but we will talk of that later.'

Daniel had the King's attention, and he continued, 'What

will you do with Hlomela when Gamba's family are all dead, kill her too? You can hardly marry her off to anyone after this. All Bulawayo is aware of her shame. The most sensible solution would be to send one of Gamba's relatives after him and bring him back·to marry Hlomela. Let him buy off Umzeila's injured pride and pay you lobola for your daughter. You'll be able to set the bride-price as high as you wish. His family is hardly likely to quibble.'

Lobengula's anger gave way to an expression of scowling concentration. Suddenly he smiled and flung an arm about Daniel's shoulders. 'Days spent working the land in your valley have not dulled the trader in you, my friend. Your words tell me this. Whatever befalls, be it good or bad, it must be made to yield a profit. Very well, I will take your advice.'

Lobengula turned to his eldest son who had heard all that had been said in the room. 'Tell the Indunas there are to be no killings. Then send orders for my impis to return – and take these women out with you.' Lobengula waved his wives away impatiently as Hlomela's mother crawled to his feet and began showering kisses upon them.

As they went, Lobengula smiled at Daniel. 'Gamba will need to call on the generosity of all his family if he is to meet the bride-price I shall ask for Hlomela.'

Nyamatakah left the room without a word, but his eyes betrayed the burning humiliation he felt. His father, King of the Matabele, had allowed a white man to alter an important decision that concerned tribal custom. Nyamatakah found it humiliating. He shared the views of the young warriors of the Matabele impis that all white men must be made to respect the authority of the King. If they did not they should be driven from the land. No one, not even an elder son, would question a decision made by the King. One day he, Nyamatakah, would rule the Matabele. He vowed that things would be different then.

Daniel had seen Nyamatakah's eyes as he turned away. 'Your son grows tall, Inkosi. One day soon he will command an impi.'

Lobengula snorted, but the derision was allied to a father's pride. 'Oh yes, he will be an Induna, but to be a King he must learn to see further than the tip of a spear. I hope he will have the wisdom to keep his brother, Lundi, close by him at all times. That boy is a thinker.'

'I came to Bulawayo today to return Lundi to his family . . . but there is another reason why I am here. I would like to talk to you of a treaty, Inkosi.' Daniel used the Matabele word for 'Great Chief', the closest word they had for 'King'.

'You too? I am surrounded by white men who want treaties . . . concessions, call them what you will. They are as persistent as flies about a sick cow. Everywhere I turn, they are there. Their clamour threatens to deafen me. Am I to hear it from you too now?'

'I'm not seeking a concession. My heart is with the Matabele. I believe the treaty I have in mind is in the best interests of your people. Let me tell you my thoughts.'

For a full hour Daniel sat with the King and told him why he thought a treaty between the Boers and the Matabele would be advantageous to Lobengula and his people. Lobengula asked a number of questions, but none that Daniel had not asked himself many times. He had the answers.

When Daniel ended, Lobengula sat for many minutes, his chin resting on his chest, saying nothing.

When he finally looked up, he said, 'You have echoed the fears I have kept locked in my heart for many years. To speak of them, even to my closest advisor, would be taken for weakness. A King must not doubt his own invincibility, or that of his army. To do so is to destroy the pride of his people. Yet you have put these thoughts into words – and offered me a solution. It may not be the right answer, my friend. I do not share your confidence in the Boers, but I accept that the Matabele have little choice. However, such a treaty cannot be made without the consent of the Council of Indunas. I will call them together and we will discuss this. Now, so much talking has made me thirsty. We will drink.'

It was dark when Daniel left Lobengula's house. As he made for the opening in the wooden stockade that surrounded the building, the slim figure of a girl slipped quietly from the shadows. Daniel halted uncertainly as she dropped to her knees and touched his feet with her forehead. Rising quickly, she whispered, 'I thank you for my life – and the lives of

Gamba and his unborn child. Your name will always be praised in our hut.'

It was Hlomela. Before Daniel could make a reply, she pushed something into his hand and ran off as quickly as she had appeared.

When he reached the store Daniel paused in the light shining from one of the windows and examined his unexpected gift. It was a pouch made from leopard skin and heavily decorated with white, green and black beads. Inside was a tightly wrapped package. Hlomela had presented Daniel with a good luck charm of the type that ingangas made up for young lovers, in order that their dreams might be fulfilled.

With a smile, Daniel tucked the pouch carefully inside a pocket. The charm appeared to have worked for the young couple. He hoped it might have retained some of its power for him.

What was probably of far more importance was the knowledge that he had gained some influential friends among Gamba's family.

CHAPTER THREE

The full Council of Indunas met two days after Daniel's talk with Lobengula. The discussions lasted for a week. Daniel would have preferred the meeting to have taken place in secret, but this was not the Matabele way. The Indunas sat around in a circle in the central cattle pen, surrounded by Matabele tribesmen and concession seekers. Daniel had no doubt that the decision of the Council would be immediately communicated to Rhodes.

The Indunas were almost equally divided on the question of a treaty with Transvaal. Only a final speech by Lobengula decided the issue. When a vote was taken, the decision was made to sign a treaty of friendship with the Transvaal Republic.

When the treaty was duly drawn-up, during the morning of the seventh day, Uiys Toblin signed on behalf of the Transvaal Republic. For the Matabele, Lobengula's 'X' was followed by the marks of half-a-dozen senior Indunas.

The celebrations to mark the signing of the treaty lasted for two days, then Uiys Toblin headed south with three ox wagons – and the treaty.

Daniel rose early the following day, to prepare for his return to Insimo, He had just finished washing when a young white man, in a state of exhaustion, staggered into Bulawayo, calling for Daniel. It was young Jannie Van Eyck. He carried alarming news. A strong force of Mashona warriors had made a surprise attack on the Insimo valley, killing a number of herd-boys and carrying off Nathan, Daniel's seven-year-old second son.

Jannie had been hunting some miles away when the incident happened. He heard of it only when he returned, many hours later. He had immediately set out to fetch Daniel. It was dusk by then, but he had ridden through the night, leading a spare horse. His first horse went lame before half the journey had been accomplished. The second collapsed and died twelve miles short of Bulawayo. Leaving the horse and saddle behind,

Jannie Van Eyck ran through lion-infested country during the two most dangerous hours, those that linked night and day.

Leaving the exhausted young hero to be put to bed, Daniel left Bulawayo accompanied by Wyatt, leading behind them all the horses they were able to borrow from the Europeans camped outside the Matabele capital.

By changing horses at frequent intervals, Daniel hoped to reach Insimo late that afternoon, twenty-four hours after the abduction of Nathan.

The two aching riders reached the valley when the sun was poised over the western hills. They found the house shuttered and barred as though to withstand a siege, but as Daniel slid from his horse, staggering as his tired legs took his weight, the door was thrown open. Elvira ran to him, their two younger children standing frightened and confused in the doorway.

Inside the house, Elvira explained in detail exactly what had happened. She confirmed what Daniel had already guessed. The dead Matabele herd-boys had put up a brave but futile fight against Nathan's kidnappers.

Later, Daniel questioned the other herd-boys who had witnessed the swift raid and they all agreed that there had been at least a hundred warriors in the raiding party.

It was an unheard-of number for the Mashonas to gather together. Unlike the Matabele, the Mashona did not regard themselves as belonging to a single nation, owing allegiance to a King, or paramount chief. The Mashonas lived in small villages, or family units, each independent of its neighbour. Their way of life had been dictated to them, to a large extent, by their Matabele overlords. Any hint of a Mashona federation would have brought the full weight of Lobengula's wrath down upon them. It was not an entirely satisfactory way of life, but a small group was easier to hide among the nearby hills when a Matabele raiding party was sighted. Not until one travelled beyond the accepted range of the annual Matabele raids were Mashona villages of any size sighted.

Daniel was questioning one of the herd boys about the raiders, when an aged Mashona said suddenly, 'These men were Mashona – but they were not warriors of the people.'

'What's that supposed to mean?' Daniel looked sharply at the speaker.

'They were the Mondoro's men. Guardians of the House of Chiefs.'

The unexpected news startled Daniel and brought back uneasy memories of many years before. 'Are you certain? Why would they come here to carry off my son?'

'They were the Mondoro's men,' repeated the old Mashona doggedly. 'I have been to the House of Chiefs many times. I recognised some of the warriors. As to why they took your son – who are we to question the warriors of a God?'

There was a murmur of agreement from the Mashona workers and one of the Matabele herd-boys spat on the ground contemptuously. 'The Mashona cringe in fright at the sound of wind in the trees. There is not a brave man among them.'

The comment brought a howl of protest from the Mashonas. The herd-boy who had spoken shifted his spear to his right hand and glared at them defiantly.

'There's been enough blood spilled,' Daniel snapped. 'It's a pity I didn't have this information at Bulawayo. I would have ridden directly to the House of Chiefs and saved a day. That day could make the difference between life and death. If you're going to remain in this valley you'll remember you *all* work for me – and it's to me you give your loyalty, not to a Mondoro.'

Daniel wished Jannie Van Eyck had been able to return to Insimo with him. The only other white man in the valley was Aaron, who was now a man of seventy years of age. He could not accompany Daniel on a wild rescue raid. Eventually, Daniel decided he would set off at dawn the next morning, accompanied by six of his longest serving Matabele herd-boys, each armed with a brand-new Winchester rifle. The guns were part of a consignment confiscated by Senhor Farrao from an American vessel caught trading with the Pombeiros, a hundred miles downriver from Sena. Each of the revolutionary rapid-firing rifles held fifteen shots, giving the small rescue party the fire power of a hundred men.

During the night, Jannie Van Eyck returned. He was tired but determined not to be left out of the rescue attempt. He brought news that Lobengula himself was on his way with his personal bodyguard – an impi of fifteen hundred seasoned warriors. Lobengula sent word that he would reach Insimo late the following day. He urged Daniel to wait for him before going in pursuit of the Mashona kidnappers.

Daniel was relieved to know he would have the backing of Lobengula's Matabele, but he had no intention of delaying his departure a moment later than was necessary. He set off with Jannie Van Eyck and the herd-boys before the sun put in an appearance above the horizon, riding into a beautiful, multi-coloured dawn that quickly pushed back the blanket of thin cloud draping the rocky hill-tops.

Gradually they left the high plateau behind and entered an area of broken hills and dense shrub. When the sun was at its height, they came in sight of the House of Chiefs, with Mondoro's rocky summit behind the circular stone building.

They had been expected. As the eight men slowed their horses to a walk and advanced in an open formation, a white clad figure came out to meet them. It was one of the Elders of the House of Chiefs.

The old man had no weapon visible, but Daniel was taking no chances. He kept his rifle trained on the approaching man until he stood before them and held his arms out wide, palms forward.

'I come alone – to take you to your son,' he said to Daniel.

'If he's been harmed in any way—' Daniel began, but the old man shook his head.

'He is well, although he will welcome the chance to return to his mother and father. He is but a child.'

Daniel looked suspiciously at the Elder, suspecting a trick. 'Why was he taken from his home and brought here in the first place?'

'It was an unfortunate mistake. It arose as a result of a visit to the White Mondoro by some Portuguese soldiers.'

Daniel was still not sure the Elder was telling the truth. The House of Chiefs was two hundred miles from the nearest settlement. He had never heard of them venturing this far inland.

' One of the Portuguese was an important man. He spoke of you, telling the Mondoro you now lived in a valley between this place and the great kraal of Lobengula. The White Mondoro expressed the wish that he might see you again – or one of your sons. Through him, the Mondoro said he would be able to foretell the future of our land for as long as the child had years to live. There were those who overheard the Mondoro's words. They were repeated many times until they reached the ears of the Chief of the Mondoro's army – but by now they had become a command. Anxious to please the Mondoro, the army was taken out to seek your child. The rest you know for yourself.'

The old man looked at Daniel's lathered horse, standing with drooping head, too tired to seek out the few blades of grass that had forced a way through the dry, hard-packed earth. 'Come. You have ridden far and must be tired. You and your men will need to rest before you take the boy.'

Daniel did not doubt the Elder's words, and his relief at knowing Nathan was safe was overwhelming, but he still exercised caution. 'I'll come inside – but alone.'

To Jannie Van Eyck, he said, 'If I'm not out by sunset, go back and tell Lobengula.'

If the old man was offended by Daniel's words, he did not allow such feelings to show. Bowing to Daniel, he said, 'As you wish. Follow me.'

Daniel led his horse through the opening in the massive walls of the House of Chiefs and almost immediately saw Nathan playing in the dust with a number of other children. When he saw his father, Nathan ran to him with a cry of delight. Then, the moment of reconciliation over, he was anxious to return to his young friends, giving Daniel a casual assurance that he was well, puzzled that such a question had been asked.

It was an embarrassing anti-climax to the 'rescue'. Leaving Nathan with his friends, Daniel was led away to a meal, prepared for him by women of the Mondoro's household.

After eating, Daniel was told the White Mondoro wished to speak to him. He agreed to the meeting, but only began to bathe after he had seen Nathan led out and handed over to Jannie Van Eyck.

The blind medium had grown older and frailer in the years since Daniel had last met him, but his memory was as sharp as ever. Running his sensitive fingers over Daniel's face, he nodded happily. 'The years treat you kindly, White Man.'

'I have a good life.'

'It is well. I am sorry it took an unfortunate misunderstanding to bring you back here.'

'It's a misunderstanding that may yet have tragic consequences, Mondoro. Lobengula is coming with a very large impi. Unless I can persuade him to turn back, your people must flee for their lives.'

'They will not leave without me and I am too old to run. Neither will you stop Lobengula, although I do not doubt you will try. I was aware when the Scatterer first came to the Great House of the Chiefs that he had been chosen by Chiminuka to end my life. Let Chiminuka's will be done. I die a happier death than will Lobengula.'

The White Mondoro raised his sightless eyes to Daniel. 'It matters little what the Matabele do to me now. I have given a long life to Chiminuka. I die happy in anticipation of receiving his reward. He will open my eyes to see the things that have been hidden from me in this life. But there is sorrow in my heart for those who must die with me and who enjoy no such wonderful hopes.'

The Mondoro's thin voice died away and there was a silence between the two men for perhaps three minutes. Then the medium of the Spirit God, Chiminuka, shivered violently. 'Go now, White Man. Take your son home. You can be proud of him. He will guard your heritage well, and increase it tenfold.'

The import of the Mondoro's words was not lost on Daniel. 'Nathan is my second son, not my heir.'

'I know this, White Man – and your first born will prove himself truly a man. But this is the child favoured by Chiminuka. It is he who will carry your line.'

Daniel and his party rode twenty miles before darkness overtook them. They made a dry camp among the tumbled granite rocks on the top of a low, kopje. The herd-boy sent ahead to find the camping site had surprised and shot a nice sized klipspringer on the hillside. As it roasted on a spit, a drowsy Nathan sat in the crook of Daniel's arm, leaning against his father and trying hard to stop his eyelids from closing. He was a contented and tired little boy. As Daniel held him he tried to be happy about the bright future predicted for his seven-year-old son – but he could not forget the Mondoro's prediction that Wyatt would not inherit Insimo.

The next morning they met up with the impressive impi led by Lobengula. Driven on by the urgings of their King, the impi moved fast. Lobengula, bedevilled by gout, the same ailment that had made a cripple of his father for so many years, was travelling in a wagon drawn by a team of salted horses. Inside the wagon, Lobengula reclined in a battered old armchair, presented to him by Daniel some years before.

Roaring at his driver whenever the wagon jolted his gouty leg, Lobengula's voice boomed out even louder when the wagon slowed on the ascent of a hill. Immediately, the warriors of the impi crowded around and, taking a grip on horse or wagon, ran it to the top of the rise.

It might have been a comic scene had Lobengula not been on his way to deal out death and torture to the warriors of the Mondoro.

Lobengula was overjoyed to see Nathan and Daniel reunited. After dangling the child on his knee for some while he gave him a small, boxed hand-gun that had been a present from one of the hopeful concession seekers.

In a bid to take advantage of Lobengula's jovial mood, Daniel explained about the mistake that had led to Nathan's abduction. He begged the King to turn around and return with his impi to Bulawayo. Daniel added that the Mondoro regretted the deaths of the herd-boys and would be willing to make generous compensation to their families. He went on to suggest that the King himself should choose cattle from Daniel's herds. He, in turn, would claim them from the Mondoro.

Lobengula's mood underwent an immediate change. 'No. The Elders of the House of Chiefs are men of the Rozwi tribe, the ancient leaders of the Mashona. If they go unpunished the Mashona will follow their example. No Matabele will be safe in his own country. I will have the heads of every warrior who raided the Insimo valley – and their families shall die with them. Come with us, trader. Bring your son and let him witness Lobengula punish those who carried him off from his home.'

Daniel argued with Lobengula, but only succeeded in angering him. Finally, he said, helplessly, 'The Mondoro was right. He told me you would not be turned aside.'

'The White Mondoro has always concerned himself over much with my future. He once told me I would scatter my own people. It was true . . . but I scatter only those who oppose me. Now it is my turn to play the soothsayer. I predict that the Mondoro and his people have only a few hours left upon this earth. I will remain at the House of Chiefs until I see my words come true.'

Lobengula rode away towards the House of Chiefs and Daniel watched him go, helpless to do anything to save the gentle old Mondoro. Daniel's six herd-boys rode with Lobengula, having begged for permission to go on the great raid with their King. On their return Daniel would have first-hand knowledge of the fate of the White Mondoro and his people.

CHAPTER FOUR

Lobengula's expedition against the House of Chiefs was proclaimed a great victory and celebrated as such in Bulawayo. For the first time in his reign, Lobengula bowed to custom and allowed the women prisoners to be used by senior herd-boys for the ceremonial 'washing of the spears'. To many of the younger warriors it seemed that the greatness of the Matabele had returned once again.

Daniel did not attend the celebrations, so sickened was he by the report on the raid, given to him by his herd-boys. The White Mondoro was dead. As predicted by Chiminuka, he was slain by 'the Scatterer'. But it was doubtful whether the far-seeing God had anticipated the manner of the medium's death. Lobengula had expressed curiosity about the whiteness of the albino's skin. Was he a white man through and through, or was there perhaps a black man like his fellows beneath the white skin?

In order to satisfy this passing curiosity, one of Lobengula's Indunas had the helpless old medium flayed alive. Relating the incident without a flicker of remorse, the excited herd-boy said, 'He was white all through – as white as you, but he screamed like a Mashona.'

The following day the herd-boys left Insimo for Bulawayo. Because of the prowess they had shown in slaughtering the inhabitants of the House of Chiefs, they had been accepted as warriors in Lobengula's impi.

Daniel did not go to Bulawayo again until November, when he received an urgent message that Lobengula wished to see him.

When Daniel arrived at the King's kraal he found a full meeting of the Council of Indunas in progress – and Farewell Loveday was with them. A murmur of anger arose from the Indunas when Daniel put in his appearance, but it was quickly silenced by Lobengula. Calling Daniel to him, the King placed in his hands a folded piece of paper, which showed evidence of having passed through many hands.

Without his customary greeting, Lobengula said seriously, 'When you were last in Bulawayo you used your friendship with me to obtain a treaty of peace between the Matabele and the people of your bearded friend. Read, trader. Is this the piece of paper we signed?'

Puzzled, Daniel read. His watchers, anxiously awaiting his reaction, saw astonishment and then anger register on his face.

'This is not the treaty that was signed here! That was a document professing friendship and co-operation. This makes it sound as though the Matabele have agreed to become the subjects of President Kruger. No, it most certainly is *not* the treaty.'

There was a gasp of anger from the assembled Indunas and, as the murmur of their voices gathered in strength, Daniel realised that the anger was no longer directed against him.

But Lobengula was still to be convinced. 'It is easy to put two strokes with a pen on a piece of paper and say "This mark was made by the King of the Matabele." But each white man makes a mark different to any other. Is this not the mark made by your bearded friend?'

Daniel examined the almost illegible signature at the foot of the page. 'It certainly *looks* like Uiys Toblin's signature, but only he would know for certain. Toblin is an honest man. He wouldn't try to cheat you in this way. I'll fetch him here to confirm what I've just told you. This is not the treaty that was signed here, in my presence.'

Now it was Lobengula's turn to look surprised, 'You have not heard? Your friend is dead. Killed by Bechuana tribesmen as he passed through their country after obtaining the treaty.'

The shock of the blunt statement rocked Daniel. 'The Bechuana are not in the habit of attacking white men who pass through their country.'

The easiest road from Bulawayo to the capital of Transvaal – or to anywhere south of Matabeleland – passed through Bechuanaland. Since the country had become a British Protectorate it was considered one of the safest routes in southern Africa. A number of ugly suspicions began to raise themselves in Daniel's mind. 'If he was killed by the Bechuana, what happened to the real treaty – and how did this worthless piece of paper find its way here?'

'Be careful how you handle that "worthless piece of paper", Mister Retallick. It's British Government property – and I understand your friends, the Boers, put great store by it.'

Farewell Loveday stepped forward and took the 'treaty' from Daniel's hand. 'This was sent to Sir Hercules Robinson, Governor of the Cape Colony, by the government of Transvaal. The accompanying letter claims the treaty was negotiated for them by Uiys Toblin. Sir Hercules asked me to bring it here and verify its authenticity. He'll be delighted to have the assurances of King Lobengula and yourself that the document is a forgery. However, it says very little for the morality of your friends, the Boers, that they should seek to tarnish the honour of a dead man by rewriting his hard-won treaty in such a way.'

'I'll know more about "tarnished honour" when I learn the truth about Toblin's death,' retorted Daniel. 'There are a great many people with good reasons for stopping a treaty of friendship between Transvaal and the Matabele from going through.'

'Perhaps. But *if* Toblin was killed by someone else it would appear the Transvaal government wasted no time in taking advantage of the fact and altering the document he had signed.'

Daniel refused to be drawn into an argument with Farewell Loveday. Turning to Lobengula, he said, 'I'm sorry this has happened, Inkosi. I'm convinced that whoever killed my friend is responsible for forging that treaty. I'll go to Bechuanaland and learn the truth.'

'I will give you an impi. They know how to get the truth from a Bechuana. It is time Chief Khama was taught that travellers to and from Matabeleland are under my protection. I will ensure they are not harmed in the future.'

'This isn't the time to go to war with the Bechuana,' said Daniel hastily. 'They're under the protection of the British now. Whatever you do, don't give Great Britain an excuse to send soldiers to Matabeleland. Repudiate the treaty you've just been shown and leave things at that for the time being. I'll return to Insimo now and collect my partner, Aaron. He was a friend of the Bechuanas in his early trading days.'

Farewell Loveday had listened to the exchange between Daniel and the King with barely concealed irritation. He was extremely jealous of the influence Daniel had with the Matabele ruler.

'I suggest you follow the advice you've just given the King,' he said to Daniel. 'Bechuanaland *is* now a British Protectorate and a full investigation into Toblin's death has already been carried out. You'd do well not to meddle in matters that don't concern you.'

'As it happens, this *does* concern me. Uiys Toblin had three wagonloads of trade goods with him when he left Bulawayo. They belonged to me. No one can question my right to find out what's happened to them. What else I learn in the process need worry only the men responsible for the death of Uiys Toblin.'

With this parting shot, Daniel took his leave of Lobengula and the Council of Indunas, and set out for Insimo.

Daniel and Aaron arrived at the border with Bechuanaland to find their way barred by a European officer of the Bechuanaland Border Police, backed by a large party of uniformed native police.

'I'm sorry, sir,' he replied, in answer to Daniel's indignant question. 'The border's closed. The tribes are fighting each other a little further on. It's not safe for travellers. If you're heading south, I suggest you follow the river on the Matabele side and go through Transvaal.'

'We're not passing *through*. We're on our way to see Chief Khama.'

'I'm sorry,' the policeman repeated. 'As your safety can't be guaranteed anywhere in the country, my orders are to allow no one to pass.'

'It's a pity someone didn't warn Uiys Toblin before he was murdered,' said Daniel angrily. 'I think this is a ploy to prevent us from learning the truth about his death.'

'Come, Daniel. We are doing no good here. The policeman has his orders.' Aaron turned his horse and walked it back the way they had come.

When Daniel caught up with him he was still furious. 'I'm not giving up. They're not going to keep me from seeing Khama.'

'Of course they aren't . . . but we couldn't discuss anything in front of him.' Aaron jerked his head in the direction of the policeman. 'He is called a "Border Policeman", I think he said. When I was trading with the Bechuanas there were no such things as borders – and I am too old to start recognising them now. Besides, we are simple men, Daniel. Can we be expected to look at the sand of the Kalahari Desert and say, "This piece here is Matabeleland – that piece a foot away is Bechuanaland"? Of course not. We'll ride back along the road until we're out of sight, then head westwards for a few miles.'

They crossed the border shortly before dusk, in an area of shallow, semi-sterile soil and stunted trees. Almost immediately they encountered another patrol of Bechuanaland Border Police. Fortunately, the men of the patrol were so busy talking and laughing among themselves that they passed over the fresh tracks made in the sandy soil by the horses of Daniel and Aaron, without noticing them. Barely concealed by a clump of thin shrub, the two anxious men pinched the nostrils of their mounts, acutely aware of the clear tracks leading to their unsubstantial hide-out.

When the patrol had passed out of sight, Daniel and Aaron headed into the desert to make their night-camp.

For the next few days they kept to the desert, staying well clear of the Bechuana villages and the tiny, desert-edge settlements. The going was hard but they kept on until their water ran out and they were forced to seek the people they had so carefully avoided until now.

They had wandered further into the Kalahari than they realised. Before long the thirsty horses began to stagger beneath the burden of their riders. To have continued riding would have killed them. But Aaron was an old man. He could not walk in the heat of the day.

They travelled for most of one night. When Aaron tired, Daniel helped him on his horse and they went on until the horse sank to its knees. Daniel coaxed it to its feet again and Aaron walked beside it for perhaps three or four miles, then he declared he was unable to take another step.

The two men lay down to rest. Before the extreme heat of the day became totally unbearable, Daniel pulled up as many bushes as he could, piling them into a heap. He made Aaron crawl beneath the meagre, makeshift shelter and both men rested until evening.

When the sun sank towards the horizon, the two men set off again, heading eastwards towards the sparsely populated region of Bechuanaland. Before they had been walking for an hour Aaron began staggering alarmingly. Daniel knew they could go no further without water. At dawn, leaving Aaron with the horses, Daniel set off, praying he would find a Bechuana village before the sun rose too high.

He had travelled for no more than two miles when he saw a diminutive figure jogging across the sand ahead of him. Crouching low, the man's eyes were studying the ground as he went. It was a Bushman.

Daniel shouted and the Bushman looked up from the faint tracks he was following. For a few moments he stood poised to run, uncertain of this strange man who staggered towards him, shouting and waving his arms. Panic gripped Daniel and his instinct was to shout louder, urging the Bushman to stay where he was. Fortunately, reason returned in time. Forcing himself to slow to a walk, Daniel raised his arm in greeting and croaked, 'I come in peace.'

It had been many years since Daniel had last spoken the Bushman language and the words came out with difficulty. But the Bushman understood – and stayed.

'I have a friend . . . and horses. Over there,' Daniel waved a hand vaguely. 'We are without water.'

The Bushman nodded. 'I have seen you.'

'You've seen us . . . but didn't come to offer help?'

'Many of my people have died because they offered help to the white man.' He put out a tentative hand to within an inch of Daniel's rifle. 'This is not a friend to the Bushman.'

Unslinging the rifle from his shoulder, Daniel held it out. 'Take it. It's yours in exchange for water.'

The Bushman shook his head. 'Such things are for the white man . . . and for the Bechuana. Not for a Bushman.'

From a small pouch slung about his neck, the Bushman took a small, wooden pipe. It was empty and he made the motions of filling it. Daniel reached inside a pocket and pulled out his tobacco pouch containing two large plugs of tobacco. He handed them to the Bushman who, after a moment's hesitation, handed one of them back.

'I will show you water,' he said. 'But first we will fetch the other white man.'

Instead of retracing Daniel's footsteps, the Bushman set off at an angle to them. Ten minutes later Daniel saw Aaron lying beside one of the horses on the hot sand. The other horse was attempting to graze the barren ground. Following the contours of the undulating land, Daniel had walked in a half-circle.

Aaron heard Daniel coming and raised his head eagerly. 'Daniel . . . that you? You've got water?' He croaked the words through cracked and dry lips.

'We're all right now. I've found a Bushman. He'll take us to water.'

With the Bushman's help, Daniel lifted Aaron to his feet and then tried to persuade the exhausted horses to come with them. Neither horse would move. Daniel tried again and again. Then the Bushman tugged at his sleeve.

'Leave them. Water is not far.'

To Daniel's astonishment, the Bushman led them no more than a hundred yards from the spot where Aaron had been lying. There was a slight depression in the ground here, no more. Certainly nothing that Daniel could see in the surrounding plant life to advertise the presence of water.

The Bushman knew better. Digging in the sand like a badger, he dug a hole as deep as his arm in the soft sand. Then, from nearby, he scraped away surface sand and produced a pointed hardwood stick, the tip hardened in some long-ago Bushman fire. With this stick he was able to dig still deeper, scooping the sand out behind him.

Soon the sand being excavated from the hole came out darkened with moisture. A few minutes more and the Bushman was satisfied. Squatting back on his heels, he waited, looking down into the hole.

After some minutes, he grunted in satisfaction. Rising to his feet, he said, 'There is water. Drink.'

When Daniel looked, he saw water oozing from the sand to form a clear puddle at the bottom of the hole. Unslinging his water bottle, he held it in the bottom of the Bushman's water-hole until it was half full. Then he carried it to where Aaron lay panting in the sun.

Aaron downed the half-bottle of water without once removing it from his lips, then croaked for more. But Daniel's next thoughts were for the horses. They had smelled the water. Half-crazed with thirst they would have trampled sand into the primitive water hole had Daniel not beaten them back. He satisfied their immediate thirst by pouring water in Aaron's cupped hands and allowing them each a single bottleful. They would all rest here tonight and drink their fill during the cool night hours, before moving off in the morning, before the sun rose.

So engrossed was Daniel with watering the horses that he did not see the Bushman leave. When he next thought of him, the Bushman was already a mile away, jogging along, head down, following the tracks he had left when Daniel called him. To the Bushman it mattered little that he had saved the lives of two Europeans. He would have been equally indifferent had they both died. They were not his people.

By morning Daniel and Aaron and their two horses were much improved after the well-watered rest and they were able to resume their journey.

That day they came across the first of a number of small, family communities and by evening reached the kraal of Khama, the Bechuana Chief. They received an unpleasant shock. The benevolent Chief Aaron had known during his trading days had died many years before. In his place was a very different man. Mission-educated, Chief Sekete Khama sported tattered European clothing, boasted of having only one wife – and had forced monogamy on his bewildered people. Had it not been for the support of the British government, Sekete would have been deposed and a more tractable Chief elected to rule the tribe. But Sekete was popular with the British government. He ruled as they wished him to rule. He was also important to the Mission authorities, being their most illustrious convert in the whole of Africa. Starved of success elsewhere, they magnified his importance out of all proportion. Each new attempt to emulate his European 'protectors' was flashed around the world as an example of positive missionary influence.

It seemed that forbearance was not one of the qualities instilled in Sekete by his training. When he heard that Daniel and Aaron came from Matabeleland, he accused them of being Matabele spies. Daniel tried repeatedly to tell the Bechuana Chief they were not interested in carrying tales back to Lobengula, but, when questioned about Uiys Toblin, Sekete Khama became furious. Storming from his hut, he called on the warriors of his bodyguard to arrest the white men and throw them into a nearby hut to await the arrival of the police.

The Bechuana police arrived the following day, a group of native policemen led by the same European who had turned them back on the border. He seemed more amused than angry at the manner in which they had disobeyed his instructions. He told them, almost apologetically, that he would have to arrest them and take them to Shoshung, the capital where the Bechuana Commissioner had his office. It was not an unpleasant journey. The trooper displayed a lively interest in the way of life in Matabeleland and was pleasant company.

When they reached the office of the Commissioner, the trooper gave Daniel a quiet but ominous warning about pursuing the manner of Uiys Toblin's death. 'It's a subject best forgotten,' he said. 'No good will come out of it – for you, or anyone else.'

Sir Sidney Shippard, Her Majesty's Commissioner for the British Protectorate of Bechuanaland, was a man who had been in Africa for most of his administrative life – and he was a man not used to having his actions questioned.

He informed Daniel that a full investigation had been carried out into the manner of Uiys Toblin's death. The matter was, he told Daniel, 'unfortunate'. But he went on to say that Toblin had brought his death upon himself. He was travelling with a party of Boer hunters who were known troublemakers. They had provoked an argument with a number of warriors, led by Sekete Khama's brother. During the brief ensuing battle Toblin had been fatally wounded.

When Daniel asked the names of the Boer 'troublemakers', Sir Sidney Shippard said he did not know them. To the question of where the Boer had been buried, he received the surprising reply that Toblin had been carried away by his companions.

Next, Daniel asked how many more men were killed or wounded on both sides, but at this juncture the administrator cut his questioning short.

'I have put everything I know in a report to Sir Hercules Robinson, the Governor of the Cape Colony. That report is confidential and I am not at liberty to discuss the matter. Of far more importance to me at the moment is the matter of your illegal entry into this Protectorate. I could have you fined, or imprisoned. Instead, you will be escorted back to Matabeleland as soon as possible.'

Sir Sidney Shippard smiled at Daniel. 'No doubt your family will be pleased to see you. Your wife must be concerned at being left alone with only Lobengula's savages for company.'

'She's as safe there as anywhere else in the world,' retorted Daniel. 'And she'll need to wait a while longer before she sees me. I'm going south. To Cape Town.'

It was a spur-of-the-moment decision that startled Aaron. Before he, or Sir Sidney Shippard could argue, Daniel added, 'If you won't show me your report I'll go to see someone who can . . . the Governor of the Cape. You *can* refuse me permission to pass through Bechuanaland, Sir Sidney, but I wouldn't advise it. The alternative route will take me through Transvaal. I feel that President Kruger would be very interested to hear that you'd refused me permission to go and see the Governor. It might lead to even more speculation on the circumstances surrounding Uiys Toblin's death.'

CHAPTER FIVE

Daniel and Aaron arrived in Cape Town on the first day of January, in the year 1888. It was a bright and crisp New Year's Day, with just a wisp of cloud adorning the flat-topped mountain behind the rapidly growing town. In the harbour, a wide miscellany of steam and sailing ships displayed flags representing half the sea-faring nations of the world.

It was many years since Aaron had last set foot in Cape Town, and for once the resourceful and capable old man seemed over-awed by his surroundings. Not until he and Daniel were comfortably ensconced in the house occupied by Jacob Jacobs, a trader only a few years his junior, did Aaron relax and become the confident Jewish trader once more.

As Jacobs busied himself preparing a meal for them, he kept up a constant barrage of small talk, giving them the latest colony gossip. Only when Daniel asked him whether he had heard anything concerning Uiys Toblin's death did the old trader's manner become serious.

Turning from the pot he had been vigorously stirring, he peered at Daniel over the top of his steamed-up spectacles.

'So you were a friend of Uiys Toblin, eh? What a man he must have been. When he lived I never heard of him. Now he's dead it seems the whole world is divided between those who were his friends – and his enemies. You want to know how he died! Shall I tell you how the Boers say he died? Or would you rather hear the story put about by Rhodes' men.'

'I'd prefer to hear the truth,' stated Daniel bluntly.

'Perhaps you would. There again, you might not,' said Jacob Jacobs, ambiguously. 'Either way, you're not going to get it. The most popular story at the moment is that Toblin's countrymen had him killed because he refused to put his signature to an altered version of the treaty.'

'All right,' Jacobs spread his hands wide in a gesture of apology. 'You don't like that story? Neither do I, so I'll tell you another version. The more scurrilous gossips suggest that he died because it wouldn't suit Rhodes' ambitions to have the Matabele sign a treaty with anyone but himself – but it's a rumour that men speak of in whispers. Rhodes has the money to buy off all criticism. Anyone he can't buy has a nasty habit of disappearing from the scene. Me, I don't believe anyone. I just repeat what the gossips say. It's certain that Toblin did himself no favour by making a treaty with Lobengula. An *honourable* treaty would suit no one in today's mood.'

'I persuaded Uiys Toblin to sign that treaty with Lobengula,' said Daniel. 'It *was* an honourable one.'

Jacob Jacobs gave Aaron a pleading look. 'You think I have no troubles of my own that you should bring an honest man to my house?'

Putting a plate of steaming meat, mashed mealies and pumpkin down on the table in front of Daniel, Jacobs said, 'Get that inside you. An honest man will have the stomach for little else but good food in Cape Town today.'

Turning back to Aaron, Jacob Jacobs suddenly gave his friend a brief, lop-sided grin. 'It's been a long time, Aaron. Far too long. Tell me, what brings you to Cape Town after so many years?'

'We've come because Daniel – my partner – wants to meet the Governor. I told him you are the man to fix it for him.'

'Well now, seeing him isn't going to be easy. Governors like people to believe they are very busy men. Sir Hercules Robinson is as good a governor as any we've had in the colony . . . but that's not saying a lot. The standard's not been high. I'll see what can be done, but you'll need to give me a few days.'

Putting a meal in front of Aaron, Jacob Jacobs bustled about the kitchen for a few minutes. Then, still wearing the holed slippers he wore about the house, he left the room without a word and Daniel heard him somewhere in the garden. It sounded as though he were talking to some chickens.

'Do you really think he'll be able to arrange a meeting with the Governor?' Daniel asked doubtfully.

Aaron chuckled, 'If *he* can't we've wasted a very long journey, Daniel. Don't let his appearance fool you. After Cecil Rhodes, Jacob is probably the richest man in the Cape. He has interests in a great many businesses, some he's taken from Rhodes. He even stood for Parliament against Rhodes once.

He lost, of course. Well, you've seen him. What chance could such a man have of defeating a living legend? Nevertheless, Jacob is not a man to be taken lightly. You'll have your meeting with Sir Hercules Robinson. I'll stake my share in our company on it.'

Exactly one week later, Daniel was shown into the Governor's office. The deference with which he was greeted was an indication of the standing of Jacob Jacobs in the Cape community — for Sir Hercules Robinson was a Rhodes' man. He listened, occasionally nodding sympathetically as Daniel explained his reasons for coming to Cape Town.

'Yes, yes, I can quite understand your concern,' the Governor said eventually. 'It was a most unfortunate business. Most unfortunate. I have seen Sir Sidney Shippard's report, of course, but I'm afraid its contents *are* confidential. They cannot be released without the express permission of the Foreign Secretary. However,' the Governor leaned towards Daniel in a gesture of implied familiarity, 'I don't mind telling you I am not satisfied. Not satisfied at all. I have asked Sir Sidney to come to Cape Town and explain certain aspects of his report. I would like you to remain in Cape Town until his arrival, Mr Retallick. I realise it will probably be inconvenient, but it will not be time wasted.'

Daniel was dismayed. 'Wait until Shippard gets here? If he comes in a wagon it might take three months, plus another month for your messenger to reach him!'

Sir Hercules Robinson smiled. 'This is not your uncivilised native kingdom, Mr Retallick. I will telegraph to Sir Sidney and he will ride to Kimberley and take a train from there. Did you not come that way?'

Daniel admitted that he and Isaac had not known of the railway, and had given the hurly-burly of Kimberley a wide berth.

'The railway journey takes a mere three days, Mr Retallick, although it will be a week or two before Sir Sidney reaches Kimberley. Stay here at the Cape for a while and enjoy a holiday. Before you know it Sir Sidney will be here and you will be able to take the train on your way home.'

The Governor stood up and extended a hand to Daniel, 'Now you must excuse me. I have a very busy afternoon . . .

new legislation, you know?' He walked Daniel to the door resting a friendly hand on his shoulder. 'We will be having a party at my residence next week. You must come and tell me about your Matabele Chief – or "King", I believe he calls himself. I am quite certain much of what we hear about him is sheer nonsense. Does he really practice cannibalism?'

Daniel fretted in Cape Town for six weeks after his meeting with the Governor. Sir Sidney Shippard did not arrive until the last week in February. During this time, Daniel learned that his long residence in Matabeleland and friendship with Lobengula were well-known facts in the Cape Colony. He was something of a celebrity. Because of this he was invited to a great many social functions. Daniel attended a few but felt so totally out of place that he declined all future invitations. The Cape colonials had only the vaguest knowledge of events in the interior. Their thinking was not far removed from that which prompted Sir Hercules Robinson to ask whether Lobengula practised cannibalism.

When Daniel was called to the Governor's office during the first week in March, he fully expected to meet Sir Sidney Shippard there. Much to his surprise, the Governor informed him that the Bechuanaland Commissioner had boarded a ship bound for England that very morning, 'to confer with the British Government on certain matters'.

'However, you will be pleased to hear that Sir Sidney Shippard has admitted to certain errors in his report.' Sir Hercules Robinson's manner was brisk. 'He agrees that Chief Sekete Khama was to blame for the regrettable incident in which Mr Toblin was killed, and your wagons stolen. If you care to submit a claim, full reparation will be made to you by Chief Sekete Khama. As this claim is being supported by the British Government, you will be paid in full.'

'My wagons and their contents are not important,' retorted Daniel. 'I didn't come all the way to Cape Town for the sake of three wagon-loads of trade goods. I came to learn the truth of Uiys Toblin's death.'

'Of course, of course,' soothed the British Governor. 'It seems the whole ghastly business was a most unfortunate misunderstanding. It was reported to Chief Sekete Khama that the Boers were massing on his borders and about to invade his country. He sent his brother and three hundred warriors to investigate. They met up with Toblin and his party and mistook them for part of the Boer invading force. There was a brief skirmish during the course of which Toblin was fatally wounded. That, very briefly, is what happened. Chief Sekete Khama is most upset at his brother's impetuosity and has forwarded a substantial sum of money to Transvaal, to provide a generous pension for Toblin's widow and dependants.'

'I'm sure that will make everyone happy,' commented Daniel sarcastically. 'I'll take the railway to Kimberley then head for Transvaal to tell Mrs Toblin the good news. But Sekete Khama didn't seem very upset about his brother's "mistake" when I spoke to him. Tell me, who carried word to him that the Boers were "massing on his borders"?'

Sir Hercules Robinson shuffled through the sheaf of papers lying on the desk before him. 'I am afraid I am unable to give you an answer to that question, Mr Retallick. It is not given in Sir Sidney's report.'

'And no one can ask him because he's on his way to England.' Daniel stood up. He did his best to control the anger he felt at having been so easily outwitted by the man seated on the other side of the large desk. 'I'm sorry to have wasted your time – and mine.'

'It has not been a total waste of time for you, Mr Retallick. After all, you *have* obtained a promise of reparation for the loss of your goods. As for myself . . . ?' Sir Hercules Robinson produced one of his best, diplomatic smiles. 'I have thoroughly enjoyed your company. Perhaps the next treaty you persuade Lobengula to sign will be with Great Britain, eh?'

'My advice to Lobengula will be to steer clear of all treaties – not that he will need such advice. Lobengula once told me that white men always say one thing to his people and another to their own. Now he must realise that our written words are no more reliable. I'll give you a word of warning, Sir Hercules and it applies to Transvaal, Portugal, Germany – or any other country hoping to take advantage of Lobengula's inability to read, or sign his name. It's easy enough to concoct a treaty and find men ready to swear they witnessed its signing – but I suggest you remember that Lobengula rules a nation with close to forty thousand warriors who are itching for war. Push him too hard and that's what you'll get, treaty or no treaty.'

When Daniel left his office, Sir Hercules Robinson sat in deep thought for a long time. Then he pulled towards him a slim folder with the word CONFIDENTIAL stamped diagonally across the plain, buff-coloured cover. Opening the file, the boldly printed words on the otherwise plain fly sheet stood out in bold print.

'PROPOSAL TO DECLARE THE NATIVE PROVINCES OF MATABELELAND AND MASHONALAND BRITISH PROTECTORATES.'

Inside were two long reports, both putting forward the arguments in favour of forming such Protectorates. One was signed by Cecil Rhodes. The other bore the stamp of Sir Sidney Shippard, K.C.M.G., Her Majesty's Commissioner for British Bechuanaland.

Raising the silver cap on a squat, glass inkpot, Sir Hercules Robinson dipped a quill pen inside and wrote in quick, neat words beneath the last report.

'I feel most strongly that implementation of the policies suggested here would involve the Government of Great Britain in a great deal of unacceptable expense. There is also a very real possibility that such a course of action would provoke Lobengula and result in him taking up arms against the British Government. Should this happen, the intervention of British troops would become inevitable. Other governments, with some justification, would no doubt suggest we were engaged in occupation, and not protection.

'I agree with both Rhodes and Shippard that British influence should extend north of the Limpopo River, but I believe it might best be advanced by the enterprise of a private company having proven assets. Such a company would, of course, enjoy the full support and encouragement of Her Majesty's Government.'

Sir Hercules Robinson read through his brief footnote. Satisfied, he signed his name.

There was only one company with sufficient assets to advance British influence in Lobengula's domain. That company was owned by Cecil Rhodes.

*   *   *

Daniel stepped from the train in Kimberley in the middle of a torrential downpour. He was tired, but had found the journey from Cape Town quite incredible. Sitting on the hard padded seat of the enclosed carriage, he had watched the countryside flash past the open window at what seemed to be a frightening speed. The six-hundred-mile journey had been achieved in only three days. When Daniel had first made the same journey in a slow, creaking ox-wagon it had taken an uncomfortable two months! Standing on the exposed platform, his saddlebags slung over one shoulder and a bedroll clutched in his hand, Daniel felt more alone and vulnerable than if he had been standing in the empty, scrub-filled bushveldt.

Aaron was not with him. He would not be returning to the Insimo Valley. The aged Jewish trader had been uncharacteristically quiet for many days before they were due to leave Cape Town. Finally, on the last night, he confessed that he wished to remain in Cape Town.

'I'm an old man, Daniel,' he said. 'I can't face that long journey northwards.'

'Nonsense!' Daniel was shaken by Aaron's decision. 'You'll enjoy every minute . . . you always do.'

'I might have fooled you, Daniel. I never fooled my own body. The thought of long hours in the saddle sets every one of my old bones groaning. I have only a few years left to me, my boy . . . . No, don't interrupt me. This isn't easy for me to say.'

There were tears lurking in Aaron's eyes and Daniel fell silent. He realised his partner had given the matter deep and careful thought.

'During the months we have been here I have been reminded of so many enjoyable things I had forgotten. A drink with friends who are old men like myself. Reliving shared memories. I've also visited the churchyard often. My wife is there, you know? Perhaps it's foolish, but I feel closer to her now than at any time since she died. I would like to end my days here – and take my place at her side when the time comes.'

Daniel did his best to hide the unhappiness he felt from Aaron. 'If you're really going to be happier here . . . but Matabeleland won't be the same without you.'

'You've been like a son to me, Daniel. I shall miss you too.'

He brushed a hand impatiently across his eyes. 'Agh! Such tears! I'm just a maudlin, foolish old man. Jacob! Jacob! Where do you keep your French brandy. I want to drink a farewell toast.'

'Mr Retallick? Are you Mr Daniel Retallick?'

Daniel came back to the present. A blue-uniformed African was standing on the station platform before him.

'I'm Daniel Retallick. Who wants me?'

'Sir Hercules Robinson sent word you'd be arriving, sir. You have a room booked at the Kimberley Club. I've been sent to carry your luggage.'

Perplexed, the uniformed African looked up and down the platform for the missing luggage.

Daniel shrugged his saddlebags higher on his shoulder and handed the bedroll to the African. 'This is all the luggage I have. I'm travelling on from here by horse and they aren't built to carry sea-chests.'

Daniel's first reaction was one of annoyance that the Cape Governor should have booked a room without saying anything to him. He might have refused the offer had the weather not been so appalling. As it was, he did not relish the thought of tramping the muddy streets of an unknown town looking for a room.

'Lead on, I'm with you.'

The African shook out a large, black umbrella. Holding it over Daniel's head, he led the way from the bleak, comfortless Kimberley Station, to the unashamed luxury of a club that catered for men who had gained great wealth from the nearby diamond diggings.

Daniel was too tired to eat. Going straight to his room, he lay on his bed and soon dropped into a deep sleep that lasted until the next morning.

He awoke to the sounds of the town stirring beyond the open window. After dressing and shaving, he made his way to the dining-room. Open to residents and non-residents, the Kimberley Club was a popular eating place for all who could afford the excellent food on offer. It seemed that every table in the place was full.

However, it was not many moments before a uniformed waiter asked Daniel to follow him. He was led to a table for two, strategically placed by a window to catch the scant breeze blowing from the rain-sodden hills.

The other seat at the table was occupied by a big man whose face bore a heavy moustache and a somewhat sorrowful expression.

Daniel nodded to his breakfast companion and would have been content to leave their acquaintanceship at that had the other man not extended a hand across the table. In a rather high-pitched voice, he said, 'Welcome to Kimberley, Mr Retallick. I'm Cecil Rhodes.'

Daniel had been half-expecting such a meeting. He knew Sir Hercules Robinson had not booked a room for him out of concern for a man he had met on only a few occasions. He took the proferred hand and looked at the other man with great interest. Cecil Rhodes was a legendary figure, both in England and in Africa, but there was little about his appearance to hint at such greatness.

'I believe you and I have a mutual interest, Retallick. Matabeleland – although in my case it would be true to say that Mashonaland interest me more.'

'Why?'

Daniel had observed in Cape Town that people indulged in conversational games, skirting around a subject without making direct reference to what they wanted to say. He had grown tired of their ways.

Rhodes was momentarily taken aback by Daniel's blunt question, but he was quick to recover. With a disarming smile, he said, 'You'll pardon me, but I'm not used to speaking to forthright men. Most of them say only what they think I want to hear – and they never ask me direct questions.'

The smile grew wider. 'I'll answer you equally directly. There are two reasons. The first is that there's gold in Mashonaland. The second, that I want to see Great Britain's influence extended north of the Limpopo River.'

Daniel shrugged indifferently. 'Substitute Germany, Portugal, or Transvaal for Great Britain and you're saying exactly the same as every other concession-seeker who squats on his haunches around Lobengula's camp fires.'

Rhodes leaned towards Daniel across the table, his smile gone. 'Compare me with any man who dances attention on

Lobengula and you're making as big a mistake as comparing Great Britain with any other country . . . or persuading Lobengula to make a treaty with Transvaal and not with your own country. Why *did* you do that, Retallick?'

'Because Lobengula is a friend. I considered a treaty with Transvaal to be in the best interests of his people. Had they been honest with him I'm still convinced it would have been for the best. Trekkers are as thick as flies across the Limpopo. They're just itching to trek to Matabeleland. The only way to stop them is to call on the assistance of the Boers themselves. You can do nothing about them. The Cape is three months marching time from Matabeleland – even if Britain had an army to send. By the time they arrived a full-scale war would have broken out between the Boers and Lobengula's impis.'

Rhodes nodded. Daniel was talking a language he understood. Carefully weighing one option against another, Rhodes replied, 'What you say makes sense . . . but if Lobengula had a treaty with Great Britain we could put a great deal of pressure upon President Kruger.'

'Pressure after the event would be too late. I want no war. I have a wife and four children in Matabeleland.'

'Ah yes!' said Rhodes. 'You run cattle on two hundred square miles of some of the finest country in Matabeleland. You also have a promising gold deposit on the land.'

Seeing Daniel's astonishment, the smile returned to Rhodes' face. 'It surprises you that I know about the gold? It needn't. Kurt Henkel found the gold on your land, what is it – seventeen years ago? That's close enough. Henkel now works for me. Don't worry, Retallick, your secret is safe. The last thing I want is a gold rush to the land occupied by the Matabele. War does nothing for share prices. I intend forming a company, Retallick. One to make the old East India Company assume the proportions of a village shop. You can help me, and so become part of one of the greatest enterprises of all time. You'll also be bringing the benefits of civilisation to the natives of whom you are so fond. At the same time you can ensure that their homeland remains intact. I'll also give you a signed undertaking that the carriage of all trade goods to and from Mashonaland will rest in your hands – and yours alone.'

It was impossible not to be caught up in the enthusiasm of

this man seated across the table, but Daniel forced himself to remember that Rhodes was a shrewd and ruthless business-man. He gave nothing away without ensuring he had a return

'What am I expected to do to become part of this "glorious enterprise"?' Daniel asked.

'Persuade Lobengula to grant a concession giving me exclusive mineral rights to the whole of Mashonaland.'

Daniel laughed. 'You may not be squatting in the filth of Lobengula's kraal, Mr Rhodes, but you're a concession-seeker right enough. My guess is that Lobengula has had enough of signing pieces of paper held out to him by white men. He'll never agree. I value his friendship too much to try to persuade him.'

Daniel pushed his empty plate from him and stood up, 'You're wasting your time. Stick to Bechuanaland. You have the Commissioner and Chief Sekete Khama in your pocket there.'

'Sit down, Retallick.' Rhodes pulled a thick envelope from a pocket and pushed it across the table towards Daniel. 'I told you not to compare me with any other men you've known. Lobengula has already signed another piece of paper. Here it is. I suggest you read it before you refuse to go along with me.'

Daniel opened out the document and began to read, incredulity increasing with every line.

The Chief Lobengula, ruler of the tribe known as the Matabele, suzerain of the Mashona and Manica tribes hereby agrees to the following. In order that peace and amity shall continue forever between Her Britannic Majesty, her subjects and the Matabele people, Lobengula engages to use his utmost endeavours to prevent any rupture of the same. It is further agreed by Lobengula that he will refrain from entering into any correspondence or treaty with any Foreign State or sell, alienate, cede, or permit or countenance any sale, alienation or cession of the whole or any part of the said Matabele country without the previous knowledge and sanction of Her Majesty's High Commissioner for South Africa . . . .

The incredible document was signed with a large, somewhat shaky 'X' and the words, 'Lobengula, his mark' written alongside it. The document had been countersigned by three European witnesses. One of them was Farewell Loveday.

Daniel pushed the document back across the table to Rhodes. 'I don't believe it. This "treaty" virtually makes Lobengula a vassel of Great Britain and gives him nothing in return. There's nothing here to say that Great Britain will go to his aid if Matabeleland is invaded by the Boers.'

'There should be no need for such a clause. Now Lobengula has signed this treaty, Great Britain considers Matabeleland an area over which she has jurisdiction. Other nations will be warned off accordingly. You see, Retallick, diplomacy is always a stronger suit than violence. This document means that Lobengula cannot give any substantial concession to any national other than a Briton – and there is no company in Great Britain to match the resources of the company I'll form to exploit Mashonaland. I just made you a good offer, Retallick. I'll repeat it – once. Will you help me to get my concession? Remember, I *will* have it, whether you help me or not.'

'Then my refusal will make little difference to you. Now, if you'll excuse me . . . I'd like to put the smell of "civilisation" behind me before the day is out.'

Rhodes looked angrily at Daniel for a few moments, then he too stood up. 'You've just turned down an opportunity to become one of the richest and most influential men north of the Limpopo. You're a fool, Retallick . . . and I never give a fool a second chance.'

CHAPTER SIX

Daniel had been absent from Matabeleland for almost three months when the Greef brothers found their way to the Insimo Valley.

In a time and place where rugged individuality was the norm, Willem, Arne and Louis Greef, together with their father, Hermanus, stood head and shoulders above their fellows. Hermanus had made a home for his family in the remote hills of north eastern Transvaal. Shallow-soil crops fought a losing battle for survival around the primitive hut he built for them. When meat was needed they took their guns and hunted for it. Sometimes it was buffalo, sometimes the wild deer that roamed the wide valleys. Occasionally it was cattle owned by the few tribesmen who remained in the fastness of the hills.

There had been more tribesmen when Hermanus first reached here. Determined that their number would never pose a threat to the Greef family, he and his sons had culled them as though they were overstocked wild animals.

In their mountain stronghold, the Greefs and a few other families scattered about them, had little to do with the Transvaal Government. They neither knew, nor cared, for the ordinances published for the government of the country as a whole. The Greefs made their own laws. They paid no taxes, and no one dared venture into the hills to collect them.

On one occasion only did they bestir themselves for the benefit of their country. It was when the hated British had annexed the Transvaal and a 'people's army' of Boers rose and took it back again. Even then the Greefs were not so concerned with fighting for their homeland as taking up arms against the British. When the battle at Majuba Hill had been won, the Greefs turned their horses and went back to their home. Their departure was not regretted by their recent comrades. The Boers were hard fighters and showed no mercy in battle, but when white men threw away their guns and stood with hands raised it was accepted that they were surrendering. The Greefs did not take prisoners. Armed or unarmed, an enemy was an enemy until he had been killed.

These were the men who entered the Insimo valley from the low-veldt to the south east.

The three brothers rode close together along the valley, overtaken by a brief rainstorm that left water dripping from the wide brims of hats pulled well down, shielding their eyes. As they rode, steam rose about them from the wet horses and the hot, damp earth.

The Matabele herd-boys tending Daniel's cattle were at the far end of the valley, but the Mashonas working the early maize fields saw the riders and moved back out of sight among the whispering, sun-dried stalks of the tall plants.

The three Boer brothers saw the Mashonas. Indeed, their eyes missed nothing as they rode along, but their objective was the European-style house of Victoria, in prominent view further along the valley. From the direction in which they approached Insimo it appeared to be the only dwelling in the valley, except for the unfinished dwelling being built by Jannie Van Eyck.

When the brothers reached Victoria's home, they reined in cautiously, each man fingering the rifle he had slung across his shoulder. The house and outbuildings were clean and well up together. The Greefs were not always welcome visitors to such houses. They preferred to find tumbledown wooden shacks, where the occupants were not so fussy – or were amenable to pointed suggestion.

After a few moments of low conversation, Arne Greef swung down from his horse, handing his rifle to brother Willem. Arne was smaller than the other brothers and although none of the three men presumed to be smartly dressed, Arne's clothes were not quite so dirty as those of the others. Arne also knew some letters and was considered the smartest of the three.

Before Arne could raise his hand to knock at the door, it opened and Victoria stood in the doorway. Arne saw immediately that she was coloured and assumed she was a servant. 'Tell your boss there's some hungry travellers outside who'd appreciate a meal, and a place to sleep for the night.'

Arne Greef spoke in 'kitchen-kaffir', a mixture of English, Afrikaans and Bantu. It was fast becoming the *lingua franca* of those tribesmen of southern Africa who worked for white men. Victoria had learned the bastard language while she was in Tati, but the use of it here, when she was in her own house, made her flush angrily. She had seen the three men coming towards the house and knew they brought trouble, but her anger overrode caution.

'I'm the "boss" of this house. You'll find water in the stream coming down from the hill over there and I'll have meat sent to you. As for sleeping, you'll have to make do with the ground. There's plenty of it – outside the Insimo valley.'

Arne Greef stared at Victoria in disbelief. Then his thin lips parted in a mirthless grin and he turned to speak to his brothers, in Afrikaans. 'Did you hear that, broer? She's the boss-man here, and she's ordering us out of this valley.'

Louis, the youngest of the brothers and a simple giant of a man, sniggered. Willem, the bearded elder brother, scowled and said nothing.

Arne swung back to Victoria and his thin smile had vanished. 'No baster orders me and my brothers from any-where. Who's the owner of this valley? Where is he?'

'It's owned by Daniel Retallick . . . .,' Victoria hesitated, Elvira and her children were in their house along the valley. Therese was with them. She would not send these Boers there. 'He's somewhere around. He never goes far.'

Arne Greef assumed that Victoria was living with Daniel, but he also knew by the way she had hesitated that he was nowhere around at the moment. The grin returned, wider this time.

'Well now, if your man's away you're going to have to entertain his guests yourself.' His gaze moved from her face to her body, kept slim from years of horse-riding. 'You'll know well enough how to do that, I don't doubt.'

From his horse, Willem growled in Afrikaans. 'If you're going to hump the bitch get on with it, man. Then she can get us some grub. I'm starving.'

Arne Greef saw instantly that Victoria understood what was being said. He grabbed at her as she reached for the loaded shotgun, placed just inside the door.

Victoria slipped from his grasp and took hold of the gun, but Arne Greef managed to grasp the barrel as she brought it up. The gun went off and Arne let out a howl of pain. He staggered backwards, deafened, his left ear bloody and ragged-edged – but he had the gun.

As Louis Greef leaped from his horse, Victoria ran inside the house. There was no time to try to bolt the door. The Boer brothers would have shouldered it open before she had the stiff wooden bolt across. Neither was there a place in the house to hide from them. She fled through the rooms at the front of the house to the kitchen. Running past the startled Mashona kitchen servant, she made her escape through the kitchen doorway.

Big Louis Greef was the first of the brothers to burst from the house. He howled in delight when he saw her running up the slope, heading for the broken rocks at the top of the hill. Louis ran after her, Arne behind him, cursing the blood that flowed from his ear. Meanwhile, Willem was still on his horse. He galloped past the two running men, legs and arms flapping as he urged the horse up the slope.

Willem Greef caught up with Victoria before she reached the cover of the rocks and drove his horse at her, knocking her sprawling to the ground. As she picked herself up, he rode the horse at her again. By now the two younger brothers had reached them and Arne gripped Victoria's arm. She cried out in pain as he twisted the arm, lifting her from the ground.

'I'll teach you to draw a white man's blood, you baster cow.'

He increased the pressure on the arm and she arched her body backwards in an effort to reduce the pain.

'Louis, get her clothes off.'

The big Boer leaned over her and gripping both shoulders of her dress he ripped it from her body. Then he reached out and touched her, his loose lips wet with spittle. 'Hey, Arne. She's got a great body, broer—'

'It'll do, but you'll need to help me if you want to do something with it—'

Before Arne could say more, Victoria kicked out, her foot catching Louis Greef in the groin. He fell back on the ground, howling in pain. But Victoria's respite was brief. Willem Greef leaped from his horse, rifle held in his hand. Striding to where Victoria struggled with Arne Greef, he swung the rifle butt against the side of her head. As she sagged unconscious in Arne Greef's arms, he let her slide to the ground.

Jannie Van Eyck had been concealed among the rocks along the valley when he saw the three riders, far in the distance. Jannie had found the lair of a leopard that had been bothering Daniel's herds of late. He was waiting for dusk in the hope of putting an end to its marauding. However, strangers were sufficiently unusual in the valley for him to abandon his task.

He had left his horse at Daniel's house and he called there first to tell Elvira of the visitors, and Therese rode homewards with him. Halfway between the two houses they heard the sound of Victoria's desperate shot.

Jannie Van Eyck had left his hunting rifle with a Matabele bearer. Looking back along the path, there was no sign of the Matabele. He was probably still talking with friends at the Retallick house.

Therese had a lighter, Winchester rifle in her saddle holster and reaching across, Jannie took it. 'You stay here until I've found out what's happening.'

'No, I'm coming with you.'

There was a great deal of Victoria's determination in Therese and Jannie knew better than to argue with her.

'All right – but stay behind me.'

Jannie Van Eyck dug his heels into the horse and took off at a gallop, Therese's horse pounding along only a length behind.

Jannie Van Eyck saw the group on the hillside before he reached the house and turned the horse to cut across the soft ground towards them. By now Jannie Van Eyck was close enough to see Victoria spread-eagled naked on the ground with two men bending over her. A third, bearded man stood looking on, a rifle cradled in his arms.

The two crouching men started up as Jannie slithered his horse to a halt. Clearing the saddle, he leaped to the ground, Therese's rifle clutched in his hand.

Pushing past the men he dropped to his knees beside Victoria. A moment later, Therese was at his side.

'Ma? Oh my God – what happened?'

As Therese cradled her mother, Jannie Van Eyck looked up and saw the coarse faces of the Boers. Suddenly he realised that this was not the result of some accident. He wished his father was with him . . . this was something that was beyond his youthful experience.

'She's all right,' said Arne Greef. 'We were enjoying a bit of fun together and it got a bit out of hand, that's all.'

'You're a liar,' Therese flared. 'who are you? What have you done?'

Arne Greef had recognised Jannie Van Eyck's uncertainty and had immediately written him off as a young lad who would cause the three brothers no trouble. Ignoring him, he reached out and gripped Therese's arm. 'You've got a bit more fire in you than your Ma, girl. You should have come along a bit sooner.'

Jannie Van Eyck straightened up and in a quick movement knocked Arne Greef's hand away from Therese. As he did so he caught the movement of Willem Greef's gun coming up. He dived to the ground and rolled away. As Willem Greef came in view he fired – but Victoria was quicker. She had regained consciousness a few minutes before and while all attention was focused upon Jannie she snatched up a single shot musket left on the ground beside her by one of the Greef brothers.

She fired a split second before Jannie Van Eyck's hurried shot went wide, but Willem Greef thought Jannie Van Eyck had shot him. He fell back in a sitting position, staring at Jannie in pained surprise. Then he removed one of the hands that was clutching his stomach and held it up, staring stupidly at the red blood that glistened on his fingers.

'He's shot me, Arne. The damned baster kid's shot me.' He gave a deep groan of pain. 'Aagh! He's set my blerrie guts on fire. Shoot him, Arne. Shoot the brat.'

Arne took a single pace forward but Jannie levered another cartridge into the breech of the Winchester and Arne Greef froze.

'You'd better get him out of here.' Jannie jerked his head nervously in Willem Greef's direction, without taking his eyes from Arne Greef. Louis Greef was also in his view, standing uncertainly a few feet behind his brother. Jannie pushed his elbows closer to his body in an effort to stop the rifle from shaking. He hoped neither of the two men facing him realised just how scared he was.

'Get him out? Kill him, Jannie. Kill them all,' Victoria screamed at him as Therese struggled to hold her.

Arne Greef licked his lips and looked pleadingly at Jannie Van Eyck. 'My broer's hurt bad, man. If we don't get help for him he'll die for sure.'

'You'll *all* die if Lobengula learns you're here,' Therese snapped as Victoria reached for her ripped dress and wrapped it about herself.

'Get him out of here,' Jannie Van Eyck decided. 'And don't stop until you're well clear of the valley.'

Arne Greef nodded to Louis and turned towards the horse that grazed nearby. Louis Greef bent down and picked up his elder brother as though he were a child. The movement caused Willem Greef to cry out in pain.

'Kill them, Jannie! If you don't you'll live to regret it.'

Victoria had picked up Willem's fallen gun. Now she threw it away again in disgust. It was a percussion model and in the fall the percussion cap had fallen and been lost in the grass.

Therese was shocked by her mother's determination to have the Boers killed, but the incident had taken Victoria back to her days, long ago, at Tati. She hated the Greefs with all the intensity of the hatred she had once had for Andreus Van Niekerk and the Australian miners who had abused her body.

Jannie Van Eyck followed the Greef brothers to their horses and slipped a heavy, large-bore elephant gun from its holster on Louis's horse.

'You can't send us off without guns,' Arne Greef protested. 'You might as well kill us here. With a badly wounded man and no guns we'll be a target for every thieving kaffir we come across.'

'Then you'd better keep clear of "thieving kaffirs" and everyone else on this side of the Limpopo. I'm still not sure I shouldn't be handing you over to Lobengula. You'd best get going before I change my mind.'

'We're going.'

Willem Greef was slung upon his horse by Louis. Sagging painfully, he rode away, his brothers supporting him on either side.

'Help me get Ma into the house,' said Therese with her arms about her mother. Victoria had sunk to the ground, overcome by a blinding headache that blotted out all thoughts of the Greef brothers.

'Some of the Mashonas are coming. Get the women to help with your Ma. I want to make sure those three leave the valley.'

'Jannie – take care,' Therese called after him and Jannie Van Eyck lifted a hand in acknowledgement.

At the head of the valley, the Greef brothers, Arne and Louis, bound Willem's stomach wound with a strip of his own dirty shirt. He was then transferred to the younger brother's horse and with Louis holding him in the saddle before him, they rode away from Insimo.

When Jannie returned to the house, Victoria was lying on the bed in her room, the curtains drawn to keep out the painful light. When Jannie looked in at her, she asked, 'Where are they? Where are those three Jaapies now?'

'They've left the valley. It's all right, they won't be back.'

'Won't they? One of them's badly wounded. Do you think they are going to go away and forget all about us? If he dies they'll be back here – with their friends. You should have killed them all – or let me do it for you. It's the only way with men like that. Let them live and you'll go in fear of them for the rest of your life.'

Victoria saw Jannie's confusion and she suddenly softened. He knew nothing of the life she had once led – and Victoria hoped neither he nor Therese ever would. She reached out her hands to both of them. 'It's all right, take no notice of me. I thank God you were in the valley. I wouldn't be alive now if it weren't for you.'

'I should have taken them to Lobengula,' said Jannie. 'But I wasn't sure—'

'It doesn't matter now,' lied Victoria. 'But until Daniel returns we'd better post armed Matabele boys around the house – Daniel's house too. They might try something there.'

She put a hand to her head, grimacing at the acute pain that had returned. 'You attend to that, Jannie. I think I'll rest for a while.'

*   *   *

Willem Greef died two days after arriving home. He was buried on Greef land, alongside the graves of his mother and the four Greef children who had not survived the rigours of Transvaal frontier life. He was laid in the ground in a rough coffin, constructed from planks of wood torn from the platform of an old trek-wagon.

At the shallow graveside, Hermanus, the bearded patriarch of his diminishing family, wept bitter tears at the loss of his eldest son. Then, no sooner had he and the two surviving sons set foot inside the dilapidated wooden shack than he knocked Arne to the ground with a blow that belied his sixty years.

Arne, bewildered, scrambled to his feet only to be knocked down again. He stayed on the floor, complaining bitterly at the treatment meted out to him, but a booted foot put a stop to his whining.

'Get out! You hear me, boy? Get out . . . and you.' Hermanus jabbed a finger at his slow-thinking youngest son. 'You'll not sit here enjoying your brother's birthright while his killer walks and breathes. No one kills a Greef and forgets about it, d'you hear me? Get out, both of you and bring this boy back here.'

Arne and Louis Greef had told the old man that Willem had been shot by Jannie. They had said little about Victoria.

'I want to see the baster who shot my Willem and sent his two brothers scuttling away with their tails between their legs, like two scared mongrels. Bring him to me here.'

'But—'

'You want knocking down again? Bring him back, I say. Until you do I don't want to see either of you on this land. If you think maybe it's too much for the two of you then take the Pretorious boys with you – and the du Toits. God's teeth that should be enough to bring back one coloured boy. Get out now . . . Go!'

CHAPTER SEVEN

The house for Jannie Van Eyck and Therese was nearing completion. The roof was on and the doors hung. It needed only the internal fittings and window glass. The glass was on its way by slow ox-cart from the Cape Colony.

Jannie and Therese visited the house most days. It somehow brought their wedding day closer and gave their marriage a feeling of reality. In here, Therese could make-believe that they were already married and she was mistress of her own home. She led Jannie by the hand from room to room, discussing yet again where they would place each item of, as yet, unmade furniture. It was a large house, but Therese was already finding accommodation problems.

The young couple were on one of their daily visits to the house when Therese stopped in the centre of the room that was to be their bedroom, and said, 'You know, Jannie. I think we should have had another bedroom built.'

'Another? We've got three. How many visitors do you expect us to have?'

'Well, there's your father. We'll need to keep a room for him, but I'm not thinking of visitors. I'm wondering about rooms for . . . the babies.'

'Babies?' The thought of children, his and Therese's, gave Jannie a strange feeling in the pit of his stomach. Family life was something he knew little about. From as far back as he could remember he had led a nomadic life with his father and, once the last of his half-sisters had married at the early age of fifteen, without the influence of a woman in his life. Jannie had never thought about it with any thought of regret. There had been something indescribably comforting about nights spent around a smoky camp-fire with the stars above and the sounds of the bush all round. Jannie Van Eyck had learned to enjoy the thrill of topping a hill and seeing a panorama of unknown land laid out before him. He had believed it to be as full a life as any boy could wish for. Yet, sometimes he and his father would spend a few nights in a house, or even a cabin in the hills, with a family. A husband, wife and children. On such occasions, Jannie's heart ached for something he had never known. The pleasures of family life. The feeling of *belonging* somewhere.

'. . . of course there'll be babies. At least as many as Daniel and Elvira.'

Jannie's astonishment was so genuine that Therese broke into a peal of amused laughter. Then she hugged him tightly to her. 'Oh Jannie! I do love you so much.' She looked up at him. 'Surely you'd thought about us having babies?'

Jannie grinned down at her. 'Of course . . . but I hadn't got as far as them actually being *born*.' He kissed her and, as she clung to him, he whispered, 'If we're going to have so many babies, oughtn't we to make an early start?'

His hands slid down her body and Therese let him have his way for a few minutes until she felt her need rising to meet his own. Then she gripped his exploring hands in her own and whispered breathlessly, 'Not yet, Jannie. Not now. You've been very good. You can wait a while longer . . . please. I want you too . . . very much. Don't make it difficult for me.'

Jannie's hands came up to hold her shoulders and she relaxed. 'I'll be worth waiting for, Jannie. I promise you.'

They left the unfinished house hand-in-hand, happy in the knowledge that each had so much to give the other. They had almost reached the horses when Jannie's keen, hunter's ears caught the sound of a snapping twig in some nearby under-growth. He knew instinctively that the sound had not been made by an animal.

The horses were still twenty paces away, their reins wrapped loosely about the lower branches of a Mopani tree.

The memory of the visit by the Greef brothers was still fresh in Jannie's mind. Squeezing Therese's hand so hard that she stopped her happy chattering and looked at him questioningly, he hissed, 'Act naturally, but walk faster. Someone's watching us from the bushes. When I say "Go", run for your horse and ride for the herd-boys' compound. Fetch them back here – armed. No questions now. Go!'

Therese sprinted for their horses. Startled, both animals drew up their heads and snorted, tugging at their reins. Therese unlooped the rein and leaped to her horse's back. Jannie stayed behind, keeping between Therese and the unseen watcher in the bushes until he saw her mounted. Now he too ran. He reached his horse just as big Louis Greef crashed from the bushes ahead of him and grabbed the animal's reins.

Jannie snatched his rifle from the saddle holster and, holding it in both hands, struck out at Louis Greef. The Big Boer uttered a single grunt of pain, then dropped to the ground.

The sudden flurry of activity frightened Jannie's horse. With empty stirrups flapping, it cantered away along the path. Jannie was given little time to curse his luck. No more than a hundred yards along the path, two riders emerged from the undergrowth and flanked Therese.

Jannie shouted and threw the rifle to his shoulder, but he dared not risk a shot for fear of hitting Therese as the horses swerved from one side of the path to the other. Eventually Therese was forced from the path and all three horses and riders crashed out of sight in the dense undergrowth.

The next moment he heard a shout from nearby and a bullet whined no more than a foot above Jannie's head. It cut through a leafed twig and sent it spiralling to the ground in front of him.

The urge inside Jannie to run to the spot where he had seen Therese forced from the path was overwhelming, but commonsense fought a winning battle. There were at least four men out there somewhere. One of them looking at him over the sights of a rifle at this very moment. He would be dead before he took half-a-dozen paces.

All these thoughts went through his mind in the fraction of a second. As he threw himself into the undergrowth beside the path, a second shot ricocheted from a tree beside him.

Crouching low, Jannie ran for the nearly completed house. The last twenty yards were across a clearing. He took it in a desperate sprint, waiting for another shot. It never came.

Vaulting through a window space, Jannie crouched beneath the sill, peering out, hoping to catch a glimpse of his adversaries. As he waited he checked his gun, wishing he had Therese's fifteen-shot Winchester. His gun was a very large bore, double-barrelled hunting gun. Both barrels were loaded, but the remainder of his ammunition was in a pouch on his horse.

'You in there—' The shout came from the bushes about fifty feet from the window where he crouched. 'We want you, not the girl. Come on out with your hands in the air and we'll let her go.'

The voice was Arne Greef's. Jannie had begun to suspect that the two shots had been no more than warnings. Now he was certain. The Greefs wanted him – and they wanted him alive! The thought gave him an uncomfortable prickly feeling at the back of his neck. But if it meant they would release Therese to get him . . . .

'Let her get on her horse and go. When I see her ride away I'll come out, not before.'

Jannie could just make out the sound of hoarse whispering, followed by a hastily stifled guffaw. Then there was the unmistakeable sounds of a struggle – and Therese screamed.

Jannie's knuckles turned white and his grip tightened on the hunting rifle. He raised his head to look over the sill and a well-aimed bullet splintered the woodwork of the window-frame, only inches away.

Jannie was helpless against the unseen besiegers, but less than half-a-minute later the same voice called again, 'You were too eager. *Now* you can look, but raise your head slowly and carefully.'

Jannie followed Arne Greef's instructions in time to see Therese pushed into view from the undergrowth. She had been stripped of all her clothes and Arne was holding her from behind, using her as a shield between himself and Jannie.

'You see this? This is what you should have been getting when that house of yours is finished. Now, do as you're told, or we'll show you what else you'll be missing – and my bet is that she'll be more lively than her mother was. Do you think you'll enjoy watching that?'

All the time Arne Greef was talking he was walking towards the house and now he was standing between Jannie and the place from which the unknown marksman had just fired at the window frame.

Jannie slid the barrel of his rifle over the sill and called, 'Now it's your turn to listen. I'll kill Therese rather than let you and your friends have her. This is a ten-bore hunting rifle with a hair trigger and it's pointing straight at Therese's heart. You can shoot me dead, but my finger will twitch just enough to send a bullet straight through Therese – and straight through you as well. Are you listening to me very carefully now?'

Arne Greef realised his mistake. His lips were suddenly dust-dry and he licked them nervously. 'You wouldn't kill her. You—'

Jannie drew back the hammer of one barrel and the click as it locked in place sounded to Arne Greef like the gate of hell being opened.

'Shoot, Jannie! Don't take a chance. Don't let them have me!'

Therese's shrill shout was all Arne Greef needed to reach a decision very quickly.

'Don't shoot! What do you want me to do?'

'Let her go – now.'

Arne Greef released Therese's arms and she took a step forward, unable to believe she was free. When she was quite certain she ran to the house and Jannie helped her through the window, the rifle still pointing unwaveringly at Arne Greef's heart.

'Hold this a moment – and be careful with that trigger.'

Jannie handed the hunting rifle to Therese while he pulled his shirt over his head and passed it to her.

The shirt did not reach to Therese's knees and hung in drapes about her body, but neither she nor Jannie were concerned with appearances.

Arne Greef still stood in the clearing in front of the house, hardly daring to exercise a muscle. He started nervously when Jannie Van Eyck called to him again from the shadows inside the house.

'Tell your friends to come out of hiding and throw their guns down on the path by the door. They'd better take it slow and easy. If they make me jump you're a dead man.'

'You heard him,' Arne Greef called over his shoulder. 'Come out and do as he says, *all five of you.*'

For a few long moments nothing happened. Then there came a stirring from the undergrowth. One by one, five men stepped into view, Louis Greef among them. Walking along the path leading to the house, they threw down their guns, then assembled self-consciously alongside Arne Greef.

'One of you go and fetch two of the horses here. You . . . the big man, you do it.'

Louis Greef looked to his brother and Arne Greef inclined his head.

The horses could not have been far away because Louis Greef returned only minutes later leading Therese's horse and another belonging to one of his companions.

'Go out to your horse and ride off,' Jannie said to Therese. 'I want to see you safely away before I leave the house.'

Therese looked as though she might argue, but Jannie said, 'Hurry, Therese. If they rush us we'll have no chance. I've got only two bullets in this gun.'

Therese scrambled awkwardly through the window. With the shirt flapping loose about her she ran to her horse.

Mounting the animal, Therese looked uncertainly towards the window where Jannie waited. Giving him a brief, unhappy wave, she galloped away along the path that led to the Retallick house and the compound of the Matabele herd-boys.

Not until she was out of sight did Jannie step into view through the window. He walked slowly to the horse that had been brought for him, his rifle pointing at the group of sullen Boers the whole while.

'Now move well away from those guns – as far as you can go.'

Jannie waited until they reluctantly shuffled to the edge of the clearing. Then he swung up to the saddle of the Boer horse. Kicking his heels in the animal's flanks, his elation escaped in a loud whoop as the horse leaped away.

The shout of victory died in his throat. The horse had hardly stretched out in a full gallop when there came the crack of a rifle, fired at point-blank range. Shot through the heart, the horse crashed to the ground, sending Jannie flying through the air over the beast's head.

The heavy rifle flew from his hand and, as Jannie staggered to his feet and looked about for the weapon, a grinning Boer stepped from the undergrowth behind him and knocked him to the ground with a blow from the gun that had brought down the horse.

*   *   *

Uiys Toblin had built a home for his family on a splendid farm a few miles to the north of Pretoria. Daniel made his way there from Kimberley, pausing en route to marvel at the vast gold diggings of the Witwatersrand. Here thousands of men from two dozen countries and many varied walks of life, dug deep down through the soil of the Transvaal, seeking the elusive ore.

Not all the miners worked for themselves. Many toiled for Cecil Rhodes – so many that Daniel was left wondering why Rhodes was so anxious to obtain a concession to search for more gold in Lobengula's territories. The more Daniel thought about the matter, the more convinced he became that mining was incidental to the grand plans Cecil John Rhodes had for the lands north of the Limpopo River. Daniel believed that if Rhodes gained so much as a toehold there he would somehow succeed in bringing the whole Matabele empire crashing about Lobengula's ears.

When Daniel reached the Toblin farm, he was delighted to find the Boer hunter, Jaconus Van Eyck there. After he had expressed his sympathy to Uiys Toblin's widow, Daniel told her and Van Eyck of his talk with Sir Hercules Robinson, and of the Governor's 'inquiry' into the death of Uiys.

Alice Toblin listened quietly until Daniel mentioned the pension Chief Sekete Khama had agreed to pay her.

'I'll have no blood money from the Bechuana – or from the British. They were responsible for Uiys's death, I'm certain of that. Paying me a pension won't give Uiys back to me. Not even the deaths of those who ordered his killing will do that – and, God knows, I want them dead!'

'*Ordered* his killing? Do you have any proof?'

'Proof? How do you obtain proof when so many lies are being told? *I* know who's responsible, but I don't want to talk about it anymore. Ask Jaconus. He knows, he was there.'

Choked with emotion, Alice Toblin fled from the room, greatly distressed. The Toblins had been a close and happy family. The death of Uiys, and the manner in which it had occurred, was a tragic blow to them all.

To Jaconus Van Eyck, Daniel said, 'Is what Alice said true – you were with Uiys?'

'I was with him.'

Jaconus Van Eyck spoke slowly and deliberately past the

large pipe that was a near-permanent feature of his weathered, bearded face. 'Half-a-dozen of us were on our way to Bulawayo to get Lobengula's permission to hunt, when we met Uiys coming down the trail. He was as excited as I'd ever seen him. When he showed us the treaty we knew why. We all agreed the treaty was more important than hunting, so we turned about and came back with him.'

Jaconus Van Eyck removed the pipe from his mouth and cradled the warm, wooden bowl thoughtfully in his hands. 'I suppose we were all hoping to be a part of history, as it were, and share in poor Uiys's glory.'

He replaced the pipe between his teeth. 'It brought very little glory – but a whole nest of trouble. We were halfway across Bechuanaland when up rode Chief Sekete Khama's brother and a bunch of mounted Bechuanas. He didn't seem pleased to see us. I got the impression right there that he'd been expecting to find Uiys on his own. Anyway, he ordered us to turn around and go back to Matabeleland. None of us was keen on doing that, so next he tells us we're to go along with him. That idea had even less appeal and we refused. Uiys told Sekete Khama's brother that the road through Bechuanaland had been guaranteed by the Cape Government, so he'd better have a very good reason for stopping us. Sekete Khama's brother got angry and the next minute he upped and shot poor Uiys. Then he and his men rode away, leaving us alone.'

Daniel frowned. 'He shot only Uiys and allowed the rest of you to ride away?'

'There was a bit of a fracas. One of the hunters got in the way of a bullet aimed at Uiys – but yes, that's about the way of it. Uiys was shot three times. He was the one they were after. There is no doubt of it.'

'Damn Rhodes and his scheming,' Daniel cried angrily. 'He's behind this – I'm sure of it – but it will never be proved. What I *do* know is that if I hadn't persuaded Uiys to sign a treaty with Lobengula he'd be alive today.'

Jaconus Van Eyck grunted noncommittally. 'I think Rhodes, or the British, really wanted to get their hands on the treaty. But Sekete Khama's brother became scared at what he was doing. He and his men rode off as though the ghost of Andries Potgieter was ofter them. Uiys lived for two days and before he died he gave me the treaty for safe-keeping. We buried Uiys alongside the road and I delivered the treaty to Pretoria myself—'

Daniel interrupted Jaconus Van Eyck. 'Before we go any further – are you *absolutely* certain it was Bechuanas who killed Uiys? It couldn't have been natives from Transvaal?'

Jaconus Van Eyck looked puzzled. He shook his head vigorously. 'They were Bechuanas. I know Sekete Khama and it wasn't the first time I've met his brother. Besides, why should anyone from here want Uiys killed? He'd just signed a peace treaty between the Boers and the Matabele – something the Transvaalers have been urging President Kruger to do for many years. Uiys would have been a hero when he reached Pretoria.'

'Perhaps the treaty didn't give Transvaal as much as Kruger wanted?'

Jaconus Van Eyck looked at Daniel, not understanding. 'What are you suggesting? That Uiys was killed by Boers and *not* by the British? That's ridiculous, Daniel. Why, nobody in Transvaal knew about the treaty.'

'If the British knew, then we must assume that someone in Transvaal knew too. Did you read the treaty yourself?'

'Uiys showed it to me before he died. It promised friendship and mutual co-operation between Lobengula and Transvaal—'

'Nothing about Lobengula committing his army on behalf of Transvaal in the event of war? Or throwing his country open to Boer hunters, travellers and traders?'

'Nothing at all.' Jaconus Van Eyck removed the pipe from his mouth. 'What are you saying, Daniel?'

'The copy of the treaty, allegedly sent out by the Transvaal Government, bore no resemblance to the one I helped negotiate between Uiys and Lobengula. I saw the copy that Farewell Loveday claimed was sent to Sir Hercules Robinson, at the Cape.

'Then it's a forgery.'

'Yes – but who's responsible, Britain, or Transvaal? Someone will know in Pretoria. I'll go there and get the truth.'

'That's not a good idea, Daniel.' Jaconus Van Eyck spoke slowly and thoughtfully. 'I don't believe Uiys was killed by his own people – he was respected too much – but I don't doubt the government in Pretoria saw his death as an opportunity to alter the treaty to their advantage. They believed he was the only white man who knew exactly what the treaty contained – and who'd believe a kaffir if he complained he'd been cheated? Now you want to go to them and say *you* know the treaty's been altered? Think, Daniel. Only a few years ago they were slaughtering the British on the battlefield for the sake of our country. One more British death isn't going to break the heart of any Boer. Keep well away from Pretoria – and forget the treaty. I hear that Lobengula's repudiated it anyway.'

Reluctantly, Daniel was forced to admit that Jaconus Van Eyck was right. He had come as close to learning the truth concerning Uiys Toblin's death as any man ever would. Besides, he could change nothing now. Rhodes had come up with another treaty that gave Britain the lead over Transvaal. No doubt one treaty would cancel out the other and the interested countries would begin jockeying for position all over again. The only thing that was certain was that whoever won – Lobengula would be the loser.

CHAPTER EIGHT

Daniel rested for two days at the Toblin farm and the daily routine of life on a working cattle farm made him yearn for his own home in the Insimo valley. He had been away from home for six months and the Matabele winter had begun. It was time to be thinking of the next season's crops, and perhaps the formation of a new herd.

Then Daniel's plans received a setback. He, Jaconus Van Eyck and Alice Toblin were seated around the table, finishing lunch, when one of the Toblin servants came running to the room, eyes rolling in fright. He gasped out his news, not to Alice Toblin, but to Jaconus Van Eyck.

'Baas! Many men coming to the house from Pretoria. They carry guns. I think they look for the Ngesi.'

The servant used the native word for 'Englishman'.

The two men leaped to their feet and Jaconus Van Eyck looked through the window. Turning back, he smiled, 'They don't need to send a hundred men to arrest an Englishman – not even you, Daniel. Something must be happening. It's the Pretoria militia. They don't turn out as a rule for anything less than full-scale war.'

Outside the house the mounted commando stopped at the well in the yard to water their horses and Jaconus Van Eyck introduced Daniel to their commander, Major Peter Colenbrander.

The Boer commander shook Daniel's hand, then scrutinised him carefully. 'Daniel Retallick? I've heard of you – you're a trader, from Matabeleland. Is it merely a coincidence that you're in Transvaal at the same time as a Matabele army's crossed the river to raid our settlements?'

It was obvious that Daniel's surprise was genuine. 'I don't believe it! The last thing Lobengula wants is trouble.'

'I'll go along with that,' agreed Jaconus Van Eyck. 'Where did your information come from, Major. Someone's got it all wrong.'

'It's true enough,' replied Major Colenbrander. 'The reports have come in from too many people. I think you'd both better come along with us. You might be able to help us find out what it's all about.'

Major Colenbrander's commando was comprised of a hundred of the toughest men Daniel had ever seen. Heavily bearded men with well weathered faces, they carried their guns with the familiarity of men who knew how to use them well. Wearing heavy cross-belts packed with spare cartridges, each man was a walking arsenal. This was the type of force for which the Boers were to become justly famous in ensuing years. A mobile, hard-hitting commando, able to ride long distances, feed off the land – and hit the enemy hard when and where it was least expected.

On the way north riders were constantly intercepting the commando, bringing news of the progress of Lobengula's impis. It seemed the Matabeles had crossed the Limpopo River, marched swiftly inland for about ten miles, then turned south east. They were now heading for the mountainous region lying close to the lands claimed by the Portuguese.

No reports had yet been received of attacks on the Boer settlements along their route, but the northern Transvaal communities were in a state of near-panic. Tales of atrocities by the Matabeles and their Zulu kinsmen had frightened Boer children around countless camp-fires for many generations.

As riders came in and reported to Major Colenbrander, the commando constantly changed direction, to intercept the impis, but soon the messengers became unnecessary. The impis were moving fast, and in a straight line now, approaching the homeland of the Buvenda tribe.

Daniel thought that this tribe must be the target of the impis, although why Lobengula should risk incurring the wrath of the Boers by attacking such a little known and relatively inoffensive tribe was beyond his understanding.

As more information came in, Daniel found the cross-border incursion even more puzzling. This was no ordinary raid. The warriors were moving in two columns, indicating there were two impis, a fact borne out by the observation that the warriors of each column carried shields with differing impi colours. Reports put the total number of Matabele warriors at about four thousand men – outnumbering the Boer commando by forty-to-one.

By now the impis were in the heart of Buvenda country – yet not a single kraal had been attacked and not a Buvenda tribesman molested. Moreover, the few Boer farms in the area were being carefully by-passed by Lobengula's warriors.

Even Major Colenbrander now agreed that this was *not* a raiding party in the normal sense. The Matabele impis were after something particular, and they were wasting no time reaching their objective. On some days it was estimated that they were covering fifty miles between dawn and dusk.

When the commando eventually met up with the impis it came as a sudden surprise. Toiling up the side of a steep range of hills, they came out on the ridge – and saw the two columns of Lobengula's warriors moving across the undulating veldt beneath them.

'Jesus Cristus! Look at them.' The hoarse-voiced remark came from a young member of the commando. The Matabele made an impressive sight. There were not two but *three* impis, plus half of Lobengula's own bodyguard – the latter armed with modern, cartridge-firing rifles. The Boer estimate of four thousand warriors had been a conservative one.

The Indunas leading the impis were also very much alert. No sooner had the Boer horsemen topped the ridge than the impis merged into their traditional 'head and horns' battle formation and turned to meet the threat posed by the commando. The shields of the warriors formed a solid phalanx, a mile wide and at the centre of the battle line were the warriors armed with rifles.

Major Colenbrander began to look worried as the impis slowly moved up the slope towards his commando. They advanced, stamping their feet to the ground with every other step, and rattling heavy knobkerries on the taut hides of the cow-hide shields.

'If I've got to fight, *I'll* choose the battle-ground,' the Boer commander muttered. 'It won't be on an exposed hill-top like this.'

'I doubt if the Indunas want a fight,' Daniel said quickly. 'They're trying to frighten you away. Get your men to back away from the ridge. I'll go down and speak to them.'

'I'll come with you,' grunted Jaconus Van Eyck, gnawing at an empty pipe. 'Unless I'm mistaken, Gamba's regiment is down there. He came with me on a hunting trip to the Mazoe valley a few years ago. We're old friends.'

The news that Gamba had already re-established himself with the tribe came as a surprise to Daniel, but if he was indeed Induna of one of the impis, it was good news. Gamba and his family were deeply indebted to Daniel.

As Daniel and Jaconus Van Eyck rode slowly down the hillside, the advancing impis halted and their three Indunas stepped from the ranks and walked together to meet them.

The youngest Induna was apparently the one in charge of the mysterious expedition. Tall, even by Matabele standards, he carried himself with a proud bearing that bordered on haughtiness. He nodded his head seriously to Jaconus Van Eyck, but it was to Daniel he spoke first.

'Greetings, trader. You are far from home. I have yet to thank you for the lives of my family – and for persuading the King to accept me as husband for his favourite daughter.'

Daniel thought Lobengula had been wise to waste no time in placing Gamba at the head of one of his strongest impis. Gamba was a man born to command – and he possessed a deep sense of loyalty.

'You too are far from home, Gamba . . . and your presence angers the Amabhunu.' Daniel used the name by which the Matabele called the Boers. 'Why have you crossed the river?'

'You do not know?' Gamba was genuinely surprised. 'I thought that was why you and the hunter were here.' His expression changed suddenly and became one of grim anger. 'Then the men on the hill are not here to help you. They were sent to attack us. Had you not been with them there would have been a battle. *They* would not have asked us why we were here.'

'Why *are* you here?' Daniel repeated.

'Because of Lobengula's love for you, trader. The Amabhunu have twice raided your valley. The first time they attacked the Mambari woman – the one who lived in Khami when I was a boy.'

A horrified shock went through Daniel. Gamba was talking of Victoria.

'Was she badly hurt? What happened?'

Gamba shook his head. 'I don't think she was hurt,' he nodded to Jaconus Van Eyck. 'Your son drove them from the valley, hunter. But one was badly hurt.'

'Good boy!' Jaconus Van Eyck felt a sudden urge of pride but it was tinged with surprise. Jannie was a skilful hunter, but he was also a very gentle boy. So gentle that Jaconus had always been worried about him. He had believed that, faced with a situation where he must kill a man, or be killed himself, Jannie's nerve would fail him.

'You said there was a second raid . . . ?'

Gamba acknowledged Daniel's question with a quick nod of his head, but now he was looking only at Jaconus Van Eyck. 'The Amabhunu came again and this time they carried your son away with them.'

Jaconus Van Eyck's pipe dropped from his mouth and he made no move to pick it up. 'You're certain of this, Gamba? There's no possibility you've made a mistake?'

'None.' Gamba beckoned to someone in the ranks of his warriors and a young man trotted forward. It was Takwire, one of Daniel's senior herd-boys.

Takwire told the story of the two raids, adding a postscript of his own. 'Young boss Wyatt sent two herd boys to tell the King of the raids. He and I followed the trail of the Amabhunu to the river. We did not cross but waited until Gamba came. The young boss wanted to come with the impi, but Gamba sent warriors to take him back to Insimo.'

Daniel's own pride in Wyatt was lost in his concern for young Jannie Van Eyck.

'Do you know the names of the men who have my son?' Jaconus Van Eyck put the question in a gruff voice to Gamba.

'Yes, they are known to the Buvenda tribesmen. Their name is "Greef" and they live only a few hours march from here.'

'I know where they live – and I also know the Greefs. God help my Jannie.' Jaconus Van Eyck retrieved his pipe and tried to fill it with fingers that trembled uncontrollably.

'Perhaps they'll hand him over to the Transvaal authorities,' said Daniel with hollow optimism. 'When it's learned what happened at Insimo they'll let him go.' It sounded no more convincing now it had been said.

'Oude Baas Greef and his boys are what are called "Poor Whites" in the Cape. Here in Transvaal, where there are so many families with nothing, a "Poor White" is about as low as man can get. He has no one to look down on but kaffirs and coloureds. They'll know Jannie's coloured.'

Jaconus Van Eyck turned away abruptly and Daniel said gently, 'I'll go and tell Colenbrander what's happening.'

'Tell him also he can catch me up. I'm on my way to the Greef's home.'

Before riding up the hill to Major Colenbrander and the commando, Daniel suggested to Gamba that he and the impis should now return to Matabeleland, leaving the Boers to deal with the Greefs.

Gamba refused. He had been sent by Lobengula to punish the men who had raided the Insimo valley – Matabeleland – and bring Jannie Van Eyck back. If Gamba returned to Bulawayo unable to tell Lobengula of the fate the Greefs had suffered, he would be in disgrace once more.

Before Daniel was halfway up the slope to where Colenbrander waited impatiently, the impi were on the move again, jogging along after Jaconus Van Eyck in the mile-consuming pace they could maintain for hour after hour.

Major Colenbrander showed less concern for the events in the Insimo valley than in the continuing presence of the Matabele impis on Transvaal land, when Daniel gave him the explanation.

'I'll concede that they had some justification for crossing the Limpopo River in the first place,' he said grudgingly. 'But they should have reported what had happened to the nearest Burghermaster. Tell them to return to Matabeleland and leave us to deal with this matter.'

'They take their orders from their King, not from me, Major. Besides, they don't trust you. They want to see justice done.' Daniel pointed to the hunched figure riding ahead of the Matabele. 'So does Jaconus Van Eyck. It's his boy the Greefs have carried off.'

Jannie Van Eyck had a rough journey to the Greef homestead, deep in the fastness the Boers called the Spelonka Mountains. The Greef brothers were short of horses and Jannie was hauled along behind one of them, at the end of a long rope securing his hands to Arne Greef's saddle. At times he had to run to keep up with the pace set by the horsemen. If he fell he was dragged along, tearing clothing and skin until he was able to regain his feet and stumble after his jeering captors once more. At their infrequent stops he was subjected to constant taunting and an occasional beating. He was also kept short of food, forced to rely on the scraps the Boer brothers threw to him.

When the party eventually arrived at the Greef farm, Jannie Van Eyck was staggering along, as stiff-legged as a drunken man, his mind numbed by pain and fatigue.

As he stood swaying splay-legged at the end of the slack rope, his hands held out before him, Hermanus Greef came from the dilapidated timber shack and walked slowly around him, viewing Jannie's pitiful state with obvious satisfaction. To Arne, he said, 'So you've brought him back, eh? You've made him suffer a little?'

'He's suffered, Pa,' Arne Greef jerked on the rope. Jannie Van Eyck staggered and almost fell. 'He's come all the way from Matabeleland on the end of this.'

'Good!' Hermanus Greef's voice was thick with emotion. 'He'll stretch your rope still more when I've finished with him.'

Turning to Jannie Van Eyck, he said, 'You speak Afrikaans, boy?'

'Better than your two sons,' Jannie replied painfully.

Arne Greef tugged savagely at the rope and Jannie Van Eyck fell heavily to the ground.

Hermanus Greef kicked Jannie viciously in the ribs. 'Answer my questions and don't try to be clever to your betters, boy. You know why you've been brought here, eh?'

Jannie Van Eyck said nothing and his silence earned him another kick.

'You're the sort who never learns, boy. Too much to say when you'd do best saying nothing, and a closed mouth when you should be answering questions. All right, I'll tell you why you're here. My boys have brought you to me because you killed their brother – my eldest son, Willem. Nobody kills a Greef and lives to boast of it.'

Reaching down, Hermanus Greef took a cruel grip on Jannie Van Eyck's hair, lifting his head clear of the ground.

Glowering into his face, he repeated, 'No one, you hear me, boy?'

'I didn't kill him, I'm sure I didn't. I shot, but missed. He was shot by the woman he'd raped.'

'He's lying, Pa. He killed him. You know that. Willem told you so himself.'

'You hear that? Are you calling my poor, dead son a liar now? And what's this about raping a woman? My boys told me it was only some coloured bitch. Are you telling me they're all liars now?'

'She was coloured, Pa,' said Louis Greef.

'Of course she was – and so is this murdering . . . lying . . . little . . . no-good . . .' Each word was accompanied by a kick and Jannie was left sobbing in pain.

'What we going to do with him, Pa?' asked Arne Greef.

'Do? We'll make him suffer a bit. Then you and Louis can string him up to the baobab tree over by Willem's grave and leave him there to rot. It will serve as a warning to the kaffirs – and to anyone else who thinks of taking on the Greefs.'

Giving Jannie Van Eyck a final kick, Hermanus Greef stumped back to the rundown Greef shack.

The Greef boys, with their friends, the Pretorious and du Toit brothers, celebrated their return with the aid of cheap Cape brandy that left them lying on the ground when they fell in a drunken stupor. When they came round they were violently sick. Before they recovered from their excruciating hangovers, they repeated the process once more.

The orgy of drinking came to an end only when the cheap brandy ran out and Hermanus Greef's irritability exceeded his hospitality. Then the Pretorious and du Toit brothers tottered off to find their horses and set off in opposite directions to ride home.

Half-an-hour later, and ice-cold sober, the Pretorious boys were back, declaring to the disbelieving Hermanus Greef that the whole Matabele army was heading along the valley towards the Greef homestead.

'Matabele? What the hell you talking about? You boys still drunk? You'd better sober up pretty damn quick or your Ma will play hell with you.'

'We're telling you, Oude Baas. They're coming this way. Thousands of 'em. They must be after the coloured boy—'

'Then you'd better get him out of sight. Arne! Louis! Wake up and come out here, you good-for-nothing pair. There's work to be done.'

Hermanus Greef was still not certain the Pretorious brothers were telling the truth, but he was taking no chances.

He was too late. The Pretorious brothers had been so amazed at seeing the Matabele impis advancing towards the Greef shack that they had missed Daniel, Jaconus Van Eyck and Major Colenbrander's commando, riding ahead and to one side of the impis.

Suddenly they came into view and the Pretorious boys did not wait to see more. Turning their horses, they bolted along the valley, away from both impi and commando, leaving the Greefs to face whatever was to come.

Arne and Louis Greef had dragged themselves reluctantly from their beds. Now they stood in front of the sagging doorway, puffy-eyed and bad-tempered, glowering sullenly at the newcomers.

'Good day, to you,' Hermanus Greef addressed the three men who rode up to the shack. 'I'm relieved to see you,' he jerked a thumb in the direction taken by the Pretorious brothers. 'My neighbour's boys. They've had too much good Cape brandy. They thought you and your men were a Matabele raiding party.'

Hermanus Greef broke into a throaty laugh, but Major Colenbrander cut his amusement short. 'The Matabele impis are along the valley, scarcely half a mile away. They've been sent by Lobengula because you've been raiding inside his country.'

'Raiding? Me?' Hermanus Greef was not a quick-thinking man and he played for time, wondering where Major Colenbrander's interest lay. It was unthinkable that he should take the side of kaffirs, even Matabele kaffirs, against a white man. But Colenbrander was obviously a man of influence and authority. Hermanus Greef had never found a man of the major's standing sympathetic to his own views. 'I'm too old to go off raiding, Major. It's as much as I can do to get on a horse. Why, I haven't left my home for more than two years now—'

'Then it's your sons we should be speaking to,' Daniel cut in on the old man's prevaricating. 'They've raided my valley twice. The first time they attacked a woman. The last time they carried off Jannie Van Eyck.'

'Jannie's my son,' interjected Jaconus Van Eyck. 'Where is he?'

Hermanus Greef's eyes opened wide, 'You . . . you're not Jaconus Van Eyck . . . the hunter?'

'I am, and right now I'm hunting my son. What have you done with him?'

Hermanus Greef's throat suddenly felt very tight and dry. 'You've got it wrong, Jaconus. My boys have been to Matabeleland, yes. I admit that. They had some fun there too, they tell me. But their fun was with basters – coloureds, man. They know how to treat white women. I've taught them that, out of respect for the memory of their dear mother, God rest her soul. As for your boy – well, what would they want with the son of Jaconus Van Eyck?'

'My son, Jannie, is a "baster",' Jaconus Van Eyck rasped. 'I'm asking you for the last time, Oude Baas. Where is he?'

Daniel barely had time to register Major Colenbrander's startled expression at the news that Jaconus Van Eyck's son was coloured, for at that moment the Matabele impis emerged from the bushveldt.

As the commando milled about in confusion, Gamba issued his orders briskly. Within two minutes of their arrival, the Greef homestead was totally surrounded by four thousand Matabele warriors. As Gamba strode forward to join the group talking to Hermanus Greef, the warriors began rhythmically beating on their shields, a sound that quickly filled the air and struck terror into Arne and Louis Greef.

There were angry muttered protests from the men of the commando as Gamba arrogantly pushed his way between their horses to take his place with Daniel and the others. Gamba ignored them.

Pointing to Hermanus Greef, he said, 'Is this the man who hunts women and boys in our land.'

'No, he is an old man. His sons are the hunters.'

'Then we will take *them* back to King Lobengula.'

'Wait, Gamba. There is much talking to be done. First of all we must find Van Eyck's son.'

'My warriors have found him . . . .'

The conversation between Daniel and Gamba was in Matabele, but Jaconus Van Eyck understood enough to register relief at Gamba's words. The relief died when Gamba turned to him and Jaconus Van Eyck saw the sadness on his face.

'I am sorry, hunter. He hangs from the great tree behind the house, a rope about his neck.'

Jaconus Van Eyck's eyes closed and for a moment he swayed as though he would fall, but as Daniel took a quick step towards him he opened his eyes and the expression in them brought Daniel to a halt. Looking past Daniel, he said to the Induna, 'Show me.'

Inclining his head, Gamba walked away with Jaconus Van Eyck following.

'What was that all about? Where are they going?' Major Colenbrander moved to Daniel's side and looked after the departing men with barely concealed irritation. He did not speak the Matabele language. 'There's too much going on here that I don't understand.'

'Then let me enlighten you. Gamba is taking Jaconus to where his son is hanging from a tree. Murdered by your countrymen here, no doubt. When he comes back he'll expect to take the Greefs back to Matabeleland to stand trial before Lobengula.'

In the silence that followed Daniel's words, the rattling of Matabele war-shields sounded very, very loud.

Hermanus Greef broke in upon Major Colenbrander's troubled thoughts. 'You can't hand me over to kaffir justice. I'm a white man – a Boer, the same as you. All right, I had the boy hung, but he'd killed Willem, my eldest. How was I to know he was Van Eyck's son. He was a baster. You know voortrekker law, Major. You look after your own and expect help from no one. If you have trouble with kaffirs, or basters, you've got to stamp on it quick. If you don't you'll be murdered in your bed.'

'I wouldn't tell that to Gamba, if I were you. Your "voortrekker law" doesn't go down well in Matabeleland.'

Daniel looked at Major Colenbrander. 'The next move is up to you, Major. Your decision here is going to be an important one for future relations between Lobengula and Transvaal.'

'Perhaps – perhaps not,' Major Colenbrander looked angrily at Daniel. 'You've tricked me, Retallick. You and Jaconus. If I'd known all this was the result of a scrape between the Greef boys and some coloureds, I'd never have allowed things to go this far. I'd have ordered Lobengula's army out of the Transvaal Republic, double quick.'

There were murmurs of agreement from the listening Boers of his commando.

'What you see here isn't a tenth of Lobengula's army,' stated Daniel. 'Think of that before you risk upsetting Lobengula. Provoke a war and within six months there won't be a living soul for a hundred miles south of the Limpopo. Oh, I don't doubt you'd win in the end, you've got the guns that Lobengula lacks – but the cost of winning will be so high that you'll be unable to move across the Limpopo to follow up any success you might have. The British would. Your action will hand them Matabeleland on a golden plate. Ask yourself whether one murdering old man and his two vicious sons are worth such a price – and you'd better make up your mind quickly. Here come Jaconus and Gamba now.'

Jaconus Van Eyck carried the body of Jannie in his arms and Daniel had never seen such anguish on a man's face. As Jaconus laid his dead son on the ground at Hermanus Greef's feet, a few of the men in Colenbrander's commando removed their wide-brimmed hats out of respect. Most did not and Daniel's conviction grew that the Boers would never allow Gamba to take the Greefs back to Bulawayo.

'Look at him, Oude Baas. There's my boy. Look at him, I say!'

Hermanus Greef lowered his eyes to Jannie's body, then quickly looked away again.

'He took a fearful beating before he died, Oude Baas. Was that your work, or that of your boys?'

Hermanus Greef looked to Major Colenbrander for some sign of support, but the commando leader was not yet ready to commit himself.

'He . . . he fought us. He was a brave boy. I give him that . . .

he fought like a man. I'm sorry—' Hermanus Greef choked on his words.

'He was hardly eighteen years old, Oude Baas. A gentle boy. A good boy. I don't believe he killed your son. Killing a man just wasn't in him. Even a thieving, no-good son like yours.'

When Hermanus Greef made no reply, Jaconus Van Eyck spoke to Major Colenbrander. 'I'm making a formal complaint of murder against Hermanus Greef and his two sons. Will you take them in custody to Pretoria for trial?'

There was not a sound from the men about the commando leader as they awaited his reply.

Colenbrander knew whatever decision he made now would be criticised by someone. He chose the way that would be acceptable to the majority of those who rode with him, knowing that they represented Boer opinion.

'I'd like to take them in for trial, Jaconus, out of personal respect for you – but I must face the facts. The case would never reach a court and I'd be the laughing stock of Pretoria. This is voortrekker country – and the voortrekkers make their own laws. You know that – you've been one of them for most of your life. Why, it's not even certain this corner of the country belongs to us. Pretoria and Lisbon have been arguing about borders for months.'

Hermanus Greef's relief was evident and his face twitched in a nervous smile.

'Would your answer have been the same had my boy not had coloured blood in his veins?' Jaconus Van Eyck asked the question quietly.

'Yes.'

'There has been enough talking.' Gamba was one of the very few Matabeles who understood Afrikaans. He had been following the arguments of Colenbrander and Jaconus Van Eyck closely. 'Lobengula sent me to find the men who raided his country and attacked those who enjoy his protection. I have found them. I will take them back to Bulawayo now.'

Daniel translated Gamba's words for Major Colenbrander.

'Tell the Induna there are procedures to be followed in such cases. Lobengula should complain to the Transvaal Government. The matter will be looked into . . . but I must remind him it was Lobengula himself who tore up Toblin's treaty. He can't expect much sympathy from President Kruger.'

'That's right, Major. You tell this kaffir-boetje to take his broers back where they came from. We've fought for this country. No kaffir's going to come in and lord it over a white man. If you want some help you can count on me and my sons.' Hermanus Greef had regained much of his confidence after hearing Cólenbrander's words.

'The Amabhunu did not listen to my words,' said Gamba, coldly. 'I was not asking him if I could take these men. I was *telling* him.' Gamba had earlier silenced the shield-beating, now he signalled with his hand and it began again, sounding even more menacing than before, and causing the Boer commando to look nervously towards their commander.

'For God's sake, Major. Don't back yourself into a corner. Sit down and talk to Gamba. You've got a hundred men's lives in your hands. Whichever way you look at it, the Greef's aren't worth such a price—'

Pale-faced, Major Colenbrander said stubbornly, 'My men knew what might happen when they volunteered to come out with me after the Matabele. There's an important principle involved in this.'

Daniel groaned. The last thing the situation needed was a man who was determined to write himself into the history of the Transvaal Republic. He appealed to Gamba.

'Back your warriors off while we talk about this. Lobengula didn't mean you to come here and start a war!'

'I have my orders, trader. These men must be taken to King Lobengula.'

'Damn your orders, Gamba, and your principles, Colenbrander. You're both talking over the dead body of my son as though he never existed at all. There *is* another way. *I'll* show you what it is.'

Jaconus Van Eyck strode the few paces to where his horse stood, loose-reined. A double-barrelled hunting rifle, twin to the one Jannie had owned, hung by its sling from the saddle horn. Jaconus lifted it down and, before anyone realised his intention, he swung around and fired. Once . . . twice.

The two Greef brothers were standing beside the cabin, leaning carelessly against the peeling bark of its wooden walls.

Jaconus Van Eyck's first shot knocked big Louis Greef back against the wooden wall before he pitched forward to lie on his face, arms and legs twitching in dying convulsions.

Arne made an attempt to run, but he had no sooner turned sideways than the second heavy bullet shattered his ribs, piercing both lungs before embedding itself in the wall of the shack. Arne fell back against the wall and slumped to the ground where he sat coughing up his life's blood.

As the second shot echoed back from the surrounding hills, the drumming of the Matabele warriors faltered and died. For a few moments the valley was hushed and still. The unnatural silence was broken by a howl of anguish that had an animal quality about it. The sound released an angry outburst from the Boer commando.

'Arne! Louis!' Hermanus Greef sank to his knees beside Arne Greef as his life bubbled away within arm's reach of Louis Greef's now-still body.

'Jaconus, man! That was sheer bloody murder.'

Jaconus Van Eyck pulled the empty cartridges from his rifle and thumbed two new shells in their place. After a quick glance towards the Boer commando, he slipped the strap of the heavy rifle over his shoulder. 'No, Major. It's voortrekker justice. You were telling me about it a few minutes ago, remember? You should be grateful to me. I've just saved your life – and the lives of your men.'

Turning his back on Major Colenbrander, Jaconus Van Eyck spoke to Gamba. 'You've done all that Lobengula asked of you, Induna Gamba. When you return to the King, tell him that the gun of his friend, Van Eyck, robbed you of the men you sought. I offer him no apology for avenging my son's death. Tell him that, Gamba. He'll understand.'

'I understand too, hunter. Better, I think, than your own people.'

Gamba called to his men and they responded to his words, shouting happily as they formed up in marching formation. Gamba was taking them home.

Before he left, Gamba turned to Major Colenbrander and spoke to him in passable Afrikaans. 'I say this to your face, so no man can say another used words that were not mine. I was sent to find the Amabhunu who had come to our land and attacked those who enjoyed Lobengula's protection. My King did not say, "It does not matter because those who were attacked were not Matabele." There is only one law in our land. Lobengula's words do not have two meanings: one for white, another for black. When I tell him what has been said here today, he will not be pleased.'

In a single sweep of his arm, Gamba encompassed all the men of the commando and Colenbrander himself. 'The road to Lobengula's kraal is no longer open for you and your people. There will be no hunting. No concessions. The days of friendship between our peoples are over.'

With great dignity, Gamba walked to the head of his warriors and gave the order for them to march northwards, taking the shortest route to the Limpopo River, no more than forty miles away.

CHAPTER NINE

When Wyatt and the Matabele trackers returned to Insimo with news that Jannie had been taken over the river to Transvaal, Therese had known she would never see him alive again. When Jaconus Van Eyck broke the news of Jannie's death to her, she accepted it with an outward calm that deceived everyone except her mother.

Jannie Van Eyck was buried in the tiny Insimo valley burial ground, beside the grave of Philippe, the one-time Pombeiro. It was here, during the simple burial ceremony for the boy who would have been her husband in such a short while, that Therese's composure cracked. Standing between the graves of the two men who had meant so much to her during her short lifetime, she suddenly broke down and, weeping inconsolably, was led away by Victoria.

Daniel quickly learned all the details of the two raids on the Insimo valley. He determined that before he left the valley again he would establish an efficient system of look-outs and armed guards. There would be no recurrence of the incidents involving the Greef brothers.

Jaconus Van Eyck agreed to remain in the valley and help Daniel carry out his plans. He knew it would be advisable to stay away from Transvaal until the killing of the Greefs was no longer a contentious issue there.

His decision was received with great relief by Elvira. Daniel would be spending many more weeks away from her, on his trading trips. After Jannie had been carried off responsibility for the valley rested with her. It was a difficult task. Both the Matabele herd-boys and the Mashona farm labourers resented taking orders from a woman.

Daniel's homecoming was heavily clouded by the tragedy of Jannie Van Eyck's death. There was uncertainty in the air too about the future of the Matabele kingdom. Despite all this, Daniel felt the anxiety and strain of recent months fall away from him. He was home again.

Late in the night after the funeral of Jannie, Daniel rose from his bed and made his way out to the verandah surrounding the house. Lighting a pipe, he stood gazing out at the valley, silvered by the light from a full moon. He had crept quietly from the bedroom, thinking that Elvira was asleep, but it was not many minutes before she joined him. Barefooted and wearing only a long, white nightdress, she slipped noiselessly from the house and he started as she slipped an arm about his waist.

'Is it so difficult to sleep by my side in a comfortable bed?' she whispered.

Daniel hugged her to him. 'It's what I've longed for more than anything else during the months I've been away. Every night when I laid my blanket down in some uncomfortable hollow in the bush, I hoped I might wake up and find myself back here, with you and the boys.'

'And your body has returned to us – but where are your thoughts, my husband?'

'They are here too, but they travel beyond today . . . this night. I'm wondering what the future will bring for Wyatt and Nathan, Adam and Benjamin. Lobengula is under tremendous pressure to open up his country to Rhodes and his friends. How can I prevent him from signing away the future of his people – and the future of our sons too? Wyatt will soon be a man. He'll want—'

Elvira's finger found his lips and pressed them closed. 'Shh! You praised Wyatt for behaving like a man when he and the herd-boys tracked the Boers. It was true, he did – but his pleasure at your words was that of a young boy. Let him be my young son for a while longer. Too many children have to grow up before their time. Poor Jannie was one.'

Daniel felt her tears warm against him and his arm tightened about her.

'Look out there, Daniel,' Elvira whispered fiercely. 'With so much beauty to be seen how can men's minds grow so ugly?'

'I don't know. Perhaps the Devil moved in while God was admiring the view – and I'm afraid of the same thing happening to Lobengula. If he's not careful he'll be so taken up with the presents and promises made to him by Rhodes and his agents that he'll not be aware he's sold the inheritance of his people.'

'Suliyana is concerned too. She came here with Lundi, while you were away. Spiteful kraal gossip had upset her. It's being said that Lobengula is twice the man his father was about the girth, but possesses only half his cunning. The truth is that drink is severely affecting his thinking. He now has a passion for champagne and brandy cocktails. A wagonload of drink was sent up for him from Bechuanaland, just before he signed the treaty with Great Britain.'

'I must talk to Lobengula about that. I'll need to go to Bulawayo in a few days time, to ask permission for Jaconus to remain at Insimo.'

'In a few days time it will be as though you have never been away — but tonight is a homecoming.' Elvira took his hand. 'Come to bed, my husband.'

Later, after Elvira had given Daniel the love she knew he needed, it was her turn to find sleep elusive. Although she had not admitted it to Daniel, she too was concerned about the future. Not only for her children — but for her husband. Suliyana had remained at Insimo for a week. During that time she had spoken honestly of matters that would have been dangerous to mention to a Matabele woman.

Drink was only one of Lobengula's problems, albeit the one that was most evident to other men. He could see his enemies growing stronger beyond the country's borders, while the Matabele fell further behind in both wealth and military strength.

The latest blow to fall concerned the Barotsi tribe, beyond the Zambezi River to the north of Matabeleland. Lobengula heard disquieting rumours that the Barotsi Chief, Lewanika, was contemplating a treaty with Rhodes and sent a senior Induna to investigate.

The Induna returned laden with presents from the Barotsi Chief ... but the gifts made the Induna's news no more palatable. Lewanika had *already* granted a concession. Permission to prospect and mine for minerals had been granted to a private concession-hunter — who had promptly made for Kimberley where he sold it to Rhodes!

The news found Lobengula in a sober state and plunged him

in a state of deepest despondency. Matabeleland was now totally surrounded by lands to which the white men's influence had extended. Matabeleland stood alone.

The 'treachery' of the Barotsi – for this was how Lobengula viewed the concession, hit Lobengula particularly hard. For as long as the white men had been crowding his borders, Lobengula had always looked upon the road north as his ultimate escape route. If a white invasion came, Lobengula intended to emulate his father and retreat northwards, leaving the white men to fight over Matabeleland like greedy dogs over a bone. Suddenly this escape route had been closed to him. Now Lobengula knew without doubt that one day the Matabele would have to fight the white men. The ways of the two peoples were too far apart for them ever to stand side by side in friendship and the Matabele were too proud to submit to the protection of one of the European countries who coveted their land. They, like the whites themselves, were used to going their own way, taking the respect of others for granted.

It was a situation that gnawed at Lobengula's heart night and day. It became bearable only when he drank heavily. As a result, he drank heavily for most of every day.

All these things Suliyana told to Elvira who, in her turn, worried for Daniel. She knew how deeply committed he was to securing for the Matabele the right to retain their identity and independence. He would feel the impending disaster almost as keenly as Lobengula, and would become totally involved on their behalf. He could do nothing else. The Insimo Valley was Lobengula's tangible recognition of Daniel's commitment – and the Insimo valley was to be Daniel's legacy to his sons.

Daniel found Bulawayo unchanged. It was hot and noisy and smelly. Perhaps the grass-thatch 'beehive' huts sagged a little more than when he had left, but their ageing lines were blurred by the thick pall of dust that hung over the Matabele capital. Kicked up by the hooves of the great Matabele cattle herds, the dust was stained red by the rays of the setting sun.

Lobengula was seated by the 'indaba' fire – the fire around which the tribal officials conducted the business of the Matabele. Lobengula was drinking brandy from a wicker-clad jar, surrounded by the usual miscellany of Europeans. Concession-seekers and would-be hunters, they preferred the warmth and hospitality of Lobengula's fire to the lonely dangers of the bushveldt. Most of them had been here when Daniel left to go south — but he was quick to observe that there was not a Boer face among them. Gamba had kept the promise he had made to Major Colenbrander.

Lobengula boomed a loud greeting to Daniel. 'Welcome home, trader! You've been away far too long. Come, sit beside me and tell me about your journeys.' Lobengula looked about him at the noisy throng. 'No, we will go to my house, away from these noisy children.'

Struggling to his feet, the King leaned heavily on the shoulders of members of his bodyguard and preceded Daniel to the house. He was fifty-two years old now and age had dusted his hair with grey. He was also a very big man, taller and heavier than his father had been — and quite as unsteady on his feet.

Inside the hut he ordered one of his wives to put a light to the ready-laid fire, then stood unsteadily before the fireplace, warming his hands. Beaming genially at Daniel, he said, 'I hear your travels have taken you far, my friend?'

'Very far, Inkosi. I have spoken to the Governor in the Cape Colony, to Cecil Rhodes — and visited the family of my friend Toblin in Transvaal. I returned from there with Jaconus Van Eyck. I would like him to remain and work with me at Insimo. He is a good man. I will vouch for him.'

'He is also a brave man. Tell him I grieve for the son he has lost. He may stay.'

Lobengula eased himself into his large, leather armchair and exhaled his breath gratefully. Then he looked critically at Daniel. 'You have lost weight. Gamba told me of the troubles you and he had with the Boers. I do not like making enemies of white men, but the Boers can never again be the friends of the Matabele.'

'The great tragedy is, had Toblin not been killed the treaty would not have been altered and the Boers would have done the work Gamba set out to do.'

'You believe this? Do you think the Boers would have meted out justice as did your friend Van Eyck? Kill two white men to avenge the death of one who was neither of their people, nor mine?'

'I believe that if a Boer gives his word, it will be kept,' declared Daniel firmly.

'I accepted the word of your friend Toblin, but his countrymen twisted those words to suit themselves,' Lobengula reminded Daniel.

'There are always men at hand to take advantage of a situation. Both sides were quick to use Uiys Toblin's death. I've seen the treaty you made with the British, Inkosi. It's not a good one for your people.'

Lobengula scowled angrily. 'I signed no treaty with the British.'

Daniel could not believe the King was serious, 'I saw the treaty myself. It bore your mark – and that of Umnombati, and was countersigned by the Reverend Loveday. The British are using the treaty to warn off Transvaal, Portugal and the Germans.'

'If by signing such a treaty the white men would cease from pestering me I would happily sign. More than half my day is spent listening to their pleas.'

'A treaty must be carefully worded if it's not to arouse anger among others – unless it also guarantees that your battles will be fought for you. As things are, you've signed a treaty that gives you nothing. Britain can sit back while you wage war with your neighbours. Then, when you're all too weak to fight any more, they'll march in waving their treaty and take all they want.'

Lobengula tried desperately to pull his alcohol-dulled thoughts together – but failed. He roared angrily for one of his wives and a big, anxious-looking girl hurried in and dropped to her knees in front of the King.

'Go and fetch Umnombati.'

The junior wife momentarily forgot the awe in which she held her royal husband. 'Umnombati is a very old man. He sleeps—'

'Then wake him. Tell him his King wants him here now.'

The wife scrambled to her feet and fled from the room. Lobengula reached for the brandy flagon. It was empty and he threw it across the room in a fit of childish pique.

'You'll see,' he mumbled. 'You'll see, trader.' Suddenly struggling to his feet, spurning Daniel's hand, Lobengula made his heavy way outside, to where the men about the Induna fire were still drinking heavily. Here he took a brandy jar from one of the concession-seekers.

Umnombati arrived supported by two of his wives. He was now a very old man indeed, being well over ninety years of age. The flesh on his body had shrivelled away, leaving the wrinkled, leathery skin hanging on a skeletal frame.

The man who had for so long been the senior Induna of the Matabele nation raised a hand in a palsied salute to his King. Beside him his two wives also trembled, but they were unable to claim the excuse of age. They were scared. In their experience a man of Umnombati's status was not called from his bed in the night by the King unless he had incurred extreme royal displeasure. When such a thing occurred the whole family of the unfortunate man were likely to suffer whatever fate was meted out to the miscreant.

But there was no such fear in Umnombati, 'You sent for me, Lobengula. I am here.'

Lobengula grunted. 'The trader says he has seen a treaty signed between the Matabele and the British. It is a bad treaty, he says. Have I asked the advice of the Council of Indunas on such a matter?'

'The King of the Matabele is a King indeed. He does not consult with his Elders before doing that which he knows is right for the people.'

'No riddles, Umnombati. The trader says the treaty bears your mark too. I have said I signed no treaty. We await your words.'

Umnombati turned his face towards Daniel. 'The King has signed no treaty.'

Lobengula relaxed. 'There! I told you the truth. You should know by now that a King does not lie. His word can be believed by all men.'

Lobengula carried the jar of brandy to his lips and poured a frightening amount of the contents down his throat. When it was lowered to the ground, he said huskily, 'Go now. We will talk again, trader.'

Umnombati had been moved from his distant kraal to Bulawayo many years before. As befitted his age and position in the tribe, his hut was close to the King's house. Daniel walked with him and apologised for being responsible for having the old Induna brought from his bed.

'I am grateful that I can still perform a service for my King. But you are right, trader. It *is* a bad treaty for our people.'

'Then Lobengula *has* signed a treaty? But you said—'

'Would you have me call my King a liar before those who drink about his fire? To admit that the son of my great friend, Mzilikazi, was so stupid with drink at the time he did not realise what he was doing? The mark on the paper was made by a drunken man – not by a Matabele King. Lobengula has forgotten . . . so should all men.'

'The British won't let him forget, Umnombati.'

'If it were not this treaty it would be something else. The white men will squeeze the Matabele nation tighter, and tighter . . . and tighter still. One day they will feel it slipping from their grasp, like an over-ripe fruit. When that day comes there will be war. I think the Gods must have willed it, trader. So be it. Is it not better for a young Matabele warrior to die fighting for a nation that is still great and proud, than to live to old age with a white man standing between him and the sun?'

CHAPTER TEN

Elvira had not seen her father for some years and she was very concerned because there had been no news from him for many months. Daniel waited only until he was quite certain that Jaconus Van Eyck could run things at Insimo before announcing that the whole family would make the long journey to Sena.

The trip needed a great deal of planning. Daniel intended taking the proceeds of two seasons trading with him. Such a journey required the King's permission and Lobengula gave Daniel the road in late July 1888. The King also insisted on sending two hundred warriors along, turning the family trek into a major expedition. With a full dozen wagons drawn by slow-plodding oxen, it would be at least a month before they reached the home of Senhor Farrao.

But although it was a planning headache for Daniel, it was a great adventure for the four boys. Their excitement had reached fever pitch long before it was time to leave Insimo. Even Therese caught their mood and smiled happily for the first time since Jannie Van Eyck's death.

Therese was accompanying the Retallicks, mainly to help Elvira with the boys, but also because Victoria and Elvira agreed it would be good for her to get away from Insimo for a while. Therese spoke fluent Portuguese and should prove a great asset on the long journey through Mozambique.

The wagons and escort set off from Insimo on a wonderfully crisp and clear winter's day, with landmarks up to fifty miles distant standing out clearly against the sky.

All the Mashona workers turned out to wave them off as they left the house behind. Further along the valley, the Matabele herd-boys set up a continuous ululating cry that echoed from the rocky crags and startled their charges.

It was a good beginning for a happy trek that progressed without incident for the first two hundred miles. By then they were passing through an area abounding in cool, clear streams and spectacular, tumbling waterfalls.

One evening they camped early, in order to allow the boys to try their hands at fishing. There was no guard set. There were a few Manicas in the area, but they kept well clear of Lobengula's escorting warriors. Suddenly, a warning cry went up from one of the Mashona wagon drivers who had been exploring further along the valley where they had camped.

Immediately, the relaxed and carefree camp became a scene of confused activity. The Matabele ran for their spears and shields, and Daniel helped Elvira round up the boys. Lifting them to the dubious safety of a covered wagon, he snatched up his own rifle and ran along the narrow twisting valley after the Matabele escort.

The cry from the wagon driver had given the warning that armed men were coming. Suddenly, ahead of him, Daniel heard the knobkerries of the Matabele warriors begin beating against their long shields and he knew the information had been correct. Rounding a turn in the valley, Daniel's heart sank. The 'armed men' were riders – and there were almost as many of them as there were Matabele in the escort. As he watched they formed up with some semblance of order, rifles at the ready, in preparation for the attack of the Matabeles.

The warriors of the escort were armed only with the broad-bladed assegais. A battle would be a one-sided affair. A single volley would be sufficient to cut down many of the Matabele warriors and they would never get close enough to use their broad-bladed stabbing spears against mounted men.

Fortunately, the warriors were advancing in their customary slow and deliberate manner. Daniel was able to reach them and push ahead of their advancing ranks before either side took any positive action. He called on the horsemen to hold their fire. Much to his relief, a blue uniformed horseman broke from their ranks and a very young, fresh-faced Portuguese officer came to meet him.

'Who are you, senhor? Why do you bring an army of armed tribesmen to Portuguese territory?'

Ignoring the territorial claim, Daniel replied, 'My name is Daniel Retallick. My wife is the daughter of Senhor Farrao, Captain General of the North West District. We are bringing our children on a visit to their grandfather. The tribesmen are an escort provided for us by King Lobengula of the Matabele.'

The young Portuguese army officer's manner underwent a remarkable change at the mention of Senhor Farrao. 'My apologies, Senhor Retallick . . . but can you halt your warriors before there is a fight?'

The Matabele warriors were closer now, the short assegais already drawn back in readiness for battle.

'Get your men back out of the way – quickly,' Daniel snapped at the Portuguese officer. 'I'll need a few minutes to cool the warriors down. Don't come close until I call you.'

Jerking the reins of his horse, the Portuguese officer cantered back to his men and waved for them to follow him along the valley, away from the Matabele warriors.

Believing the soldiers to be running from them, the warriors howled in disappointment. They had not yet blooded their spears. There was not an Induna with them. Lacking his authority they would have broken ranks and pursued the Portuguese had Daniel not shouted them down, emphasising his words with a warning shot.

When he had their attention, he said, 'There will be no battle. The horsemen are Portuguese soldiers. They have come to escort my wife to her father.'

His words brought grumbles of disappointment from the younger warriors – the 'Mahaja', the unremittingly disgruntled young heart of Lobengula's army. Too young to have taken part in the fighting that marred Lobengula's accession to the Matabele throne, they listened enviously to the tales of battle, related about the camp-fires by older warriors. Each of them was eager for the day when he too would take part in a battle worthy of retelling again and again.

There would be no glory for them today, but Daniel did not breathe easily until the warriors lowered their shields and began chaffing each other in a slightly embarrassed manner, as tension eased.

Daniel called the Portuguese officer and took him to the wagons to introduce him to Elvira, Therese and the boys. The young Lieutenant's name was Carlos St Anna, a name with a familiar ring. Looking at him more closely, Daniel saw that the features of the young man closely resembled those of the officer he and Elvira had known so well before they were married.

'You are the son of Colonel Francisco St Anna?'

'*General* St Anna.' The young Lieutenant corrected Daniel proudly. 'You know him?'

'We both knew him very well. Your father commanded the garrison at Sena when I lived there. He was not very much older than you are now, in those days. He and my husband fought against the Pombeiros together,' Elvira smiled at Lieutenant St Anna, uncomfortably aware that Wyatt was staring at his father with undisguised hero-worship. He had been told little about Daniel's earlier days in Mozambique. Lieutenant St Anna also showed rather more deference to the man he had at first mentally dismissed as just another Englishman. Albeit one fortunate enough to be married to a prosperous and influential Portuguese of very good family.

Daniel was unaware of the rise in his status. He was more concerned with Lieutenant St Anna's open admiration for Therese. She was very aware of his regard, serving to increase Daniel's disquiet. Daniel's earlier years were so far removed from his present way of life that they might have involved another man – but there was one memory that Daniel could not forget. It concerned an incident that had occurred not very far from the valley where they now camped. He had ridden away from that spot on a blustery, grey day many years ago with Victoria beside him, doing his best to keep between her and the bodies that hung, wry-necked, from a tree beside the path. One of the dead men was Mariano, Therese's true father. He had been executed on the orders of Lieutenant Francisco St Anna . . . father of the man who had just carried Therese's hand to his lips!

Daniel realised with a start that Lieutenant Carlos St Anna was speaking to him, 'You will be able to resume your acquaintanceship with my father when you reach Quelimane. He is now Commander-in-Chief of the army in Mozambique and his office is there.'

'But we're not going to Quelimane. We're on our way to Sena. To visit Senhor Farrao.'

'Forgive me! I was forgetting that news could not possibly have reached you yet. Captain General Farrao is no longer at

Sena. The Governor of Mozambique was recently recalled to Portugal. Senhor Farrao has been appointed Acting Governor, in his place. He is now, of course, at Quelimane.'

Now Daniel knew why the mention of Senhor Farrao had made such an impact on the young Lieutenant. Elvira's father had become the most powerful man in the ancient Portuguese colony of Mozambique.

Lieutenant St Anna insisted that the Matabele escort should now return to Bulawayo. He would escort them for the remainder of their journey, first to Sena, in the hope of finding a suitable boat to take them to Quelimane, and then downriver to the Portuguese port.

Daniel sent the Matabeles off with a message for Lobengula, commending the men on the manner in which they had performed their duties and they left well pleased with themselves.

The next night, Daniel and the Portuguese soldiers outspanned in yet another of the attractive, well-watered valleys which abounded in the Manica Mountains. As they sat about the fire Lieutenant St Anna told Daniel the reason why he was in the area. Acting Governor Farrao had sent him to remind the Manicaland Chiefs that their allegiance lay unequivocally with Portugal.

The Chiefs were anxious to assure Lieutenant St Anna that they needed no reminding. Living in great style only a few miles to the east of their lands was Manuel Antonio de Souza Gouveia, a Goanese landowner of mixed Portuguese and Indian parentage. His slave-trading links with the Arabs were extremely profitable and enabled him to maintain a large force of armed retainers. Because his vast estates bordered an area that was the subject of dispute with all those parties interested in Central Africa, the Portuguese bestowed upon him the title of 'Captain General of Gorongoza', charging him with the task of securing the loyalty of all Manica Chiefs in the disputed area.

The Portuguese authorities had made a good choice. Gouveia believed in rule by terror and his methods were terrifyingly effective. A Manica sub-chief complained to the Governor of Mozambique about the high taxes Gouveia was levying on his people. Captain General Gouveia's response was to send his private army to Manicaland to 'visit' the sub-chief. They returned to Gouveia's stronghold driving herds of captured livestock before them. Not one of the sub-chief's people remained on the lands that had been theirs for as long as men could remember. The Manica women and children were sold into a life of slavery. The men, together with the old folk, had their throats cut by Gouveia's mercenaries.

On the way to Sena, Lieutenant St Anna explained that it was necessary to make a slight detour, in order to call on Captain General Gouveia. He had some dispatches to deliver from the Acting Governor. Lieutenant St Anna spoke with the air of apologetic embarrassment adopted by all Portuguese of breeding, when they were forced to deal with Gouveia. To them, Gouveia was an 'animal', to be kept well away from cities and other places where civilised people gathered. At the same time, they recognised the need for such a man to act as a 'guard dog' along the uncertain borders of their territory.

Daniel had heard many rumours of Gouveia, the scourge of Manicaland. Yet, when the wagons creaked to a halt outside the huge, rambling, grass-thatched house on Gouveia Mountain and the Captain General came out to greet his visitors, the first sighting of the Goanese 'monster' came as a great anticlimax. Manuel Antonio de Souza Gouveia, was a small, insignificant man whose manners as a host could not be faulted. He bowed unctuously over Elvira's hand, and drooled over Therese. He was cooler in his welcome to Daniel, but that was only to be expected. Rhodes had done nothing to improve the already strained relationship between British and Portuguese.

When the Captain General learned of the contents of Daniel's wagons, his manner towards him thawed considerably and he asked if he might examine the ivory Daniel was carrying to the coast.

'Certainly. I wouldn't deny any man the opportunity to view the finest ivory in Africa,' Daniel replied, the trader in him coming to the fore.

Gouveia gave him a non-committal grunt, but when he had examined a sample from each of Daniel's wagons he showed much more enthusiasm.

'We have fine elephants here in Gorongoza too,' he said.

'But you are quite right, this is first-class ivory. What price do you expect it to fetch on the coast?'

Daniel named a price that was considerably higher than he would have asked from Senhor Farrao.

Gouveia shrugged. 'You *might* receive such a price, if you are prepared to wait for a buyer.' He then made an offer that was lower than Daniel's quote, but still higher than Daniel would receive from Senhor Farrao. 'I will pay you in gold. You can take it with you, or call here for it on your return.'

'I'll settle for a note drawn on a Quelimane bank,' said Daniel.

'As you wish. Then it is agreed?'

'It's agreed.' Daniel shook Gouveia's limp, pudgy hand. A deal concluded here suited him well. Senhor Farrao was now the Acting Governor General of Mozambique. He would not want to concern himself with matters of trade – and without the heavily laden wagons, Daniel and his party would be able to travel much faster across the unhealthy Mozambique plains.

Then Gouveia revealed some of the character that Daniel had expected to discover. 'The girl who travels with you – Therese. She is yours to sell?'

'She's not up for sale. She's the daughter of a friend.' Daniel wondered what Gouveia's approach would have been had he known she was also the daughter of one of the most famous rebels Mozambique had known.

'Ah! But you will have some influence with her? You could persuade her to remain here? It would prove very rewarding for you, Senhor Retallick.'

'Rumour has it that you've enough wives already.'

'I have *many* wives, Senhor. Enough . . . ? No, I think not.'

'Well, however many you have would be too many for Therese. She wants a one-woman man – and before you become too interested, I suggest you have a chat with General St Anna's son. I think he too has an interest in Therese.'

Daniel hoped the warning would deter Gouveia, but he determined to give Gouveia Mountain a wide berth on the return journey.

Later that evening, after a splendid meal, Daniel went for a walk about the grounds of the house, while Elvira prepared the younger boys for bed. In a quiet, enclosed garden that boasted a pool and a tiny waterfall, Daniel surprised a dark-eyed girl who looked to be part-Arab. He knew instinctively that she was one of Gouveia's 'wives'. She did not run away, as he thought she might. Instead, she stared at him with bold brown eyes. Then her tongue touched her upper lip briefly, and she gave him a smile that carried an unmistakable invitation.

At that moment a guard rushed from one of the buildings adjoining the garden and in angry Arabic ordered the girl inside.

Daniel smiled, remembering Gouveia's words. The Goanese Captain General might consider he could manage more wives, but Daniel doubted if they could be kept out of mischief.

To Daniel it had been no more than a harmless incident, quickly forgotten. But Gouveia had observed the brief encounter from the balcony of his house and there was no amusement in his expression.

Daniel's family-wagons and the Portuguese escort had hardly passed out of sight the next morning when swift punishment was meted out to the bold-eyed concubine.

She was dragged screaming from the harem to the same garden where her indiscretion had taken place. As she fell to her knees, sobbing and begging for mercy from the man to whom she belonged, the remaining ladies of Gouveia's harem were brought out. They were to witness the fate that would be theirs if they too forgot themselves and raised their eyes from the ground to look at another man.

Two men were also brought to the garden, their hands bound behind them. Slaves from the Sudan, they had been emasculated to provide Gouveia with harem guards. Their crime was twofold. First, they had allowed the erring concubine to slip past them to the garden. Secondly they had not reported the matter to their unforgiving master.

As the women of Gouveia's harem watched in horror, too frightened of the Captain General to avert their eyes, the woman and two men died, their throats slit by an Arab. The executioner was an Arab butcher, employed to kill animals in the special manner dictated by the religion of Captain General Gouveia's frequent Moslem guests.

CHAPTER ELEVEN

The visit to Gouveia's home had a strangely sobering effect upon the family party that had set off from Insimo in such high spirits. The Captain General of Gorongoza could not be faulted as a host, yet even the two youngest children had lapsed into unaccustomed silence in the somewhat sombre atmosphere of Gouveia's home.

Accompanied by Lieutenant St Anna's mounted escort they made fast time to Sena. Unfortunately, the only vessel available here was an ancient, open steam launch of about thirty-five feet in length. It had been at the fortified village for two months, having broken down en route to the garrison town of Tete, further upriver.

The launches master-cum-engineer was quickly located in a nearby native village and sobered up by St Anna's men. He grudgingly admitted that the engine of the launch *might* be repaired in a few days – given the services of a number of strong men, and a competent blacksmith.

The repairs in fact, took seven days and Elvira made the most of the time spent in her childhood home. She entertained neighbouring prazeros and proudly introduced her family to old family servants. When word went around that Elvira was at Sena, old friends came from miles away to admire the boys and tell Elvira how well married life agreed with her.

The children were in great danger of being thoroughly spoiled by the time the launch was repaired, but when Daniel heard the first wheezing strokes of the aged steam piston, he wondered whether spoiling his family might not be preferable to risking their lives on the Zambezi River in such an aged and decrepit vessel.

Indignantly, the owner of the steam launch assured Daniel that he and his vessel had been navigating the river between Tete and the sea for twenty-five years, and both were good for another twenty-five.

Much of the family's belongings had to be left behind at

Sena, for lack of room in the boat. In addition to Elvira, Daniel, the boys and Therese, Lieutenant St Anna insisted on accompanying them, with six of his soldiers.

Elvira shared Daniel's opinion of the old steam launch, but to the four boys this was the most exciting part of the long journey. The water in the river was low and, as the boat coughed and spluttered its way down-river, vibrating with every slow beat of the engine, it frequently ran aground. It seemed that soft mud banks abounded just beneath the surface of the sluggish brown water on every bend.

The engine of the launch had insufficient power to drag the vessel off the mud against the current, and it became the duty of Lieutenant St Anna and his soldiers to plunge into the water and heave the boat clear. During this operation, which occurred at least a dozen times each day, Daniel and Wyatt stood guard with their rifles, ready to scare away the crocodiles.

Once they had chugged past the sleepy, Portuguese village of Shupanga, the going became easier. The river widened out considerably and soon they were steaming easily through the mangrove swamps of the Zambezi estuary. Here they encountered a new hazard as the progress of the antiquated launch became subject to the ebb and flow of the tide.

There were many crocodiles here, and schools of hippopotami. Their great, water-polished bodies threatened disaster on more than one occasion when they bobbed to the surface of the water in the path of the launch. In the stillness of the night, when the boat's engine was silent and the occupants of the launch had bedded down in the bottom of the boat, lions and leopards could be heard growling and coughing among the lush undergrowth on the shore. The passengers slept with soldiers in the bow, amidst the carelessly stowed luggage, and Daniel and his family in the stern, behind the stacks of short, cut logs that fuelled the furnace of the launch.

There was little opportunity for romance in such a cramped and gregarious setting. Yet Lieutenant Carlos St Anna and Therese managed to make considerable progress. Unable to take long walks ashore, they were often to be seen sitting close together in the bow of the boat. Carlos St Anna would ostensibly call her attention to distant landmarks, or features on the river, using the opportunity to touch her, his head close

347

to hers as she pretended not to see the object in question.

In the evenings the young couple would sit talking together in a low whisper, long after the other passengers in the launch were asleep. In this way they learned much of each others thoughts and hopes.

They were talking together on the night disaster struck the small party. It was the second night in the fetid mangrove swamp. The master of the launch had hoped to clear the unhealthy, mosquito-ridden area by dusk, but the craft had been able to make little headway against a strong tide. Tying up alongside the bank at dusk, the occupants of the launch ate a hastily prepared and unappetising meal. Then, with the exception of the young couple, they settled down to sleep, doing their best to ignore the persistent and irritating mosquitoes that abounded in the swamps.

Daniel felt he had hardly closed his eyes when he was awakened by the hand of Lieutenant St Anna. He sat up quickly, 'What . . . ?'

'Shhh! Listen.'

Daniel became aware of a sound that was like nothing he had ever heard before. At first he thought it was the roll of distant thunder, but it did not die away as did thunder. Instead the rumbling continued, growing louder with every moment that passed.

'What is it?' Daniel whispered.

'I don't know.'

The sound appeared to be coming closer. Beside Daniel the children began to stir.

'Wake the boatman,' said Daniel. 'Perhaps he knows . . . .'

The Portuguese boatman was already scrambling to his feet. In the moonlight, Daniel saw the man's abject fear as he hurriedly crossed himself.

'Madre Maria! A bore – a big wave. It is heading upriver. Get your family ashore – *everyone* ashore. Quickly! Make for the highest ground you can find. I must slacken off the mooring ropes or they will break and my boat will be lost.'

The passengers were already awake by this time and Daniel hurried to get them together. The huge wall of water, rushing upriver at twenty miles an hour made a deafening sound. Shouting at Elvira to follow him, Daniel snatched up the bewildered four-year-old Benjamin, who was beginning to cry. Stepping ashore, he reached back for Wyatt who was carrying Adam, his second youngest brother.

At that moment, the advance swell of the bore reached them, raising the level of the water by three feet. It took Wyatt beyond Daniel's grasp. Seconds later the giant wall of water struck. Daniel was bowled over and carried away, the sheer weight of the water threatening to crush him. He was flung against the rough clinker-planking of the launch, then tumbled end-over-end and carried upriver with the bore.

He was saved by a dense tangle of mangrove root, just when he feared his lungs would burst. Gripping tightly to the slimy, tangled roots with his free arm, he held on against the pull of the water, his other arm still tight about the limp body of Benjamin.

Just when Daniel felt his lungs could hold the air in them no longer, his head broke clear of the water and he was able to breathe again. Almost immediately, his feet touched bottom and he sank knee-deep in mud.

Benjamin was more dead than alive, but as Daniel floundered to the low river bank, the child began coughing and whooping as his lungs expelled water and sucked in air. Moments later Benjamin began to struggle frantically in Daniel's arms.

'It's all right . . . . It's all right, son. We're safe.'

Daniel's breathless attempt to calm his son was successful. Moments later father and son lay side-by-side on the bank, gasping in air together. Then, still breathless, Daniel rose to his feet and scooped up his young son. They had to find the others.

The deafening boom of the phenomenal tidal bore still filled the air, but it was receding. Somewhere along the river bank, Daniel heard a voice calling in Portuguese for help. Daniel squelched his way towards the sound, at the same time calling at the top of his own voice to Elvira and the remainder of the boys.

He found a soldier wedged in an uncomfortable, but not dangerous position among the roots of another mangrove tree. The soldier was easily extricated and new voices could be heard calling in the darkness along a hundred yard stretch of the river bank. When he heard Elvira's voice calling in answer to his own, he made his way towards her.

Elvira was close to the boat and Nathan was safe with her. They had been fortunate. The boatman had succeeded in slackening the rope at the bow of the steam launch – but not the stern rope. When the advance swell arrived, the launch was lifted in the water and slewed broadside on to the bore. With tons of water thundering down upon it, the boat was thrown on its side, spilling out the occupants. Elvira and Nathan clung to a part of the boat sheltered from the main weight of the tidal wave. The boat now lay on its side, securely wedged in the mud.

Wyatt and Adam were still missing, but as panic rose in Elvira, Daniel assured her they would be found. He squeezed her hand confidently, but he had spoken with more optimism than he felt.

'I'll help you to search.' Elvira was distraught. Wyatt was her eldest son and they had always been very close.

'You stay here. Wyatt's a sensible boy. He'll make for the boat as soon as he can and he'll expect to find you here waiting for him.'

Leaving Benjamin with his mother, Daniel set off upriver in the path of the bore. He occasionally met with soldiers making their way back to the boat, but he found no sign of either Wyatt or Adam.

Behind him, Daniel heard a cry as the boat was righted and, water-filled, floated low in the water. Beneath the boat was the body of a soldier, the first casualty of the freak tidal wave.

Daniel stumbled along the muddy bank, calling the names of his two boys and was soon joined by Lieutenant St Anna. Therese was safe. She had been hurried inland by the young Portuguese officer moments before the wave struck. Only the two boys and a soldier were unaccounted for and Daniel prayed that he would find the boys safe and together.

Lieutenant St Anna brought Daniel a rifle and cartridge belt, recovered from the launch locker. There were crocodiles and hippopotami here, both dangerous to an unarmed man.

Two hundred yards along the bank they met the missing soldier, limping his way back to the boat. In answer to their question he replied that he had neither seen, nor heard anything of the boys. He also informed them that there was a deep creek, extending a long way inland, only a short distance upriver. It could not be crossed in the darkness.

Ignoring this warning, Daniel and Lieutenant St Anna continued to search the bank until they arrived at the creek. The soldier had been right. It *was* impassable. As Daniel stood on the edge of the deep water he heard an asthmatic wheeze from a clump of reeds not twelve feet from where he and Carlos St Anna stood. There was also the sound of great teeth tearing at something and Daniel realised a crocodile was feeding in the darkness.

Querulously, he called, 'Wyatt? Adam?' There was no reply. Sliding back the safety catch on his rifle, Daniel sent a bullet crashing into the reeds.

There was a startled grunt from the ugly amphibian as it splashed into the water and glided away in the darkness. Fearful of what he might find, Daniel edged his way through the reeds, feeling the way with his feet. He had not gone far when the toe of his boot touched something that gave slightly. Reluctantly, Daniel reached down and touched the still form. It was the part-eaten carcass of a buck that had been caught up in the flood waters.

Daniel and Lieutenant St Anna traced the extent of the creek for more than half-a-mile before accepting that it would be impossible to cross on a rising tide. Returning to the mouth of the creek, they met soldiers coming to help in the search for the missing boys.

As the party trudged back towards the launch in a dispirited silence, the words of the late Mondoro of the Great House of Chiefs sprang to Daniel's mind, to add to his concern. He had said it would be left to Nathan to continue the family line. Was this the way Wyatt was to die?

There was no sleep for anyone during what remained of the night. The boat had to be baled-out and an effort made to assess the damage to the vessel. Daniel and Elvira worked together in silence, neither daring to put into words the fears that dominated their thoughts.

As dawn began to lighten the sky above the still-distant ocean, Daniel and the soldiers set off upriver once again. Few of them entertained any hope that the boys were still alive. Had they escaped from drowning, they would have had to contend with the night-hunting creatures inhabiting the dense thickets of the swamp. But no one questioned Daniel's determination to learn the fate of his two sons. They would search for as long as was necessary.

The creek they had encountered during the night was still deep, but wandering along its bank they reached a spot where the far bank jutted to within a stone's throw of their own. Here, Daniel and Lieutenant St Anna decided to swim across, leaving the remaining soldiers behind.

The undergrowth on the far side of the creek was very dense and it took the two men three hours to cover an estimated mile along the river bank. The flash-flood had claimed many animal victims along here. One dead buck was lodged twelve feet high, in the fork of a tree and they saw the bloated carcass of a hippo, swirling grotesquely downriver, four stubby legs pointing to the sky.

Another half-mile and Lieutenant declared that it would be useless to go on.

'To search further would be foolish,' he said sadly. 'I know how you must be feeling, Senhor, but you have a responsibility to the other members of your family. Soon the tide will turn again. What if there is another of these bores? We must be there to help them.'

In his heart, Daniel knew that St Anna was right. Nevertheless a stubbornness born of despair would not let him return to the launch without one last effort. Looking along the river, he pointed to a sharp bend, some three hundred yards distant. 'We'll go as far as the bend. Then we'll turn back.'

Wearily, St Anna nodded his head and set off behind Daniel, both men pausing every few yards to raise their hoarse voices in futile shouting.

They had covered almost three-quarters of the agreed distance when suddenly Daniel stopped and held up a hand to halt St Anna.

'Listen!'

The thick, damp undergrowth effectively muffled most sounds and the two men listened for a full minute without hearing anything. Daniel cupped his hands to his mouth and bellowed with all the power in him.

'ADAM! WYATT!'

Both men waited and the silence was as heavy as before – then they heard a faint cry.

'There! Did you hear it?'

'It might have been no more than an ape,' St Anna said doubtfully. 'Do not build your hopes too high—'

'An ape, be damned!' Daniel shouted. 'That was a child. I'm certain of it. WYATT . . . ? ADAM . . . ? Where are you?'

The reply was no more audible than before, but this time both men agreed that it came from well inland, and some way ahead.

Ignoring the creepers and thorns that tugged at him, Daniel fought his way through the undergrowth until he fell. Climbing to his feet, he called again.

'WYATT . . . ? ADAM . . . ?'

As the sound of his voice died away, Daniel's fingers dug into the palms of his hands and his lips moved silently in unfamiliar prayer.

'Pa . . . . We're here. We're here . . . .'

It was the voice of five-year-old Adam. As tears of uncontrollable relief sprang to Daniel's eyes, Lieutenant St Anna tugged at his sleeve. 'It came from this direction.'

Fifty yards further on, the two men came to a clearing. There, on the far side, perched in the fork of a tall tree were the two missing boys.

'Pa!' Adam wriggled delightedly in his brother's arms, but Wyatt neither released him, nor uttered a sound of greeting. Daniel's fears rose once again. Climbing the tree, he quickly learned the reason for Wyatt's peculiar behaviour.

Both boys were cut and bruised as a result of their experience in the river, but Wyatt had additional problems. Always susceptible to insect bites, he had spent the long dark night prey to the countless mosquitoes. Frightened of releasing the grip he had on his restlessly sleeping brother, he could do nothing about the blood-sucking insects. He was barely aware of the dawn's arrival, so swollen and tightly closed were his eyelids, and the face about them.

As if this were not enough Wyatt had swallowed so much salt water during the terrifying minutes he had been caught in the clutches of the bore, that it had affected his larynx. His voice no more than a painful whisper, he had heard Daniel calling long before his young brother. Unable to call out himself, he could not make his brother understand what he was trying to tell him.

When Daniel reached the two boys he had to prise Adam free of his brother's life-saving grip. Adam clung to his father desperately for a few minutes before being lowered to Carlos St Anna.

Bringing Wyatt down proved much more difficult. He had crouched in the tree, out of the reach of most wild animals for twelve hours. Blinded, he dared not move or shift the grip he had on his brother. Now he suffered from agonising cramp in almost every muscle.

When Daniel eventually brought him to the ground, the eleven-year-old boy clung to him as though he were still a baby and Daniel saw tears squeezing their way between the slits where his eyes were hidden. Wyatt was trying to speak and when Daniel brought his head close to his son's lips he heard his hoarse, almost inaudible whisper.

'I . . . was . . . scared, Pa. I was . . . scared.'

'Scared? No, son, not you. You're as brave a man as any I know.'

Choking back his own emotion, Daniel settled his eldest son more comfortably in his arms and set off to return the way they had come. He remembered the remainder of the Mondoro's prophecy: '. . . your first-born will prove himself truly a man.'

Daniel offered up a silent prayer to the Mondoro's Spirit God, Chiminuka. He asked him to accept Wyatt's brush with death as being sufficient to satisfy the prophecy and wipe the slate clean. . . . .

CHAPTER TWELVE

By the time the battered steam launch wheezed into the harbour at Quelimane, Wyatt had succumbed to a severe bout of malaria. Consequently, the reunion of the Acting Governor of Mozambique with his daughter and grandchildren became a desperate bid to organise doctors and other medical staff.

Within a few days, Daniel, Adam, and three of the surviving soldiers were also struck down with the same illness. To the Portuguese, it confirmed their widely held belief that the Zambezi estuary was so unhealthy as to be uninhabitable.

Daniel and Adam recovered quickly, aided by generous doses of quinine, but Wyatt hovered between life and death for three long weeks. Then, one morning, he opened his eyes and smiled at his mother. The fever was gone. For the first time in all those weeks, Elvira, gaunt with worry, felt able to leave his bedside.

From that day, Wyatt grew steadily stronger, but not until late October, when the family had been in Quelimane for two months, was he strong enough to leave the house. By now Daniel was anxious to return to Matabeleland, hoping to arrive there before the rains began in earnest.

Now it was Elvira's turn to spring a surprise. She and Daniel were talking in their bedroom, in the Governor's official residence. Busying herself re-arranging flowers in a great, windowsill bowl, she said, 'I think it might be better if we remained here until the rainy season was over.'

'Stay in Quelimane? There's work to be done at Insimo. Wyatt is well enough to face up to a slow journey home now.'

'Perhaps . . . but I think I am not.'

Daniel was puzzled and Elvira smiled at his confusion. 'It would be sad after presenting you with four sons if I should lose what I am quite convinced will be a daughter.'

Daniel's incredulity quickly changed to undisguised joy. 'You're sure . . . . ?'

Elvira nodded happily. 'I was certain before we had the

accident on the river. I said nothing then because I was afraid I might lose it . . . and you had enough to worry about with Wyatt.'

'Worry . . . ?' Daniel took Elvira in his arms and hugged her happily. 'I think it's wonderful news!' Smiling down at her, he asked, 'When will the baby arrive?'

'Early in March – and it *will* be a girl, I know.'

'Then we'll wait for her here in Quelimane. You'll have the best medical attention that's available. Now, let's go off and tell the good news to your father, and the boys.'

It was very hot in Quelimane during the rainy season. Hot and uncomfortably humid. The whole Retallick family spent a few weeks in the hills to the north of the city, but returned in time for the Christmas festivities.

For the four boys in particular, Christmas in Quelimane was a wonderful experience. It had always been a special time, a day for exchanging presents . . . a family occasion. But here, in Quelimane, in the heart of the Catholic Portuguese Colony, it became far more. They enjoyed the sight of streets of decorated houses, and were overawed by the pomp and beauty of the Christmas morning service in Quelimane's great church.

All of Quelimane's society was at the service. As he left, afterwards, Daniel found himself walking beside General St Anna. Ahead of them were Elvira, the boys – and Carlos St Anna, walking beside Therese.

'They make an attractive couple . . . but I remember seeing a face like that many years ago, when I too was a young Lieutenant. Am I mistaken, or is there Pombeiro in that girl?'

'There is, Francisco. Her mother is Victoria and the man she believed to be her father was Philippe. He died some years ago, a pardoned man.'

'I remember,' said General St Anna, non-committally. 'You say she *believed* him to be her father. Who is her *real* father?'

'I think you know the answer to that: Mariano.'

General Francisco St Anna allowed his breath to escape in a heavy sigh, 'The events of Vumba's kraal occurred almost twenty years ago. Has Victoria forgotten?'

Daniel shook his head. 'No, she has never forgiven you, or your countrymen.'

'Then there can be no question of marriage between Therese and Carlos?'

'Marriage? Are you serious?' Daniel looked at the well-dressed men and women leaving the church about them. 'Therese is a very nice girl, Francisco . . . but she is a Mambari – of mixed blood.' The use of the Matabele word had been automatic. 'Carlos is your son. Son of the General commanding the Portuguese army in Mozambique. Therese would never be accepted by your people.'

'You are mistaken, Daniel. This is Mozambique, not Mother Portugal. Here, I am a great soldier, with estates to match any in the land. In Portugal I am nobody. When I visit there you will find my name on no society guest list. Indeed, I hardly merit a salute from a non-commissioned officer. This is my home and here today I can see at least four women who are coloured – yet accepted by all. They, like all the other women, are dressed for the day. Tomorrow they will be in working clothes, kerchiefs about their hair, helping the workers in the fields. Judged not by colour, or breeding, but by the help they give to their husbands, and the manner in which they run their houses. *This* is the world to which Carlos belongs. It is to such a community he will bring a wife.'

Ahead of them, Therese laughed at something Carlos said to her and leaned towards him. Their hands met and held for a few moments, then fell away.

'I'll speak to Victoria,' said Daniel. 'But I promise nothing. She's a very determined woman.'

'If she were not there would be no daughter of Mariano to cast her spell upon my son. But you are going to be here for many months. I think it will be better if I send Carlos off on another expedition to the interior. The seasonal rains of Manicaland should be sufficient to dampen the ardour of the most passionate young man.'

After the excitement of the Christmas celebrations, life in Quelimane went on as indolently as before. The humid heat provided all the excuse the Portuguese needed to carry out only the minimum of work.

Then, one airless day in mid-January, Senhor Farrao sent a messenger to bring Daniel to his office.

When Daniel arrived, he found the Acting Governor pacing

the room, ignoring the perspiration that stood out on his red face. With no preamble, he strode to his desk, picked up a newspaper and thrust it at Daniel. 'Read this. It's that damned man Rhodes again. He and your Matabele King.'

The newspaper was an English language weekly from the Cape Colony. The headlines spread from edge to edge of the front page. 'RHODES OBTAINS EXCLUSIVE CONCESSION FROM MATABELE KING'. Beneath, in slightly smaller print, it added, 'Lobengula signs at last. Rhodes gets the lot.'

Daniel read on. The more he read the greater became his dismay. If the report were true it meant that Lobengula had given Cecil Rhodes a truly remarkable concession that gave him everything but the throne of Matabeleland.

Daniel lowered the newspaper, thoroughly bewildered. What could have happened to persuade Lobengula to grant such a concession — and to Rhodes, of all people? With his particular brand of ruthlessness, Rhodes would trample the Matabele into the ground.

'You think that is bad? The newspaper does not tell half the story. By the same boat I received a letter from the Portuguese Ambassador in Cape Town. He tells me Rhodes intends using the concession to commence mining in Mashonaland. I am protesting most vehemently, on behalf of my Government. Mashonaland is Portuguese territory. If Rhodes brings his miners there it will be an act of aggression against Portugal.'

Daniel had every sympathy with Senhor Farrao and could understand his anger, but it did not explain why the Acting Governor had sent a messenger for him.

'Because King Lobengula is your friend, you understand him. Why is he doing this?'

Daniel shook his head sadly. 'Lobengula is no longer the man I once knew. Certainly not the Jandu you met at Sofala. I don't think he is the man his people chose to lead them. He takes his own road now, helped along by brandy and champagne.'

But no matter how much Lobengula had changed, it seemed he still valued Daniel's friendship and advice. Before the month was out, a weary Induna, with an escort of only a dozen

Matabele warriors reached Quelimane, looking for Daniel.

The Portuguese soldiers, hastily called from the garrison barracks immediately surrounded the unfamiliar warriors and ordered them to surrender their weapons. The Matabeles knew nothing of what was being said and refused to give up their guns. An ugly situation was saved by Wyatt Retallick. He rode upon the scene and recognised the men as Matabeles.

His identification caused a great stir in Quelimane, where the Matabele were known only by rumour and exaggerated reputation.

Escorted by a rapidly increasing number of Portuguese soldiers, the warriors were brought to the Governor's office to await Daniel's arrival.

Daniel and Elvira were walking along the nearby promenade when the Acting Governor's messenger found them and they both hurried to Senhor Farrao's office.

Daniel recognised the Induna as a member of the Council of Indunas and treated him with a respect and warmth that did much to restore the Induna's bruised dignity. He had travelled far through a foreign land to reach this strange kraal where the houses were higher than the tallest Matabele tree. On the ocean beyond the town great creatures swam through the water belching smoke. It was a new and frightening world here. Not until he began talking to Daniel could the Induna overcome his awe and discharge the trust placed in him by his King.

'I have been sent by Lobengula to bring you back to him. The King has great need of you, trader. He has put his mark only on those papers given to him by white men he thought he could trust. Yet now it is said he has given away our country. This man Rhodes claims he may dig holes for gold wherever he wishes – even in the garden of the King. Lobengula has asked other white men to tell him the truth of this, but it seems the writing on the paper tells different things to all men. No two of them say the same thing. He needs you to tell him the truth of this, trader.'

'You've come a long way, Induna – yet you needed to journey only as far as Insimo. There you would have found a man who would not lie to you. Jaconus Van Eyck is an honest man.'

'He is all the things you say. Lobengula called for him when the Boers came to Bulawayo, demanding that their wagons be allowed to cross the country of the Mashona. They wished to seek new lands on the far side of the Zambezi River. Your friend sent them home again. Before they left they laughed in the face of Lobengula and said they would be back. Lobengula was so upset at this he has sent two Indunas to England, to speak to your Queen about the men who trouble him.'

Daniel found it difficult to hide his astonishment. 'Two Indunas have gone to England, to see Queen Victoria?'

'Yes, the missionary Loveday has gone with them – and the King sent Van Eyck to act as his personal interpreter. He thought it important that the Indunas be accompanied by at least one honest man.'

'Van Eyck's gone . . . ? Who's looking after Insimo?'

'The Mambari woman, Victoria.' The Induna came as close to a smile as any very tired man could. 'Lobengula sent an impi to guard your valley and help her with the work – she chased them away, firing a gun over their heads. She said they would eat more than they would earn for you.'

Daniel smiled briefly too. He had seen Victoria roused – and a Matabele Induna, scornful of a woman's ability to do a man's work was guaranteed to anger her.

'Please come, trader. You are Lobengula's friend. He needs you. He told me to tell you he is a blind bull surrounded by a pack of wild dogs. Now they are fighting among themselves, but the King fears that one day they will all rush in together and tear him and our country to pieces.'

'From what I have heard, Lobengula has already handed the country to them by giving Rhodes a concession.'

'Others say this too, but the missionary, Loveday, told the King that Rhodes is an important man. He said that if Rhodes is allowed to dig for gold he will drive all other white men away. The Commissioner from Bechuanaland also came to see Lobengula. He said it would please your Queen if Rhodes was granted a concession to dig for gold.'

Daniel sucked in his breath angrily. 'If men like Sir Sidney Shippard are mixed up in this, it's little wonder that Lobengula doesn't know which way to turn.'

'It is so, trader . . . and this man Rhodes has done nothing to chase away other white men. There are now more of them at Bulawayo than ever before. They bay like jackals about the fire.'

The Induna studied Daniel's face and read the indecision there. 'The King needs you, trader,' he repeated. 'My people need you.'

'You must go,' Elvira said quietly. 'Lobengula has done so much for us. The valley – everything we love – he has given to us.'

'But what can *I* do to help now?' They talked in English so that the Induna would not understand what was being said. 'It's too late to help him. I've told him time and time again to sign nothing. The moment I leave the country he scrawls a cross on the first piece of paper that's held out to him. As for sending Jaconus to England . . . !'

Daniel looked pointedly at the swelling of Elvira's body. 'Besides, there's the baby. I can't leave you now.'

'You will not leave me. I will come with you.'

Daniel opened his mouth to protest again, but Elvira reached a hand quickly to his lips. 'Please, let us not argue, Daniel. If we leave right away we will be home long before the baby is due. We *must* go. In your heart you know this. Lobengula is making a desperate plea to you for help. He believes, as do I, that you are the only one who can do anything for him.'

Daniel was not convinced that he would prove to be the saviour everyone was expecting, but Elvira was right. He could not refuse Lobengula's call. Whether or not Elvira accompanied him could be decided elsewhere.

To the Induna, he said, 'Come, I will arrange for you and your men to be given a place where you might rest. We will return to Bulawayo together.'

CHAPTER THIRTEEN

Senhor Farrao had grave misgivings about the family returning to Matabeleland at such a time and he did his best to dissuade them. That night, at dinner, he told them that all the news filtering from Matabeleland was bad.

'There is a very strong likelihood that Lobengula is no longer in control of the country,' he declared. 'I have it on good authority that the young warriors are on the verge of revolt.'

'The best authority on what is happening in Matabeleland is the Induna who arrived here today. Events may be moving too fast for Lobengula's liking, but there's nothing to suggest his leadership is threatened. The Mahaja are always complaining. They are young warriors – and young warriors want war. I've heard it all before. So has Lobengula. He and his senior Indunas listen to the wild talk of the young warriors and they smile. There is fire in the bellies of young Matabele men. They want to marry and raise families – but they can't do this until Lobengula grants them the right to wear a warrior's head-ring. Traditionally, this isn't done until they've proved themselves in battle . . . so they're anxious to fight someone. It's the way things have always been.'

'I hope you are right,' replied Senhor Farrao, gloomily. 'You will pay a high price if you are not.' The Acting Governor did his best to shake off his apprehension. 'But as you are determined to leave, I will do what I can to smooth your long journey. I have arranged for my own boat to take you upriver to Sena. I have also sent a runner to Captain General Gouveia, asking him to bring horses there. They will be faster than oxen for your wagons.'

Observing the look that passed between Daniel and Elvira, he added, 'I am aware of your feelings towards Senhor Gouveia. Unfortunately, he is the only man in the whole of the interior who owns horses.'

Senhor Farrao raised his own glass to them, 'What more can I say, except . . . go with God.'

* * *

The river voyage to Sena was pleasantly uneventful. The experience of Senhor Farrao's boatmen, a bright moonlit night and a flood tide all combined to take them through the worst of the Zambezi swamplands during the night hours, when the heat was not so unbearable.

At Sena they found that Gouveia had not yet arrived with the horses. They also learned they had missed Lieutenant St Anna by only two days. He had left Sena for his father's estates, a hundred miles upriver. Here he intended gathering militiamen to strengthen his small force of regular soldiers before moving on Manicaland to remind the Chiefs of their allegiance to Portugal.

The realisation that she had missed Carlos St Anna by so short a time proved too much for Therese. The thought of perhaps never seeing the young soldier again made her realise how much he had come to mean to her. She had wanted to remain at Quelimane, believing he would soon return there, but Daniel insisted that she return to Insimo with him. He and Elvira had every sympathy with her, but they also had a responsibility to Victoria – and Daniel could not tell Therese of the objections he knew her mother would raise to a marriage with Francisco St Anna's son.

Therese left during the night on Senhor Farrao's sole remaining riding horse, leaving Daniel to fume at Gouveia's delay in reaching Sena.

It was another week before the Captain General of Gorongoza arrived, and the reason for the delay became immediately apparent. He and his men had been slaving. More than a thousand wretched women and children, yoked and tied, were herded to the far end of the stockade where they were closely guarded by men of Gouveia's 'army'.

Daniel's anger at the delay and its cause was shrugged off by the Captain General. This was Portuguese territory. What happened here mattered to no one but the Portuguese themselves.

It was no time to get into argument with one of Mozambique's most powerful men. Choosing a number of good riding horses, and taking along a guide, Daniel set off for the St Anna estates at Tete.

He arrived just too late to witness the wedding of Therese to

Carlos St Anna. Although arranged in a hurry, the marriage was no hole-in-the-corner affair. It took place in the small town's church, attended by friends and employees of the St Anna family.

The priest who had conducted the marriage made no apologies for his part in arranging the ceremony.

'A nice young girl who rides alone across a hundred miles of unknown country, to be with the man she loves deserves the blessing of the Church. Am I to say I will not marry them and allow them to go off and live together in mortal sin? No, Senhor Retallick. I say Mozambique has need of such spirited women. I told Carlos he had better marry her quickly, before some other young man came along and snatched her up.'

Therese stood beside her new husband and looked at Daniel with a mixture of defiance and happiness, coupled with a desperate wish for him to express approval of her marriage.

'Your mother is going to be very angry with me, Therese.'

'If she's ever had to make up her mind between doing something everyone else said was wrong – and losing her man, she will understand.'

Daniel thought of Victoria's love for Mariano . . . and later for his brother, Philippe. But Therese knew very little of her mother's early life. Victoria had worked very hard to ensure it remained a secret. Even so, Daniel knew she was not going to approve of this marriage.

To Therese, he said, 'I know Carlos has got himself a fine wife. His father will agree: We've already discussed it—'

Before he could say more, Therese flung herself at him. 'Thank you, Daniel. I *knew* you'd understand – you and Elvira. Please tell Ma . . . tell her I love her too. I *want* her to wish me well. It's just—'

'I know, Therese. She *will* understand, I promise you . . . but she'll probably never admit it to anyone. Go away now and write a letter to her. I'll take it with me.'

Pushing her away gently, he clasped Carlos St Anna's hand. 'Treat her well, Carlos. As soon as you're able, pay a visit to Insimo. You'll be made very welcome there . . . by everyone.'

Elvira shared Daniel's hopes for the young couple, but most of her thoughts now were for the life that was making its presence felt inside her. The delay at Sena had set back the plans she and Daniel had made, and brought the date the baby was due uncomfortably close.

Declining an invitation to spend a few days at Captain General Gouveia's mountain home, Daniel told the Goanese he was taking an easier route well to the south. It would take him through the long valley where the Rozwi Queen, uTshwebe, had her home.

'Why do you choose that particular route?' One look at Gouveia's face told Daniel that the question had not been asked from idle curiosity.

'uTshwebe is a friend. I arranged the marriage of her daughter to Lobengula, King of the Matabele.'

'Indeed? uTshwebe made a great many unwise alliances. She will make no more.'

'uTshwebe's dead?'

'Yes. I hope your friend Lobengula will not feel too distressed at the loss of one of his mothers-in-law. If he is, tell him Captain General Gouveia of Gorongoza may soon give him the opportunity of lodging a personal complaint. I am thinking of taking my army of four thousand men to receive an assurance from *him* that he acknowledges allegiance to Mother Portugal.'

Daniel laughed aloud at Gouveia's bravado. 'You'll need more than four thousand men. Lobengula has ten times that number – and none of them are slaves who will run at the sound of the first shot.'

Gouveia blinked when Daniel mentioned the strength of Lobengula's army, but he tried not to let Daniel see how much the information had impressed him. 'We shall see who will run.'

As the Captain General of Gorongoza rode away, Daniel was left with a feeling that he had just averted a foolhardy and bloody attack on Lobengula and the Matabele.

Travelling through the Manica Mountains, it became apparent that Gouveia had punished uTshwebe and her people ruthlessly. There were no signs of life in the hills for twenty miles about the deep valley and, when they reached the spot where the kraal had stood there was nothing left but a giant mound of ash covering the valley floor. The story of uTshwebe and the mystery of the scar she carried over her heart had passed into legend.

The valley had become a place of ghosts and shadowy memories and Daniel drove the wagons on, heading for less haunted country.

They were making good time now, although, after leaving the Manica Mountains, they crossed a narrow belt of tsetse fly country and lost four horses.

They were no more than sixty miles from Insimo when a large party of Mashonas began following them, running from the shelter of one rock to another along the ridges of the hills about them and hurling insults at the party.

Daniel fired a couple of shots in return, but they were warning shots only, aimed at persuading the Mashonas to keep their distance.

Not far ahead was a rolling plateau. Once there, the Mashonas would drop behind and the incident would be over. The Mashonas realised this too and a few of them hurried to get ahead of the wagons. Making their way through the tumbled granite boulders they reached a point as close as they dared to the wagons and their small Matabele escort.

Waiting until the leading wagon passed below, one of the Mashonas sprang to his feet and hurled a spear, running away without waiting to see where it fell.

The success of his throw exceeded all he could have hoped for. The spear smacked against the flank of one of the four horses harnessed to Elvira's wagon. Unhurt, but startled, the horse reared and shied. The sudden commotion frightened the other horses – and they bolted.

Elvira had the reins herself. She heaved back on them, trying to bring the horses under control, but there was no stopping them now. As they pounded along the valley, the wagon swayed and bounced alarmingly behind them. It had not been built to travel at such a speed. The four boys were in the wagon too and as they tumbled about, Wyatt fought his way forward until he too had a grip on the reins, adding his strength to that of his mother.

The horses had just begun to respond to the combined pull on the reins, when one of the front wheels of the wagon struck a large rock and splintered in a dozen pieces. The wagon tilted alarmingly. Then, accompanied by the screams of Elvira and the two youngest boys, it crashed on its side, Elvira falling inside and Wyatt being thrown clear. The weight of the wagon pulled the two rear horses to the ground and the leading horses slithered to a halt, to stand sweat-flecked, quivering with fright.

Daniel reached the wagon at the same time as the shaken but unhurt Wyatt. They both crawled inside the shattered wagon as native drivers from the other wagons ran to their aid and extricated the horses from a tangle of harness.

'Don't try to move,' said Daniel, as Elvira began throwing off the various items of clothing, cooking utensils and stores surrounding her.

'I'm all right,' insisted Elvira, to Daniel's great relief. 'Find the children . . . .'

Adam and Benjamin were howling noisily, but both boys crawled unaided from the rear of the wagon. Only Nathan remained in the wagon, amidst a pile of smashed boxes. He was clutching his arm, his face contorted in pain. Holding the limb up for inspection he said, 'I think it's broken, Pa—' with that, the nine-year-old boy fainted.

Wyatt and Daniel pulled Nathan from the wagon and an inspection of the arm revealed an irregularity, halfway between wrist and elbow. The bone had not broken through the skin and by the time Nathan regained consciousness, it had been splinted and tightly bandaged.

Daniel was confident the arm would heal satisfactorily, but he was far more worried about Elvira. She protested vehemently that she was well, but the attack and the overturned wagon had been a very frightening experience for her and, when she thought Daniel was not looking, he saw a grimace of pain cross her face.

The goods from the overturned wagon were quickly distributed among the remaining wagons and Daniel pushed on faster than before.

They reached the Insimo valley the following day, their arrival greeted by shrill howls of welcome from the Mashona women working in the fields, and cries of delighted greeting from the Matabele herd-boys.

Daniel drove hard for the house and not until she was

actually sitting in her own kitchen did Elvira finally admit that she felt unwell. When Daniel helped her to her bedroom, she sank on the bed with a groan of pain.

Panting heavily, she said, 'I think you had better find Victoria, quickly, my husband. I do not think our baby will wait any longer.'

Daniel shouted for Wyatt to ride off and find Victoria, but news of their return had already reached her. She rode up to the house before Wyatt had caught a horse.

Victoria took the news that Elvira was in labour with a typically efficient calm. She sent servants scurrying about the house, fetching and carrying. After a brief visit to Elvira she went to the kitchen to organise the things she was going to need – but all the time her eyes were searching for Therese.

When she did not see her, she put the question Daniel was dreading.

'I'm sorry, Victoria . . . it's a long story – but she's well, very well,' he added hastily to allay Victoria's sudden fear. 'She's married . . . eloped. But she's very happy. I went to see her—'

There was a loud crash as the large porcelain bowl Victoria was carrying slipped to the ground and smashed on the stone floor of the kitchen.

'Therese is . . . WHAT?'

'Married.' A cry came from the bedroom and Daniel took Victoria's arm. 'I promise you she is well . . . . Can we talk about it later. Please, Victoria, Elvira needs you.'

The cry from the bedroom was repeated. With a great effort, Victoria put the thoughts of her daughter to the back of her mind and hurried to Elvira.

The birth of Elvira's daughter was swift – and tragic. The child was born dead, killed by the accident that had hastened her arrival into the world.

Elvira grieved deeply. She had desperately wanted to give Daniel a daughter. Daniel was unhappy too. He blamed himself for not insisting that Elvira remain in Quelimane.

'I should have *made* you stay,' he repeated for the umpteenth time. 'Your father will say so too.'

'My father will say nothing. A woman's place is with her husband. He knows that as well as any man.'

Daniel was seated on the edge of Elvira's bed and she reached for his hand, fighting back her tears. 'Our baby was conceived in love, and she died loved. God will welcome her. Of that I am certain—'

Elvira's voice broke and Daniel held her to him until she slipped into a deep, exhausted sleep.

The baby was buried in the tiny cemetery, beside Philippe and Jannie Van Eyck. It was here too, beside the grave of her late husband, that Victoria came to read the letter that Therese had written to her. In the quiet of this place she finally came to terms with the knowledge that Therese was married to the son of Francisco St Anna, the man who had killed her true father. It was not easy, but once Victoria had made her decision a calmness came to her that would remain for the rest of her years. The ghost of Mariano had finally been laid. Therese had never known Mariano. She had thought of Philippe as her father, and had loved him. In return, Philippe had treated Therese as though she was his own daughter – and had loved her too.

Victoria would do nothing to destroy her daughter's happiness. Therese's father was buried *here*, at Insimo. Mariano had never been. Therese would receive her mother's blessing for a long and happy marriage.

CHAPTER FOURTEEN

The decision to send two senior Indunas to England had been made by Lobengula – but the seed had been sown by the Reverend Farewell Loveday!

For very many years Loveday had toiled in Matabeleland with little reward, either spiritual or monetary. He accepted that the conversion of the Matabele to Christianity would not be possible without a great deal of support, both inside the country and without. For this reason he approved of Rhodes' plans for settling the country. Loveday believed the European would bring with him Christian standards that the Matabele would ultimately accept.

Conversion of the Matabele was Farewell Loveday's first, idealistic aim. He had other ambitions too. Over the years he had seen men for whom he had obtained concessions grow rich on the proceeds of ivory sales. More recently he had carefully set the stage for the greatest coup of all, on behalf of the man who emulated the mythical Midas, turning all he touched to gold.

The exclusive mining concession granted to Rhodes was certain to make a number of new millionaires among the directors of the company being formed to exploit Lobengula's lands. Farewell Loveday had confidently expected to receive a substantial reward for his part in the great venture. Instead, he had been virtually ignored during the final stages of the lengthy negotiations, his place taken by three men sent to Matabeleland by Rhodes himself. When Loveday hinted he would like to be included among the shareholders of the new company, he was curtly informed that the shares were already fully subscribed.

It was clear that Cecil Rhodes' plans for Matabeleland and Mashonaland left no room for gratitude. Farewell Loveday decided to take steps to force the hand of the great man.

A few well-chosen remarks to Lobengula were sufficient to

set his plan in motion. Lobengula believed he had thought of sending his Indunas to England. But when they set off with Jaconus Van Eyck as official interpreter, Farewell Loveday was with them.

The news that the party was on its way to England to see Queen Victoria seriously alarmed Rhodes. He had gained a concession from Lobengula, but this was only the first move in his ambitious plans. He was aiming for a charter from the Queen for his company. With such a charter, backed by the might of Great Britain, a man could mould his own Empire. He would be a virtual dictator of all the lands at his disposal.

But the granting of such a charter was by no means a foregone conclusion. Already the Cape newspapers were eagerly printing stories that Lobengula was having second thoughts about his generous concession. Indeed, one or two smaller papers had published notices, purporting to be signed by Lobengula, repudiating the concession. The same newspapers also carried reports by knowledgeable hunters, expressing doubts about the reported extent of Lobengula's territory.

Such arguments and criticism mattered little to Rhodes. He was used to such outbursts of feeling against him – but he *was* concerned about Lobengula's motives for sending the deputation to London. He believed the Indunas must be carrying messages for Queen Victoria. If the two tribal elders reached England and fell into the clutches of the anti-Imperialist press, it might well spell the end of his carefully laid plans for Southern Africa. The Indunas had to be stopped.

Stopping the Reverend Farewell Loveday did not prove to be as simple as Rhodes would have wished. The Matabele missionary had served the great man for many years and was well aware of the extent of his considerable influence.

While the whole of the Bechuanaland Border Police were out scouring roads and paths, and even the wide wastes of the Kalahari Desert for the travellers, Jaconus Van Eyck was guiding them southwards, through Transvaal.

When the Bechuanaland authorities failed to intercept the Indunas, Rhodes realised they must have taken the Transvaal route. He mobilised the British Consul in Pretoria, and his own Company officials in that country, in a bid to locate them.

Rumour and counter-rumour came to him, but still the ill-assorted party eluded capture.

Then, one day, the London-bound group reached Kimberley.

Busy administrator though he was, Rhodes never ordered another to carry out a difficult task when it could be performed by himself. He sent for the Reverend Farewell Loveday.

The meeting took place in a ramshackle hut owned by Rhodes and located close to the Kimberley Club. It was furnished in a spartan manner, ill-suited to a millionaire, yet it was here that Rhodes carried out much of his work when he did not wish to be disturbed by the various activities and acquaintances to be found in the Kimberley Club. Rhodes also slept here on occasions on an ancient iron-frame bed in a corner of the room.

When Farewell Loveday entered the hut he expected to be greeted with an outburst of angry recrimination from the man whose interests he had served in Matabeleland for so long. Instead, Rhodes was the perfect host. In the rather bizarre setting, Rhodes behaved as though he were entertaining in a grand mansion. After pouring Loveday a drink, he enquired after his health, that of his family, the situation in Matabeleland – and then Loveday's journey, and the two Indunas he was escorting to London.

Farewell Loveday replied equally politely and it was Rhodes who was forced to breach the thin veil of affability hiding the real purpose of the meeting.

'You know, of course, that my concession for all the mineral rights in Lobengula's lands is an accomplished fact now? All the conditions have been met and the documents lodged with the British Government.'

Farewell Loveday took a steady sip of his drink. 'I too have a concession granting me mineral rights to a large section of Matabeleland. All relevant conditions of this have also been met – and it pre-dates your concession by some two years.'

'I don't believe you,' Rhodes said angrily.

Farewell Loveday shrugged. 'I'm quite confident that I can prove my claim to any interested party, and it so happens that both the Indunas travelling with me were witnesses to the concession.'

'Is this the only reason you are going to London? To prevent me from obtaining a charter? You are acting from spite, no doubt!'

'No, I am carrying a letter from Lobengula to Queen Victoria.'

'What does it say?'

'I think that is a private matter between King Lobengula and Queen Victoria.'

Rhodes looked at Farewell Loveday with renewed suspicion. 'I can prevent you from travelling. I have only to telegraph the Governor at the Cape and your natives will be stopped and sent back to Matabeleland, where they belong.'

'You can do that, Mr Rhodes, but there would be an awful fuss about it.' The Reverend Farewell Loveday was using his mildest missionary manner. 'I've already telegraphed the Governor to say we're coming. No doubt a great many members of the Church and the Native Societies will be at the station to meet us.'

Farewell Loveday stood up. 'Thank you for the drink. You know where to find me if you wish to speak to me again.'

Farewell Loveday left the untidy shanty and walked through the streets of Kimberley filled with an unusual exhilaration. He had taken on Cecil Rhodes, the most powerful man in Africa, and had successfully bluffed him, of that he was certain. Rhodes wanted nothing to cause even the slightest upset in his plans for a chartered company. He would send for Farewell Loveday again. If not here, then certainly in the Cape Colony. At that meeting, Rhodes would agree to whatever terms Farewell Loveday dictated. Rhodes would never forgive him, of course . . . but at least they would *both* be rich enemies.

Three days later the small party from the vast and sparsely populated land to the north of the Limpopo River stepped from the train to the bustle of southern Africa's largest and busiest city. In Kimberley, Farewell Loveday had groomed the Indunas for their foray into European social life by persuading them to adopt the white man's clothes, but neither Farewell Loveday nor Jaconus Van Eyck had been able to prepare them for the revelation of European technology.

It began with the railway train. At first, the Indunas had viewed it with terror. Fear had turned to wonder when the train picked up speed and they had not been devoured by the fire-devils that lived deep in the heart of the engine.

When they reached Cape Town and viewed the ships, carriages and great houses, the Indunas realised they had much to learn about the ways of the white man.

Here in Cape Town, the Reverend Loveday suffered a minor setback to his plans. He had sent details of his proposed journey to the Governor, Sir Hercules Robinson, hoping to gain official backing for the Indunas. He should have known better. Rhodes had carried out his threat and telegraphed Sir Hercules.

The Governor refused to meet Farewell Loveday. He sent a message to say that although he was not able to prevent the small party from continuing their journey to London, the visit stood no chance of succeeding. Without his official backing the delegation would *not* be seen by Queen Victoria. Neither would any letters purporting to come from Lobengula be accepted by Her Majesty.

Farewell Loveday bullied, cajoled and pleaded until he finally arranged a meeting between the Indunas and the Governor. It was doomed from the outset. Sir Hercules Robinson demanded to see the letter from the Matabele King to Queen Victoria and wanted to know what verbal messages the Indunas carried. When neither was forthcoming, he dismissed the whole party from his presence. If they wished to waste time and money on an uncomfortable voyage to England they were at liberty so to do – but he would make quite certain the visit achieved nothing.

Rhodes had effectively demonstrated the power and influence he had in the Cape Colony, but Farewell Loveday was not beaten yet. The following morning he was waiting in the Governor's office when Sir Hercules Robinson arrived to begin the day's work. He had decided to show Lobengula's letter to the Governor.

It made startling and unexpected reading. Making no mention of Rhodes' controversial concession, Lobengula complained to Queen Victoria of Portuguese incursions in his country and spoke of Boers massing on his southern borders. He asked for the Queen's protection and, for the first time ever, set out the boundaries of his territories claimed by the Matabele nation. It took in not only the whole of Mashonaland but Manicaland too!

Suddenly, Farewell Loveday's mission to Britain took on a whole new meaning. With this letter entered in the official British Government records, it would add millions of pounds to the share value of any company which had Lobengula's concession.

Sir Hercules Robinson had the letter carefully copied, and three days later Cecil Rhodes arrived in Cape Town.

Rhodes went straight to the hotel where Farewell Loveday was staying. It was a different Rhodes from the ill-tempered man who had ridden rough-shod over Loveday in Kimberley. Today, Rhodes was friendly, benevolent ... almost apologetic. Of course Loveday *must* go to London. The delegation *would* be made official. Rhodes himself would see to this. As for the concession that Loveday himself held . . . .

When Cecil Rhodes left Farewell Loveday's room some hours later, the two men had agreed to merge their Matabele concessions, to their 'mutual advantage'.

Later that same day, Sir Hercules Robinson wrote to the Colonial Secretary in London, informing him that a mission from Lobengula would shortly be arriving in England. He requested that they be shown every diplomatic courtesy – and that arrangements be made for them to meet Her Majesty, Queen Victoria.

Unknown to any of the men who were celebrating their good fortune, there was another letter. Carried in a pouch strung about the neck of one of the Indunas, it never left his person. This letter was to be given only to the Queen of England. It complained to Her Majesty of those men who wanted so desperately to dig for gold in Lobengula's territories, that they lied and cheated in order to obtain concessions. He asked Her Majesty for her advice and her urgent assistance in keeping such men out of his Kingdom.

Had Rhodes known of the existence of this second letter he might not have been so eager to send the Indunas to London. In the long term, of course, the letter would make little difference to events in Africa. The letter carried by the Induna was a *personal* message from the King of Matabeleland to Queen Victoria.

The *other* letter was the one that would be passed through official channels and receive Government recognition. History would ignore Lobengula's personal plea.

Lobengula had displayed a lack of faith in Farewell Loveday, but his guile had been defeated by the subtle workings of the white man's protocol.

Lobengula's two Indunas were presented to Queen Victoria on 2 March 1889. On that same day, six thousand miles away, Daniel entered Bulawayo and was hurried into the presence of the King. Lobengula struggled to rise from his cow-hide throne and hugged Daniel as he would a long absent brother.

'It has been too long, my friend. Much too long.'

Holding Daniel at arm's length, Lobengula saw the strain of recent events on his friend's face and became momentarily struck with remorse. 'It sorrowed me to hear of the loss of your new-born child. It was fortunate it was only a girl child. However, Suliyana is sending your wife a gift—'

'Suliyana has cause for grief too. Her mother is dead, killed by the Portuguese.'

'Yes, word reached us from her people while you were away. I have sent a letter to the Queen of your country, telling her that the Portuguese are invading my lands and killing my people. I have asked for her help.'

Daniel winced, but Lobengula never noticed and continued, 'I would send impis against them myself, but the Portuguese live far away, and I have troubles close to my home kraal.'

'You certainly have, Inkosi. What's this concession you've signed with Rhodes?'

'I remembered your words and was careful what I said to the men belonging to Rhodes. We talked much before I made my mark. It was a good concession, when we spoke eye to eye. But writing words on paper seems to change them. They come back to the ears with a different meaning.'

'I had hoped you'd learned that lesson before I left. What on earth made you sign yet another concession?'

'The Induna Muvandi assured me that this was good for us. It offered guns – many guns, for the impis. I was told this man

Rhodes would give the Matabele much more than any other man.'

Daniel knew Muvandi, and liked him well. He was one of the few truly pro-European Indunas ... perhaps *too* pro-European.

'Rhodes will also *take* more than any other man in return,' retorted Daniel, grimly. 'Do you have a copy of this concession?'

Lobengula called one of his wives. She hurried away to return in a few minutes with a loosely rolled sheet of thick paper. As Lobengula unrolled the document, Daniel caught a glimpse of Muvandi. He was sitting impassively among a large group of fellow-Indunas, his eyes fixed upon the ground at his feet.

The concession began with a wealth of legal jargon, binding the signatories and their heirs and successors to the terms set out in the document. Daniel's eyebrows rose as he read of the gifts promised to the King. One hundred pounds a month, a thousand Martini-Henry breech-loading rifles, a hundred thousand rounds of ammunition – and a gunboat on the Zambezi River, or five hundred pounds in lieu!

But if the Rhodes faction was being uncharacteristically generous, the rewards the millionaire was gaining in return were truly stupendous. To Rhodes went complete and exclusive charge over all metals and minerals in Lobengula's domain, together with full power to do *all things he deemed necessary to win and procure the same.*

Daniel read the document through twice to ensure he had missed nothing. Lobengula watched his face anxiously.

'Is it true what men say, trader? Have I given away the lands of the Matabele?'

'Pretty well. You've given Rhodes great powers.'

'Does it mean Rhodes can send his men to come inside the King's kraal and dig for gold?'

'It does.'

'Even beneath my own house?'

'If that's where he thinks he'll find gold, yes.'

Lobengula's gaze sought and found the Induna whose advice he had followed in signing the treaty.

'Muvandi, friend to my father. Trusted Induna of my Council. You have betrayed the Matabele people.'

Muvandi rose slowly to his feet, his eyes still on the ground. As though in a trance, he picked his way through the seated ranks of his fellow Indunas until he stood before Lobengula.

'It is as my King says.'

'The light of day has seen enough of you and yours. Go!'

Muvandi raised his head now and met the King's anger with cool pride. 'I go, Inkosi, because it is your order, but I have served our people in the way I thought best. Bayete!'

With this last salute to his King, Muvandi turned away, pausing briefly before Daniel.

'Goodbye, trader. Today I am a dead man.'

These were Muvandi's last words. The Induna walked from the King's kraal, scorning the escort of jeering warriors who jostled him as he made his way to the place of execution. Daniel looked towards Lobengula, but the King had sunk back upon his cow-hide throne and was calling for beer to be brought to him. It would have been a waste of time for Daniel to plead for Muvandi's life. The King needed a scapegoat. Muvandi filled the bill.

Minutes later Muvandi had been clubbed to death by the King's executioners. It was only a beginning. For years the Matabele people had witnessed the ever-increasing encroachment on their lands by the white men. Many blamed Lobengula for not taking up arms against them. But no one dared air his opinion. The Mahajas, the young warriors, had been spoiling for a fight with the white men for years, but Lobengula had held them firmly in check. Now they vented their pent-up frustrations on the family of the man who had been publicly branded as the white men's tool.

All that afternoon and evening the Mahajas rampaged through Bulawayo, seeking Muvandi's many wives and children, slaying them where they were found.

As darkness fell and the effect of excessive beer-drinking took a firm hold on the young warriors, they cast their nets still wider. Anyone even remotely connected with Muvandi was hunted down and killed. Friends, servants, in-laws. All were targets on this bloody night.

When the sun rose again on Bulawayo, its rays fell on three hundred corpses, sprawling grotesquely where they had been slain. It had been the night of the Mahajas. Many of the white men who idled their lives away around Lobengula's fire heeded the warning. They were not welcome in the land of the Matabele.

Some 'asked for the road' that day. It was a request that was granted to them immediately. Others, less confident of the King's goodwill, simply saddled a horse and rode breakneck for the border. Their actions may have been dictated by panic, their fears premature, but the message spelled out by the slaughter was clear. The white man was not welcome in Matabeleland – and the Mahajas, at least, were prepared to kill to keep them out.

CHAPTER FIFTEEN

In London, the two Indunas were taken to Windsor Castle to meet Queen Victoria. So impressed were the Matabele Elders with what they had already seen of London that they were fearful of meeting the ruler of such an incredible country. They cowered on the floor of the room where they waited her arrival, and nothing the palace officials or Jaconus Van Eyck said would persuade them to rise to their feet.

Eventually, the doors were thrown open and Queen Victoria entered the room. The two Indunas, peering childlike through their fingers at the most powerful ruler in the world were amazed. They saw a tiny woman who would not stand as tall as Lobengula's chest. What was more, she was smiling!

The Queen found the two men charmingly amusing, but insisted that they should rise to their feet to speak to her. With Jaconus Van Eyck interpreting, she asked them about their long journey, how they were enjoying Great Britain, then questioned them about their own families – and about Lobengula.

This was the moment for which the men had been waiting. The senior of the two drew himself up to the full height of a Matabele Induna and delivered the King's letter to her personally, in accordance with the instructions he had been given. In order that there should be no mistake, he had also learned the contents by heart. Now, through Jaconus Van Eyck, he told them to the Queen of Great Britain.

'King Lobengula sends his greetings. His body is well, but his mind is much troubled by those who come in your name, demanding that they – and they alone, should be allowed to dig for gold in his country. He begs you, as a great and wise ruler, to tell him what he should do?'

Queen Victoria was taken as much by surprise at the Induna's plea as were the officials about her. Without realising the full implications of her reply, she gave the Induna advice that, in any other circumstances, would have been perfectly sound.

'Tell Lobengula he should consider all such applications very carefully. It is not wise to put too much power into the hands of the man who comes first and exclude other deserving men. A King gives a stranger an ox – not the whole herd. Otherwise, what would strangers arriving at the King's house after, have to eat?'

It was a simply homily, but as Jaconus Van Eyck translated for the Indunas, he realised that the Queen's advice provided Lobengula with sufficient justification for withdrawing the Rhodes concession, thus blocking the millionaire's bid to gain a royal charter for his company. He smiled at the consternation among the officials.

Farewell Loveday was also aware of the implications of the Queen's words and his dismay was evident.

Fortunately for the fortunes of his company, Rhodes was himself in London. When Farewell Loveday repeated the Queen's words to him, Rhodes acted swiftly.

The Queen's untimely advice could cause trouble only if Lobengula received it in time to block the granting of a Royal Charter. While the Indunas were sent on yet another tour of military establishments, farms and impressive homes occupied by Company dignitaries, Rhodes telegraphed instructions to the Cape Colony. He ordered that all arms and money promised to Lobengula under the terms of the concession MUST be delivered immediately. In the meantime, he redoubled his efforts in England to have the coveted charter granted in the quickest possible time.

Rhodes worked hard and fast. Soon he had won over the vast majority of those opposed to the formation of a chartered company vested with almost unlimited power. Some he persuaded by charm. Others, who possessed particular influence, by the simple expedient of giving them a place on the board of the new company. His directors now included two Dukes and many other peers – one a son-in-law of Queen Victoria, prominent politicians and many of the country's soundest businessmen. Given time, the granting of a charter to such an august body was inevitable. But time was the one opponent Rhodes had not yet won over.

At the end of March 1889, the Indunas were close to exhaustion as a result of their strenuous programme and they announced that they wanted to go home. They had proved there *was* a Queen of Great Britain. She had given them a photograph of herself and a gold medallion to present to Lobengula. They had also been given the benefit of her wisdom. It was time to return to Matabeleland.

Not until the Indunas, Van Eyck and Loveday, were a day out from England did they discover that the ship on which they were taking passage had cargo on board for South America and would be calling there first. The Indunas would cross the Atlantic ocean twice before landing at Cape Town to begin the long land journey to Bulawayo.

It was August before the party returned to their homes after an absence of almost a year. They were received by the King and that night was spent in noisy celebration. Not until the sober light of day broke over Bulawayo did Lobengula have time to think about the words of the Queen whose photograph stared sternly but regally from the wall of his home.

'The Great Queen spoke wise words,' Lobengula repeated for the sixth time. Sprawled in his great, shapeless armchair, his chin sunk on his great chest, he spoke to Suliyana who busied herself repairing a hole in a faded brown trade blanket. 'The men who came from Rhodes lied when they said it would please the Queen if I gave him a concession.'

'But you *did* give it to him,' said Suliyana, brusquely. 'Just as you have signed others, in the past. It is being said by the Mahajas that all the lands won by Mzilikazi's spear are being lost by Lobengula's pen.'

'Who says this?' Lobengula roared, his head coming up. 'They will learn respect riding a stake—'

'There will be no names.' Suliyana bent low over the blanket and peered at her handiwork. 'One day you will need the young warriors to prove they can fight as well as they talk.'

After a long, brooding silence, Lobengula said gruffly, 'Do you think I have failed my people? Have I signed away the inheritance of our son?'

Suliyana put the blanket down slowly and gave Lobengula a look that was filled with sympathy . . . and love. 'You have done all that could be done. Mzilikazi would have gone to war

– and lost all. There is a time for all men. For the white man it is now. He is coming, whether or not he has his "concession". You might as well try to stop the sun rising as try to stop him. But, at the end of the day the sun sinks again. So it will be with the white man. All that you can do . . . all that any King might do, is to keep our people together. Ensure that when the white man's sun goes down there is still a Matabele nation. It will take much patience. You will need to fight our own people more fiercely than the white man.'

Suliyana carried the blanket close to her eyes for a final time. 'There is no other man who can do this. It is the duty of a King.'

'I wish I could be certain,' Lobengula rubbed a big hand wearily over his face. 'Sometimes I feel I have failed everyone. My father. My people. You—'

'Ah no! Jandu, the man I married, is no more. You are now Lobengula, King of the Matabele, and I am your Chief Wife. I have given you a son who will one day rule in your place. You consult me when you take a new wife, and you do not beat me. Because of these things I am respected above all women, even though I am not of the Matabele. You have not failed me, Inkosi. For as long as the Matabele listen to your wisdom you will not fail them either.'

After sitting in silence for some minutes, Lobengula struggled heavily to his feet and made his way towards the door. 'It is another day. I must take my place beside the indaba fire and listen to the problems of those who believe I have none of my own.'

Pausing beside Suliyana, he rested a huge hand lightly on her head for a brief moment. 'Have beer sent to me, wife. It is going to be a long day.'

His interpreting duties over, Jaconus Van Eyck returned to the Insimo valley. His arrival was warmly welcomed by Daniel and the Retallick family. The Boer hunter seemed tired and subdued, but it was not until Jaconus, Victoria and the Retallick family sat down to dine that evening that the reason for his reticence became known.

Jaconus Van Eyck told of the visit to the Queen at Windsor, and of her reply to the Induna's question. Daniel was jubilant. 'Then the troubles of the Matabele are over. The Queen of

England agrees with him. Lobengula now has all the justification he needs to repudiate this latest concession.'

Jaconus Van Eyck shook his head slowly and firmly. 'It's too late for that. Nothing Lobengula does will stop Rhodes now. The Royal Charter will be granted long before news of Lobengula's change of heart reaches the Queen. Besides, Lobengula has changed his mind so many times in the past that the British Government doesn't take him seriously any more.'

'They may not take him seriously in London, but Lobengula is King of Matabeleland. They'll *have* to take him seriously here.'

'No, Daniel. Rhodes is the man of the moment in London. He's the idol of the country and has the backing of the most influential men in the land. Britain will go to war if Lobengula tries anything. I realise it's unfair, but that's the way things are. Right at this moment, Rhodes can do no wrong.'

Jaconus Van Eyck fidgeted uncomfortably, toying with the knife resting beside his plate. 'I spoke to Rhodes in London before I left. He . . . he asked me to work for him.'

'What work could Rhodes possibly have for an honest man?' Daniel spoke with bitterness. 'He's got his concession . . . and it sounds as though he'll have his charter too. What more is he after?'

'He wants to occupy Mashonaland. Send in white pioneers to colonise the country.'

Jaconus Van Eyck's words left his listeners stunned.

'It sounds unbelievable, I know,' he continued, hurriedly. 'But Rhodes' plan makes sense. In London it's no secret that the Portuguese are out to grab as much land as they can before the borders of all lands to the north of the Limpopo River are fixed. It's equally certain that Boers from Transvaal are gathering, ready to grab a chunk of Mashonaland for themselves. It's the same old situation, all over again . . . only this time they've got to *do* something, or Rhodes will beat them to it.'

'Is Lobengula expected to sit back while white men divide up his lands between them?' asked Victoria, incredulously.

'It's too late for him to do anything,' said Jaconus Van Eyck. 'Yes, it's wrong. I know that . . . we all know. But every country with interest in this part of the world has its eyes on Lobengula's kingdom. Some are quite prepared to go to war to prevent the others from moving in. The Church is involved too, Daniel. Protestant, Roman Catholic, and Dutch Reformed. You know which is going to be best for the Matabele . . . . Lobengula has to get the best deal out of it that he can – and I think he'll get that from Rhodes.'

'Does this mean you've already made up your mind to work for Rhodes?'

'Yes.' Jaconus Van Eyck's manner was apologetic. 'I know you'll think me a turncoat, but I'm *not*. Hell, man, I'm almost as fond of old Lobengula as you are, but I reckon I can do more for him from inside Rhodes' organisation than outside. There's also a great chance for me to make something of my life from this. Rhodes is promising land and fifteen gold claims to every man who goes to Mashonaland with his column, together with whatever credit is needed to make a go of things.'

'Rhodes can afford to be generous with land that doesn't belong to him!' Daniel retorted angrily. 'God, Jaconus! You know the Matabele. Can you see them standing by and doing nothing while hundreds of white men march in and take over Mashonaland? They'll fight Rhodes and his "pioneers" every foot of the way.'

'That's what I told Rhodes. He doesn't agree. He says the concession gives him permission to mine anywhere in Lobengula's land – and to take whatever action he deems necessary to win ore and hold it. He says he needs a small army to do that and claims the authority is in the concession. All right, offering lands to those who go in for him is exceeding anything envisaged by Lobengula, but Rhodes has to keep men in the country somehow. If they leave, the Portuguese will move in. They're already fitting out an expedition to move into Mashonaland, from Mozambique. When I left London a very heated exchange was taking place between the governments of Britain and Portugal. Once Rhodes moves in he'll help to keep the Matabele and Portuguese apart.'

'The distance between Mozambique and Matabeleland has been sufficient to keep them apart so far,' retorted Daniel. 'This is just another of Rhodes' ploys, to justify his empire building . . . only this time he has the backing of Britain.'

'All eyes are on this part of Africa now, Daniel. It's a fever that's spreading throughout Europe. Either Britain gets a foot in the door, or another country will. That's the truth of it.'

'When are Rhodes' "pioneers" moving into Mashonaland?'

'Not until he has the charter. It will take some organising too. It won't be until next year, at the earliest.'

'Will you be staying at Insimo until then?'

'No, Daniel. Rhodes' original idea was to come straight through Matabeleland to Mashonaland. I managed to persuade him there would be far less chance of trouble if he kept his column well clear of the Mahajas. He wants me to go to Mashonaland with Selous and find a route for the pioneers that will take them as far as the Hunyani River.'

Daniel knew Frederick Courtenay Selous. One of the finest hunters to have found his way to Africa, he had brought ivory and skins to Lobengula in the past. In return, Selous had been granted permission to travel wherever he wished in the King's lands. Selous had stayed at Insimo on more than one occasion. Rhodes had employed two honest and skilful men as his scouts. Daniel hoped he would be as fortunate in the choice of the remainder of his force. Much would depend upon their level-headedness.

'You're free to leave whenever you wish, Jaconus. Until then you're a welcome guest in this house. You will be, whenever you pay us a visit – but I must tell Lobengula about Rhodes' plan. If he hears it from someone else he's likely to do something foolish.'

Abruptly, Daniel rose from the table and left the room. The Matabele nation was poised on the brink of disaster. Things were moving too fast. Unless he was able to slow them down the Matabele nation was doomed – and with its passing would go the life Daniel had carved out for his own family.

Daniel made his way to the stream not far from the house and sat upon a rock beside the tumbling water. He had once found gold here – the very mineral Rhodes claimed to be seeking, using it as an excuse to change the map of Africa. With a sudden chill of alarm, realisation came to Daniel that the concession gave Rhodes the right to seek gold in the Insimo valley – and Rhodes already knew it was here!

He heard the sound of footsteps on the path. A few moments later Elvira seated herself beside him. 'I knew this was where I would find you. It is where I come when things are troubling me. Wyatt does too, I have seen him.'

'A twelve-year-old boy shouldn't have troubles,' said Daniel, more gruffly than he intended, as she took his hand.

'He shares your troubles and mine,' replied Elvira softly. 'He loves us both. He loves this valley too. It is the only home he has known.'

'I know that. It worries me—'

'You are afraid this man Rhodes may change things for us?'

'The plans Rhodes has will change things for everyone. Us, the Matabele, the Mashona, Rhodes himself, perhaps – but most of all for Lobengula. He is fond of telling me how Mzilikazi was forced to move from Transvaal when the white men crowded the Matabele. Lobengula was a young boy at the time, but it's written on his memory as though it happened only yesterday.'

'Do you think he will move with his people?'

Daniel shook his head. 'He can't. The Mahajas will refuse to follow him. They will stay and fight to the death. Besides, Rhodes has his eyes on the country to the north too.'

Elvira was silent for a while, then she said, 'Perhaps the changes will be enough to keep the Matabele happy. If Rhodes brings them medicine and schools—'

'The changes will benefit only Rhodes and his men. For the Matabele it will mean the end of their way of life. They will never recover from the loss of freedom, and the shattering of their pride.'

'What will you do, Daniel?'

Elvira winced in the darkness as the tension in Daniel caused him unwittingly to squeeze her hand painfully.

'I've got to persuade Lobengula of the futility of fighting. It won't be easy, I would fight myself if I were him. Somehow I have to prevent the Matabele from scoring the one last victory they're ever likely to achieve in their short history as a nation. I'll tell Lobengula to allow Rhodes to take Mashonaland . . . even though my whole being screams out that Lobengula and his impis should drum Rhodes and his pioneers all the way back to the Cape Colony. The damnable thing is that neither Lobengula nor his people will ever understand my motives for stopping them going to war. They'll probably think *I've* sold out to Rhodes too.'

'Lobengula will know the truth – and so will I. You are an honourable man. Whatever you do, wherever you go, my love goes with you. It always has, my husband.'

Worried at the disappearance from the house of both his mother and father, Wyatt was coming along the path towards the stream when he saw them silhouetted together against the moonlit skyline. With the light-footed tread of a natural hunter, he turned and returned the way he had come. The situation in the land was causing both of them great anxiety, but while they enjoyed embracing in the moonlight, all was well at Insimo.

CHAPTER SIXTEEN

When Daniel reached Bulawayo, he found the Matabele King enjoying one of his rare sober spells, with its accompanying improvement in health. A Scots doctor, on a visit to Matabeleland had given Lobengula a morphine injection for gout and the pain had disappeared almost immediately. So impressed was Lobengula, that when the doctor insisted that he give up drinking in order to effect a more permanent cure, he had readily agreed. Daniel knew that the joyful sobriety would be of short duration, but he was happy to be able to take advantage of it now.

Lobengula's initial reaction to Rhodes' plans was one of great anger. As Daniel explained the full implications of the move to occupy Mashonaland, anger turned to despair.

'What can I do? How can I prevent this man Rhodes from stealing the land of my people?'

'You must do nothing, Inkosi. Even more important, you must prevent your Mahajas from doing anything.'

Lobengula eyed Daniel suspiciously. He trusted Daniel more than any other white man. More than any man – black or white, but could he really be trustworthy when he belonged to a race to whom lying, cheating and scheming came as naturally as breathing?

'You are asking much of me and my people. White men prepare to march into our lands and seize them, yet I must do nothing? The whole world will wonder what manner of man it is who rules the Matabele.'

'Those to whom such things matter will know you are a *wise* King. A ruler who has the ability to evaluate a very difficult situation.'

'Don't try to flatter me, trader.' Lobengula frowned. 'That is not the way to persuade me to do what you suggest. You should know this by now.'

'This is far too serious a matter for flattery, Inkosi. As I see it, you have two choices. You either allow Rhodes to take his men to Mashonaland – or you fight.'

'My Mahajas . . . and many of their Indunas, would say there is no choice. We must fight.'

'If you fight, your impis *might* win the first battle, but it will be the last victory they will ever have. Rhodes can call on many men for help. They will come armed with Maxim guns – guns with which two men can fight as thought they are an army. If every one of your warriors fought as fiercely as though he were *ten* men, your army would still be beaten, just as Ceteswayo was beaten.'

Ceteswayo was a Natal Zulu King, the last of the true Zulu Kings. Disastrously defeated in their first battle with Ceteswayo's army, the British had returned to annihilate the Zulu's, removing for all time the threat they posed to European expansion in Southern Africa.

'Allow this to happen and you'll find Rhodes will not be satisfied with Mashonaland. He'll take Matabeleland too.'

Lobengula brooded morosely for many minutes. Then, the fire gone from his eyes, he looked up at Daniel. 'It is as you say. I am no longer a King, but a hunted animal. The hunters drum their shields behind and alongside me. There is only one way for me to go. I will send no impis to fight Rhodes' men, but I must keep the news from my Mahajas for as long as is possible. Only the most trusted members of my Council will know. In return, Rhodes and his men must stay well away from Bulawayo. If he comes into contact with my warriors I cannot answer for their actions. This is understood?'

'I think Rhodes is already aware of this.'

'This is too important a matter for there to be any uncertainty. I want you to go and find this man Rhodes. Tell him I am not pleased with what he is doing. I have never said white men could go to Mashonaland, but I will not make war if he keeps his men far from Bulawayo. When I learn his men are on their way to Mashonaland I will send my impis on raids to the north and west. Their paths will not cross that of his men.'

Daniel nodded his approval. 'Your decision is a wise one, Inkosi. You have given your people time they would not otherwise have. Use it to train your warriors in the use of guns Rhodes has sent to you. It might make him think twice before he takes advantage of the Matabele again.'

Lobengula nodded. 'Your words are the words of a friend,

trader. Go now. When you return, tell me what is in the heart of this man Rhodes.'

Cecil Rhodes was at Kimberley, celebrating the news that Queen Victoria had granted a charter to his British South Africa Company.

Daniel read the details of the charter in a Kimberley newspaper before going to visit Rhodes and he was astounded by the power it bestowed upon the company.

Bounded by Mozambique, Transvaal and British Bechuanaland, the charter stipulated no northern or western boundaries. Within this vast, ill-defined territory, Rhodes could 'assume powers of Government and administration, enact ordinances and maintain a police force.'

In other words, Her Majesty Queen Victoria had made Rhodes the dictator of a vast territory, twice the size of the British Isles, with expansion prospects not limited by the sea, or by prior claims.

It was an awesome mantle for any man to don, yet Rhodes was as cheerful and carefree as if he did not have a care or responsibility in the world. He was celebrating with brandy and champagne in the Kimberley Club, only a handful of close friends about him.

Rhodes recognised Daniel immediately and stood up to grasp his hand. In his high-pitched voice he called for a waiter to come and serve Daniel with a drink.

'Welcome to Kimberley again, Retallick. You've heard the news, of course? Yes, everyone's heard by now. Well, what are you doing here? Come to join my Company?'

There had been much time to think along the way and Daniel had devised a plan he hoped would secure the future of the Insimo valley, whilst achieving a guarantee for Lobengula of the route of Rhodes' column.

'No, Mister Rhodes, but I'll raise my glass and hope it brings peace and prosperity to all those who live and work in Lobengula's lands. I'm here to speak to you about your plans for Mashonaland.'

The transformation was astonishing. Rhodes' jocularity vanished. Before Daniel could say more he was hustled to a small room nearby. Slamming the door behind them, Rhodes founded on Daniel. 'What do you know about my plans for Mashonaland? Who's been talking? I'll have no loose-tongued employees in my Company.'

'It's as well I *was* told, or the bones of your "pioneers" would have been scattered among the hills of your promised land. The British Government would be throwing your charter on their funeral pyre.'

'Don't try to stop me, Retallick!' Rhodes' high, effeminate voice was shrill with anger. 'I won't let anyone, or anything stop me now—'

'Stop you? Why on earth should I want to stop you?' Daniel took a sip of champagne and brandy from the glass that had almost been knocked from his hand in Rhodes' haste to remove him from the party in the club lounge. 'I'm here to offer you a proposition. You keep your men well clear of Bulawayo when they're on their way to Mashonaland and I'll persuade Lobengula to allow you through without trouble.'

Rhodes had already agreed to route his column of pioneers well clear of Bulawayo, but this was no guarantee that it would not be attacked. He looked at Daniel, evaluating his offer.

'You'll do this? Why?'

Daniel shrugged. 'My home is in Matabeleland. The last thing I want is war. If Lobengula's Mahaja go on the rampage, not even Lobengula will be able to control them.'

Rhodes frowned suspiciously. There was far more to this than Daniel had disclosed. 'No one wants war, Retallick. Not even Lobengula . . . but, all right, if you do this for me, what do you expect in return?'

'I want your company to forego all mineral rights in the Insimo valley.'

Rhodes stared blankly at Daniel for a moment, then enlightenment spread in a slow smile across his face. 'Ah yes . . . your personal gold mine.' He pretended to think. 'I'm not certain I can give you such an assurance, Retallick.'

Daniel placed his glass heavily on the desk beside him. 'Then I've wasted my time and yours, Mister Rhodes. The men of your column can expect Lobengula's impis to oppose them every inch of the way – and they'll be coming in force.'

Daniel strode towards the door, but Rhodes reached it first.

'You've ridden seven hundred miles to avert a war, and to

secure a future for your family, yet you're ready to accept "perhaps" as a "no"? You have children?'

'Four boys.'

Cecil Rhodes grimaced in what might have passed for assumed envy. 'You're a lucky man, Retallick. *You* will never lie awake at night, wondering what is going to happen to everything you've worked for when you're dead and gone. You've got sons to continue your life's work. Part of *you* will live on through your boys. Surely you can spare me a few minutes of your time . . . for their sakes?'

Rhodes was mocking Daniel, he was calling Daniel's bluff and knew he would stay as long as it took to get what he had come so far for.

'For their sake I'll go much further. When your men try to enter Mashonaland they'll find Lobengula's impis waiting for them. I'll be there with them – and I'll have taught them to use your own guns against you.'

'I believe you, Retallick,' Rhodes sighed, then smiled. 'I had hoped to secure at least a share in the only confirmed gold find in Lobengula's country – but you've worked hard for all you've got, just as I have. I won't interfere with your sons' birthright. You ensure a troublefree passage to Mashonaland for my pioneer column and I'll have all mineral rights in your valley ceded to you and your family.'

'I'll need it in writing.'

'Of course. You'll have it by sundown.'

The meeting had become a business transaction, something Rhodes understood and was in the habit of conducting swiftly and conclusively.

He thought he now knew his man. 'Now, come and join my party. Help us celebrate the granting of my company's charter. It's an historic moment, Retallick. Come and be a part of history.'

'No thanks. Ask me again in ten years' time. If there's still cause for celebration then, *I'll* throw a party for *you* – and invite Lobengula along to enjoy it with us.'

News of the granting of the Royal Charter to Rhodes' company spread over southern Africa with the speed and heat of a bushfire. From the Zambezi valley, Lieutenant Carlos St Anna marched a sick and weary army deep into the heart of

Mashonaland. They passed through places where the tribes-men had not heard the Portuguese tongue since the sixteenth century, when the Monomatapa and his people suffered total defeat and years of subjugation and humiliation.

When his gallant little army was too ill to march another weary foot forward, Lieutenant St Anna planted the Portu-guese flag on a low hill and proclaimed the Portuguese pro-vince of Zambo, encompassing much of Mashonaland and all Manicaland.

On his way through these almost empty hills and upland plateaus, Lieutenant St Anna flushed out a few prospectors from the Cape Colony who had somehow eluded Lobengula's impis. He ordered them to leave.

His actions brought strong protests from the British Gov-ernment in London. One morning, Senhor Farrao's servant drew the curtains in the Acting Governor's Quelimane house and saw six British warships riding at anchor, no more than a cannon-shot offshore.

This was a time when the British Empire was still gathering strength. Portugal, on the other hand, was teetering on the brink of economic and political collapse. After a brief but acrimonious exchange of diplomatic notes between London and Lisbon, Lieutenant St Anna and his men were ordered to abandon their newly acquired province.

To the south, the Boer trekkers gathered yet again, deter-mined that the Queen of Great Britain would not rob them of potentially rich trekking grounds by a signature on a piece of paper.

Rhodes hurriedly arranged a meeting with President Kruger, leader of the Transvaal Republic. Kruger entertained his own hopes of expansion. He wanted land to the east of his tiny Republic, in order to gain an outlet to the sea. Accepting Rhodes' half-promise of support in this direction, Kruger agreed to restrain the disgruntled trekkers.

It seemed that, for the moment, Rhodes had successfully defended his unborn empire against the threat posed by its neighbours.

Early in 1890, Rhodes' ambitions received an unexpected boost. It had been pointed out to the Colonial Office in

London that the Queen's advice to Lobengula's Indunas had brought the newly Chartered British South Africa Company close to disaster. Governmental steps were taken somewhat tardily to remedy the matter.

A letter from the Queen was sent out from England, explaining that the Chartered Company represented not one man, but many hundreds. It was a clumsy attempt to convince Lobengula that by granting the concession to Rhodes, he had acted in accordance with Queen Victoria's earlier, rather more honest advice.

As though aware that the letter might provoke a degree of scepticism in the Matabele King, the Government iced its unpalatable pill with an elaborate and colourful coating. The letter was sent from England with an escort of four officers of the Household Cavalry! They arrived at Lobengula's kraal in the height of summer, dressed in full ceremonial uniform.

Unfortunately, the letter was as clumsily worded as was the attempt to disguise its duplicity. It was open to a very wide interpretation.

Whilst the hot and uncomfortable cavalrymen performed elaborate sword drill for the benefit of Lobengula and his enthralled court, Farewell Loveday and other representatives of Rhodes toiled to rewrite the letter in order that it should set out their case in a manner more likely to impress the King.

No one ever knew whether Lobengula was more impressed by the letter, or the cavalrymen. Whichever it was, Rhodes had won yet again. The King dropped all objections to the concession.

1890 was to be Cecil Rhodes' most triumphant year. A Member of the Cape Assembly for many years, he was now made the Colony's Prime Minister.

All that remained was for his pioneers to move into Mashonaland and give him an empire that reached out for fifteen hundred miles from the Cape of Good Hope.

CHAPTER SEVENTEEN

The pioneer column set off from Kimberley on 6 May 1890 and by mid-June it was camping on the spot where Uiys Toblin had been murdered more than two years before.

When the column moved off from here, heading northwards, it made a brave sight. Two hundred pioneers with a hundred wagons and more than two hundred Bechuana natives were escorted by four hundred men of the company's newly-formed police force – many of its members drawn from the Bechuana Border Police. With spare horses, oxen, and goats belonging to the Bechuanas, the column extended for more than two miles and raised a dust cloud visible ten miles away.

Crossing into Matabele territory on 25 June, the column set a course that would take it diagonally away from Bulawayo. Passing to the south of the Insimo valley, the column then swung northwards and established a fort fifty miles from the Retallick home. It was close to the great ruins of the House of Chiefs, where once the White Mondoro had passed on the words of the God, Chiminuka. The new fort was named 'Fort Victoria', in honour of the British Queen who had bestowed her official blessing upon Rhodes' ambitious venture.

Daniel rode with Wyatt and Nathan to Fort Victoria late in August, when the company of police, left as garrison, had been there for a fortnight. Most of the British South Africa Company Police were living inside the wood and earthwork fort. A few more enterprising men had constructed wood and dacca huts nearby, staking a claim in what they hoped would be the first town of any size along the road between Kimberley and the new capital of Mashonaland, which was to be sited two hundred miles to the north.

There was plenty to excite the boys in and about the fort. They were allowed to examine two small artillery pieces and were given a brief but noisy demonstration of the fire power of one of the forts' Maxim guns, each capable of firing five hundred shots a minute. The fort also boasted a single Gatling gun. The ten rotating barrels were sufficient to keep a whole impi at bay – or destroy it if an Induna was foolish enough to press home the attack.

Daniel found much to interest him in his talks with the policemen manning the fort. Many of them were less than enthusiastic about Rhodes' much publicised 'pioneers'. They pointed out that the British South Africa Company Police taking part in the great adventure were being paid five shillings a day. It was a good sum, but less than the amount paid to the pioneers they were protecting.

When the roads and forts had been completed, the task of the Police would be to run the forts and ensure that the rough-cut roads remained open. Meanwhile, the pioneers would be disbanded, each man given six months' rations, a rifle and ammunition, and allowed to choose three thousand acres of land. In addition, he could register fifteen gold claims in his name.

Despite their jealousy of the pioneers, the men at Fort Victoria realised they had played a unique role in history. To a man, they were proud to be on the payroll of Rhodes' British South Africa Company.

The pioneer column reached its destination on 12 September. In the shadow of a steep-sided kopje, close to the source of the insignificant Makabusi River, the Union Jack was run up in 'Fort Salisbury'. The Chartered Company had arrived.

For a while, everything went exactly as Rhodes had planned. His pioneer column had reached its destination without incident. Lobengula's impis did not put in an appearance, and the Boers remained on their own side of the Limpopo River.

Less certain was the future reaction of the Portuguese. Talks held in London and Lisbon to establish a border between Mashonaland and Mozambique had broken down. The Portuguese thought the British brash and avaricious. For their part, the British were contemptuous of a decadent country, living on past glories and unwilling to face the facts of late nineteenth-century life.

While the politicians in Europe drew tentative lines on paper maps, those who rode between the weathered granite peaks of the disputed land played a very different game.

Guided by Jaconus Van Eyck, the men who were to administer Mashonaland on behalf of the company, went to Manicaland. Riding from one major kraal to another, they signed treaties of friendship with every Chief and Induna they found. The Administrators returned to Fort Salisbury well satisfied. As far as the company was concerned, Manicaland was securely under its jurisdiction.

They had reckoned without Captain General Manuel Antonio de Souza Gouveia. When news of what had happened reached his mountain stronghold, the Goanese half-caste mustered his army of slaves and set out for Manicaland. The Chiefs and Headmen needed reminding that they were vassals of the *Portuguese*, forbidden to make treaties with others.

Gouveia's methods were direct and absolute. Those Chiefs who admitted signing treaties with the British South Africa Company had their throats cut in front of their subjects. The Headmen of smaller kraals were forced to watch as Gouveia's bloody mercenaries pillaged their villages, raping women and putting men and children to death. Then they too suffered the fate of greater leaders.

Rumours of Gouveia's atrocities quickly reached the ears of Senhor Farrao in Quelimane, and Archibald Colquhoun, Rhodes' Administrator in Fort Salisbury. Both men were dismayed . . . but for differing reasons.

Of the two, Senhor Farrao's feelings were prompted by more humanitarian reasons. There had been disquieting reports of Captain General Gouveia's method of government before, but nothing approaching the present scale. He despatched his old friend General Francisco St Anna to Manicaland with orders to find Gouveia. The Captain General of Gorongoza was to be informed that the eyes of the world were upon him. Such barbarism as he and his men had practised in the past must cease. If it did not, international pressure would force Portugal to relinquish any claim upon Manicaland.

Archibald Colquhoun saw only that by killing off all the signatories to the company's treaties, Gouveia had made it very difficult for the British South Africa Company to prove its right of administration over the same territory. He despatched a force to bring Gouveia's campaign of retribution to a halt.

Captain Forbes and forty company police troopers made their way to the heart of the Manica Hills. Here they learned that General St Anna and Captain General Gouveia were visiting the kraal of one of the more important Manica Chiefs.

The small troop approached the site of the Chief's kraal quietly and cautiously. Such caution was well advised. A trooper, sent ahead to reconnoitre, returned with the news that the two men *were* in the kraal – and they had an escort that outnumbered the company troopers by at least ten to one.

The kraal was situated on top of a hill. St Anna and Gouveia were parleying inside, but the Portuguese and native troops were camped nearby, guarding the approach route.

Captain Forbes had been sent to Manicaland to stop Gouveia intimidating the local Chiefs. How he achieved this end was left entirely to his own discretion. Studying the Portuguese camp and the kraal on the hill beyond, he decided upon a bold move. Thirty of his men rushed the Portuguese camp and took the unsuspecting soldiers completely by surprise. They captured all the weapons, stacked with military precision, close to the cooking fires.

While this action was taking place, Forbes himself led the remaining ten troopers up the hill to the Chief's kraal. Grabbing St Anna and Gouveia, Forbes and his men backed away down the hill with them.

The Manica Chief's warriors danced alongside them all the way, making threatening gestures with their spears . . . but it was all a charade. The Chief was overjoyed to see the bloodthirsty Gouveia a captive in the hands of his enemies. The angry gestures of his warriors was no more than an insurance, should the Captain General of Gorongoza somehow manage to effect an escape.

There was to be no escape. The two high-ranking Portuguese officials were given horses and led away by their audacious captors.

General St Anna's silent but angry dignity contrasted sharply with the demeanour of Captain General Gouveia. Convinced that he was to be brought to justice for his many atrocities against the unfortunate tribes of Manicaland,

Gouveia begged for mercy, grovelling at the feet of Forbes whenever the opportunity presented itself.

Both prisoners were taken to Fort Salisbury, where their arrival caused great consternation. After a lengthy discussion between Administrator Colquhoun and his advisers, it was decided to send them to Cape Town, for eventual repatriation to Portugal.

Daniel learned of General St Anna's capture when a message reached him at Insimo. The General would be arriving at Fort Victoria early in December. He asked Daniel to meet him there.

The rainy season had started early and Daniel and Elvira set off for Fort Victoria in torrential rain. It made travelling difficult and river crossings were hazardous in the extreme. There were three rivers to cross along the route. At the second they were delayed for three days, the fifty mile journey taking them five days to complete.

They were afraid they might have missed St Anna, but the same difficulties in travelling had affected the party in which the two Portuguese prisoners were travelling. The old friends were reunited in the officers' mess at the fort.

Francisco St Anna had been deeply humiliated by the manner of his capture, but he knew there would be little sympathy awaiting him in Portugal. Crestfallen and haggard, he still managed to greet Elvira and Daniel with warmth and affection. After kissing and embracing Elvira, he held her at arm's length, looking at her with undisguised admiration.

'Ah, but you are a beautiful woman, Elvira. I should have married you myself before Daniel came along. You have grown more attractive with the passing of time . . . .'

Releasing her reluctantly, Francisco St Anna grasped Daniel's hand in both his own. 'And you, my friend? You are well?'

His hands dropped to his sides and some of the pleasure ebbed away. 'It is good of you to come and see me. I am sorry it has to be in such circumstances.'

'You are being well treated, Francisco? Is there anything you need?' Daniel put the questions in a bid to break the unhappy silence that fell between them.

'Anything I need? No, Daniel – at least, nothing you can give to me. My career is at an end. I return to Portugal in disgrace. An embarrassment to my Government. What can *anyone* give to me?'

'I'm sorry, Francisco. Perhaps things aren't as bad as you think. My father will do all he can to help you, you know this,' Elvira spoke optimistically, but she too knew the truth. She was Portuguese. General St Anna's shame at his ignominious capture would embarrass his country. He would never be forgiven for allowing himself to be captured without putting up a fight.

Francisco St Anna shrugged miserably. 'I am afraid that my shame will fall upon your father too. It is very sad. He and I have for many years asked the Government in Portugal for money to build fortresses in Manicaland. It was not forthcoming. We have asked for more soldiers, and for a rapid solution to the border problems. All these years – and nothing. Now your father and I must suffer for the incompetence of our Government.'

Turning to Daniel, General Francisco St Anna said, 'All governments seek others to pay for their own shortcomings, Daniel. This is the reason yours has allowed Rhodes to move into Mashonaland with his company. If he fails in his venture your Prime Minister will merely shrug his shoulders. It will have been the failure of a business venture, no more. It will have cost your country nothing at all. If Rhodes succeeds? Ah yes, then the outcome will be different. Rhodes will become a nobleman and your Government will take over the administration of the country from his company. It will become part of the empire of Great Britain.'

Daniel and Elvira spent the remainder of that evening trying to cheer up the depressed General, but without any noticeable success. Captain General Gouveia joined them for a while. He complained about his accommodation, the rigours of the journey – and the manner of their capture. He assured Daniel in a loud voice, that Metropolitan Portugal would demand a high price of the British for insulting the Captain General of the Province of Gorongoza. When it became clear, even to the insensitive Gouveia that he was held in contempt by Daniel and Elvira, he gave them a stiff bow and was escorted back to his sleeping quarters.

The following day the clouds temporarily rolled away and the troopers escorting the two Portuguese officials announced their intention of taking full advantage of the unexpected break in the weather and riding for the Bechuana border.

When his horse was saddled, and the escort waiting, General St Anna suddenly asked after Victoria.

'She's well,' replied Daniel. 'She misses Therese, of course.'

'Therese is a fine young girl. A good wife for my son. I think too that she will be a good mother, one day very soon.'

Elvira began to express her delight, but General St Anna had more to say to Daniel. 'My son does not yet know he is to be a father. He has been in the north, in Zumbo, for many months. I beg a favour of you. Get the news to him before he hears of my disgrace. Perhaps his mind will then be too full of thoughts of his unborn child to seek revenge for what has happened to me.'

The escort showed signs of impatience and General St Anna swung himself up to the saddle. 'I can accept with dignity all that has happened to me, but I fear my resolve would break if I were to lose my only son because of it. I send him my love . . . and love also for the grandchild I may never see.'

The capture of the two senior Portuguese officials was to be the last item of good news Cecil Rhodes received for a long time. Within a matter of only a few months, great cracks began to appear in Rhodes' dream of a brave new colony to add to the British Empire. It began with the onslaught of the rainy season. The skies above Mashonaland opened and it rained as never before in living memory. So much rain fell that new rivers burst forth from the mountain sides in roaring torrents, carving great fissures in the hillsides and flooding the valleys below. Rivers that were seldom more than sluggish brown ribbons of life, swept aside their banks and poured over the countryside in a swirling torrent of death and destruction.

The pioneers who had set up camp on rich, low-lying lands had to flee for their lives, many losing all their scant but precious possessions to the rising waters. A few huddled in what shelter they could find and sat the season out. Others left.

Those who had thought to find gold lying on the ground, waiting to be picked up, discovered that centuries of natives had been well aware of the value placed upon the yellow metal by Arab, Portuguese and others from across the seas. The land had been well prospected and mined. There *was* gold in the mountains of Mashonaland, but it would take experts to locate it, and a great deal of hard work would be expended in the winning. Disillusioned, many of these men left too.

Meanwhile, Britain signed an agreement with Portugal, 'freezing' the undefined frontier between Mashonaland and Mozambique. This did not prevent a remarkable outburst of public indignation in Portugal when General St Anna and Captain General Gouveia returned to their motherland. The two men were bitterly criticised for falling such easy prey to the invading army of Cecil Rhodes.

The wrath of the masses spilled over to include all things British. The embassy in Lisbon was wrecked, Britons were manhandled in the streets and posters adorned the walls of Lisbon, exhorting the populace to burn out the British. Students at Portugal's universities enlisted in a volunteer 'army', it's avowed intention to sail to Mozambique and liberate Manicaland. There was no shortage of brave young men, and subscriptions poured in to purchase arms and send the student army on its way.

While all this was happening, a 'Native Protection Society' in London published a series of articles sympathetic to Lobengula, criticising the manner in which Rhodes had dispossessed him of his lands. The articles told of a naive and innocent native who had been robbed of his birthright by a grasping adventurer.

It mattered not that only a year or two before, the same newspapers and magazines that now supported the campaign had printed horrific tales of the Matabele King's atrocities committed against his neighbours. This was the kind of campaign that sold newspapers.

Coupled with the persistent rumours that there was no gold to be had from Mashonaland, the increasing public sympathy for Lobengula caused the shares of the British South Africa Company to drop in value alarmingly.

Rhodes' troubles did not end here. Incensed by the manner in which Rhodes had taken possession of Mashonaland, a party of Boers announced that they intended trekking to Mashonaland, brushing aside President Kruger's plea to them.

Their leader was Jan Potgieter, the same man who twenty-three years before had led a Boer commando to the Matopos Hills to fight for Kanje against Lobengula.

Two hundred Boers gathered at a crossing place on the Limpopo River. Opposing them across the wide expanse of muddy water were no more than thirty British South Africa Company policemen. Had the policemen tried to prevent a serious attempt to cross the river they would have been blown out of existence by the large bore elephant guns carried by the Boers.

It was this scene that Jaconus Van Eyck saw when he came along the north bank of the Limpopo River, having ridden hard from the Bechuana crossing-place, many miles away. Jaconus Van Eyck had been to Kimberley and discussed the situation on the Limpopo with Rhodes. He was arriving with a possible solution . . . if only he could persuade the men of Potgieter's party to listen to him.

He arrived not a moment too soon. For days the Boers and the Company Police had faced each other across the river, the Boers occasionally taunting Rhodes' men. More than once when Boer sympathisers came visiting the trekkers, the taunts were accompanied by empty brandy bottles, which fell equally harmlessly in the wide Limpopo River.

Today was different. There was an air of excitement in the Boer camp, and far more activity than usual. Oxen were being inspanned, horses saddled, and surreptitious glances cast across the river. Grim-faced, the Lieutenant in charge of the troopers was deploying his men and giving them last-minute instructions in a low voice.

When the Lieutenant learned that Jaconus Van Eyck came direct from Rhodes with new instructions, he was relieved to hand over responsibility for the ugly situation to him.

Jaconus Van Eyck's first order was for the troopers to pull back to the shelter of the bush, more than a hundred yards from the river bank. The move brought a cheer from the intending trekkers. They thought they had scored a bloodless victory, but Jaconus Van Eyck soon enlightened them.

'You men . . . across the river,' Jaconus Van Eyck hailed them in Afrikaans. 'I've just come from Mister Rhodes. He has a proposition I am to put to you.'

'We don't care if you've just come from Jesus Cristus,' mocked Jan Potgieter. 'We're coming across.'

'Listen to what I have to say, Potgieter. Then, if you still want to cross you'll be welcome – on British South Africa Company terms.'

'We're not going to be dictated to by any Ruineck. Hell, we have as much right over there as Rhodes – more, in fact. You know that, Jaconus.'

'I'm not here to argue about rights. Rhodes has occupied Mashonaland with the backing of the British Government and by agreement with President Kruger. He says if you . . . any of you, want to come to Mashonaland you're welcome to ride-off farms for yourself, the same as his pioneers. All he asks is that you abide by company law.'

Jaconus Van Eyck's words provoked a stir of interest among the Boers, but Jan Potgieter remained scornful. 'Company laws are for Ruinecks. We're coming over, Jaconus. Don't try to stop us.'

Jan Potgieter kicked his heels in his horse's flanks, repeating the process until the horse reluctantly picked its way through the stones at the river edge and entered the dark brown water. One of the Boers, a rifle resting lightly on the saddle horn in front of him, followed suit. The remainder of the mounted men milled about uncertainly, waiting to see what would transpire.

When the two horses were chest deep in the river, Jaconus Van Eyck raised a rifle to his shoulder. Jan Potgieter was watching, but he kept going, expecting a warning shot. His companion had less faith in Jaconus Van Eyck's intentions and brought his own rifle up.

The crack of the shot echoed across the flat surface of the river. Shot through the head, the Boer's horse dropped sideways. The rider barely had time to kick his feet free of the stirrups before he too fell in the water. He came up coughing water . . . and minus his gun.

'Jaconus! What do you—?'

Jaconus Van Eyck's rifle cracked again. Potgieter's words were cut short as his own horse fell dead and he too was flung in the river beside his floundering companion.

Jaconus Van Eyck reloaded his rifle swiftly but calmly. Bringing it to his shoulder he fired yet again. A mortally wounded crocodile threshed the water in a death frenzy, twenty feet from the two men. Jan Potgieter and his companion shouldered each other out of the way in their frenzied haste to gain the Transvaal bank once more.

With one bullet in his gun, Jaconus Van Eyck waited tensely for the remainder of the Voortrekkers to make their next move.

Suddenly, one of the Boers laughed and the tension was broken.

'Hell, I never knew you could move so fast, Jan! That Krokodil could have been given a running start and still drowned in the wake you left behind. It was a pleasure to watch, man.'

The laughter spread among the others. Then the man who had made the remark called across the river, 'I'd like to cross the river, Jaconus. On British South Africa Company terms.'

'You're welcome. Make your way to Fort Salisbury and see the Administrator. He'll give you all the papers you need to file a claim. Any more of you coming across?

Less than a third of the would-be trekkers crossed the river to place themselves under the protection of the British South Africa Company. One of them was Jan Potgieter, who carefully avoided looking at Jaconus Van Eyck.

The numbers were sufficient to break the strength of the trekking party. As the tracks of their late companions' wagons cut a double furrowed track in the direction of Fort Salisbury, the remainder wheeled their wagons about and returned to the free and independent State of Transvaal, where laws were made by their own kind.

CHAPTER EIGHTEEN

Coming to terms with the Boer trekkers seemed to mark a turning point for Rhodes. Shortly afterwards, the Reverend Farewell Loveday solved the delicate problem of the Chartered Company's right to dispose of land it had not been given – and he did it with typical Loveday deviousness.

Farewell Loveday was deeply disappointed with the lack of spiritual progress in Matabeleland. The arrival of the pioneers in Mashonaland had made no impact on Lobengula's tribe at all. Loveday conceded that the process of civilising the Matabele could not be speeded up, but the thought that public opinion in Europe might possibly force the company to withdraw filled him with alarm. Missionary considerations apart, the Reverend Farewell Loveday had a considerable monetary stake in the success of the British South Africa Company's venture.

For many years a nondescript German had been trying to win a concession from Lobengula, with a notable lack of success. Now he was in Bulawayo once again and he was amazed when Farewell Loveday came to him with a proposition. The missionary would persuade Lobengula to grant him a major concession. In return, the German would immediately sell it to Rhodes. For this he would be paid a great sum of money, be given a substantial block of shares in the British South Africa Company, and allowed to prospect in Mashonaland.

Not unnaturally, the German jumped at such an unexpected opportunity. Ever since the all-embracing mining concession had been granted to Rhodes, the Europeans frequenting Bulawayo had been eager for the smallest crumb dropped their way. Yet here he was being offered the opportunity to join the man who had been given the whole loaf.

Lobengula was still unaware of the freelance missionary's total involvement with Rhodes and he shared many of his thoughts with the white man he regarded as a friend. His hatred of Rhodes now amounted to an obsession. When he had been drinking heavily, he became morose and bitter about Rhodes' trickery. Time and time again he declared that Rhodes was occupying Mashonaland illegally and his followers had no right to the land that had been given to them.

It was this argument that the anti-Rhodes campaigners were using. Rhodes himself was aware of the gaping loophole in the concession he held from Lobengula.

By playing upon Lobengula's hatred for Rhodes, Farewell Loveday convinced the King that if he were to grant a concession to someone else, specifically giving them the right to allocate farms, lay out townships and generally distribute the land as *they* thought fit, it would throw Rhodes and his company into utter confusion. The pioneers could be ordered to leave their farms and the Chartered Company would collapse.

Farewell Loveday's scheme worked better than he had dared to hope. Lobengula signed away his interest in Mashonaland on an evening when brandy and champagne combined with his burning resentment of Cecil Rhodes to cloud his judgement. By the time he was sober again, the concession was ten miles along the Kimberley road. The British South Africa Company now owned a concession to confound even Rhodes' most persistent critics.

Daniel received the news of Lobengula's latest folly with sad resignation. It was not yet known that the concession had passed to Rhodes' hands, but Daniel had none of the King's faith in the Reverend Farewell Loveday. He believed that the missionary would sponsor nothing likely to benefit the Matabele.

Daniel had little time to worry about the matter. Other things were happening that would involve him deeply.

In February of 1891, the Portuguese student 'army' arrived at the tiny Mozambique port of Beira. Ill-prepared and lacking even the basic training for an African campaign, they camped on the unhealthy marshland, inland from the port. Very soon malaria and dysentery struck their ranks, undermining morale if not enthusiasm. Determined to strike at least one blow against Rhodes, they appealed to the Portuguese army in Mozambique for assistance and were reluctantly given basic instruction in the art of war.

This was the news that Daniel and Wyatt were given when they passed through Fort Salisbury on their way to Tete to make good the promise Daniel had given to General Francisco St Anna.

The administrative capital of Mashonaland was a diverse conglomeration of huts and shanties. Some were built in the Mashona style, of mud and thatch. Others were constructed from locally-cut logs. Not a few incorporated planks of seasoned wood from pioneer wagons, broken up when the column reached its objective.

The disastrous rains of the summer had ended, but no supply wagons had yet been able to ford the still swollen rivers to the south. The men living in Fort Salisbury were short of food and clothing. In some cases men walked about barefooted, their boots having rotted on their feet as a result of the unprecedented wet season.

Daniel and Wyatt stayed to take part in a hunt not far from the embryo capital. They flushed out a small herd of reedbuck and seven were killed. They also bagged two impala, a sable, an eland . . . and two elephant. It was enough to ensure that the small community would have full bellies for a week or two.

Tete lay in the Zambezi valley, two hundred miles north east of Fort Salisbury. The terrain here was different to that of the high, Mashonaland plateau. Game was plentiful, one herd of elephant they saw containing more than eighty of the great beasts.

Daniel enjoyed seeing so much thriving wild life, but he derived the greatest pleasure from the company of his son, and the opportunity to share the experiences of the journey with him.

Wyatt had a quick mind, and was a deadly shot with his Gibbs-Melford .450 rifle, but he much preferred to stop and observe animals rather than shoot them. There were times when Daniel was concerned that Wyatt's nature was far too gentle for the harsh environment in which they lived, but he consoled himself with the knowledge that the Matabele herdboys held Wyatt in high esteem. They did not show such respect to any man, or boy, who did not meet with their very high standards. On this journey, Daniel quickly learned that his son was as much at home in the bushveldt as he was himself.

They reached Tete six days after leaving Fort Salisbury and received a reception that was more hostile than any Daniel had known during his travels in Mozambique. Tete was a much larger settlement than Sena and there were many more white faces here. For a while it seemed he and Wyatt might be sent back to Mashonaland. Not until he told them he carried a message from General St Anna to his family did they allow Daniel and Wyatt to proceed – under escort.

At the St Anna estate they were met by a delighted Therese. In her arms she carried a month-old baby son.

'Daniel . . . Wyatt,' Therese kissed each of them in turn. 'It's wonderful to see you—' Suddenly her expression changed and she looked at Daniel anxiously. 'There's nothing wrong? I mean . . . with Ma?'

'No, your mother is well and sends her love . . . to both you and Carlos – she doesn't know about this one yet.' Daniel placed a finger beneath the baby's chin. It pushed the tip of its tongue between pursed lips and began making noisy sucking noises. Daniel smiled, and then became more serious.

'I'm really here to speak to Carlos. I saw his father when he and Gouveia were taken through Mashonaland. He sent a message, urging Carlos not to seek revenge for his capture.'

All the happiness left Therese's face. 'I think you may be too late. I had a letter from Carlos a month after his father was taken. Carlos was *very* angry. Since then I have had two more letters. He seems to have thrown himself body and soul into raising an army to take back Manicaland for Portugal. I've written to him but I don't think any of my letters have reached him. I'm worried about him, Daniel. Upset too . . . he doesn't know about our baby yet.'

'Where's Carlos now?'

'The last letter came from somewhere along the Zambezi, well beyond Zumbo. But the messenger who brought it said he thought Carlos was going to cut through Mashonaland to the fort at Macequece before going on to Beira.'

Daniel frowned. 'If he's on his way to Beira he'll be going to aid the student army there. They've sworn an oath to chase Rhodes and his company from Manicaland.'

Therese looked at Daniel with wide-eyed concern. 'Will there be a battle?'

'I'd like to be able to say "no", Therese. But the Company Administrator at Fort Salisbury knows the students are on their way. He's sent reinforcements to Umtali with orders to prevent them from coming any further. I'll go there to see what's happening. I might prevent Carlos from doing something foolish.'

'I'm coming with you.'

'Impossible! Who'll look after the baby while you're away?'

Therese's chin came up in a defiant attitude that reminded Daniel she was Victoria's daughter.

'The baby will come with me.'

'It's out of the question. Wyatt and I will need to travel fast—'

'The St Anna horses are the best in Mozambique. I'll have no difficulty keeping up with you. My baby will be happy enough in a sling, in front of me.'

Therese looked at Daniel defiantly. 'Either we travel with you, or without you. I have more reason than you for wanting Carlos to remain alive. I doubt if he will take unnecessary risks once he has seen his own son.'

'She's right, Pa. I'll help carry the baby. It can't weigh very much.'

With Wyatt on Therese's side, Daniel capitulated. 'All right. We'll leave first thing in the morning. In the meantime someone will need to tend our horses. They've got a hard journey ahead.'

They set off escorted by a dozen mounted Manicas, armed with ancient flintlock muskets. At midday they struck the Luenha River, a tributary of the Zambezi, and followed it for a hundred miles to its source in the Inyanga Mountains.

Here they passed through the ruins of Chief Vumba's village. It brought back many memories for Daniel. Here he had found Victoria – and Sam Speke was buried nearby. Daniel tried to find the grave, but all traces of it had disappeared many years before. It was here too that Mariano,

Therese's true father had died. But the gallows' tree had long since been cut down for firewood and Mariano's daughter and grandson passed the spot with no hint of a ghost to haunt them.

There were few tribesmen in the hills now. Many of the Chiefs and Headmen had signed treaties with the British South Africa Company and, as a result, had received visits from Gouveia's slave-army.

Leaving the ruins of Chief Vumba's village behind, Daniel led the way through the Manica mountains to the isolated Portuguese fort of Macequece. Much to his surprise he found it occupied by troopers of the Chartered Company's police.

The troopers were piling up guns, general stores and great mounds of ammunition on the fort's parade ground and were in high spirits.

'Well .... We don't often see women in these parts – leastways, not an English woman!' The speaker was a young, sun-tanned Police Captain, the commander of the troop.

Daniel returned the Captain's greeting without enlightening him as to Therese's nationality. 'We didn't expect to see you here, either. What's happened? Where are the Portuguese?'

Contemptuously, the officer jerked a thumb in the direction of the coast, almost two hundred miles away. 'Gone. Ran like rabbits. Most of them while the battle was still on.'

'A battle?' Daniel looked to where Therese leaned wearily against her horse, surrounded by British South Africa Company troopers. The men, starved of any form of family life, were attracted equally by Therese and the young baby in her arms. 'Were there any casualties?'

The young Captain laughed. 'None ... unless you count Trooper Green. He found the Portuguese wine store and quite literally drank himself to death! They tell me there's only one better way to go.'

'How about the Portuguese? Did they suffer casualties?'

'A great many. I counted forty-nine bodies, and they carried many of the wounded away with them. Their tactics were quite unbelievable. They made no attempt to take advantage of cover. Our position was a few hundred yards from here and, before they broke and ran, they came on as though they were on parade! It wasn't a battle, we just picked them off. I didn't want a repeat of such slaughter, so I came to the fort to parley with them this morning – and found they'd scarpered! Just ran off, leaving everything behind them!'

Aware that Therese had extricated herself from the group of admirers and was advancing towards them, Daniel broke in quickly, 'A Portuguese officer – Lieutenant St Anna? He wasn't among the casualties?'

Therese had reached them now and, as the Captain turned to greet her, Daniel added, hurriedly, 'This is Lieutenant St Anna's wife and son.'

'Oh!' The Captain's manner changed abruptly and for a moment he looked embarrassed. 'I'm sorry. Yes, I'm afraid Lieutenant St Anna was a casualty.'

'NO! He's dead?' Therese's agonised cry brought a hush to the parade ground.

'Wounded . . . but rather badly, I'm afraid.'

Daniel discovered he had been holding his breath. He released it noisily.

'Where is Carlos now?' Therese's voice came out as a hoarse whisper.

'We sent him to Fort Salisbury. There are no doctors here, and without one—' The Police Captain looked at Therese's anguished expression and bit back the words he was going to use. 'He'll be looked after well at Fort Salisbury.'

'When did he leave?' Daniel asked.

'Two days ago. In a wagon.'

Daniel and Therese exchanged glances.

'I'll feed my baby, then we'll leave. We can travel a lot faster than any wagon.'

Therese, brought up among the Matabele, quite unselfconsciously pulled a milk-swollen breast from her dress and put the teat in her baby's mouth. As she walked through the gaping troopers towards her horse, Daniel would have followed, but the young Captain caught his arm and drew him back.

'Don't let that young lady build up too many hopes. I don't think her husband will survive the journey to Fort Salisbury.'

They caught up with the Chartered Company wagon carrying Carlos St Anna that same evening. It had travelled no further than the fifteen miles from Fort Macequece to the police fort at Umtali.

The four-man police escort decided to remain here when Carlos St Anna began dribbling blood. They considered that taking him to Fort Salisbury would be a wasted journey. Far better to let him die at Umtali and save them all the discomfort of a long wagon trek.

Although so seriously wounded, Carlos St Anna was conscious. When he saw Therese and the baby his eyes opened wide with joy and astonishment. It was doubtful whether he even saw Daniel and Wyatt. As the badly wounded young Portuguese Lieutenant struggled to speak to his wife, Daniel felt an emotional lump rise in his throat. It threatened to choke him. Placing an arm on Wyatt's shoulder, Daniel led him from the room, leaving the young couple alone with their baby son.

The Commanding Officer of the police fort, a florid-faced Captain had been standing in the doorway. He closed the door behind them and asked, 'What are your plans now?' Adding, apologetically, 'We're a mite short on accommodation – especially for women and babies.'

'We'll most likely stay here for a few days, until Lieutenant St Anna's a bit stronger. Then I'd like to take him to my home, in the Insimo valley. You've no objection?'

'None at all. He's not a prisoner . . . we're not even at war with the Portuguese. The whole business was too damned ridiculous for words, especially in view of this—' He dug into a breast pocket and pulled out a crumpled telegraph form addressed to the Company Administrator in Fort Salisbury. It was from the Governor of the Cape Colony. It stated that agreement had finally been reached between Great Britain and Portugal on the border dispute. It went on to set out a number of readings in latitude and longitude. Scribbled beneath them were the pencilled words, 'Fort Macequece – Portuguese. Fort Umtali – British.'

'So a lot of men have died for nothing,' said Daniel bitterly, handing back the telegraph message.

'Many more than we'll ever know,' agreed the Captain. 'Those Africans who fell victim to Gouveia – and the Portuguese Student batallion. I heard tell they were dying like flies in the Mozambique marshes. What a waste of bright young men.'

414

'A waste indeed,' agreed Daniel, looking to where Wyatt stood talking to some young troopers, only a few years his senior. Daniel hoped his son would never blindly follow any cause to such an inevitable end.

Daniel, Wyatt, Therese, Carlos and the baby left the Umtali fort the following morning. Therese would not stay a moment longer, declaring the fort to be unhealthy for a man with damaged lungs. Carlos travelled in the same wagon that had brought him from Macequece, and Wyatt drove. Therese, the baby safe in an improvised cot, was in the back of the wagon with her husband and did her best to protect him from the worst of the jolting they encountered.

The wagon had been loaned willingly by the Fort Umtali Commanding Officer. He would arrange to have it collected at some future date, when the Chartered Company had a police troop passing close to the Insimo valley.

They moved slowly, Wyatt picking his path carefully. Nevertheless, that night Carlos was restless and feverish and, when morning came, he was noticeably weaker.

After a hurried discussion on whether to carry on, or remain where they were for another twenty-four hours, Daniel said anxiously, 'Perhaps we should have left Carlos at the fort. The journey is proving too much for him.'

'He *couldn't* have stayed at the fort,' cried Therese. 'There was no one there who cared whether he lived or died. In fact, they were *hoping* for him to die. I could see it in the way they looked at Carlos . . . and at me. Here, he is with those who love him. His wife and child. His friends. If he dies—' Therese choked on the words. She began to cry softly, disturbing the baby who lay in her arms.

Daniel stepped forward to comfort her, but thrusting the baby at him, she fled to the wagon where Carlos lay restlessly sleeping.

They remained at this camp for two nights, but the condition of Carlos St Anna showed no improvement. At night it was cool in these mountains and the cold air made him cough. Each bout of coughing left his pillow flecked with blood. His fever was worsening too. Daniel believed the fever to be caused by the bullet, still lodged inside him, but the nearest surgeon was still many miles away, at Fort Victoria.

Then Daniel remembered that when he had come this way in company with Jandu and Suliyana, many years before, Suliyana had taken them to a hot springs that the Manicas claimed to have strong healing powers. It was hardly likely that the waters could heal a bullet wound, but the air about the steamy pools would be warm. Carlos would be more comfortable there.

They set off immediately and reached the springs the next day. Therese thought that a bathe in the hot, mineral rich waters would be good for Carlos, if only to remove the dust and perspiration of their travels.

Daniel, assisted by Wyatt, lifted the wounded man bodily from the wagon. As they carried him between them, Carlos cried out that he had an excruciating pain, high in his back. As the bullet wound was in his chest, Daniel thought the pain must have been brought about by the rough wagon ride. However, when Carlos was stripped for his bathe, Daniel saw a small lump, just above the right shoulder blade of the wounded man. Protruding from it was something that might have been a small piece of jagged bone.

Pointing it out to Therese, Daniel said, 'It could be that the bullet has passed through his chest and ended up there, damaging a rib.'

'What can we do about it?'

'*We* can do nothing. If only there was a doctor closer than Fort Victoria. An operation to remove the bullet might make all the difference.'

That night Carlos St Anna's fever worsened. By morning he was in a state of delirium, knowing nobody. Daniel deliberated for a couple of hours before making up his mind. He knew what had to be done, but had been reluctant to face up to the inevitable. He would have to try to find the bullet.

When he went to speak to Therese, he found her with Carlos, whose breathing was now very ragged. 'Someone's got to try to get that bullet out, Therese. Carlos may die in the attempt, but he *will* die if it isn't removed.'

Therese nodded. 'I know. You do it Daniel, please.'

The surgical 'scalpel' was a hunting knife, honed to razor-sharpness and heated in the red-hot ashes of the fire. With a white-faced Wyatt holding Carlos firmly on his side, Daniel poised, the knife held over the irregular lump on Carlos' back. He made a swift stroke, the knife slicing deep into the muscle of the wounded man's back.

Carlos cried out and began to struggle, but Wyatt held him tight. Then Therese began to speak softly to her husband and slowly he quietened. With the point of his knife, Daniel probed the wound and a sliver of bone was removed. He probed again, deeper and this time the point struck something hard – and slipped away.

Doing his best to stop his hand from trembling, Daniel eased the point of the knife further into Carlos' body. Carlos screamed with pain as Wyatt exerted all his strength to pin him to the floor of the wagon. Daniel prised upwards and at first thought the knife had lodged in another piece of bone. Then, with a suddenness that took him by surprise, the blunted nose of a long bullet from a .450 Martini Henry rifle came into view and clattered to the wooden floor of the wagon.

The operation was over.

Looking down at the bullet, Daniel's hand suddenly began to shake uncontrollably and he backed away, leaving Therese to dress the wound from which the bullet had been removed.

That evening, Carlos St Anna's fever subsided and he slept well. The next morning when he woke he asked for food, but neither Daniel nor Therese dared voice the elation they both felt.

They remained at the hot springs camp for four more days until, on the final evening, Carlos St Anna held his baby son in his arms for the first time.

When Therese returned to the Insimo valley with a baby and her wounded husband, it was as though history had thrown up a copy of Victoria's arrival, many years before. It could have been a difficult homecoming. Although she had sent a blessing to her daughter and Carlos St Anna, Victoria had believed she might find it very difficult to welcome the son of Francisco St Anna to her home. Now, the circumstances of their arrival, and the sight of the pale-faced, gaunt young man propped up in the wagon with her grandson in his arms, won Victoria over completely. One day the young couple would return to

Mozambique, but, until then, Victoria would do everything to make their stay with her a happy one.

Carlos and Therese were still at Insimo in August when Senhor Farrao arrived from Mozambique, accompanied by a mixed escort of Portuguese troops and British South Africa Company Police. The latter had been supplied by a startled Administrator, to whom Senhor Farrao had reported after riding unchallenged half the width of Mashonaland, from the Mozambique border.

Senhor Farrao was still the *de facto* Governor of Mozambique, but he had been recalled to Lisbon. He knew the summons was a prelude to his dismissal. His fall from favour had been inevitable after the defeat suffered by the student batallion at the hands of the Chartered Company's police.

Senhor Farrao had never been overawed by the importance of his position and he would not allow his imminent dismissal to destroy his outward composure. His only complaint was that the Portuguese Government could have dismissed him on the spot, permitting him to return to his estate at Sena without forcing him to suffer the perils and discomforts of a long return voyage to Portugal.

Although the story of his own downfall was distressing to Elvira, he had far grimmer news for Carlos St Anna.

Public indignation at the numerous setbacks suffered by Portugal in Africa reached a crescendo when students of the ill-fated 'army' returned to their homeland. Defeated in battle and decimated by malaria, the survivors stepped ashore broken in both health and spirit. Seeking someone on whom to vent their anger, the populace turned on the only available man who had held a post of responsibility in Mozambique. That man was General Francisco St Anna.

The unfortunate General was blamed for the lack of fighting spirit in the colonial troops. His accusers conveniently forgot that the battle had been forced upon the Mozambique authorities by the ill-trained and unprepared students from the mother country.

Stripped of his army rank, Francisco St Anna maintained a dignified silence while the populace howled for more blood. It was rumoured that the Portuguese army council were drawing up papers to have him tried for cowardice.

One day, after being stoned and reviled whilst walking the streets of Lisbon, Francisco St Anna returned to his home, placed the barrel of a loaded revolver to his temple, and pulled the trigger.

The newspapers reporting his death, carried on the same page an article written by a sympathetic student. The student told of the bravery of Francisco St Anna's son, who had fallen at the battle of Macequece, while leading the students in an assault upon the enemies' position.

Such was the fickleness of public opinion, the brief article was sufficient to have Francisco St Anna belatedly cleared of the charges that had driven him to self-destruction.

Posthumously restored to his former rank, General Francisco St Anna was given a warrior's funeral. Meanwhile, the Portuguese finally accepted that their great days of colonial glory were over. It had been a long, hard lesson.

CHAPTER NINETEEN

In the same month that Senhor Farrao arrived at Insimo, the Reverend Farewell Loveday left Matabeleland and moved to Fort Salisbury. It was a hasty departure, and the reason was not hard to find. Rumours had reached Bulawayo that the land concession Lobengula had granted to the German, at Farewell Loveday's insistence, had found its way into the hands of Cecil Rhodes.

Farewell Loveday had got away with much in the past because of his association with Mzilikazi, but he knew he had pushed Lobengula's patience too far on this occasion. It was time for the scheming missionary to seek the company of white men.

Loveday arrived in Mashonaland's administrative capital a wealthy man, although his missionary record was less than impressive. During the whole of his time in Matabeleland he could not claim a single convert to Christianity, and the bloody raids carried out by Lobengula's impis against his neighbours continued unabated.

In Fort Salisbury, Farewell Loveday found new and untried fields of endeavour in which to exercise his pastoral prowess. Wagon loads of whisky and dubious Cape brandy were arriving regularly — and the capital could already boast Mashonaland's first brothel, set up on the kopje, just outside town.

While Senhor Farrao was still at Insimo, a large impi passed through the hills north of the valley, on its way to punish a Mashona Chief with a kraal close to Fort Salisbury. This unfortunate Chief had refused to pay his annual tribute to Lobengula, believing that the white men who now occupied the land would protect him.

The mistake cost him his life together with the lives of his family and everyone else who happened to be in the Chief's kraal on that fateful day.

The raid, in Chartered Company territory, caused a furore in Fort Salisbury. Farewell Loveday's voice was raised louder than any other in condemnation of the bloody act. From the pulpit at the town's church he declared vehemently that Christian standards might only be taught to the Matabele with sword and gun.

The Administrator of Mashonaland lodged a protest with Lobengula about the raid, but he received short thrift. The Matabele King told him bluntly that he had said nothing when men of the British South Africa Company entered Mashonaland without 'asking for the road'. He had not complained when they built huts on land that was not theirs. He had even held back his warriors when they clamoured to be allowed to attack the white trespassers. But the white men must not imagine that such forbearance meant he had abandoned his subjects, the Mashonas, to the white invaders. They still enjoyed his 'protection' and would suffer his retribution whenever they offended him. If the white men had no stomach for Matabele justice, he declared, then perhaps they should leave the country?

Lobengula did not add that the ranks of his impis were full of generations of Mahajas who had never faced the guns of the white men in battle. They had not learned to respect their weapons and their tactics, as had their fathers and grandfathers. These young warriors knew only that the white men had invaded their lands and their King would not send them to war to win it back.

The Mahajas needed warfare. The whole structure of the Matabele nation was built around the impi. No young warrior would be accepted by a Matabele woman as a husband until he had 'washed his spear' in the blood of an enemy – and a Mashona who had not paid his dues to Lobengula was considered an enemy.

As if to emphasise his right of life or death over the unfortunate Mashonas, the scale of Matabele raids into their country gradually increased. Some of the farms pegged out by the Europeans lay directly in the paths of many of these sorties. Mashona farm labourers going about the business of their white employers were slaughtered as indiscriminately as their unemployed kinsmen in remote kraals and villages. It became increasingly apparent to even the most optimistic observer that a clash between whites and Matabele was inevitable.

* * *

In the Insimo valley, the Retallick family and those who worked there were strangely remote from the problems of the outside world. The distant rumbling of white discontent in Mashonaland and the frustration of Lobengula's warriors were far removed from them. For Daniel, the two years to mid-1893 were the best he had ever known. Wyatt was now sixteen years old and Nathan thirteen. Both were doing a man's work. Adam and Benjamin were younger, but they too enjoyed working with Daniel and their brothers in the fields and pastures of their valley home.

Daniel's proudest moments came at the end of each hard day's work. He sat his horse overlooking the Insimo valley, four sons at his side, and looked at what he had achieved in more than twenty years of work here. Along the valley herd upon herd of fat, healthy cattle grazed some of the best grass in the land. The Matabele herd-boys, almost as content as their charges, lolled in the shade of hill-top rock formations, or called out to friends in singsong voices that echoed from hill to hill.

On the slopes of the hills, Mashona workers cultivated acre after acre of tall maize. There was enough food here to meet the needs of both white settler and Matabele warrior. Daniel was friends with both.

It was lonely for the women in the valley, especially when Therese returned with her husband to the St Anna estates in Mozambique. Yet, had anyone suggested to them that there was another way of life, both would have scoffed at such an idea. In the fastness of this corner of Matabeleland, the residents of Insimo had discovered contentment.

The end of this settled and happy way of life was brought about by a tragically simple incident that took place on a mild April day in 1893, seventy miles away, close to Fort Victoria. Sometime during the day, part of the telegraph line linking Fort Salisbury and Fort Victoria with the Cape Colony was cut and a length of copper telegraph wire stolen.

A troop of British South Africa Company Police quickly discovered the culprits living in a nearby kraal. Brought to justice, they and their Headman, Gomella, were fined a large number of cattle as a salutary example to others. To the surprise of the District Administrator in Salisbury, Gomella paid his very heavy fine without complaint – indeed, with a remarkable readiness!

Not until he received a strongly worded complaint from Lobengula did the Administrator understand why. The cattle did not belong to the Mashona Headman. They were Lobengula's, sent to Gomella to graze on behalf of his Matabele overlord.

The cattle were returned to Lobengula with due apologies from the Chartered Company, but the incident did not end here. Gomella had given away the King's cattle. He had failed in his duty and had made Lobengula look foolish.

Early in July, a huge Matabele impi crossed the Shashi River, the unofficial border between Mashonaland and Matabeleland. The warriors descended upon the area about Fort Victoria, intent on teaching the Mashonas a lasting lesson. Gomella was captured and disembowelled in view of his terror-stricken family, then they too were hacked to death.

On previous occasions, such retribution would have been sufficient . . . but this was a large impi. Many of the Mahajas were unblooded. Determined to return to their homeland as men, they went on the rampage in a savage welter of blood-letting.

The Matabele killed Mashonas wherever they found them. For the first time, the residents of Fort Victoria witnessed at first-hand the handiwork of one of Lobengula's impis. They watched helplessly as farm labourers, house servants, and even the 'nannies' of white children were put to death by every means known to the unpractised but resourceful Mahajas.

In all this wild orgy of blood-letting, not one European was harmed, although many had belongings and livestock stolen. As they crowded inside the earthwork walls of the police fort with a handful of Mashona survivors, they clamoured for action from the Chartered Company's Police, demanding that the Matabele be driven away.

Meanwhile, their blood lust unsatiated, the impi sent their Induna to arrogantly demand from the Europeans that the Mashonas inside the fort be handed over to the warriors. The Induna thoughtfully promised that the Mashonas would be slaughtered well away from the river, in order that the fort's water supply might not be contaminated.

The Company Police refused to hand over the cowering Mashonas but, outside the fort, the Matabele terror continued unabated. Eventually, the Chartered Company Administrator arrived from Fort Salisbury with a large force of Police. Ordering the Induna to take his impi back to Bulawayo, the Administrator threatened to open fire on the Matabele warriors if they had not obeyed his order at the end of an hour.

When two hours had elapsed, the Administrator sent his men from the fort, to determine whether the Matabele had gone. On their way out of the town the troopers passed the mutilated bodies of dozens of Mashonas, men, women and children. By the time they caught up with the retiring impi they were in no mood to accept the Induna's protest that he was returning to Bulawayo, as ordered by the Company Administrator.

The Captain in charge of the troopers retorted that the impi was not moving *fast* enough. He ordered his men to open fire. About thirty Matabele warriors were killed instantly and the troop drove the remainder before them to the river crossing. Once there, they watched the Matabele warriors cross, then turned about and returned to the fort.

The impi passed through the Insimo valley on its way back to Bulawayo, still smarting at what they considered to be an unprovoked attack on them by the white troopers. Their Induna had been killed in the brief exchange of fire and they were now led by Nyamatakah, Lobengula's eldest son, the heir to the throne of Matabeleland.

Meeting up with Nathan who was out with some of the herd-boys, Nyamatakah imperiously demanded cattle for his hungry and dispirited men. Nathan replied that he would have to ask his father. Before he had even finished talking, some of Nyamatakah's warriors walked up to the herd and plunged their spears in two of Daniel's best milking cows. The remainder of the herd, many heavy with calf, panicked at the scent of blood and began running.

Nathan remonstrated angrily with the warriors, but when he attempted to draw his rifle, his arms were pinned to his side by Matabele warriors.

It was an ugly moment. It would no doubt have been much worse had Daniel not come along, attracted by the commotion. Seeing the warriors holding Nathan, he knocked their arms away and rounded on Nyamatakah.

'Has the son of the King become a thief? Has he taken to stealing the cattle of his father's friends?'

'I have not stolen. I asked for them . . . as a friend,' Nyamatakah replied, surlily.

'I told him to ask you, but his warriors started killing our best milking cows,' Nathan retorted indignantly.

'My men are hungry. We have travelled far.' Nyamatakah's anger matched Nathan's. This white man before him was no different to those who had attacked the impi without provocation. Nyamatakah would have killed Daniel – and every other white man and woman in the valley, but if he did he knew he too would die – and at the hands of his own father. This man was Lobengula's friend and was afforded his personal protection.

Daniel was aware of Nyamatakah's thoughts. He could also see this was an impi that had run into trouble and been badly mauled. Many of the warriors were nursing wounds inflicted by rifle bullets. From the direction in which they were travelling, those rifles would have been in the hands of white men.

'Your warriors may kill six of those cattle.' Daniel pointed to his beef herd, further along the valley. 'You will take them with you and make your cooking fires elsewhere. No impi has entered this valley since it was given to me by your father, before you were born. You are welcome here whenever you choose to come in friendship, but not when you travel with men who have blood on their spears.'

Smarting at the snub, Nyamatakah said angrily, 'One day the blood will be that of the white men. Then the Matabele will go where they please.'

The unpleasant incident in the valley might have been forgotten had not Jaconus Van Eyck arrived a few days afterwards. He gave Daniel details of the Matabele raid in the Fort Victoria area.

'This is only the latest in a whole series of incidents, Daniel,' he said when they were seated on the verandah, that evening as the sun went down beyond the hills. 'But it's brought things to a head. Something has to be done – and quickly.'

'This raid only lasted so long because Nyamatakah was in the impi,' explained Daniel. 'He was out to prove something and wanted to return home to act it all out in front of his father and the tribe. I've seen it all before, Jaconus. The warriors are never going to stop raiding, but I'll have a word with Lobengula.'

'It may be too late in the day for words. Rhodes has promised the settlers that he'll put an end to the raiding. He's called on them to form companies of mounted volunteers and is recruiting in the Transvaal. He's promising six thousand acres and gold claims to every man prepared to fight the Matabele to a standstill.'

The information shocked Daniel. 'He's doing WHAT? Why, an army of Boer mercenaries would commit more atrocities than a Matabele impi! Damn the man! He could almost have planned this whole business of the telegraph wire himself.'

'No, Daniel. Rhodes is genuinely concerned about the situation in Mashonaland. Many settlers are talking about leaving if the Matabele raids continue. He's *got* to do something.'

'Nevertheless, Rhodes is using this whole sorry business to his own advantage. Mashonaland hasn't fulfilled its promise. It's not the pot of gold he was led to expect. Now he's out to get Matabeleland. God, Jaconus! That man has no scruples at all. He'd sacrifice us all to get what he's after.'

Daniel had sprung to his feet and was pacing about as he spoke. Suddenly he stopped in front of Jaconus Van Eyck and looked down at him. 'All right, Jaconus, you're not making a social visit. What do you want me to do?'

'Nothing. As I've said, it's far too late to do anything. I'm here to suggest you take your family to Fort Victoria. They'll be safe there.'

An expression of incredulity took over Daniel's face. 'Leave the Insimo valley and everything I've built up here? After all these years? Never. There's too much of me here . . . part of you too, Jaconus. Young Jannie's grave is still tended every week. No, I'm grateful to you for coming all this way to warn me, but I'm in less danger from Lobengula's impis than I will be from Rhodes' Boer mercenaries.'

* * *

In spite of his assurance to Jaconus Van Eyck, Daniel discussed the question of leaving the Insimo valley with Elvira, when they lay side by side in bed that night.

She listened in silence as he told her of the Fort Victoria raid by Lobengula's impi, and of Rhodes' preparations for war. Then, quietly she asked, 'What do you *really* believe is going to happen, Daniel?'

'Lobengula has never broken his word to us about anything. He told me we'll always be safe in this valley. I believe him.'

'Then there is nothing more to be said. I trust him too. We've faced trouble before and come through. We'll do the same again. This is where we have brought up our children and watched them grow towards manhood. They would not be happy anywhere else . . . and neither would I. We stay, my husband. The Insimo valley is our home.'

CHAPTER TWENTY

When Daniel went to Bulawayo, a week after Jaconus Van Eyck's visit to him, he found far more Matabele impis than usual encamped about the Matabele capital. None of the Mahajas attempted to interfere with his progress, but many hostile glances were cast in his direction.

It was a relief to reach Lobengula's house and have the King greet him warmly at the doorway, in full view of his people. But once inside, with the door closed behind them, the Matabele King launched into a fierce attack on Rhodes.

'Have you heard what his men did? They fired upon my impi. Shot my warriors. Nyamatakah was with them. He might have been killed!'

'There's likely to be a lot more killing, Inkosi. The men of Rhodes' company are angry about your raids. They say it's impossible to carry on normal life in Mashonaland while they continue.'

'Mashonaland belongs to me. I will do as I wish there. The Matabele have always raided the Mashona.'

'I know, but Rhodes and his company weren't there before. Can't you cut down on your raiding? Make an effort not to provoke him?'

Lobengula sat down in his battered old armchair wearily and one of his wives hurried across the room with a calabash of beer. Lobengula waved her away irritably.

'You think *I* provoke *Rhodes*, trader? I ask no more than that my people be allowed to live as they always have – no more than that.'

'Times are changing rapidly, Inkosi. The Matabele *must* change with them.'

'No!' Lobengula roared the word. His wives who were in the room rolled their eyes nervously at the anger of their King. 'Raiding is an essential part of the Matabele way of life. The prowess that the Matabele warrior learns on the raid makes him unbeatable in war. Our ways have made my people great.

If the impis of the Matabele can no longer march across the hills of their own land and listen to the wind singing among their spears they cease to be the Matabele. If it were not for this man Rhodes I would do as my father did . . . take my people, my cattle and belongings, and go north across the Zambezi. But Rhodes sends his men there too.'

Daniel felt desperately sorry for Lobengula, but he did his best to be practical. 'You would need to fight hard to conquer new lands. Such battles would leave you with a much weaker nation. You must try to make peace with Rhodes. It's your only chance.'

'I have tried to live at peace with *all* white men. All my reign I have tried. Can you tell me of one white man who has lost his life at my hands . . . or at the hands of my warriors? No, I have treated them as though they were my own sons. In return they show me nothing but ingratitude and contempt. Tell me, you are my friend, what more can I do?'

Lobengula was King of the Matabele. He represented life or death to hundreds of thousands of men, women and children. Yet he was a very lonely man. The duplicity of Farewell Loveday had hit him particularly hard. Lobengula had trusted him, spending many hours talking over his problems with him. Now there was only Daniel, and his visits were all too infrequent these days. The King sat in his chair, a picture of total dejection. In his heart he knew that war with the white men was inevitable . . . and he entertained few doubts about its outcome.

Resisting the almost overwhelming urge to place a comforting hand upon the King's shoulder, Daniel said, 'Try to hold your warriors in check, Inkosi. I'll go to Fort Salisbury. If there is anything to be done, I'll do it.'

'Thank you, trader. You alone among your people are a true friend. Go in peace.'

Lobengula hoped desperately that Daniel would succeed in averting war. All the same, he sent out messengers, recalling six thousand warriors who were at that moment raiding north of the Zambezi River. While he awaited their arrival, he deployed other impis along his borders and on all roads leading to the capital.

Returning to Insimo, Daniel collected Jaconus Van Eyck and Wyatt. He rode first to Fort Victoria, then northward along the pioneer road to Fort Salisbury. In both towns Daniel saw clear preparations for war. Men were going about their business with that peculiar cockiness they adopt when a battle is imminent. Part bravado, it was also an attempt to cover their fears.

In Fort Salisbury, Daniel was given a short and unsympathetic hearing by the Chartered Company Administrator. Daniel had hardly begun to explain the purpose of his visit before he was rudely interrupted.

'If you're here to discuss peace, Mister Retallick, then you're talking to the wrong man. I suggest you go back and speak to your friend, Lobengula.'

'I've just come from Lobengula. He doesn't want war.'

'His warriors *do*. I have received two reports only today of Matabele impis firing on British South Africa Company Police patrols.'

'Come with me and talk to Lobengula. Bring these reports with you. I guarantee that those responsible will be punished—'

'As far as I am concerned, *Lobengula* is responsible. I will carry out whatever action I deem necessary to punish him. If Lobengula is so anxious to avert war, tell him to come *here* and see *me*. I will listen to him, but only if he leaves his army behind in Bulawayo.'

As he left the Administrator's office, Daniel saw a large troop of well-armed men riding out of Fort Salisbury, heading south.

Wyatt and Jaconus Van Eyck were waiting for him. Jaconus nodded towards the departing men. 'They're on their way to join up with columns from Fort Victoria and Fort Tuli. That's not all. We've just come from the telegraph office. A mixed column of Bechuanaland Border Police and Boers is in the country and another is expected from the Cape within a few days.'

Daniel's anger and frustration spilled over. 'You tried to tell me this was the spontaneous reaction of the settlers to Lobengula's raids, Jaconus. You must know now that's nonsense. These preparations for war have been going on for weeks – probably months. Lobengula's raids on the Mashona are no more than an excuse for Rhodes to invade Matabeleland. I've said so all along.'

'There's something else I think you ought to know, Daniel . . . Rhodes is in Mashonaland.'

'Then why didn't he come to speak to me at the Administrator's office?'

'He's not in Fort Salisbury. He's camped at Chief Macheke's village.'

Daniel was puzzled. Macheke's village was about seventy miles from Fort Salisbury, on the track to Umtali and the Mozambique border.

'I don't believe it. Why would he be skulking there when all the action is being directed from Fort Salisbury?'

Then suddenly, enlightenment hit Daniel with all the force of a blow to his stomach. There was only one man who could effectively stop open warfare between the Matabele and the Europeans. That man was Cecil Rhodes.

The Governor in Cape Town would be fully aware of this. Sir Hercules Robinson had been replaced by Sir Henry Loch – and Loch was not a Rhodes Company man. If he learned what was happening, he might *order* Rhodes to put a halt to warfare between the forces of the Chartered Company and Lobengula – but only if he were able to contact Rhodes.

By remaining at Macheke's kraal, Rhodes had effectively cut himself off from all communications with the outside world. He could be ordered to do nothing. It was the final, carefully thought-out detail in his well-laid plans.

Daniel found Cecil Rhodes relaxing outside his tent on a hill overlooking the Macheke River. He showed no concern at the unexpected arrival of Daniel and Wyatt.

'Hello, Retallick. We're both a long way from home. Is this your son? He's a fine looking boy. Sit yourselves down and have a drink. What'll you have, eh?'

'I'd rather talk, Mister Rhodes. About ways to stop a bloody war.'

'War?' Rhodes was in a jocular mood. 'Who'd want to make war on such a lovely day as this?'

'Mister Rhodes, I'm pleading with you. You *have* Mashonaland. It became yours without a fight because Lobengula promised that was the way it would be, and he's a man of honour. Had he attacked when your pioneer column was crossing any one of a dozen rivers, he could have cut your men to pieces.'

'Of course he could. I knew that. But you told me he wouldn't. I believed you. In return I promised to make no claim on the Insimo valley. Neither will I. That means we are *all* men of our word. What more is there to be said?'

'A whole lot more, as well you know. Lobengula has done his best to remain at peace with Europeans, in spite of all the provocation he's received from your company—'

'Provocation?' Rhodes squeaked the word excitedly. 'Provocation, you say? That's ugly talk, Retallick. If anyone has been provoked it's my company. No sooner do we begin to make a go of things – acting within the terms of our concession, I would point out, than this . . . this SAVAGE orders his army here to kill all our workers, or send them scurrying to the hills, afraid to show their faces in the light of day. Sometimes they are gone for weeks. I can't run a company like this, Retallick.'

'The Matabele have always raided the Mashona. They see no reason to stop now . . . but, if you come with me to talk to Lobengula, he'll not only listen, he'll come more than halfway towards satisfying your complaints. He wants peace.'

Cecil Rhodes snorted. 'Then he's got a damned funny way of showing it. That's all I can say.'

'Come and talk with him. You might even find you like Lobengula. You're both big men – and both have much to gain . . . or lose. At least come to Fort Salisbury and call in your various columns until we've had time to discuss the matter.'

'I can't. I may have smallpox in my party. That's why I'm remaining here. We can't have that spreading through the country, can we?'

Daniel looked about him at the men of Cecil Rhodes' party, each of whom looked the picture of health. Those who had heard Rhodes' words were grinning openly.

Daniel turned back to Rhodes in desperation. 'Mister Rhodes, I've never begged anything from anyone before but I'm begging you now. *Please* come and talk to Lobengula.'

'I'll bear it in mind . . . when I come in to Fort Salisbury.'

Daniel's shoulders sagged as he conceded defeat. He walked away from Rhodes filled with bitterness. He knew the Macheke camp would not be broken up until the columns of armed Europeans were beyond recall. He would have been even more bitter had he known, as Rhodes assuredly did, that the value of shares in the British South Africa Company had leaped to a new high on the London market. News had been 'leaked' that the Chartered Company was expanding into Matabeleland.

'What will you do now, Pa?' Wyatt asked the question as they turned their horses towards Fort Salisbury.

'Telegraph to the Governor in Cape Town. I'll ask him to order the Mashonaland Administration to stop all aggressive action against the Matabele. Then I'll go back to Lobengula and get him to pull his impis back to Bulawayo, clear of trouble. I can think of nothing else at the moment.'

Unknown to Daniel, Lobengula had also decided to approach the Governor in the Cape Colony. He sent off three Indunas with a message to Cape Town. One of them was his brother. Escorted by the European who had taken on the task of running Daniel's Bulawayo store, the three Indunas got as far as Tati. Here, their escort left them and went off to find himself a drink. During his absence the three Indunas waited patiently until they were approached by a group of Bechuanaland Border Police, demanding to know their business. Within minutes a bitter quarrel had broken out. Two shots were fired, and two of the Indunas lay dead on the ground. Lobengula's brother was the lone survivor – but not for long. He fell ill with a mysterious sickness and died within a few days of his murdered companions.

When news of the three deaths reached him, Lobengula became angrier than any of his people had ever seen him. For a few minutes the overweight, self-indulgent sovereign became once again the Warrior-King his people had elected to lead them. Rising from his throne of animal hides, he seized a spear from one of his bodyguard. Drawing back his arm, he hurled the weapon high in the air, towards the distant skyline where the sun was climbing into the sky above Mashonaland.

Pointing to where the spear stuck quivering in the ground, Lobengula cried, 'My impis will follow the path of the spear until they meet with the white man. Then they will KILL! KILL! KILL! His feet shall trample our lands no more.'

The roar of approval that rose from the throats of the Matabele warriors sent creatures fleeing through the bushveldt two miles away.

It was war at last.

By the time Daniel and Wyatt reached Fort Salisbury, the first pitched battle between the Matabele warriors and the forces of the Chartered Company had already been fought only a few miles from Insimo.

Filled with a variety of emotions, Elvira and the three boys had watched the six hundred men of the Fort Victoria column ride through the Insimo valley on their way to war.

The boys were filled with excitement at the sight of so many horsemen. Elvira was dismayed at such tragic evidence that Daniel's mission had failed. Whatever the outcome of the fighting, things would never be the same for any of them again.

Elvira climbed the hillside behind the house with the boys, following in the wake of the column. From here they heard the first volley of rifle shots in the battle between the two opposing forces. Minutes later there came the steady and monotonous chatter of the Maxim guns as they poured bullets into the packed ranks of the Matabele army. When the screams of the wounded began to make themselves heard above the din of battle, Elvira took her children back to the house.

Safely inside, Elvira made her way to her bedroom and kneeled before a silver and mother-of-pearl crucifix. Here she prayed. She prayed for the Matabele and for Daniel too. She knew that part of him was dying in the fighting going on beyond the hill.

The battle ended in a decisive victory for the men of the Fort Victoria column. More than two thousand Matabele warriors were killed, such was the killing power of the Maxim gun. It was also an indication of the recklessly brave tactics of the impis. But even Lobengula's great army could not afford to sustain casualties in such appalling numbers.

When news of the battle reached Fort Salisbury, where

Daniel had been denied use of the telegraph because of 'war requirements', he and Wyatt rode for home as fast as their horses would carry them. At Fort Victoria they obtained fresh mounts and, accompanied by Jaconus Van Eyck once more, galloped home to the Insimo Valley.

All was well at Insimo, but a number of wounded Europeans were being looked after in the house, and twenty men of the Fort Victoria column had been left behind by their Commanding Officer to guard against a possible attack by wandering Mahajas who had fled from the battlefield.

There was news too of a second battle, fought closer to Bulawayo – but on this occasion the Maxim guns had succeeded in scything down only *one* thousand Matabele warriors.

That night Daniel and Elvira slept little. Daniel grieved for Lobengula and the loss of so many of his warriors. Beside him, in the darkened room, Elvira clung to him tighter.

'What are you going to do now, Daniel?'

'I must go to Lobengula. Somehow this slaughter has to be brought to an end. I'll try to persuade him to surrender to the Commander of the troops from the Cape. That way he'll become the Queen's responsibility and not Rhodes'. He might even be able to appeal to her and obtain an honourable settlement.'

'Will Lobengula listen to you?'

'He *must*. The whole future of his people depends upon what he does next. A wrong move now and the Matabele will no longer exist as a nation.'

'This means very much to you, my husband, I know . . . but I wish you were not going. I have a feeling . . . a deep, empty feeling in here.' She placed his hand on her breast.

'I must go, Elvira. Everything we have here we owe to Lobengula. He's been a very good friend to us. Now, more than ever before, *he* is in need of a friend.'

Elvira clung to Daniel and, when he slept with his arms about her, she wept as she had never cried before in all the years of their marriage.

CHAPTER TWENTY-ONE

Daniel rode off the next morning with Jaconus Van Eyck. Both Wyatt and Nathan accompanied them. Wyatt would have come anyway, but Nathan pleaded that history was being made all about them and he was seeing none of it.

Nathan was not so certain he enjoyed history in the making when they passed the site of the first big battle. The stench was appalling. Around the battlefield vultures waddled and flapped in uncomfortable awkwardness, so gorged they were unable to leave the ground. When the party stopped for a meal a couple of miles on, no one felt like eating.

They arrived at Bulawayo mid-morning the following day and discovered that all that remained of Lobengula's capital was a wide expanse of smouldering ashes. The forces of the Chartered Company were in camp nearby and as Daniel picked his way through the ruins of the once-great kraal, a man approached him. It was an Afrikaans blacksmith who had been employed by Lobengula, mainly to keep the guns of his personal bodyguard in working order.

The two men clasped hands and Daniel said, 'It's good to see you . . . but how did you escape from this?'

'I didn't have to. Lobengula sent for me. He told me he was setting fire to Bulawayo, but that I wouldn't be hurt. I wasn't.'

'Do you know where he's gone?'

'North, that's all I know. I wish I thought he'd make it to safety, but he's got Major Forbes and two hundred men on his tail.'

'What was his mood when he spoke to you? Do you think he'll run until he's across the Zambezi, or will he stand and fight?'

The blacksmith shook his head. 'You know Lobengula better than me. He doesn't want to fight . . . he never has, but he's got his best impis around him now and they're just as keen for war as Rhodes.'

Daniel glanced up at the sky, Huge, brooding clouds were

pushing up from the east, threatening the sun. 'The rains will be here soon. Perhaps they'll cool everyone's tempers.'

When Daniel returned to the horses he suggested that the boys should return to Insimo accompanied by Jaconus Van Eyck.

The boys protested vigorously. So did Jaconus Van Eyck.

'You're not heading north alone, Daniel. Half the men with Forbes are Boers. They'd all as soon kill an Englishman as a kaffir. No, I'm coming with you.'

In the end, Daniel agreed that they would all go on together, reassessing the situation if it appeared likely they might run into trouble. They set out immediately, following the broad trail left by Lobengula's fleeing nation.

It was not long before they began meeting small groups of Matabele, all heading back towards Bulawayo. These were stragglers who had been overtaken by Forbes. They had decided to return to the ruins of their city, rather than risk becoming embroiled in a battle.

Once Daniel saw a family he recognised as kinsfolk of one of Lobengula's Indunas. In reply to Daniel's questions they told him that the King had indeed gone northwards. So too had Forbes, although when he caught up with the King, the company man would no doubt wish he had not. The family would not elaborate, but Daniel was left with the impression that Forbes was being drawn into a trap.

After threatening for so long, the rain began to fall the following day. Large drops stung their faces as the two men and two boys followed Lobengula's trail.

They passed more refugees now. Significantly, they were all women and children. Then, on the bank of the river where there were signs that a great many people had made camp, Daniel found the charred remains of Lobengula's old armchair. Now he knew that the forces of Major Forbes must have been pressing close to the Matabele King when they passed over the river.

Daniel decided to make the river crossing immediately, for fear the waters would rise during the night and make the river impassable.

They gained the far bank safely, but had advanced no more than a hundred yards when they suddenly came upon armed

Europeans wearing the crossed cartridge belts favoured by Boer commandos.

After identifying themselves to the other men's satisfaction, Daniel was subjected to urgent questioning. 'What's it like on the other side of the river? Are there any Matabele over there?'

'Not unless you count women and children . . . . But what's happened? Where's Major Forbes?'

'Major Forbes is no longer in charge. If you want to speak to someone it had better be Commandant Graaf.'

The Boer outriders did not elaborate, but led them to an uncomfortable camp, about a mile ahead.

Commandant Graaf and Jaconus Van Eyck greeted each other by their first names and it was apparent by Graaf's manner that they knew each other well.

'Agh, man! This whole chase has been a bloody shambles from start to finish, eh? This "Major" Forbes couldn't lead a party of drinkers to a booze-up. I had to take over from him or we'd all be dead now. We've got a hundred and thirty men here, many of them wounded, and another thirty-four back there somewhere. God knows what's happened to them. We've fought the whole Matabele army most of the way here.'

'Well, once across the river you'll be clear of them,' Daniel assured the Commandant. 'But I'd get across quickly if I were you. We've had rain and the river might rise very quickly.'

'You've no need to tell me that,' said Graaf bitterly. 'That's how we lost touch with Allen Wilson and his men.'

Graaf raised his voice, shouting to his men to break camp. His exact words were, 'Get your butts off the ground and ride like hell out of here.'

The demoralised column rode away without Daniel once seeing Major Forbes, the official Commanding Officer of the column. But he was not given long to concern himself with the squabble between Graaf and Forbes. Half a mile along the trail they encountered a very large Matabele impi. A roar went up from the warriors and Daniel and the others backed away nervously, keeping their distance until Daniel recognised the tall Induna who ran from the ranks of his warriors to meet them. It was Gamba, Lobengula's son-in-law.

After exchanging greetings, Daniel told Gamba he was seeking Lobengula.

'Every white man there ever was is seeking the King.' commented Gamba drily. 'But you are his friend, trader. I will take you to him.'

As Daniel and the others led their horses beside Gamba, Daniel questioned the Induna about the progress of the war and asked whether he knew what Lobengula was hoping to do. Gamba's replies were evasive and noncommittal.

Late in the day they forded another river. The trail they were following now passed through an area of tall, green-leafed Mopani trees. The ground was soft underfoot and with Gamba's impi trailing some way behind, it was as quiet as a cathedral. Then, as they approached a clearing, visible some way ahead through the trees, Gamba tried to head them away, to one side of the clearing, but Daniel called him to a halt.

'Wait a minute . . . . Can you hear anything?'

In the ensuing silence they all heard the low drone of millions of tiny wings beating the air.

'Flies.' Daniel exchanged glances with Jaconus Van Eyck. Both men thought of the thirty-four men missing from Commandant Graaf's column.

Ignoring Gamba's plea that it was not good for them to go to the clearing, Daniel mounted his horse and urged the animal forward, closely followed by the others.

At the edge of the clearing, Daniel saw that his fears were realised. Reining in his horse he called back to Wyatt, 'Take Nathan back out of the way. There's no need for either of you to see this.'

Wyatt did as he was told without question, ignoring Nathan's protests.

Daniel slid from his horse and walked into the clearing, with Jaconus Van Eyck a pace behind him. The buzzing of the flies was aggressively loud here and they hovered in great clouds over a gruesome scene.

Daniel had found Allen Wilson and his men. Their naked bodies were piled in an untidy heap in the centre of the clearing. They were horribly mutilated, but Daniel was able to recognise two of them he had met in Fort Victoria. Jaconus Van Eyck had known them all.

Daniel found himself searching the recesses of his mind desperately for an appropriate prayer, but the words eluded him. Gamba had come silently to his side and he said quietly, 'They did not die alone, trader. Four hundred of my bravest warriors died with them.' Gamba gazed at the bodies and in a voice filled with respect said, 'Yes, these were men of men, and their fathers were men before them.'

Gamba had paid the men the ultimate compliment of a Matabele warrior, but Daniel left the clearing deeply distressed at the unnecessary waste of so many lives.

The next morning they met up with another Matabele impi. This one was much smaller than Gamba's, containing no more than a hundred men. The Induna in charge was Nyamatakah, Lobengula's eldest son. With him was his brother Lundi. They had been guarding a pass in the hills to the east while Lobengula passed by. Now they were on their way to rejoin him, frustrated that they had not yet been involved in any action.

Lundi grinned self-consciously at Wyatt, but Nyamatakah scowled when the Mahajas of Gamba's impi shouted of the many men they had killed in battle.

'I have not yet washed my spear in a white man's blood,' Nyamatakah said loudly.

'There is no need for such words before a man who is your father's friend,' snapped Gamba.

'It is not long ago that *all* white men claimed to be the King's friends,' retorted Nyamatakah. 'Now we are fleeing north. We will have a new land, and who knows . . . perhaps a new King. Remember that, Gamba. For now you can return to the Shangani River with your impi. Chase the white men back to where they came from. I will take the trader to the King.'

Gamba looked at Nyamatakah suspiciously, but the heir to the Matabele throne rounded on him angrily. 'That order came from the King. Go!'

'My brother likes to hear his own voice. He thinks he is King already.' Lundi spoke the words quietly to Wyatt, so that his brother would not hear.

All that day Daniel, Jaconus Van Eyck and the two boys travelled with Nyamatakah's impi, without the royal Induna saying a word to them. Towards the evening, Daniel edged his horse towards Van Eyck.

'I'm not happy, Jaconus,' he said, in a low voice that would not carry to the boys. 'Gamba was bringing us in a straight line, due north. Now we've swung away to westward.'

Jaconus Van Eyck nodded. He had noticed that Lundi too was uneasy and twice he had seen the royal brothers arguing.

That night they camped in an area of broken rocks, building their fire some way from the fires of the impi. Daniel ensured the horses were left saddled in readiness and the two men and Wyatt took turns in maintaining a guard. Wyatt had the last two hours of the night and drowsily he watched the colours of dawn begin to chase away the night shadows. He must have dozed off for a few moments, but woke suddenly to hear a voice whispering hoarsely in his ear, speaking Matabele.

'Wyatt! Wyatt! Wake the others. Go . . . quickly.'

It was Lundi.

As Wyatt shifted stiffly, Lundi added, 'Leave everything and go now. My brother means to kill you all.'

Wyatt shook the others hurriedly and as they came awake the low voices of Matabele warriors could be heard moving towards them between the broken rocks on the hillside.

Wasting no time, Daniel checked that they were all ready then signalled for them to sprint for the horses.

As they rose to their feet the Matabele warriors saw them and set up a howl that raised the hackles on Nathan's neck. It was a sound like nothing he had ever heard before. He made it to the horses but then hopped around frantically, one foot in the stirrup while his horse, startled by the suddenness of his arrival, pranced away from him.

Daniel gave him a heave from behind and, when Nathan was safely mounted, vaulted to the saddle of his own horse.

As they galloped from the shelter of the rocks, a small party of warriors ran in an attempt to head them off, but Jaconus Van Eyck fired his rifle from the saddle and one of the Matabele fell to the ground, the others hurriedly losing all enthusiasm for the chase.

Behind them the thwarted warriors began shooting wildly . . . and suddenly Daniel's horse stumbled. He was not certain whether it had been hit or if it stumbled on a piece of rock, but it was sufficient to bring the horse to the ground. Daniel just managed to shake his feet free of the stirrups before the horse rolled over.

The horse tried valiantly to rise, but one of its back legs was broken and Daniel snatched his rifle from the saddle holster and ran.

The others had seen him fall and gave him covering fire from about a hundred yards away. The Matabeles had also seen the incident and were running in pursuit. Some were brought down by the rifle fire, but there were many more to take their places – and they too were firing.

A searing pain burned through Daniel's left leg as a bullet struck him behind the knee. For a couple of paces he tried hopping, dragging the wounded leg behind him. The pain proved too great. Turning to face his pursuers, he fired twice, downing two warriors. Then he was forced to stop to reload.

The Matabele warriors who had been spread out across the hillside closed in upon him. Daniel snapped the breech of his gun shut and shot the nearest warrior. The second cartridge misfired. An assegai flashed down, sending Daniel staggering backwards. He fell and immediately another warrior stabbed down at him, pinning Daniel to the ground.

Daniel lay helpless, aware that he had been severely wounded. Strangely, he felt no pain now.

The knot of warriors about him parted and Nyamatakah stood above him. Quivering with excitement, Nyamatakah raised his assegai. As Daniel looked up at him, a hole suddenly appeared in Nyamatakah's chest and blood blossomed around it. A moment later Lobengula's son dropped dead at Daniel's feet.

The death of the Induna brought Daniel a brief respite. Then as the warriors began to howl in anger, Daniel heard Wyatt's cry.

'Pa . . . ! Pa . . . ! I'm coming . . . .'

Turning his head with difficulty, Daniel saw Wyatt galloping his horse towards him, elbows and legs flapping wildly, a look of anguish on his face.

'No, Wyatt! Go back, son . . . .'

The words were a despairing croak in Daniel's throat as his mind flashed back to the words of the White Mondoro, spoken on the hilltop fortress, high above the Great House of the Chiefs. *'I see a hand stretching towards you. . . . . It holds a spear . . . . There are many spears pointing at your people . . . .'*

'Wyatt, go back! For God's sake go back.'

A shot from point blank range brought down Wyatt's horse. It fell to the ground and lay with legs and head twitching. '*Your heart weeps . . . but the tears are not for yourself.*' Wyatt bounced up, running. Seeing no one but his father.

As Wyatt plunged into a flailing mêlée of arms and assegais, Daniel remembered another day, an older Mondoro. '*Your first born will prove himself truly a man . . . .*'

Miraculously Wyatt fought his way through the warriors before being hacked to his knees at Daniel's side.

'*. . . . Truly a man.*'

Wyatt died calling his father's name. Daniel managed to grasp his son's hand before the assegais of Nyamatakah's impi stabbed out his life too.

'*. . . The second son will carry your line.*' Nathan almost confounded the Mondoro's prediction, and Elvira came close to losing two sons that day. Sobbing with anger and grief, Nathan was kneeing his horse towards the impi when Jaconus Van Eyck snatched the reins from his hands and led him away from the place where his father and brother had died.

As the two horsemen galloped out of sight, Lundi looked about him at the bodies of his people . . . and those who had been his friends. Tears rolled down his face. They were for his friends. He did not look at his brother. After a few minutes, Lundi turned and took his place at the head of his late brother's impi and he set off to find Lobengula.

Behind him the clouds gathered, building up far away over the hills that surrounded Insimo. In the valley the wind bowed the heads of the tall maize plants as it ran ahead of the rain, and touched the blooded spears of Lundi's impi. '*The spears and the wind sing together . . .*'

The wind whispered a dirge through the mountains and woodlands of Matabeleland. It touched the hair of Cecil Rhodes as he left the telegraph office in Fort Salisbury, rustling the messages proclaiming victory clutched in his hand.

Lobengula never learned of the death of his friend. He died on the road north. Some say he was poisoned. Others plump for suicide. A few claim he died a victim of smallpox. One or two, those who had known him well, believed the loss of his father's nation broke his heart.

The Matabele King was never again seen by a white man after firing Bulawayo as a funeral pyre for the Matabele nation, and many refused to accept the stories of his death. For many years men claimed to have seen the last Matabele King in many remote corners of the African continent.

What can never be disputed is that the wind touched upon triumph and sorrow, victory and defeat on this stormy December day. It drew from them all the seeds of discontent and scattered them far and wide across the land, there to flourish and multiply. One day those seeds would burst forth in a blood-red harvest for all men, black and white to reap.

When that day came, the final prophesy of the White Mondoro, made to the last King of the Matabele would be fulfilled.

'One day it will be the Mashona who rule all the people who now bow before Mzilikazi. The sons of your sons, and those of others here will witness the fulfilment of my words . . . and they will remember.'

E. V. Thompson
Chase the Wind £1.95

The prizewinning story of love and bitter destiny in Cornwall more than a century ago . . . For the men who dug the Cornish earth of Bodmin Moor, the flourishing copper trade brought little but poverty and exploitation. Josh Retallick, son of a respected local family, and the wild Miriam, daughter of a drink-sodden miner, explored together the wild moorland until fate swept them apart.

'A keen eye for detail . . . astonishing energy' SUNDAY TIMES

Harvest of the Sun £1.75

A magnificent saga of passion and conflict in Africa. The ship was bound for Australia. Aboard, Josh Retallick and Miriam Thackeray, prisoners destined for the convict settlements – until their vessel was wrecked on the Skeleton Coast of South West Africa. Far from their Cornwall origins, the two strangers in a hostile land meet Bushmen and Hereros, foraging Boers and greedy traders in an alien world of ivory tusks and smuggled guns.

'A host of characters and adventures' MANCHESTER EVENING NEWS

Ben Retallick £1.75

In the Cornwall tin mines of the early nineteenth century, death was the working man's constant companion. Ben Retallick grew to sturdy manhood among the miners and fisherfolk through hard and hungry years. Cruel fate stole away Jesse, his dark-eyed love, and Ben searched through hiring fairs to find her again . . .

E. V. Thompson
The Music Makers £1.95

In the troubled countryside of Ireland, the 1840s were the bad years, when the potato crops failed and the spectre of hunger stalked the landscape. Against this backdrop, prize-winning novelist E. V. Thompson spins the tale of Liam McCabe, one-time fisherman of Kilmar, who turned his hand to politics and offered his hungry fellows a gleam of hope. Never far away, the women in his life, Kathie the winsome fiddler's daughter and Caroline, dazzling lady of the aristocracy, whom he would need as he faced a host of enemies and a web of corruption — the source of a nation's torment.

The Dream Traders £1.95

The China opium trade of the 1830s was a maelstrom of greed, intrigue and misery — the way to power and wealth for the men who traded in drug-steeped dreams — and it spawned a conflict that would change the course of Asia's history. Luke Trewarne was a young Cornishman who came to China to make his fortune, but he fell in love with a country, an ideal, and a beautiful Chinese water gipsy . . .

Wilbur Smith
Wild Justice £1.95

It began in the Seychelles. A seductive, ice-cool blonde slips through customs. Once on the plane, she is revealed as a deadly terrorist, well versed in the art of jet hijacking. At Johannesburg, the stench of death is only a bullet away for the plane's 400 eminent passengers. Anti-terrorist chief Peter Stride sets out to find the sinister power-brain behind a band of ruthless fanatics — a search carrying him across continents towards an explosive climax in the scorched deserts of Galilee.

Fiction

☐	**Options**	Freda Bright	£1.50p
☐	**The Thirty-nine Steps**	John Buchan	£1.50p
☐	**Secret of Blackoaks**	Ashley Carter	£1.50p
☐	**Hercule Poirot's Christmas**	Agatha Christie	£1.50p
☐	**Dupe**	Liza Cody	£1.25p
☐	**Lovers and Gamblers**	Jackie Collins	£2.50p
☐	**Sphinx**	Robin Cook	£1.25p
☐	**Ragtime**	E. L. Doctorow	£1.50p
☐	**My Cousin Rachel**	Daphne du Maurier	£1.95p
☐	**Mr American**	George Macdonald Fraser	£2.25p
☐	**The Moneychangers**	Arthur Hailey	£2.50p
☐	**Secrets**	Unity Hall	£1.75p
☐	**Black Sheep**	Georgette Heyer	£1.75p
☐	**The Eagle Has Landed**	Jack Higgins	£1.95p
☐	**Sins of the Fathers**	Susan Howatch	£3.50p
☐	**The Master Sniper**	Stephen Hunter	£1.50p
☐	**Smiley's People**	John le Carré	£1.95p
☐	**To Kill a Mockingbird**	Harper Lee	£1.95p
☐	**Ghosts**	Ed McBain	£1.75p
☐	**Gone with the Wind**	Margaret Mitchell	£3.50p
☐	**Blood Oath**	David Morrell	£1.75p
☐	**Platinum Logic**	Tony Parsons	£1.75p
☐	**Wilt**	Tom Sharpe	£1.75p
☐	**Rage of Angels**	Sidney Sheldon	£1.95p
☐	**The Unborn**	David Shobin	£1.50p
☐	**A Town Like Alice**	Nevile Shute	£1.75p
☐	**A Falcon Flies**	Wilbur Smith	£2.50p
☐	**The Deep Well at Noon**	Jessica Stirling	£2.50p
☐	**The Ironmaster**	Jean Stubbs	£1.75p
☐	**The Music Makers**	E. V. Thompson	£1.95p

Non-fiction

☐	**Extraterrestrial Civilizations**	Isaac Asimov	£1.50p
☐	**Pregnancy**	Gordon Bourne	£3.50p
☐	**Jogging From Memory**	Rob Buckman	£1.25p
☐	**The 35mm Photographer's Handbook**	Julian Calder and John Garrett	£5.95p
☐	**Travellers' Britain**	} Arthur Eperon	£2.95p
☐	**Travellers' Italy**		£2.50p
☐	**The Complete Calorie Counter**	Eileen Fowler	80p

☐	**The Diary of Anne Frank**	Anne Frank	£1.75p
☐	**And the Walls Came Tumbling Down**	Jack Fishman	£1.95p
☐	**Linda Goodman's Sun Signs**	Linda Goodman	£2.50p
☐	**Dead Funny**	Fritz Spiegl	£1.50p
☐	**How to be a Gifted Parent**	David Lewis	£1.95p
☐	**Victoria RI**	Elizabeth Longford	£4.95p
☐	**Symptoms**	Sigmund Stephen Miller	£2.50p
☐	**Book of Worries**	Robert Morley	£1.50p
☐	**Airport International**	Brian Moynahan	£1.75p
☐	**The Alternative Holiday Catalogue**	edited by Harriet Peacock	£1.95p
☐	**The Pan Book of Card Games**	Hubert Phillips	£1.75p
☐	**Food for All the Family**	Magnus Pyke	£1.50p
☐	**Just Off for the Weekend**	John Slater	£2.50p
☐	**An Unfinished History of the World**	Hugh Thomas	£3.95p
☐	**The Baby and Child Book**	Penny and Andrew Stanway	£4.95p
☐	**The Third Wave**	Alvin Toffler	£2.75p
☐	**Pauper's Paris**	Miles Turner	£2.50p
☐	**The Flier's Handbook**		£5.95p

All these books are available at your local bookshop or newsagent, or
can be ordered direct from the publisher. Indicate the number of copies
required and fill in the form below

10

....

Name_____
(Block letters please)

Address_____

_____

Send to CS Department, Pan Books Ltd, PO Box 40, Basingstoke, Hants
Please enclose remittance to the value of the cover price plus:
35p for the first book plus 15p per copy for each additional book ordered
to a maximum charge of £1.25 to cover postage and packing
Applicable only in the UK

While every effort is made to keep prices low, it is sometimes
necessary to increase prices at short notice. Pan Books reserve
the right to show on covers and charge new retail prices which
may differ from those advertised in the text or elsewhere